ABOUT THE AUTHOR

M. A. Anderson has always had a love of things that go *'bump in the night'*, and that's why she enjoys writing dark fantasy.

Having a love of books and reading from an early age, from the age of eight she wrote short stories and song lyrics and progressed to playwriting in her teens.

She is an Australian author who writes Urban fantasy, Supernatural crime thrillers, Contemporary and Paranormal Romance.

You can find out more about M. A. and her books on her website: http://www.m-anderson.com.au or join her on popular social media sites.

EVIL NATURE

ഇ)ൽ

M. A. ANDERSON

Bella Luna Books
Australia

Copyright © 2019 M. A. Anderson
Brisbane, Australia

This edition published 2019
Bella Luna Books, Australia

Cover design by Maggie Anderson

ISBN: 9780648483601 (paperback)

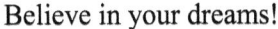
Believe in your dreams!

"There are more things in heaven and earth, Horatio,
Than are dreamt of in your philosophy."

Hamlet: Act 1, scene 5

CHAPTER ONE

Reece stood with his arms folded and stared at Andre's brother in disbelief. How was he here? Why was he here? It was difficult to get his head around the fact that Jacques was alive, *again*, and his best friend was dead. Being identical twins made it even harder to deal with because looking at him made the gaping hole in his heart hurt like hell. He even sounded more like Andre now because the hint of French accent he once had was gone. The PI's scrutinizing gaze remained on the vampire standing in the doorway. "How can you possibly expect us to believe you? Why should we after everything you've done?"

Jacques reached inside his unbuttoned, calf-length black jacket and produced a glass vial containing a gray powdery substance and held it at eye level. "Because, my dear Detective, this contains some of my brother's ashes," he said, his dark gaze moving from the small bottle in his hand to the four suspicious faces, "and you have a quantity of his blood stored for emergencies. Am I correct?"

"So?" Reece stepped away from the others and stood in the center of the office, his hands on his hips. He wondered how Jacques knew about Andre's blood. How long had he been alive and why had he been keeping tabs on them?

"So that means with both of those elements and a sorcerer's assistance we can bring my brother back from the realm of the dead. That is what you want, isn't it?"

"How do we know what he's tellin' us is true?" Ed remained beside Sarah, arms folded, his disbelieving eyes steadfast on their nemesis.

"Because I am living proof." Jacques spread his arms wide. "How else could I stand here before you now? You saw me die and yet here I am."

Ed glowered at him. "You're a liar and a murderer. Maybe you made us see what you wanted us to see. Maybe you've been alive all this time just waiting for a chance to scheme your way back into our lives. Andre is *dead*."

Sarah gripped his arm and gave him a nervous frown. She didn't think it was a good idea to antagonize Jacques. They had all been on the receiving end of his wrath once before.

"It has been done," Nathaniel said.

Reece's focus moved from Jacques to Nathaniel. "You're sure about that?"

"What I was told came from a reliable source. Someone who has seen the ritual performed." He stepped up beside Reece, his eyes never leaving Jacques for a second. He knew how his former master's mind worked. "Although I have not witnessed it myself, I believe the immortal that provided me with the information told the truth."

A satisfied smirk spread across Jacques' pale, handsome face and his left eyebrow arched. "You see. Now do you believe me?"

The PI swung his head around and scowled at the vampire. "What's in it for you? You wouldn't be here offering help unless it benefited you. So what is it?"

"How shrewd of you, Detective." He returned the vial to the inside pocket of his wool coat and stepped across the threshold. "Yes, there is something I want in return. But I shall leave that for another time." His intense gaze locked onto Reece and he searched the PI's soul. Would he do what he wanted? "Consider my offer carefully. Would you want to pass up the opportunity to have your beloved friend returned to you?"

⅊

"You need to find out Jacques' agenda before making a bargain with the devil," Ed told Reece. "Who knows what he'll want you to do."

Reece's serious gaze rested on his ex-boss. "Does it really matter? If I don't agree to whatever he wants Andre will remain dead."

"Is it worth your soul?" Sarah asked, placing a concerned hand on the PI's arm.

"He'll want you to agree before he tells you what he wants you to do.

You know that, right?" Ed frowned at him, wondering why Reece had agreed.

"Yeah, I'm well aware of how Jacques' mind works." He folded his arms. "But I don't see any way around it."

"Who the hell resurrected that monster anyway?" Ed growled. "Now we have two of them to deal with." He paced the length of the office then spun around. "Do you think he's in league with Drac? It's funny how Jacques showed up after he left."

"Who knows?" Reece shrugged and stood up from off the corner of his desk. "All I know is if there's a way to bring Andre back then I don't have a choice."

"But you do have a choice," Nathaniel said.

Reece's eyes moved to the huge vampire. "What are you saying?"

"You know what I am saying. Do you really want to be in league with Jacques?"

"So you think I shouldn't agree to his offer and leave Andre dead."

"Jacques will not bring your friend back immediately. He will test your loyalty first. It could take weeks, months, or even years." Nathaniel folded his arms across his broad, muscular chest.

"Would Andre want to return knowing the price you had to pay?" Sarah's concerned eyes stared into his.

Reece gave a heavy sigh and tears stung the backs of his eyes. "I want my friend back."

"You have other things to worry about," Ed told him. "What about the Charlotte situation?"

"I honestly don't know, Chief."

"You'll forgive her, won't you?" Sarah asked. "You know she wouldn't intentionally do anything to endanger our lives? She was under Vlad's influence."

"Yeah, I know. But it still doesn't change anything. Andre and Arianne are dead." He walked over to the window, leaned against the frame and gazed out at the night.

"You still love her, don't you?"

Reece eyed the priest over his shoulder but didn't reply.

CHAPTER TWO

The next afternoon, Sheriff Lozano was in his office trying to call Reece to no avail. He frowned at his phone and gave a heavy sigh. *Why isn't he picking up?* He tried Andre's cell. No answer there, either. The sheriff had some well-earned vacation time coming and planned to visit Los Angeles. He wanted to organize a time to meet with the PI and his team as he had found something significant he wanted to share with them. He'd discovered certain information while doing some research that would rid the world of monsters once and for all, at least the otherworldly kind. There would always be human monsters. Lozano was pleased to be able to offer his assistance. He'd learned a lot while working with Reece and his team and wanted to return the favor. He sighed again and stared at his phone willing it to ring. Maybe they were working a case and couldn't answer right now. Lozano hoped that's all it was, knowing what they did for a living.

The sheriff opened his laptop and typed in the airline he'd chosen to fly with. He had a couple of days to organize himself and wanted to get to LA as soon as possible. He knew he'd be putting himself in harm's way, but he had to tell them what he'd uncovered, and maybe assist while he was there. Now that he was aware of the creatures roaming the streets during the day and after dark he couldn't ignore his instincts any longer. He had to be involved in ridding the earth of such abominations. He'd come to believe it was his calling.

His official cell phone buzzed and vibrated across his desk pulling him away from his thoughts. He snatched it up and pressed the button hoping it was a return call from Reece. "Sheriff Lozano speaking?"

"Don't involve yourself in matters that don't concern you," the gruff male voice warned on the other end of the line.

Lozano pulled the phone away from his face and stared at the screen. Unknown number. He pressed it back to his ear. "Who is this?"

"Not important. What you need to know is that your friends are indisposed." He gave a throaty chuckle.

"What does that mean?" The sheriff sprang from his chair and stepped out of his office looking for one of his officers to do a trace on the call. His eyes roamed the long, windowed corridor. He spotted Simpson and waved his arm in the air to attract his attention.

The officer spotted him and hurried along the hallway. "What is it, boss?"

Lozano covered the phone. "Can you get a trace on this call? I want to know the location ASAP."

"Sure thing." The officer nodded and rushed into an empty office.

The sheriff removed his hand. "Where are they?"

"The master has already eliminated some of them. It's only a matter of time before they are all dead. That's why I'm telling you to stay away from LA. If you come here you'll have a target on your back."

Lozano wondered who'd died. He wasn't concerned for his own safety. "When you say he's eliminated some of them, you mean he's killed them?"

"What else?"

"Who?"

Silence.

"Tell me *who*?" Lozano pressed. He hoped it wasn't Reece or Andre. Maybe that's why they weren't answering their phones.

"You'll find out when you get here. I assume you're still coming."

"Yeah, I am." Now more than ever he needed to get to LA.

"You've just signed your own death warrant." The line went dead.

"Hello?" Lozano sighed and dropped the phone into the top pocket of his uniform shirt.

Simpson rushed out of the office. "The switching center couldn't determine the exact location of the call, boss. They said the phone's signal was bouncing off the cell towers near the destination but not close enough to pin point it."

"Dammit! Thanks Hank." The sheriff spun on his heel and headed back to his office. He needed to move his vacation time forward so he could be on a flight out tonight.

₨₳

Sitting at the terminal waiting to board, Lozano thought he'd give it one last try to contact Reece before he flew out. The line rang for a long time and he was about to ring off when the PI answered.

"Hello, Sheriff, what can I do for you?"

"Is everything ok? I had a strange, anonymous call telling me Dracula had killed…"

"He did." Reece gave a heavy sigh.

Hoping it had been a lie, Lozano was taken aback by the reality of the news and it took a few seconds for his mind to make sense of it. "Who died?"

The PI sighed again. "I'd prefer not to discuss it right now. It's… I'm still trying to process it myself."

The sheriff had to respect his wishes even though he wanted to know. "Ok. I understand. The reason I called is I'm on my way to you and…"

"Don't come here, Sheriff." Reece's warning was resolute. "There's nothing you can do."

"I have vacation time up and I'm coming. I don't need your permission." He heard the boarding call for his flight. "Look, I gotta go. I'll see you when I get there."

"Sheriff?" Lozano had rung off. "Shit!" Reece tossed his cell phone onto the coffee table.

"What did Sheriff Lozano want?" Sarah asked.

"He's flying here tonight."

"Why?" She sat down on the sofa and let out an exhausted sigh.

"He said he had some vacation time and wanted to spend it here."

"How long will the flight take?"

"Maybe an hour or so." Reece frowned at her. "Why?"

"I think one of us should be at the airport when he arrives."

"She's right. We have no clue where Dracula is right now *and* we have Andre's brother to deal with again," Ed told him. "Who knows what either of them is up to?"

"Lozano said he received an anonymous call about what happened here. He wanted to know who died."

"Then we sure as hell need to be at LAX when he flies in," his ex-boss said, hoisting his heavy frame out of the armchair he'd been occupying. "If they know about him his life is in danger too."

"We don't know the flight details," Reece said, folding his arms.

"Easily solved." Ed got on his cell phone. After a five minute conversation he turned to the PI. "Southwest Airlines, terminal one, 8.05 PM."

CHAPTER THREE

Charlotte remained cloistered away in the spare bedroom. She knew she'd have to face everyone soon enough but didn't have the courage to right now. She couldn't bare that Reece wouldn't look at her and her heart ached for him. He'd lost his best friend and it was her fault. They had been happy before all of this, ready to commit to a life together, and it had all changed in a moment. How could she explain it to Tommy? A single tear slid down her cheek and she brushed it away.

Once the new drama they were facing with Andre's brother was resolved she would try to reason with Reece. She had to know if there was any hope for them. A sob stuck in her throat. How could she live without him if he decided what she had done was unforgivable? A knock echoed into the compact space and Charlotte's eyes moved to the door, her heartbeat ticking up a couple of notches. Was it Reece? "Come in."

Sarah poked her head around the opening. "I just wanted to let you know we're going to LAX to pick up the sheriff. He's flying in tonight." She pushed the door back and stepped into the room. "Will you be ok?"

Charlotte nodded. "Yes." She waited a beat then said, "How's Reece doing? Is he all right?"

"He seems to be holding up ok." Sarah crossed the room, sat on the side of the bed and gave Charlotte a pained look. "I know how much you're both hurting. I wish there was something I could do."

"The fact that you're still talking to me helps. I don't think the others feel the same way."

Sarah wrapped her fingers around Charlotte's hand and gave it a reassuring squeeze. "They know it wasn't your fault. It's just going to take some time for that to sink in. I believe it will all work out, eventually."

"I wish I could be as confident." She heaved a heavy sigh. "I don't want to lose Reece. I love him so much. It breaks my heart that he won't speak to me." Another tear slid down her cheek. "Will you talk to him? Tell him how sorry I am? Tell him I love him?"

"I have tried, Charlotte, but he doesn't want to talk."

"What can I do to make him understand?" More tears slid down her face.

"Just give it some time. The expression 'time heals all wounds' really does work."

Charlotte gave her a curious frown. "How much time?"

"As much as it takes. This kind of emotional distress can't be rushed." Sarah stood up and walked to the open doorway. "I have to go. We won't be long."

"That's ok. I'll probably sleep, if I can."

The priest nodded and smiled then closed the door.

Charlotte buried her face in her pillow and burst into silent tears. She didn't feel as though she belonged here anymore. She felt like an intruder.

CHAPTER FOUR

Lozano came through the gate ten minutes after the plane landed and was surprised to see Reece, Sarah and a man he didn't know waiting for him. He rushed across the terminal and gave the PI a tight man hug. "It's good to see you. When I couldn't get in touch with you and I got that strange call I thought…"

Reece took a step back. "Yeah, I can understand that. I'm still here."

"Thank God." The sheriff's eyes roamed the terminal for Andre, Arianne and Nathaniel. He frowned and his gaze returned to Reece. "Andre?"

He nodded. "And Arianne."

"Oh no. Nathaniel?"

"No, he's fine."

Lozano let out the breath he'd been holding. "I'm real sorry, Reece. I know Andre was your closest friend."

"Yeah, he was." Tears stung the backs of his eyes and he blinked them away.

"How are you, Sheriff Lozano," Sarah said, stepping up and extending her hand. He shook it.

"Good. You?" His gaze moved to the man standing behind her.

Sarah glanced over her shoulder then turned around. "This is Lieutenant Ed Borenko. Homicide division with the LAPD."

Lozano extended his hand. "Good to meet you, Lieutenant."

"Likewise. Call me Ed, will ya. No formalities necessary."

"Thanks, Ed." The sheriff looked at Reece. "I wasn't expecting an escort. What brought you down here?"

"The phone call you received. If they know who you are you're in as much danger as we are."

The sheriff's eyes widened. "Well I appreciate you coming to pick me up."

"No problem. We need to stick together. We have a new adversary to deal with. An old resurrected one to be more precise. Shall we?" Reece gestured toward the exit and headed in that direction. Everyone followed.

Lozano caught up to him. "What do mean?"

"Andre's brother, Jacques, has reappeared on the scene."

The sheriff's face paled. "How is that possible? I thought you said he burned up in the sun. Vampires can't come back from that... can they?"

"Apparently they can. Nathaniel told me that a reliable source witnessed the ritual in Europe. All it takes is some of the deceased vampire's ashes, their blood, an awakening spell and a sorcerer who can perform it."

"Holy Mother of God!" He fingered the silver St. Jude medallion around his neck.

"Yeah. You could say that."

The group made their way out of the airport and over to the parking garage.

"So he's here to exact revenge?" The sheriff shrugged. "What?"

"He told us he can help bring Andre back from the dead." Reece pressed the remote control and the van beeped and flashed to life. He took Lozano's luggage, tossed it in the back and the four climbed inside.

"Are you going to accept his offer?"

"I want to... but it means working for him."

"You're serious?"

Reece nodded. "Deadly serious."

"We all agree he shouldn't do it," Ed told Lozano from the back seat. "But he wants Andre alive, as do we all, so..." He shrugged. "Nathaniel told Daniels that Jacques will want him to prove his loyalty before he does anything to help bring Andre back, and that could take months or even years."

Lozano glanced over his shoulder and frowned at Ed, allowing the information to circle the processing center of his brain. There had to be another way.

Heading back, Reece took a detour to his office to show Lozano the place even though it was still in a state of disrepair. When they reached the top of the landing the PI stopped in his tracks, the others pulling up short behind him on the stairs.

"What's wrong, Daniels?" Ed asked, peering around the PI, wondering what made him stop.

"Stay here," Reece whispered, pulling his pistol and easing his body across the hallway. The door to his office was ajar. Again.

Ed stepped onto the landing, pulled his weapon, and whispered, "What the hell? Not again?"

Reece raised a finger to his lips and pressed his spine against the wall beside the door.

Ed nodded and took up position on the opposite side, avoiding the squeaking floorboard in the center of the hall. No point in alerting whoever was inside.

Sarah and Lozano remained on the landing.

Reece signaled his ex-boss, counted to three with his fingers and kicked the door open. It flew back, smacked the wall and bounced off. The PI shoved it aside and stormed into the office, gun raised, Ed right behind him.

CHAPTER FIVE

"What are you doing here?" Reece asked, giving his fiancée a severe stare and stuffing his Glock into the back of his tan leather belt. "I could've shot you." He walked back to the doorway and called Sarah and Lozano inside. "It's ok. It's only Charlotte."

"I wanted to do something to help." She set the files down on the desk and came around it.

"I thought you were going to try and get some rest," Sarah said.

"I couldn't sleep so I thought I could be useful here."

Lozano stepped up to her and extended his hand. "It's good to see you again, Charlotte."

She shook it. "Thank you. It's good to see you too. What brings you to LA?"

The sheriff gazed around at the group. "I found something by accident that I thought would help us rid the world of monsters like Dracula."

Reece folded his arms. "Like what?"

Lozano turned around. "There's an ancient tome locked in the Vatican called The Grand Grimoire. It was discovered in Jerusalem in the tomb of Solomon around 1750. It's believed to have been written by Honorius of Thebes, who was supposedly possessed by Satan. It's also believed to contain occult spells including one that can eradicate vampires. I guess the devil didn't want any competition." He gave a brief chuckle.

"We know about the Grimoire. Unfortunately there's no way to get a look at its contents."

"Maybe there is," Sarah said. "Every ancient manuscript and parchment has been categorized, copied and logged on computer in the secret archives."

"And?" Reece gave her a curious frown.

She gave him a self-assured smile. "And I know someone who has access to those files."

"Did you know the book is rumored to be fire proof?" Lozano was impressed.

"Yes, but I doubt anyone has tried to find out if it's true. The book is dated somewhere around 1520 AD," Sarah told him. She looked at Reece. "I'll call and see what I can find out about the spell. We also have to recite the incantation to close the rift. With everything that's happened I haven't had time to prepare for it."

"Let's work on one problem at a time. I think getting rid of Dracula takes priority right now. We can deal with the other demons that come through later."

"Do you know where he is?" the sheriff asked.

"No. But Nathaniel knows someone who can find out." Reece's eyes moved briefly to Charlotte sitting behind his desk. What was he going to do about her?

"I've been giving this whole Jacques' offer thing some thought and I might've come up with a solution." Lozano propped himself on the edge of Reece's desk and folded his arms. "I think you should tell Jacques that you're prepared to work for him only if he brings Andre back now. Once your friend has returned then you can use the spell on Jacques and be rid of him too."

"You don't know what that monster's like," Ed said, poking his finger at the sheriff. "He wouldn't go for it. He wants to control Daniels and in doing so control the rest of us too."

Lozano raised defensive hands. "It was just a suggestion."

"Oh, yeah, sorry. Didn't mean to get all in your face." Ed stepped back.

Reece ran the sheriff's idea around his mind. "It's worth a try. What can he say? No?"

At that moment, Jacques appeared at the door. "My ears were burning. I wonder who is talking about me."

Lozano shot up off the desk and stared at him, eyes wide. He wasn't aware that Jacques was Andre's identical twin. "Andre?"

"No. He's nothing like Andre. It's Jacques." Reece's intense stare locked onto the vampire. "Why are you here?"

"Have you come to a decision regarding my offer?" He remained in the open doorway.

"As a matter of fact I have. To show good faith I'd like you to have the ritual to bring Andre back performed before I begin working for you."

The left corner of Jacques' mouth hitched up into a smirk. "And why would I do that?"

"Because you need my help as much as I need yours. I'm sure we can come to some kind of mutual agreement as to the terms of the arrangement. Don't you?"

Jacques' dark gaze moved around the group then rested on the PI. "I will take your proposal into consideration."

"I want an answer now." Reece wasn't backing down.

Neither was Jacques. "You shall have your answer when I have had time to consider it."

Reece glowered at him. "Forget it. I should have known you wouldn't negotiate."

Jacques didn't appreciate being manipulated but he did need the PI's assistance. What was the private investigator planning? He could hear the cogs ticking over in the man's brain. "Very well. I will organize the ritual. I assume you will want to be present."

"You bet. We all do."

Jacques once again crossed the threshold, stalked across the room to where Reece stood, reached around him, picked up a business card from off the desk and ran his eyes over the white rectangle. "I will be in touch once things are in motion. It may take a while." He gave the PI an intense stare, pushed the card into the inside pocket of his jacket, turned on his heel and was gone.

A satisfied smile spread across Reece's face. Would the victory be short lived?

"Do you really think he'll go through with it?" Ed asked, a note of skepticism in his voice.

"Yeah, I do. He needs our help with something big and it's in his best interest do whatever it takes to get it done."

Lozano stepped up to him. "I had no idea he looked exactly like Andre. What a head spin."

"Sorry about that. Yeah, I should've mentioned it." Reece gave him a sideward glance.

The sheriff waved it off. "Nah, all good. The question is do you trust him?"

Reece's stern gaze moved to the empty doorway. "Not within an inch of his undead life."

CHAPTER SIX

Jacques stalked out of the building, across the sidewalk and stepped into the black limousine. He despised Reece Daniels. And the fact that he now had to bend to his will instead of the other way around did not sit well with his uncompromising nature. He glanced up at the second story window with the black and gold logo Double D Investigations emblazoned across it. Would the PI and his crew help him once they knew what lay ahead?

"Let us go," he ordered.

The driver eased the limousine into the traffic heading for the Sunset Tower Hotel on Sunset Boulevard. He would arrange for the sorcerer to fly to Los Angeles to perform the ritual in the next couple of weeks and have the PI on his payroll soon after. He had plans for them all. Permanent plans.

By the time the vehicle pulled under the marquee covered hotel driveway it was almost ten o'clock. Jacques told the driver to pick him up the following evening right on sunset, handed him a hundred dollar bill and watched the car disappear into the sea of traffic before heading for the sidewalk. He was ravenous and needed sustenance. He knew there were parking facilities in the parklands beside the hotel and decided a brief stroll was in order. As he descended the steps his senses picked up on a nervous human heartbeat. His eyes roamed the row of cars in the dimly lit, tree lined space searching for the female. *Ah, there she is.* The young woman was beside her car fumbling through her purse. He drew her scent deep into his nostrils as he approached. Delicious.

"May I be of some assistance?" Jacques voice echoed around them in the stillness. The dog park was quiet at this time of the evening.

The young woman jumped backwards and spun around. "Oh! You – you startled me. What did you say?" Her hand moved to her throat and her breathing quickened.

"I asked if I could assist you." He gave her a charming smile.

"I – I can't seem to find my keys. I must've left them somewhere." Her heart rate accelerated. She was afraid of him. He enjoyed the sensation of mortal fear.

His left eyebrow arched. "Are you certain?"

"I – I think so. They're not in my purse." She held her bag open to him.

"Perhaps it would be wise to recount your movements. It may jog your memory."

"Well, I – I was at the Tower Bar with friends. But I don't remember taking the keys out of my purse." She frowned, trying to recall the events of the evening.

Jacques gestured toward the hotel. "Would you like me to accompany you back inside so you can ask if they've been handed in?"

"That's very kind of you, but…"

He extended his hand. "Please forgive me for being so rude. I'm Jacques by the way. What is your name?"

She glanced at his hand and trembled when their palms connected. "A – April." She gave him a nervous grin.

"How lovely." He gripped the young woman's wrist and gazed into her wide, frightened eyes. "Don't scream. I am not going to hurt you." His alluring smile widened into fangs as the thought crossed his mind. *But I am going to enjoy taking your life.*

☙❧

Back at Reece's apartment, everyone was preparing for bed. It was imperative that they all remain together while Dracula was AWOL and Jacques was back in town. Who knew what either of them was planning? It was the only way to keep his team and Lozano safe. As Charlotte headed down the hallway to the room she occupied Reece came up behind her.

"Charlotte?" She turned around. "I think it would be a good idea for you to go stay with Mrs. Jenkins for a while."

"Why?"

Reece sighed. "Because I need some time to sort things out without you being here."

Tears stung the backs of her eyes and she blinked to prevent them from spilling down her face. "What am I supposed to tell Tommy? He thinks we were married in Vegas."

The PI sighed again. "Yeah, I know." He shook his head. "I don't know what you should tell him."

"Well that doesn't help me at all, does it? My going there is your decision, not mine." She folded her arms, the strain evident on her face. "Are we ever going to talk about what happened?"

"At some point, yes, but not right now. I've got too much to deal with at the moment."

"And I don't?" She glowered at him. "So our relationship isn't important to you, is that what you're saying?"

"No, that's not what I'm saying."

"Then what?" She frowned up into his eyes, tears glistening in hers. Her life was crumbling around her and she didn't know how to stop it.

"Look…" He stared into her tear-filled eyes trying to interpret his feelings. His heart ached for many reasons – the loss of his friend, his disintegrating relationship with Charlotte – his uncertainty about his feelings for her. His serious gaze remained on her for a moment then he gave a heavy sigh, turned around and walked away.

Charlotte dashed into the room, closed the door and burst into tears. She had never seen the look of contempt in Reece's eyes until tonight.

"Everything ok?" Lozano asked, noticing the scowl on the PI's face.

Reece's frowning gaze met his. "Huh?"

"Is everything ok?"

"Yeah, everything's fine."

"You're sure? Coz from where I'm standing it doesn't look like it." The sheriff could sense the tension in the atmosphere and knew something was off.

"I'm heading for bed. Goodnight." Reece stalked back along the hallway to his room.

Lozano walked over to the foldout sofa bed he was sharing with Ed. "Do you know what that was all about?"

"It's a long story."

"You tired?"

Ed heaved a heavy sigh. "Not really." He sat up and leaned against the backrest. "I'll give you the abbreviated version."

"Sure."

"Dracula knew all our plans because Charlotte was tellin' him."

"What?!"

"It wasn't her fault. He compelled her when he had her prisoner."

"He what?" Lozano sat down on his side of the bed.

"Vamps can mesmerize people with their eyes. Make 'em do what they want 'em to do. It's like hypnotism. That's what Drac did to Charlotte."

Lozano rubbed the back of his neck. "Man."

"Yeah."

"So is that why Reece and Charlotte are having problems?"

Ed nodded. "Reece can't get his head around the fact that Charlotte got Andre killed."

The sheriff gave him an incredulous frown. "Yeah, but she didn't do it on purpose. The vampire made her."

Ed sighed. "Reece said it still doesn't change the fact that Andre's dead."

"Thing is, if Jacques brings him back there won't be an issue."

Ed gave Lozano an 'are you kidding me' look. "There'll still be an issue because it happened."

"Has anyone tried reasoning with him?"

"Sarah tried but it made no difference."

"Would you mind if I tried?"

Ed's right eyebrow rose. "Nope. If you think you can talk some sense into him be my guest."

"Thanks." Lozano lay down on top of the covers on the sofa bed and stared at the ceiling. He felt compelled to help Reece and Charlotte work things out, even if the PI didn't want his assistance.

CHAPTER SEVEN

Jacques stood on the balcony of the penthouse suite at 2 AM gazing at the busy street below, the glare of the headlights on the moving vehicles against the dark night lit up Sunset Boulevard, giving it an ethereal glow. He wondered if the PI would do what he needed him and his team to do. Would they end Eva Van Helsing, who had been hunting him since his return, then go in search of Dracula and finish him once and for all? Jacques was aware they had already tried and failed. Was he placing too much faith in someone who was unable to accomplish the task? Time would tell. He wanted total control over the minions of undead spread across the globe. He craved the position of principal vampire and he would do *anything* to attain it. Even murder an old comrade.

Jacques wished he could utilize the vampire hunter's extraordinary capabilities to end Vlad's life, but she was hell bent on ending his first and wouldn't back down. She'd told him she did not negotiate with blood drinkers when they had faced off in Vienna, while Jacques was on a quest to find Vlad Tepes a year ago. He had heard the vampire was there. Eva was the great, great, great, great granddaughter of Abraham Van Helsing, Dracula's nemesis, and was a far more astute adversary. She had almost ended his life with a silver dagger handed down through the Van Helsing generations, but had missed his heart only by inches during the assault. He would have killed her himself, if he could have. Unfortunately, her agility and speed had prevented him from doing so.

His eyes roamed the patrons sitting outside the Wild West style restaurant and the Starbucks across the street in search of his next meal. It would take only seconds for him to swoop down into the driveway and exit the hotel grounds. But it had to be for the perfect someone. His palate had changed since his resurrection and he favored only A+ blood types now. The others left him with a disagreeable stomach and a bitter taste on his tongue.

He spotted a young woman saying goodnight to friends on the opposite sidewalk and his eyes followed her as she made her way along a nearby side street, the carpark full. He leapt from the balcony, making sure he was not seen, and lowered himself onto the rooftop of the valet parking building, keeping his hungry gaze on her. She had wandered up the hill heading to her car.

Jacques dropped onto the driveway, straightened his attire and whipped across the busy boulevard in hot pursuit. He could smell her blood pulsing through her veins and the bloodlust enveloped him. He was a blur in the night, blending into the shadows, as he followed her to a custom pink Volkswagen Bug.

His canines extended and locked into place, his mouth salivating at the expectation of her warm A+ blood running down his throat.

He'd heard one of her female friends mention her name.

"Gabby," he called after her. He enjoyed the sadistic games he played with mortals.

The young woman stopped on the hill and turned around, frowning at him as he came toward her. "Do I... do I know you?" He was incredibly attractive and she knew she'd remember his face if she had met him before. High set cheekbones and chiseled jaw, gorgeous, dark bedroom eyes. Her heartbeat quickened. Was he going to ask her out?

"Not yet. I saw you at the restaurant." He glanced over his shoulder then returned his gaze to her. "I'm sorry for following you like this..."

She gave him a cautious smile. "That's ok. I don't remember seeing you. Were you there with friends?"

Jacques stepped closer and smiled. Her eyes widened in horror. He pushed his gloved hand over her mouth to stifle the scream he knew would come and was about to whisk her into the shadows of a narrow easement beside the high concrete fence opposite her car when something hard, fast and sharp hit him in the left shoulder blade and he released the young woman with a gasp of pain. Someone would pay for this.

"Run!" the female European voice ordered from behind him.

The young woman took off down the hill toward the restaurant, streaks of mascara running down her face as she peered over her shoulder sobbing.

Jacques spun around and came face to face with Eva Van Helsing wielding a crossbow.

He reached over his shoulder with his right hand, wrenched the arrow from his back and tossed it aside. Lucky for him it hadn't hit a major organ, although he knew it would have if she had meant to kill him.

"So, Jacques Delacroix, up to your old tricks I see." She strutted toward him, weapon raised.

"The need for blood isn't an old trick. It's a necessity for procuring my life as you are already aware." He gave her a self-satisfied smirk and stood his ground. "May I enquire why you are here?"

Her glossy plum-colored lips widened into a shrewd smile. "I think you know why."

"Mm, as I suspected. So why didn't you kill me just now?" His brooding gaze bore into hers.

"There is time."

Sirens rang out in the distance. Someone had contacted the police.

"Well, it has been enlightening chatting with you but I must take my leave." Jacques dissolved into the night.

Eva continued up the hill to her car, threw the crossbow on the floor behind her seat and climbed in. She had a stop to make.

CHAPTER EIGHT

She entered the property through the garage and stood at the open doorway into the house, her senses on high alert, her acute hearing homing in on any unusual sounds nearby. The fingers of both hands gripped a Glock 18C fully automatic pistol loaded with silver cartridges. She wasn't about to take any unnecessary chances. She peered around the doorjamb. No one. She knew the lights wouldn't be on because immortals didn't need light to see by. Their acute nocturnal vision could see clearly in the dark. She made her way cautiously up the four steps and into the back of the two-story home.

Would she find him before he found her? She hoped so.

Eva Van Helsing continued moving through the lower extremities of the house: the kitchen, the dining room, the living room then into the entry hall. *Where is he?* Her eyes moved to the upstairs landing. *He must be up there.* She crossed the entrance and eased herself up the staircase one step at a time, gun raised. If she had a heartbeat it would be thundering in her chest right now. She had been turned into an immortal back in the sixties, which had proved advantageous, especially in her line of work. Now she had all the time in the world to find and eradicate the bloodsucking vermin roaming the earth, feeding and murdering. Yes, she knew she was also one of them, but unlike some she didn't kill to sustain her existence.

Once she reached the upper level of the house, she continued forward with caution, her ears attuned to every creak and groan of the property. He could be lying in wait anywhere and she would not allow herself to be caught off guard. The hallway was in deep shadow as all the room doors were closed. Eva's nocturnal vision scanned the alcoves and statues along the lengthy hall, making sure no one was hidden amongst them. Still nothing.

He has to be somewhere.

Her eyes continued to roam the gloomy depths.

A strong arm slid around her throat, dragging her backwards along the carpeted passage. She struggled and clawed at the hand to free herself but he was far too strong. Feeling light-headed, Eva dropped her weapon. She would not give up without a fight. A burst of adrenalin surged through her body and she used both hands to pummel his. She wished she could bite it. The arm tightened around her neck until she saw glowing yellow stars before her eyes. Her vision blurred… then blackness.

When she came to, Eva was tied to a chair in the middle of the living room, Nathaniel standing before her with his arms folded across his huge, muscular chest. "How did you find me? And why are you here?"

Her dark gaze met his. "Why do you think I am here? You are a vampire and I am a vampire hunter."

"Yes, I am aware of that. But you too are a vampire."

"So? That does not prevent me from doing what I was born to do." She wriggled her wrists, trying to ascertain how tight her restraints were.

"Why are you trying to dispatch me?"

"You are Jacques' henchman. Why wouldn't I? I will have him soon enough too."

"I am not associated with him any longer. I have not been for almost three years. When he died…"

Her eyes widened. "What do you mean 'when he died'?"

Nathaniel's right eyebrow arched. "Jacques died. He burned in the sun."

She shook her head. "No, that cannot be. How is he here?"

"He was resurrected."

"*That* is not possible."

"I am afraid it is. Believe me, I wish he was not here either, but he is and we have a new set of issues to deal with."

She frowned at him. "Who is 'we'?"

Nathaniel clasped his hands behind his back and paced once then turned around. "You do not need to know that yet."

"So what do you plan to do with me? Kill me?" She raised her chin in a gesture of defiance.

"No. I am not going to kill you. But you must give me your word that you will not attempt to kill me, either."

"And why should I do that?"

"Because I believe we can work together to acquire what we both want."

"Which is?"

"Jacques' and Vlad's eternal demise."

CHAPTER NINE

The following morning, Lozano was up before anyone else. He showered, dressed, put on the coffee, and waited for whoever woke up next. Ed was still asleep on the sofa bed, snoring loudly, and the sheriff wondered how he hadn't woken up yet. Cops usually slept with one eye open and wouldn't the noise wake him anyway? He poured himself a cup of black coffee, wandered over to the window and gazed outside. He checked his watch. 5.40 AM. The sun's golden aura almost reached the tops of the high rises. He heard a sound behind him and swung around.

Reece crossed the living room and into the kitchen. Lozano followed him.

"Morning," the sheriff said. "Manage to get any sleep?"

"Not much." Reece poured himself a mug of steaming coffee and took a cautious sip. "You?"

"What do you think?" Both men's eyes moved to Ed.

"You can bunk in with me if you like," Reece offered.

"Thanks. I might take you up on that." He sipped his coffee. "So how are things?"

Reece gave him a curious frown. "What things?"

"You and Charlotte?"

"I really don't want to get into it right now. We've got enough to worry about."

"Come on, Reece, that's a cop out and you know it. You need to purge it out of your system if you expect to move on."

The PI slid his mug onto the kitchen counter and folded his arms. "What do you want me to say?"

"Look, I understand how you feel about... about losing your best friend, but it wasn't Charlotte's fault. It was beyond her control. You have to see it for what it is."

"I know it wasn't her fault."

"Well then..."

Reece raised his hand. "Just let me finish, ok?"

"Sure, sorry. Go on."

"Andre's still dead and she did have a hand in it, regardless of whether she knew what she was doing or not."

"You know that's not fair, don't you?" Lozano poured more coffee into his mug and leaned against the sink.

The PI sighed. "Fair or not, I can't get past that right now."

"What if it had been you? You know, while you were out at the abandoned motel? What if they'd compelled you and you got Andre killed?"

Reece gave him a dark stare, folded his arms and gave another heavy sigh. "Then I'd be the one in Charlotte's position and have to take responsibility for my actions."

Lozano gave him an incredulous frown. "But they weren't her actions they were Dracula's." He waited a beat. "Do you still love her?"

"I think..." He shook his head. "I'm not sure how I feel anymore."

Sarah came into the kitchen, her eyes moving around the room. "Good morning. Have you seen Charlotte?"

Both Lozano and Reece gave her a questioning stare and said, "No."

"Why?" Reece asked.

"Because she's not in her room."

"Did you check the bathroom?" He remembered Sarah telling him to check the bathroom at the Golden Nugget when he couldn't find Charlotte.

"Yes, it was the second place I looked."

The men followed Sarah back to Charlotte's room and stepped inside.

Reece stood with hands on hips and scanned the entire space. Charlotte's belongings were gone. "She left."

"How do you know?" Sarah asked.

"Her things are gone."

"Surely she would've said something... or left a note."

"Not after our conversation last night." Reece had a sheepish look on his face.

"What did you say to her?" Sarah gave him a serious frown.

Reece sighed. "I said it would be best if she stayed at Mrs. Jenkins' for a while."

Sarah folded her arms and scowled at him. "Why would you tell her to do that? Do you know how much she's hurting right now? How much she blames herself for everything that's happened?"

"I'm not the bad guy here." The PI pressed a hand to his chest. "It might be a good idea to remember that."

"Neither is she," Sarah told him, stepping into the hall. The men followed. "She didn't know what she was doing. Maybe you should get that through your head." She strutted off to the living room.

Reece gave Lozano an uncertain glance and sighed.

"She's right you know." The sheriff left Reece standing in the hallway.

The PI stalked into his room and closed the door. Why was everyone giving him a hard time? Charlotte was the one who had betrayed them all. His heartbeat ticked up a couple notches. He was annoyed and frustrated with the whole situation. Dracula had certainly pushed a wedge between him and his friends. Was he going to let that monster win? He picked up his cell phone from off the night stand and hit speed dial. Andre's voicemail kicked in. Shit. He'd automatically hit the wrong number. He listened to his friend's voice and broke down, tears rolling down his face.

☞

Later that morning, a knock on the door echoed into the living room and Ed strutted over to check through the peephole before opening it. He turned to the others and frowned. "It's Nathaniel. How is that possible?" He swung the door back. "How the hell are you here during the day?" Ed eyed the attractive woman standing beside him. "Who's that?"

"May we?" Nathaniel motioned inside.

Ed nodded and stepped out of the way. "Oh? Sure, sure." He waved them inside.

Reece got up off the sofa and crossed the room. He stood with hands on hips frowning at Nathaniel. "How are you here during daylight hours?"

The vampire raised his left hand to reveal a solid, white gold ring with a crested blue stone. "Eva gave me a daywalker ring. It is crafted from Lapis

Lazuli and has been charmed by a sorcerer." He turned to her. "Please, forgive me. This is Eva Van Helsing. She is of the Van Helsing vampire hunter family. Her great, great, great, great grandfather was Abraham Van Helsing."

"So, not only is Dracula real but so are the Van Helsings?" Why was he not surprised?

"Yes. Very much so." Eva extended her hand. "It is a pleasure to meet a fellow hunter."

Reece shook it. "We," he said, turning and glancing at the others, "hunt every kind of otherworldly creature out there, not just vampires."

"That is commendable." Eva's perceptive gaze roamed the other faces in the room and rested on Lozano. "And you have an intuitive among you. How useful."

Sheriff Lozano stepped up beside Reece. "I'm new to all of this. I wasn't sure what I was until I met these amazing people."

"You have a wonderful gift. I hope you use it wisely." Her eyes returned to Reece.

Lozano's face reddened and he wasn't sure what to say. He gave her an embarrassed smile, crossed the room and sat down next to Sarah.

"I believe you have had a number of altercations with Vlad. Perhaps we can compare notes and come up with a solution to our mutual problem." She gave the PI a suggestive smile, her seductive stare remaining on him.

Something primal shifted in his groin and he turned his gaze to Nathaniel. "I'm glad you can finally move around during the day. It'll certainly benefit the team." He could still feel Eva's eyes on him, his gut tightened.

"Yes. I am grateful to Eva for offering it to me. It will be very advantageous."

"Let's sit down and discuss what we're going to do next."

"I have already encountered Jacques. I prevented him from killing a young woman." Eva said, following Nathaniel and the PI across the room.

"Do you know where he's staying?" Reece turned his head to look at her.

"Yes, as a matter of fact, I do. He is a guest at the Sunset Tower Hotel."

"Thanks. Good to know."

"My pleasure." Her lips spread into an alluring smile.

Reece couldn't take his eyes off the woman. Her stunning face drew him in. After a long moment, he cleared his throat and turned back to the others.

Sarah noticed the interaction between them. She stood up. "Why don't you sit with the sheriff?" She knew he was in two minds about Charlotte, so why tempt fate? Eva seemed keen to retain Reece's interest.

"Thanks," he said, moving around the coffee table and taking a seat beside Lozano.

Eva lowered her curvy, tightly clad figure into an armchair and crossed one, long booted leg over the other.

Nathaniel remained standing. He, too, could sense the attraction and would speak to Eva alone later to warn her off. Reece did not need the distraction nor did he need the attention when his relationship was on the line.

CHAPTER TEN

Jacques was alone this time. No adherent entourage, no vampire army. Only him. He thought if he traveled on his own he would draw less attention to himself against the likes of Eva Van Helsing and other vampire hunters wandering the earth. The unfortunate truth was he had been wrong. She had tracked him down in a very short space of time and he was not pleased with those turn of events. It wouldn't be long before she made another attempt at ending his undead life and he would have to take certain precautionary measures to prevent that from happening.

Since his reawakening, as he preferred to call it, he didn't need to sleep. He wasn't sure why his body didn't need to regenerate, but he never seemed to tire anymore. An advantage he knew would serve him well and help to keep him alive.

He paced the hotel suite from end to end, the ceiling to floor drapes drawn so that the rooms were dark, hiding him from the sun. He hadn't dared step out onto the wrap around balcony to see if his newly reanimated immortal life also allowed him to venture into the daylight. Perhaps he would at some point, but for now he was satisfied with being back in the land of the living and making plans for his future and the demise of Reece Daniels and his cohorts. The evening had always been the time he enjoyed most, anyhow, and he still chose the shadow of night as his playground.

A knock on the door pulled him from his thoughts and his eyes moved toward it. Ah, his meal had arrived. A lady of the evening, or better known today as a stress therapist. He gave a quiet chuckle at the thought and headed for the door. Perhaps she could be useful in that regard before he devoured her. She was the kind of woman that wouldn't be missed when she disappeared. He had made sure of that.

CHAPTER ELEVEN

Sarah contacted one of the brothers she knew working in the Vatican archives and asked him if he would be willing to help her. She had saved his life from a rogue vampire once and he had vowed that if she ever needed his help he would do whatever she asked. But would he? There had been something forbidden between them, feelings neither of them could hide. He had been a novice clergyman back then but had now been at the Vatican for more than twenty years and was in a position of trust. Could she ask him to betray the laws and values of the church – corrupt as it was – to steal copies of long-hidden documentation that could rid the world of creatures like Dracula and Jacques for good? Yes, yes she could and she had to. She had no choice. The other end of the line rang for a long time. She knew she had to hold on until someone picked up. This was a matter of life and death. The human race's. She heard a click.

"Hello, Vincenzo, it's been a long time." Sarah's heart rate ticked up a notch at hearing his rich Italian accent. They had been secret lovers once and she couldn't deny the lingering feelings she still held for him, despite her love for Ed Borenko.

"Ciao, il mio amore. You need my help, yes?"

"Yes."

"What can I do?"

"What I need could get you excommunicated... or worse."

"I owe you my life, mia dolce. Whatever it is I will do it."

"I need you to send me the pages of the Grand Grimoire specifically related to vampires."

Silence.

"Vincenzo?"

"I – I cannot."

Sarah sighed. "What happened to 'I owe you my life'?"

"If it was anything else I would gladly do it, but…"

"If you don't help me many people will die. We've already lost loved ones because of him."

"Him?" Vincenzo's eyebrows rose and his face paled. He knew who Sarah was talking about.

"Yes, *him*."

"Va bene lo farò." He closed his eyes, shook his head and made the sign of the cross.

"Grazie. If there was any other way I wouldn't have asked. I hope you know that?"

"Si, I know."

"How soon?"

"I am not sure. I will need time."

"We don't have much time, Vincenzo."

"I will do my best. I will call you when I have it."

"Thank you. Please be careful."

"Always. Arrivederci, my love."

"Arrivederci." A single tear slid from the corner of Sarah's right eye and she swiped it away. Vincenzo was a long time ago. Ed was her man now. She sniffed back the urge to cry, stood up and turned around. Ed was in the doorway.

"Everything ok?" He had a worried frown on his face.

"Yes, everything's fine."

"Did you get onto that guy at the Vatican?"

"I did. He's going to help us get the pages."

"Well, that's good news. At least something's goin' right today."

Sarah walked over to him and wrapped her arms around him, burying her head against his bulky chest.

"What do ya know. That's two things." He raised her face up to his and kissed her gently on the lips.

The pair joined the others in the living room.

"How'd it go?" Reece asked.

"Vincenzo will get back to me once he has the pages."

"Great." Reece breathed a relieved sigh.

Lozano stood up. "What are you going to do about the Van Helsing woman? Do you trust her?"

Reece eyed the sheriff for a moment. "I don't know. She seems genuine in her quest to rid the world of vampires like Vlad and Jacques."

"Yeah, and every other vamp too," Ed added. "Remember we have vamp friends."

"I haven't forgotten. But I think we should use what she knows to help us. Don't you?"

Sarah knew it was a bad idea having Eva Van Helsing around. She could tell Reece was attracted to her and that would definitely interfere with reuniting him and Charlotte.

CHAPTER TWELVE

Charlotte didn't go to Mrs. Jenkins' house as Reece had suggested, instead, the next morning she traveled out of the city early and headed to the San Fernando Valley where her ex-partner lived. She and Todd Lassiter had worked missing persons for five years together before Josh Jamieson arrived on the scene. Their partnership had been dynamic and they had successfully solved many cases together before he'd decided to take an early retirement. He was fifteen years her senior, widowed, with one adult son living in Australia. She knew he would offer her a place of sanctuary while she figured out what to do next.

They'd been close at one time and had almost begun a romantic relationship. Working together had revealed the best and worst of their natures but that hadn't prevented their attraction drawing them even closer to one another. That had been eleven years ago, before she'd married Dan. She was glad it hadn't developed into anything more otherwise she wouldn't have had anywhere else to go. She didn't have close friends, well, except for Reece's team, but she didn't feel exceptionally close to them anymore. She'd spent all of her time working and raising her son so something had to give. And it had been personal relationships.

She'd called Tommy from their apartment the previous evening and had given him a happy account of events. They were still in Las Vegas having a wonderful time. She would send pictures soon. She was sorry she hadn't already. What else could she do? She couldn't tell him that her relationship with Reece might be over for good. Tommy loved Reece. How could she break that kind of news to him? No, for now she would let him believe everything was fine. If all else failed, she would have to come up with a condensed version of the truth, but not yet. She wasn't giving up on their relationship. And, at some point, when she knew she was ready to, she would face Reece and insist they talk it out. He could ignore her all he wanted for now, but he couldn't indefinitely.

Charlotte pulled the car up outside the main entrance to the ranch-style house and climbed out. The property was extensive with three horses cavorting in one of the top paddock's outdoor pens. Her ex-partner had yearned to own a horse ranch one day and he had made his dream come true. The scenery here was beautiful with a backdrop of the St Gabriel mountain range in the distance.

Todd opened the door and came around the sedan to her, arms wide, and wrapped them around her. "It's good to see you, hon. Been a while."

The minute Charlotte was cocooned in his comforting embrace she burst into tears, unable to hold back her distressed emotions any longer.

"Hey, what's wrong?" Todd held her tight while she sobbed, her body shaking against his.

After a long while, Charlotte did her best to compose herself and eased herself out of his arms. "Sorry about that. It's been a difficult few weeks." Her eyes met his sincere, concerned gaze. "Is it ok if I stay here for a while?"

Although Todd was older than her he was still an attractive man –tall, broad-shouldered, chiseled features, with graying temples. His pale blue eyes roamed her tear streaked face. "Of course it is. Stay as long as you need." He opened the trunk of her car and tugged the suitcase out then took her hand and led her into the house. She was in need of a trustworthy shoulder.

The warmth and familiarity of the man gave Charlotte solace. She knew she'd made the right decision coming here. "Thank you, Todd. You don't know how much this means to me."

"You know you're welcome here anytime." He set the suitcase down in the entry hall and turned around. "Want to talk about it?"

Charlotte sniffed back the urge to cry again and shook her head. "Not right now." She gave a thin smile. "Maybe later."

"Sure." He smiled. "You know I'm here if you need me. Right?" He rubbed her arm.

She nodded. "I know."

"Ok, well, let me show you to your room." He wheeled the suitcase down the hall, opened the double doors at the end, and dropped the bag onto the bench stool at the foot of the king size bed. "Feel like something to eat? Or some coffee, maybe?"

"Coffee would be great. Thanks." She entered the room and walked over to the bed. "I'll just take a quick shower and be right out."

"Take your time. No rush." Todd stepped into the hallway and gave her a concerned glance before closing the door. He knew she'd open up to him once she was settled in and he hoped he could help. The engagement ring on her finger hadn't gone unnoticed.

Charlotte gave a heavy sigh and dropped onto the bed. How could she convince Reece to forgive her for what she'd done? How could she forgive herself?

ᘓ

When Charlotte entered the spacious, galley style kitchen, Todd was making waffles over by the garden window which held a selection of herbs, chilies, and other accoutrements. The sweet, pastry aroma and crispy bacon smell of the breakfast dish permeated the room and drifted into her nostrils causing her stomach to give a low growl. She hadn't felt hungry earlier but now she did. She wandered past the island counter, over to the round table by the ceiling to floor bay window and took a seat, the sun's rays infusing the pane of glass warm against her back.

Todd scooped the waffle onto a plate containing crispy strips of bacon, picked up the second plate on the counter and crossed the room, placing the breakfast in front of her. "Help yourself to the butter and maple syrup," he said, taking the seat opposite and setting his plate down. "I hope you're hungry."

"It all looks so good. I didn't think I was hungry until I smelled the bacon cooking." Charlotte dropped a curl of butter onto her waffle then poured the syrup over the top and breathed in the buttery goodness.

Todd pointed across the table. "Eat up. You don't want it to get cold."

Charlotte cut into her waffle, ran the segment on her fork around the pool of sticky syrup on her plate and popped it into her mouth. She gave a satisfied sigh as the warm, sweet maple taste spread across her tongue. "Mm. How did you learn to make waffles like these?"

"My mom's recipe." His smile reached his eyes.

"They're so good." Charlotte continued to scoop syrupy waffle and bacon into her mouth.

The older man sitting across from her waited a beat then said, "Do you feel like talking about what's brought you out here now?"

Charlotte's gaze met his and she wiped her mouth with the napkin before answering. "If I told you, you wouldn't believe me."

Todd set his knife and fork down on his plate. "Try me." He wanted to help her but knew he couldn't unless she opened up to him. "Why don't you start at the beginning?" He pointed to the engagement ring still on her finger. She'd forgotten to leave it in her room when she left Reece's apartment. "Who's the lucky man?"

She hesitated. "Do you remember Reece Daniels?"

"Sure. A good cop and a genuine guy." His right eyebrow arched. "I thought he was a confirmed bachelor."

Charlotte shrugged. "I guess people change. He and Tommy get along so well. Maybe that's what changed his mind."

"I hope he knows how lucky he is." Todd's eyes remained on her. "Is he the reason you're here?"

Charlotte's gaze moved to the food on her plate. "Partly."

"So what's the other part?"

"You won't believe me."

Todd eased his six foot frame back into his chair and folded his arms. "Like I said, try me."

She shook her head. "You'll think I'm insane."

"Why don't you let me be the judge of that."

Charlotte sighed. "Ok." She searched his face wondering what he would think of her after she told him and realized there wasn't much point in backing down now. "Reece and I were eloping to Las Vegas when I was drugged and abducted from LAX. As it turns out, the kidnappers contacted him and told him to continue on to Vegas and they'd be in touch once he was there."

Todd's relaxed demeanor tightened. He sat up straight on his chair and frowned. "So what happened?"

"Reece called his team and they followed him there. I guess he knew he'd need their help to locate me so..."

"Where'd they take you?"

"I woke up in a dive of a motel somewhere in an older section of Vegas.

Someone in a hood came back and drugged me again. I thought I was going to die." A tear slipped down her left cheek and she brushed it away. "I thought they'd injected me with some kind of poison."

"How did Reece find you?"

Charlotte fingered the napkin on the table. "He didn't. I was released and ended up in the hospital. They notified the police and that's how he found me."

Todd gave a deep sigh. "Do you know who took you?"

Her eyes moved to his but she didn't answer.

"Charlotte?"

"Yes, I know who took me."

"So who was it? Did they catch him… or them?"

Charlotte shook her head. "No. He got away."

A long, uncomfortable silence hung in the air for what seemed like the longest time before Todd spoke again. "Tell me who took you."

"Before I do I want to explain about me and Reece... why we're not together right now."

"Ok." His eyes roamed her sad face and he noticed tears welling in her eyes again.

"I did something terrible, Todd."

"I can't believe that of you, Charlotte."

"Well it's true."

"What did you do that was so terrible?"

"I got two of Reece's team killed."

Todd leaned on the table top. "How?"

"The abductors messed with my mind and I didn't know what I was doing."

"What do you mean?"

"While they had me they, for want of a better word, hypnotized me into relaying information back to them so they knew what Reece and his team were planning to do."

"And they killed two of Daniels' team because of what you told them?"

Charlotte nodded without answering.

"Hon, you didn't know you were doing it. How can it be your fault?"

"That still doesn't change the fact that Reece's best friend was killed, does it?" She frowned into his eyes and another tear slid down her cheek.

"Oh."

"Yes. Oh."

"And he knows all of this? The hypnotizing thing..."

"He knows." She swiped at another tear threatening to spill from the corner of her right eye.

Todd moved over to the chair beside Charlotte and took her hand in his. "He'll come around once he's had time to process it."

"I don't know if he will, Todd. I'm afraid of losing him."

"He obviously loves you enough to ask you to marry him so I think he'll do the right thing in the end."

"I hope so."

"So who was it that took you?"

Charlotte stared into his eyes. "That's the part you're not going to believe."

CHAPTER THIRTEEN

When Reece's cell rang his gut told him it wasn't good news. He rushed across the office, snatched the phone off his desk and frowned at the screen. Caller Unknown. Something slithered deep in his belly as he pressed the button to answer the call. "Hello?"

"I want you to come to my hotel," Jacques commanded.

Reece groaned inwardly. "When?"

"Now."

"Why?"

"Because I am ready to discuss the terms of our agreement. Do you have a problem with that, Detective?"

Reece walked across to the window and leaned against the frame. "It's daytime. Why aren't you sleeping?"

"That's a long story. One I might consider sharing with you when you arrive." The line went dead.

The PI pulled the phone from his ear and frowned at the screen. Jacques was already giving him orders and he didn't like it.

"What'd the bloodsucker want?" Ed asked, hoisting himself out of a chair and crossing the office. He could tell it was Jacques by the succinct monologue of the brief conversation on Reece's end.

"I've been summoned to his hotel suite." Reece slid his phone onto the desk and dropped into his office chair.

"And you're goin'?" Ed's brow wrinkled into an incredulous frown.

"Of course I am. What other choice do I have?" He leaned forward, resting his elbows on the wooden surface. "He's the only one that can bring Andre back. If I don't do what he wants he won't help us."

"You're going to find out exactly when he's planning on doing that, aren't you?" Lozano asked. "Bring Andre back, I mean."

Reece gave a heavy sigh. "Yes, I am. But I don't want to piss him off otherwise he may change his mind. He's been known to do that before."

"And then what?" Lozano folded his arms.

"All hell breaks loose. Jacques is unpredictable." His serious gaze locked onto the sheriff. "At the best of times."

"So you plan to let him walk all over you. Is that it?" Lozano stood up and crossed the room.

"Look, you don't know what he's capable of. We do."

Lozano raised defensive hands. "I was just asking."

"Yeah, well, maybe while I'm gone Ed can fill you in. Then you'll understand why I'm treading lightly where he's concerned."

"Sure. Ok." Lozano stood beside Ed in front of Reece's desk and gave the Lieutenant a brief sideward glance.

Reece checked the wall clock, stood up and snatched his phone from off the desk. "I'd better go."

"Be careful, Daniels," Ed said.

"I will."

₞₧

Reece stood inside the elevator and watched the numbers ascend as the lift traveled up to Jacques accommodations. With every passing floor his gut tightened so much that by the time the doors opened onto the penthouse suite the vampire occupied he could barely take a breath. His eyes roamed the private foyer before he stepped out, the lift doors hissing closed behind him and he glanced over his shoulder and swallowed hard. Did he really want to be on the top floor of the Sunset Tower alone with Jacques? No, but he had no choice. Andre would remain dead unless he did what his nemesis wanted.

And what was that? He was about to find out.

The elegant door swung open and Jacques' dark-clad figure appeared in the doorway. "Welcome, Detective Daniels." He made a sweeping gesture. "Won't you come in?"

52

Reece's suspicious gaze rested on Jacques and he hesitated before crossing the foyer and entering the suite. The door closed behind him and the heavy feeling in his solar plexus dropped into his gut causing a wave of nausea. He swallowed the sickening sensation.

The room was in darkness, except for one lamp perched on a small, wooden table at the end of the sofa.

"Please... take a seat." Jacques crossed the room and sat in the single, striped arm chair across the coffee table opposite the tan, velvet three seat settee.

Reece felt his bravado dissolve as he sidled past the shin-height table and sat down on the center cushion.

Jacques rested his elbows on the armrests and clasped his hands in front of him. "So. Here we are."

"What is it you want me to do for you, Jacques?"

"In due time, Detective, in due time."

"Let's just get this over with. I'm not here for a social call."

"That's too bad. I thought you might want an update on Andre's... predicament."

Reece leaned forward. "Yes, I do."

"The sorcerer will be here next week at the earliest. He's a busy man and it took some persuasion to get him to rearrange his schedule."

"And?"

Jacques' left eyebrow arched. "When he arrives he'll perform the ritual. What else?"

"So you're actually going to keep your word?"

"Did I not say I would?" He crossed one leg over the other. "Why, Detective, did you think I would change my mind?"

"I didn't think anything. I just want it done."

"And it shall be. After you do something for me."

"I knew it." Reece sprang off the sofa.

"Well you cannot expect me to do something for you in good faith without reciprocation, can you?"

"What do you want?" Reece folded his arms. "Stop playing games and just tell me."

"I want you to find and kill Dracula. But, before that I want you to eliminate Eva Van Helsing from the equation."

Reece's incredulous gaze rested on the vampire. "She could help us."

Jacques stood. "And what makes you think she would want to. It is clear she has her own agenda."

"To rid the world of you, you mean?"

"Something like that, yes." Jacques walked over to the bar. "Drink?" He held up a decanter.

"No, thanks."

"Suit yourself."

"We've already made attempts on Dracula without success. Nothing we planned worked."

"But wasn't that because he knew your plans in advance? Didn't Charlotte Delaney provide him with the information?"

"She was compelled to deliver the information, yes. She didn't do it willingly."

"Then why have you exiled her from your group?" A satisfied smirk crossed his lips.

"I haven't. She chose to leave."

"Is that so?" He poured himself an expensive, Louis XIII Grande Champagne cognac. "I thought it was at your request."

Reece stalked across the room. "How do you know that?"

"It doesn't matter how I acquired the information. You need her to return."

"No. She's not a part of this anymore."

"You will need her help."

"I'm not doing it."

"What about your act of good faith?"

"How can Charlotte coming back be an act of good faith?"

"Because I want her on your team."

Reece dark gaze grew more severe. "Why?"

"She played a part in Andre's demise. Perhaps she can make amends for that by working for me too."

"What are you up to, Jacques?"

"As I have already explained, I want Vlad dead."

"Why?"

"That is a need to know and you do not need to know right now."

"What if I refuse to help you?"

"Then my brother remains in the realm of the dead."

"How do you expect us to finish Dracula? Do you have a plan that'll work?"

"Not at the moment, no. But I am sure we can work together to devise one that will."

"Then we'll need Eva Van Helsing's assistance."

"You do realize she is a vampire?"

"Yeah I know." Reece recalled the emotional pull she had on him and also the Lapis Lazuli ring she'd given to Nathaniel. It wasn't difficult to make that call.

"Take care where she is concerned. She enjoys playing with people's lives."

"Like you, you mean?" He gave Jacques a serious stare. "I'm a big boy. I can take care of myself."

"When it comes to Eva Van Helsing I doubt it." He gave Reece a knowing smirk.

CHAPTER FOURTEEN

The vampire hunter sat with arms folded watching Ed, Sarah and Lozano. She was bored and wondered when Reece would return. She knew he was engaged to be married but the relationship had gone sour so why shouldn't she have a little fun with him while she could? Nathaniel had warned her off, but she didn't take orders from anyone, especially not a vampire who had been in Jacques Delacroix's employ. If Charlotte Delaney was stupid enough to get into the situation she'd been in that was too bad. She would at least enjoy the hunt. If Reece wasn't interested, which she didn't believe by his reaction to her, she might consider stepping back. Maybe he felt remorseful for telling his fiancée to leave. Maybe there was a way to infiltrate his guilty feelings and use it to her advantage. Food for thought. She licked her glossy black lipstick and gave a heavy sigh.

Sarah's gaze rested on the woman and she wondered what was going through the vampire hunter's mind. Would she help them find and eliminate Dracula? Or would she use them to implement her own strategies. Either way, if it led to the demise of Vlad Tepes it didn't matter. Sarah's eyes moved to her cell phone sitting on the desk and she wondered why Vincenzo hadn't called. She hoped he could access the pages they needed without any serious repercussions. Had she done the right thing by involving him?

"I don't trust Jacques' intentions," Ed said, plonking his heavy frame into the seat behind him. "He'll get what he wants and not fulfil his end of the deal."

"Reece seems to think he'll honor their agreement." Sarah's gaze returned to the men in front of her.

Ed's brow wrinkled and he squinted at her. "And you believe that after what he put us through the last time?"

Sarah sighed. "I didn't say I believed it but Reece does. He wants Andre back and he'll do whatever it takes to make that happen."

"Yeah, well let's hope it doesn't get us all killed." Ed swung around in the office chair and stared out the window. "I wonder what's takin' so long."

Eva stood up and strutted across the office. "Jacques will have Reece doing his bidding before he follows through with resurrecting his friend. That is how he operates."

"So what do you suggest?" Sarah ran her gaze over the woman and folded her arms.

"If it were up to me I would have already ended Jacques."

Sarah's head tilted to the side. "Didn't you have that opportunity a couple of nights ago near his hotel?"

Eva gave the priest a sheepish glance. "Well, yes, that is true but..."

"But what?" Lozano asked.

"There is something I want from him first."

"And what's that?" Ed questioned.

"It is between him and me."

"Look, if you want to work with us... or need our help you better be honest about your intentions. We don't take too kindly to secrets. They can get people killed and we've lost good people already." Ed gave the woman a severe stare. She was another bloodsucker he didn't trust. Why was Reece?

"He has something that belongs to me and I want it returned. That is all I am prepared to say for now."

"So I guess the bottom line is... are you going to help us get rid of both Jacques and Drac?" Ed's dark stare deepened. His gut told him not to believe her.

"I am."

Nathaniel entered the office and crossed the room. "Good morning." He scanned the entire space then asked, "Where is Reece?"

"He's negotiating with your ex-boss," Ed told him.

"How long has he been gone?"

"A while. I'm starting to worry." Sarah's gaze moved to the closed office door.

"Have you called him?"

Ed yanked his body out of the seat and gave the vampire an incredulous stare. "What do you think? Of course we have. Goes straight to voicemail."

"If he is not back within the next half hour I will go to the hotel myself." Nathaniel didn't like the fact that Reece was alone with Jacques. Anything could happen.

"Thank you, Nathaniel, we appreciate that," Sarah said, giving him a thin smile.

"I came here because I have had word from Marcus."

"Does he know where Dracula is? Lozano asked.

"He has a location but wants to be sure before he passes on the information."

"Ok. Good. We need to find that monster soon and deal with him." Ed's eyes teared up at the thought of losing Andre and Arianne. He turned toward the window and brushed a stray tear from the corner of his eye. Dracula would pay for what he'd done.

œ)&CR;

Reece watched Jacques cross the room and take his seat. He'd heard his cell go off but didn't check it, although he knew it would be either Ed or Sarah checking up on him. Jacques was still toying with him and the PI knew he would already have certain strategic measures in place to find Dracula. So why wasn't he sharing what he knew? And why was it that Jacques was awake during the day? That was dangerous.

"You said you'd tell me why you're up during daylight hours. How is that possible?" Reece walked back to the sofa and sat down. If he could glean any information that would assist them in getting rid of Jacques he was prepared to stick around to find out.

"I don't recall saying I would tell you anything." He raised his glass of cognac to his lips and took a generous mouthful.

"What's the big secret? Got something to hide?"

"Oh, very well, if it will stop your incessant questions. Since my return I no longer require time to rejuvenate."

Reece knew that was not a good thing. Was he stronger? Is it possible he could walk in the daylight now? His eyes roamed the elegant room. Then why did the vampire have the drapes drawn? Hadn't he attempted to venture out yet to see if he could? "What else?"

"I have a taste for a certain type of blood now. I cannot drink just any kind."

"What type?"

"A positive."

"Don't you find that a bit odd?"

"Why question such anomalies when I am alive again?"

"Have you tried going outside?"

Jacques dark gaze met Reece's but there was also an element of fear behind his eyes. "No, I haven't."

"Why not? Afraid you'll fry?"

"You need not concern yourself with my well-being, Detective. You should be more concerned with locating Dracula and adhering to our arrangement."

"We're waiting on intel as we speak. Nathaniel has someone looking into it."

"Ah, yes, Nathaniel. Who would have thought he would betray me."

"That's past history, Jacques. Let's just focus on now."

The vampire stood up. "You are right. One thing at a time."

Reece wondered what Jacques meant by that. "You should see if you can go out in the sun." He wanted to know so he could be prepared for whatever Jacques had planned. Reece knew Andre's brother wouldn't let what had happened to him go unpunished. There would be definite consequences for them all once their task was done.

CHAPTER FIFTEEN

Charlotte sat staring into Todd's curious gaze. How could she explain that she, Reece and the others had been chasing monsters? How could she tell him there were vampires, werewolves, demons and other otherworldly creatures roaming the earth? She knew that once she let him into her nightmare world everything between them would change and there would be no going back. Was she prepared to ruin their friendship? He was a man of logic, so she knew he wouldn't believe her when she told him the truth. It was frightening and she wished she'd never learned *the truth* herself. When Todd found out would he want to help? He said he did, but would he once he knew how dangerous it was?

Todd clasped her hand in his. "You know you can tell me anything."

Charlotte's uncertain gaze remained on him and she shook her head. "Not this."

"Why do you think I won't believe you? It can't be that bad. Can it?"

She gave him a thin smile. "Worse."

Her ex-partner eased his body back against the seat. "Really? That bad, huh?"

Charlotte nodded and a tear slid down her left cheek.

"Hey." Todd brushed the glistening trail away with his thumb. "I know you well enough to know you wouldn't lie to me so why don't you tell me what's troubling you, so I can help?"

"That's just it... I don't want you involved in any of this. I don't want you to help."

"You're coming here has already involved me. So why not just tell me?"

Charlotte frown into his eyes and gave a short gasp. He was right. She had inadvertently put his life in danger, too. She popped up off the chair. "I shouldn't have come here. I'm sorry, Todd, I have to leave." She rushed around the table and headed for her room. She needed to go. Needed to get as far away from Todd as she could. But where would she go?

"Wait. Charlotte." He followed her.

She threw some of her clothes into her suitcase then hurried into the bathroom to collect her toiletries.

Todd stood in the doorway. "Where are you going?"

"Anywhere else but here. You can't be involved in all of this."

Todd crossed the room and turned her to face him, his hands gripping both her arms. "All of what? Tell me."

"I can't."

"Yes, you can. We've always been honest with each other and now is no different."

Charlotte stepped away from him and sat on the edge of the bed. "If I tell you it will change things between us." She glanced up at him, her brow wrinkled into a sorrowful frown. "Is that what you want?"

"I want to help you, Charlotte."

She gave a heavy sigh, stood up and walked over to the multi-paned, French doors leading onto a small balcony overlooking the paddocks and mountain range. "Do you believe in…?" Charlotte shook her head. "I can't do this."

"Yes, you can. Tell me." He walked over and turned her around to face him.

"Do you believe in things you can't see?"

Now it was his turn to frown into her eyes trying to ascertain her meaning. "What do you mean?"

"Do you have a belief that there are things out there we know nothing about?"

A shiver ran the length of his spine. Charlotte's question was bizarre and alarming. "I don't know. What kinds of things?"

"Supernatural ones."

Todd stepped backwards. "Are you saying that you were abducted by aliens or something?"

Charlotte shook her head. "No. Not aliens."

"Then what?" He folded his arms and Charlotte knew he was closing her out.

"Never mind, I have to finish packing." She went to step around him but he stopped her.

"Charlotte." He raised her chin up to meet his gaze. "Tell me."

"Demons, vampires, werewolves… those kinds of supernatural things."

His frown deepened. "So what you're saying is those creatures are real?"

"Yes, Todd, *very* real."

He gave a humorless guffaw. "You can't expect me to believe…"

"I knew I shouldn't have told you." She rushed across to her suitcase and continued packing.

"Wait, Charlotte, I want to understand."

"You can't unless you can listen with an open mind."

Todd crossed the room and gently grabbed her arm, preventing her from tossing more clothes into her case. "Ok. I'll listen." He took her by the hand and led her back to the kitchen. "Sit. I'll make us some coffee and then you can explain."

ᎧᏟᏏ

Reece arrived back at the office before Nathaniel had a chance to go after him. Jacques' revelation about himself could prove advantageous to their team and offer a way of getting rid of him in the long term. The vampire was stronger now in some respects, that was obvious, but in others he was more vulnerable, like only being able to ingest one type of blood group. Jacques was also still fearful of the sun and hadn't attempted to venture out to see if his new found strength allowed him to walk in the daylight. Another advantage for them – at least for now.

When he stepped through the door he was inundated with questions.

"So what does the bloodsucker want you… or us to do?" Ed asked, folding his arms across his protruding belly.

"Did you find out anything we can use against him?" Lozano wanted to know.

"What took you so long? We were all worried." Sarah stood up and came around Andre's desk to him.

Reece raised his hands. "Can I have a minute?" He rounded his desk and sat down.

"I am pleased you are back in one piece," Nathaniel said.

Eva sat back and observed, saying nothing.

"Well?" Ed urged. "Are you gonna tell us?"

"Ok, ok. Geez, Chief, you can be pushy sometimes."

Ed plonked down in one of the two chairs facing the PI's desk. "Yeah? Well we were concerned about your health. And with good reason. Next time, answer your Goddamn phone, will ya?"

"I appreciate the concern but I couldn't just whip out my cell and answer it in the middle of our meeting, could I?"

"Yeah, you could. The vamp isn't royalty, ya know."

Reece shook his head. "To answer your questions: as we suspected, he wants us to kill Dracula. Why, you might ask? Ego. He wants to be king pin of the vampire world. Yes, I did find out some useful information about him. Since his resurrection he doesn't need to sleep which makes him a stronger adversary. He can also only drink one type of blood now. A positive. I asked him if he's tried going out in the sun but he hasn't. He's still afraid, which is a good thing as far as I'm concerned. At least we'll know where he is during the day."

"What makes you think he hasn't tried?" Lozano asked.

Reece's gaze moved to the sheriff. "Because when I entered the suite the living area was in darkness. He had all the drapes drawn."

"And you don't think that might've been for your benefit? To make you think he was still vulnerable to the sun?" Lozano had a point.

The PI frowned. "I hadn't thought of that. But he did seem genuinely afraid to try."

"Don't be so sure about that. We all know what a manipulator Jacques is." Sarah took the seat beside Ed.

Eva popped up off her chair and strutted across the office. "The priest is right. Do not underestimate him at any time. He is cunning."

Reece's gaze moved to the attractive brunette. "Trust me, I don't."

"That is good, because if you do it will the death of you. Do you really believe he will leave Los Angeles once the deed is done? Do you think he will forget what happened to him... what you did to him? He is biding his time with you. If we do not dispatch him he will exact his revenge, without a doubt."

"Why would you say that?" Sarah turned around on her seat to look at the woman.

"Perhaps because it is the truth. Jacques is holding a grudge. Do not expect him to just walk away."

"I'm well aware of what Jacques' intentions are. I know he'll come after us once we've done his bidding. That's why we'll be ready for him. He will not take anyone else from us." Reece was adamant, remembering his partner, Dave, and how he'd died.

₧₨

Todd brought two mugs of coffee over to the table and sat down opposite Charlotte. He slid a mug across to her, his eyes never leaving her for a second. Whatever had happened to her had caused some kind of delusion in her mind. Maybe she didn't want to remember the truth, but this? It wasn't like her to create stories. He made the decision to hear her out and would help her in any way he could. But supernatural creatures? That seemed too far-fetched as far as he was concerned. She'd asked him to have an open mind. Could he? "You said you were abducted by supernatural creatures. What kind?"

Charlotte's eyes met his serious stare and she sighed. "Succubus. There were three females working for..." She stopped herself. There was no way Todd would believe her when she told him Dracula was the instigator. He would think she'd gone mad.

"For who?"

"Have you read the novel Dracula by Bram Stoker?"

Todd shifted on his chair and frowned even deeper into her eyes. "I'm not a fan of horror stories but I've seen part of the movie on television. Why?"

"The novel was based on a Wallachian War Lord named Vlad Tepes. It was believed that he was a vampire, a blood drinker, because he'd murdered thousands of people during his reign."

"What has that got to do with what happened to you?"

"Because he's real, Todd. He held me captive and manipulated my mind so I would betray the people I love."

Todd blew out a noisy breath and continued to stare at Charlotte, the look of disbelief evident in his eyes.

"I knew I shouldn't have said anything. I knew you wouldn't believe me."

"I didn't say I didn't..."

"Please don't make this any worse by saying that. I can see in your eyes that you don't. And I understand how difficult it must be for you. I didn't know any of this until I started working with Reece. That's why I left the department. I couldn't sit idly by knowing what was out there and not try to do something about it."

"You're telling me Dracula's real?"

"Yes. I could've introduced you to someone who's been chasing him for over a hundred years but right now I can't."

Todd's frown deepened. "Someone who's been chasing him for *over* a hundred years?"

"Yes, Todd. Sarah is a priest who has used vampire blood to continue to live long enough to find Dracula and kill him."

"Do you know how crazy that sounds?"

Charlotte jumped up off her chair. "Call Reece. Talk to him. Ask to talk to Sarah, too. They'll tell you I'm not making any of this up. The succubus killed several young men in Las Vegas, one was a cop. Didn't you see the news reports? Talk to Sheriff Lozano. He's in LA right now."

Todd came around the table and gripped her forearms, frowning into her welling eyes. "Ok. Calm down. I remember the Vegas murders but there wasn't a lot on the news about how those men died."

"Their life force was drained out of them, Todd. They were shriveled corpses that's why the police didn't release the information."

"All right, I'll call Reece. Please sit. Have your coffee. I'll be right back." He headed for his office.

CHAPTER SIXTEEN

Reece's cell phone vibrated on his desk and he snatched it up, not recognizing the number. "Double D Investigations. This is Reece." There was a long silence on the other end of the line and he wondered if Jacques was playing one of his games. "Hello?" The tension in his voice at the anticipation of the vampire answering him was obvious.

"Hey, Reece, it's Todd Lassiter. I know it's been a while."

The tightness in the PI's gut unraveled and he released the breath he'd been holding. "Hey, Todd, what can I do for you?" Cops always got straight to the point.

"Charlotte's here at my house. She's pretty upset. She asked me to call you."

"Charlotte's with you? I don't understand." Reece walked over to the window and gazed out at the street below.

"You know we used to work together, right? Well, she needed a place to stay for a while."

"Oh, ok." What else could he say? He thought it strange that Charlotte would go there rather than back to Tommy. Why hadn't she gone to Mrs. Jenkins'? "Is she all right?"

"Not really. She's been telling me about what happened to her in Vegas and that's the reason I'm calling."

"What did she say?" Reece hoped she hadn't disclosed the truth of their encounter.

"She's been saying some pretty messed up things. She told me she was abducted by…" He wasn't sure he could say the word; it sounded so bizarre but he needed to know if what she'd told him was true. "By Dracula."

"Shit." Reece paced.

"Shit she's having some kind of breakdown or shit it's the truth?" Todd's gaze moved through the floor length window in his study. The sun had almost set behind the mountain range, its orange aura capping the jagged peaks. The beautiful view had always given him a sense of comfort, up until now. "Reece?"

He could hear a heavy sigh on the other end of the line. "Can you meet me?"

Todd frowned. "Why?"

"Because what I have to tell you needs to be said in person."

"Ok. Sure. When and where?"

"Preferably soon. Do you know Spring For Coffee on south Spring street?"

"Yeah. I've bought coffee there a couple times."

"Good. How long will it take you to get here?"

Todd glanced at the digital clock on his open laptop and calculated the mileage in his head. "About an hour, give or take."

"I'll see you then."

"Reece?"

"Yeah?"

"What Charlotte told me… is it true?"

"Let's talk about that when we meet."

℘℃℞

Reece was at an outside table under an orange umbrella sipping an espresso when Todd pulled his silver SUV into the curb under a tree twenty feet from the café. What was he going to tell the ex-detective? That Charlotte had gone mad? He knew he couldn't betray her, no matter what was going on in their lives right now. But he also knew he couldn't tell Todd the complete truth, either. It would put his life in jeopardy and Reece wouldn't allow another innocent person's death to sit heavily on his conscience.

Todd approached the small, round table; his hand outstretched, and ducked his head as he stepped under the bright colored awning. "It's good to see you again, Reece."

The PI stood and shook his hand. "You, too. Can I order you anything?"

"No, thanks, I'm good." He sat down.

Reece took his seat and swallowed the last of his strong coffee. He'd need it. The silence between them, despite the traffic and other patrons around them, was deafening. He waited for Todd to speak.

The man across from him stared into his eyes with a questioning gaze, drew in a deep breath and asked, "Is – is Charlotte telling the truth?" Nothing like getting to the point.

"Charlotte's been through a life-changing ordeal and under a lot of pressure these past few weeks. As she told you, she was abducted and tortured…"

Todd's eyes widened and his eyebrows rose. "Tortured? No, she didn't tell me that."

Reece watched him for a moment before continuing. "Ok. What did she tell you, exactly?"

"That she'd been taken from LAX and transported to Vegas and that you'd been instructed to continue your flight and the abductors would contact you once you were there. She said a female demon, a – a succubus, had taken her to a rundown motel and she'd been drugged. She also said *Dracula* manipulated her mind so she could inform him about what you and your team were doing." His eyes searched Reece's for answers. "Is any of it true?"

The PI folded his arms and gave a heavy sigh. "Do you think it's true?"

"Come on, Reece, don't do that. Just be straight with me."

Reece's gaze moved to Todd's SUV. "Can we talk in your car?"

Todd's eyes followed the PI's gaze then returned to him. "That bad, huh?"

"I think it'd be better to discuss this in private without other ears listening in, that's all."

"Sure." Todd stood up and pulled the remote keys from his jacket pocket.

Reece followed him along the sidewalk and both men climbed into the car.

"Ok, what's so dire that we couldn't talk about it over there?" He motioned with his head at the café through the windshield.

"If I told you what I know it would put your life in danger. Is that what you want?"

Todd turned in the driver's seat and stared at Reece. "I want to help Charlotte."

"Even if it means risking your life?" He wondered what kind of relationship Todd and Charlotte had had. Had it been romantic? Was there still something intimate between them?

"She's suffering, Reece, and you're part of the reason. The other part is what happened to her. She feels terribly guilty for betraying you, and for the death of your friend and the other young woman. You know that, right?"

"Yeah, I know."

"So what are you going to do about it?"

"Right now?" He shook his head. "I don't know. I've got bigger things to worry about."

"Like what?" Todd gripped the steering wheel and swiveled further around in his seat.

"I'd prefer to keep you out of it."

"I think it's a bit late for that, don't you?"

"So you're saying you believe what Charlotte told you is true?"

"I think by your reaction I can only assume that some of what she said is… To be honest, I don't know." He shrugged. "Are you going to let me believe Charlotte is losing her mind?"

"Ok. Look." He stopped himself, trying to figure out what to tell Todd. He had been a cop, after all, and would know if Reece was feeding him hogwash. "The murders in Vegas were committed by demons. There's a rift between here and hell and that has allowed dangerous otherworldly creatures to enter and roam the earth."

"Why doesn't anyone else know about it?"

"Because those of us who do guard that information with our lives and do everything we can to deal with the creatures that come through. Can you imagine what would happen if people knew?"

"Yeah, I guess I can. What about Dracula?"

"What about him?"

"Is he real?"

"Vlad Tepes is very real and a serious threat to humanity. He manipulated Charlotte's mind to gain access to what we had planned. What do you think would happen if he did that to hundreds of people all over the world?"

Todd blew out a noisy breath. "Man."

"Yeah. That's only the beginning. Right now we're dealing with two monsters. Jacques Delacroix, Andre's brother, who just happens to be a vampire, and Dracula, who, at this point, has vanished."

"Was Andre a vampire too?"

Reece nodded. "Yeah, he was. If you are serious about wanting to help then you'll meet other vampires who work with us."

"It all seems so surreal."

"We've all felt the way you do, believe me. But after a while you come to terms with it. There really isn't a choice."

"Charlotte mentioned Sarah. Is she really over a hundred years old?"

"She's been infusing vampire blood just so she can track down Dracula. She has her own axe to grind with him."

Todd shook his head. "I feel like I've been pulled into the Twilight Zone."

"Yeah, I know what you mean." Reece gave him a thin smile. "Do you want to follow me back to my office? The other members of my team are there."

"Yeah, I do."

Reece opened the passenger door and pointed to the parking lot beside the café. "My car's in there."

"Do you still have the Mustang convertible?"

"Yep, wouldn't be without her." He stepped onto the sidewalk. "Follow me back."

"Sure."

☙ ◯ ❧

Reece opened the office door and motioned for Todd to go in ahead of him. The ex-detective took a tentative step through the doorway and his eyes roamed the faces staring back at him. "Hi," he said with a thin, uncertain smile.

The PI followed him in and closed the door behind them. "Everyone, this is Todd Lassiter."

"Yeah, I know who he is," Ed said, eyeing the man with suspicion. "What's he doing here?"

Reece directed Todd across the room. "Charlotte's at his house in the San Fernando Valley. She told him what happened to her."

"What?!" Ed forced his heavy frame out of Reece's office chair. "Why?"

"She went to Todd for help."

"Help? I thought she was goin' back to her babysitter's house." Ed came around the desk.

"I guess she had other plans."

"She didn't want to go back and have to tell her son that you weren't together anymore," Sarah confided.

"Yeah, I figured that was the reason." Reece gave her a sheepish glance.

"I want to help." Todd said, trying to alleviate the tension in the room.

"Help? How do you think you can help, Lassiter?" Ed folded his arms over his podgy belly.

"That's why I'm here. You tell me what I can do."

"Does he know about us?" Nathaniel asked.

"He knows what's out there. Well, mostly what's out there. Let me do the rounds." Reece's eyes roamed the office. "Where's Eva?"

"She said she had some business to attend to and that she'd be back later." Lozano came around the desk and stood beside Ed.

"And you let her leave?" Reece frowned.

"Yeah. How do you think we were gonna stop her?" Ed asked. "She's a vamp, remember?"

"Right. Good point. Ok, you know Ed. This is Sarah Johnson, Deacon of St. Joseph's church. That, there, is Enrique Lozano, Sheriff with the LVPD. Nathaniel, who is an immortal."

"By immortal you mean vampire, right?"

"Yes, that is what he means." Nathaniel stepped forward offering his hand.

When Todd's palm met the chill flesh of Nathaniel's he pulled back. "Sorry."

"That is all right. A common reaction I have grown accustomed to." The vampire gave him a thin, crooked smile.

Sarah stepped up to Todd. "How is Charlotte?"

"She could be better. She seems confused and conflicted. And she blames herself for the deaths of your friends."

"Yeah, well, it wasn't her fault. The bloodsucker compelled her to betray us." Ed huffed out a heavy sigh. "We understand that." His gaze moved to Reece. "Well most of us do, anyhow."

"Then maybe someone needs to tell her that. She thinks you all hate her." He turned to Reece. "Especially you."

"I don't hate her. It's… I can't get past the fact that her actions caused Andre's and Arianne's deaths. I do know it wasn't her fault but it doesn't change the fact that they're gone." He returned his ex-boss's severe stare.

"Then you should tell her. I'm sure it would give her some comfort to know that." Todd sensed there was more to it but wouldn't push the issue.

Reece's gaze turned to him. "I will, but not right now." He circled his desk, sat down and looked the ex-detective in the eye. "So, do you still want to help?"

"Yes. What do you need me to do?"

CHAPTER SEVENTEEN

Someone had called in the lone car in the derelict parking lot at the old LA zoo about twenty minutes before the patrol car pulled up behind it. When the cop arrived on scene he assumed the vehicle had been stolen, taken for a joy ride then dumped there, but as he approached the blue hatchback he could see a non-moving figure in the driver's seat. He pulled his weapon, raised his hands and called out, "Please step out of the vehicle." Still no movement or response. The cop moved with caution as he came alongside the passenger side of the car, peering through the back side window as he got closer to the front passenger door.

Why would someone be sitting up here at night alone? It's a pretty creepy place in the dark. His mind ran through the recent list of stolen vehicles. This one wasn't one of them. He could now see the driver was a woman. "Ma'am, would you please step out of the car?" Why wasn't she moving? A heavy weight sank into the pit of his stomach causing a wave of nausea. *Is she... Is she dead?* He gripped the handle and whipped the door open still holding the pistol in his shaky right hand.

℞

Reece arrived at the scene forty five minutes after the 187 call went through. He still kept a check on the criminal activity around Los Angeles and had heard the cop call in the body at the old LA zoo. Something about the description disturbed him. He remembered Dave and him coming here when they were looking for a serial killer who turned out to be a neophyte werewolf about thirteen years ago. Andre had wiped the memory of that night from his mind until after he'd told him the truth about himself. Coming back here gave him the heebie jeebies.

The flashing red and blue strobe lights of the patrol cars and ambulance made the area look like an amusement park, but this was no fun ride. A young woman had been murdered, the description bringing to mind the bodies he'd been investigating when Jacques was in town the previous time. Had he done this?

Reece approached a uniformed cop standing at the perimeter and flashed his PI license. "Ok to go through?"

"Yeah, Jim's expecting you."

"Thanks."

The PI stalked across the expansive lot and approached the hatchback sitting center stage beneath four portable flood lights. Jim Peters was crouched between the door and the driver's seat examining the body.

"Hey, Jim. What's the verdict?" Reece folded his arms and stood at the open doorway.

Jim stood up and turned around. "If I didn't know better I'd say this was the handiwork of Jacques Delacroix." Jim had gotten too close all those years ago and Reece had talked him through the truth of the murders, including that of Jim's daughter. These days, if any suspicious deaths came through his lab he'd inform the PI.

Reece's right eyebrow arched. "What makes you say that?"

His gaze moved to the pale young woman sitting in the car looking as though she'd been frozen in time, her eyes staring ahead blankly through the windshield.

"She's been completely exsanguinated and there are no visible wounds. Sound familiar?" He peeled the purple latex gloves from his hands with a snap and dropped them into his kit. "What's going on, Reece? Why do you look like you know something?"

Reece raised defensive hands. "Hey, I know nothing about this. But there is something you should be aware of."

The older man's head tilted to the side. "And what's that?"

"It could be his handiwork."

"What?!" Jim's forehead creased into an incredulous frown. "I thought he was dead."

"Yeah, I know. We all did. But he's back."

"How is that possible?"

"Can I fill you in later? Right now I'd like to know how long you think she's been here."

"A day, at least. It's funny no one called it in sooner. Maybe the kids that traipse through the old zoo thought she was just sitting here." He shrugged. "Damned if I know."

"If it was Jacques I'll make sure he doesn't do it again."

"And how do you plan to do that? He seems to take matters into his own hands and do whatever the hell he wants." Jim packed up his kit and picked it up off the ground. "If I had my way he'd be dead… for good. We miss our girl. Every day. The pain doesn't get any easier with time, no matter what people say."

Reece rested a comforting hand on the man's shoulder. "I know."

Jim knew the PI understood. He'd lost people to Jacques, too.

The pair walked away from the vehicle allowing the guys from the coroner's office to remove and bag the body.

"So how are you going to stop Jacques from doing this again? If it was him."

"I'll talk to him. We're kind of working together right now."

Jim stopped in his tracks, his serious gaze meeting Reece's. "Tell me I didn't hear what you just said."

"You heard it right."

"But why?"

"Because he said he can bring Andre back."

Jim's frown deepened. "From the dead you mean? And you believe him?"

"Yes, I do. There's some kind of ritual. It was performed on Jacques' ashes and that's how he's here."

"Pity. We'd all be far better off if he wasn't."

"Yeah, we all feel the same way. But, right now, if he can bring Andre back I'll let him think I'm doing exactly what he wants."

"Be careful, Reece. From what you've told me about him I'd be worried he won't try to pick you off one at a time."

"I'm well aware of what Jacques is capable of and I expect him to try something like that. But he won't for a while because he needs our help."

"Well, good luck with that." Jim gave a heavy sigh. "I'd better get back and take a closer look at April Langley."

"Who?"

Jim glanced over his shoulder at the car being winched onto a tray truck. "The girl from the car."

Reece climbed into his Mustang, snatched his cell from the console and pressed speed dial for Jacques. That monster was up to his old tricks again and had to be stopped. When the vampire picked up, the PI said, "I'm coming over. Make sure you're at your hotel by the time I get there." He pulled the phone from his ear and glanced at the time. "Which should take about forty minutes." He rang off before Jacques could refuse.

ℴ)(ℛ

Reece pushed open one of the double, brass and glass doors to the hotel, climbed the steps, stalked across the art deco style lobby and punched the button on the first elevator in a set of three opposite an ornate, winding staircase. He understood why this particular venue would appeal to Andre's brother. Jacques was meant to keep a low profile, so why had he deliberately killed that young woman and left her where she'd be discovered? What game was he playing with them now?

The elevator's accordion door slid open and he stepped into the confined space. Jim was right. Jacques did whatever he wanted without consideration for the consequences of his actions. LAPD will never find out who murdered April Langley and that was something that didn't sit well with him. An unnecessary death that could've been avoided. And unless someone on the homicide team figured it out it would become and remain a cold case like so many others.

The elevator stopped on the penthouse floor and when the doors opened Jacques was standing behind them. "Your curt telephone call had me intrigued. Why the haste to get here, Detective?"

Reece stepped out of the lift and pointed to the suite door. "Better to discuss it in there."

"Very well." The vampire made a gallant, sweeping gesture. "After you."

The PI eyed Jacques darkly as he passed him and entered the penthouse.

"Drink?" Jacques closed the door and headed for the bar.

"Why did you drain that young woman?"

"And which young woman would that be? There have been several." He glanced over his shoulder at the PI.

"You can't go around killing people for pleasure. You can't draw attention to yourself like that." Reece eased his body onto the sofa in the same spot he had occupied the last time he'd come to see Jacques.

"If I don't feed I'll die." He gestured with his hand. "Simple as that." Jacques wrapped the luxurious, black velvet robe around his lithe frame, took a large swallow of whatever he was drinking and sat down. "I was trying to be discreet, despite what you might think."

"Yeah? Well, leaving a body in a car outside the old LA zoo doesn't sound much to me like you were. Surely you're aware that kids and urban explorers frequent that location?"

"It has been a while since I was here. I wasn't aware. I thought it was abandoned and that no one set foot there." He swallowed another mouthful of what now looked like blood to Reece.

"What if someone had seen you? Where did you do it?"

Jacques motioned in the direction of the dog park beside the hotel. "Next door, actually. She had lost her keys and I offered to assist."

Reece poked the air with his index finger. "Offered to assist... Don't do it again. Understood?"

"I will do my utmost to curb my cravings and be more discreet. Is that what you want to hear?" He set his glass down on the small table beside his chair and clasped his hands in front of him.

"I mean it, Jacques. If you want us to work together you need to adhere to certain rules."

Jacques' dark gaze locked onto the PI. "I said I will do my best to accommodate you. What more do you want?"

Reece stood up. "I expect your complete cooperation, given the circumstances."

"By that I assume you mean my needing your help. Am I correct?"

"The deal's off if you continue to leave corpses lying around where they can be found. No killing of innocents."

The vampire huffed out a frustrated breath, although he didn't need to breathe, and a thin smile crossed his lips. "I give you my word that I will not kill any more innocents. There. Happy?"

"Not really, no. I know you too well to trust you at your word."

"You *think* you know me." Jacques gave an amused chortle and stood up. "No one on this planet has a compendium of knowledge about another person. *No one.* People divulge small portions of themselves to those they profess to love and those they are acquainted with but keep their darker natures secret. Everyone has a dark side, no matter who they are. You of all people, especially as a former detective, should understand that."

Reece couldn't argue with Jacques' logic because for once he spoke the truth.

CHAPTER EIGHTEEN

Charlotte had been asleep when Todd came back from talking to Reece and she hadn't heard him come home. She wondered if Reece had asked about her. She wished she could talk to him. Try to work out their issues before any more time passed. What if he'd fallen out of love with her? She had no answers and the overwhelming feeling played havoc with her mind. Before heading to the kitchen to see if Todd was awake yet, Charlotte grabbed some clean clothes and popped into the bathroom. She always felt less stressed after a hot shower.

When she opened the door to her room she could smell the pungent, nutty aroma of freshly brewed coffee and knew Todd was already up. He had always been an early riser, opting to get up before the sun rose to get the day started. She'd known that because she had stayed at his apartment once when they were on an early morning assignment. She appreciated him letting her stay at the ranch now and she hoped he would look at her through different eyes this morning.

Charlotte padded barefoot down the hallway, across the living room and into the kitchen. "Good morning. Coffee sure smells good." She picked up a clean mug from off the counter and poured herself a cup. "What are you making? It smells wonderful." She peered over his shoulder at the contents of the frypan on the stove top.

"Spanish omelet. Hope you're hungry."

"Famished, actually." Charlotte took a seat at the round breakfast table and sipped her black brew while Todd finished cooking. "How did things go with Reece last night?"

"Just give me a minute to finish this and I'll tell you." He folded and scooped the last omelet onto a plate and sprinkled a garnish over both, brought them over to the table and sat down. "He confirmed what you told me."

Charlotte gave him a sheepish glance. "Did he say anything else?"

"He asked how you were." Todd stretched a napkin across his lap and picked up his silverware.

Charlotte did the same. "He did?"

"Yeah, he seemed genuinely concerned about you."

A small smile crept across her face. "He was?"

"Seemed so." Todd wanted to make her feel better about her situation with the PI. He trusted he wasn't offering her false hope.

"What else did he say?"

"He told me about the rift between hell and earth. And about Dracula and Jacques." He cut a section of his omelet and popped it in his mouth. "I told him I want to help."

Charlotte set her knife and fork down. "No, Todd. You can't. It's too dangerous."

"You know me, Charlotte. I'm not the kind of man to go back on my word."

"Please, don't do this. We've lost people who were skilled in this area and it's been terribly difficult. I don't want to lose you too."

Todd reached across the table and squeezed her hand. "You won't."

"If you know anything about the supernatural at all you'll know how unpredictable situations can be. Demons have powers we have no knowledge of, vampires won't hesitate to drain you dry and werewolves, well, they're a whole different story all together. Do you really want to risk your life?"

"I was a cop for a long time, Charlotte, and a damn good one. I think I can handle myself with some training and further knowledge about the creatures out there. To think that cases we worked on could've been orchestrated by those monsters... it blows my mind. I have to do something."

Charlotte blew out a frustrated breath and tugged her had free. "Don't say I didn't warn you."

"I won't. And besides, it means we'll get to work together again."

She frowned into his eyes. "What do you mean?"

"Reece said he was going to call you about coming back to the team."

"He did?" Her frown deepened. "Why?"

"I guess he needs everyone on board."

Charlotte shook her head. "No. That can't be it. He wouldn't want me back on the team without us sorting out our issues first. Something else is going on."

Todd gave her a curious frown. "Like what?"

She stared into his eyes. "I don't know. But I'm going to find out."

ℰℭ

When Charlotte opened the door to Double D Investigations and stepped into the office she discovered Reece was alone. Where were the others? Perhaps her phone call had prompted him to send them home or out on assignment while they talked. She wondered why he wanted her back on the team and had a suspicion that it had something to do with Jacques and not her fiancé.

"Where is everyone?" she asked, her eyes roaming the empty office.

"I thought it would be good to have some space while we talked." He motioned for her to take a seat in front of his desk, the way she used to when they got together to discuss missing person cases before they became romantically involved.

Charlotte crossed the room and sat down. "Why do you want me back on the team? Does it have something to do with Jacques?"

"Yeah. He wants you involved. He said it'll make up for Andre's death."

"Didn't anyone explain to him that Dracula compelled me and that I didn't do what he wanted willingly?" She threw her hands up. "Doesn't anyone understand that?" Frustration coursed through Charlotte and her heartbeat quickened, her cheeks flushing with anger.

Reece remained in his seat on the other side of the desk. He felt the urge to move around it and offer her comfort but thought twice about doing so.

"If you mean me, yeah, I do understand, but like I said it doesn't change the fact that Andre and Arianne are dead, does it?"

"How many times do I have to say how sorry I am? I lost Andre too, you know? He was my friend as well. And, anyway, when Jacques brings him back none of it will even matter. Will it? I don't understand why you can't see it in your heart to forgive me, if you still love me. You know I would never do anything to jeopardize anyone's safety." She hoped he'd say he was still in love with her.

"Jacques is a manipulator. He may not do what he promised. He needs our help to get rid of Dracula and has given his word he'll bring Andre back before we begin working for him, but who knows if he'll stick to that agreement. Jacques only looks out for himself."

"So what you're saying is you'll never forgive me. Is that it?" Tears stung the backs of her eyes and she blinked them away.

"What do you want me to say?"

Charlotte popped up off her seat. "That you still love me and that over time we'll be able to move past this. I'm heartbroken over losing Andre and Arianne, but especially Andre. If I could take it back I would. I'd even sacrifice my life for his if it would make you happy."

Reece's astonished gaze rested on his fiancée. She was wearing his ring so she was still his fiancée for now. "I would never expect that of you, Charlotte."

"Well it's true. I know how much Andre meant to you and if I could erase the pain you're going through I would gladly give up my life."

Reece continued to stare into Charlotte's eyes without saying a word; his confused emotions even more conflicted. Somewhere deep inside he was still in love with her. That he knew. But whether or not he could move past what had happened was another matter. He realized he missed holding her in his arms, and she and Tommy being part of his life. "I would never ask you to exchange your life for Andre's. How could I? You have a son to raise."

"*We* have a son to raise. Tommy loves you too." A lone tear slid down her left cheek and she brushed it away.

At that moment, something inside Reece shifted and he came around the desk to her but didn't touch her. "Let's take it one step at a time and see where it goes, ok?"

Charlotte's heart felt just that little bit lighter. Could this mean there was a chance they could work things out? It seemed so and she would hold onto that hope. She gave him a thin smile and nodded. "Ok."

Reece's cell phone vibrated on the desk and pulled his gaze away from Charlotte. He snatched it up, noticing it was Nathaniel. "Hey, what's up?"

"Dracula is in Paris."

ஐ)ௐ

Vlad exited the limousine inside the hotel's underground parking garage and crossed the level to the small elevator. Paris was one of his favorite cities and was far enough away from the United States and the private investigator and his team to keep his whereabouts unknown. When the doors opened, he stepped into the empty lift and pressed the button for the third floor. That was one of the things he particularly liked about boutique hotels – minimum guests with plenty of privacy.

This hotel held old world charm and he enjoyed the splendid, prestige décor and surrounds. The Champs-Élysées and Eiffel Tower were visible from his suite and, if he so chose, he could walk to either in the later part of the evenings. He exited the elevator, made his way to his rooms and opened the door with an electronic key. The elegant living area was furnished with a burgundy, buttoned sofa and matching armchairs, a marble topped coffee table, black and gold cocktail cabinet, renaissance paintings adorning the walls and the ceiling to floor drapes were heavy enough to block out the sun during the day.

He dropped the plastic keycard onto the bureau and wandered into his bedroom. He had made contact with a supplier he knew in Paris and his female guest would be arriving at any minute. Once he was done with her, his contact would arrange a discreet pick up and disposal. Vlad shrugged out of his vintage, black wool jacket, slipped out of his boots and trousers and into a white hotel robe. He would savor the sexual pleasure the young woman would offer him before indulging in his ritualistic, immortal cravings.

CHAPTER NINETEEN

"So what are we gonna do about Drac being in Paris?" Ed asked, rolling an office chair across the floor and sitting next to Sarah and Charlotte. "Are we goin' over there to get him?" He folded his arms across his round belly and heaved a sigh. "You know he went there because he didn't think we'd find out where he was and follow him, don't ya?"

Reece turned from the window to face his team: Ed, Sarah, Charlotte, Nathaniel, Lozano, and now Todd Lassiter. "Yeah, I figured as much." He walked over and plonked himself down in his chair and clasped his hands on the desk top. "But we can't let him get away with murdering innocent people. He's on the hunt. Maybe he does plan to manipulate people he's chosen into doing what he wants." Reece shrugged. "I don't have any answers but the one thing I do know is we have to stop him. Not for Jacques' sake but for humanity's. He could be planning to initiate more humans so he has an army of vampires like the army he once had in Romania."

"Then we need to work out who's goin' and who's staying." Ed's gaze roamed the others in the room. "I can't go, unfortunately. I don't have any vacation time coming. I've used it up working with you." He raised a hand before anyone said anything. "Not sayin' it's a bad thing. Just tellin' it like it is."

"I think Nathaniel should come with me." Reece's gaze moved to Sarah. "And you, Sarah. You've been pursuing him for a long time and it's only fair you're there to help finally bring him down. And you have the resources we need."

Charlotte was hoping Reece would want her to come along, but he didn't ask.

"We need to organize our trip as quickly as possible. The sooner we're there the sooner we can find him and put an end to him. This time we won't let him get away."

"What do you want us to do while you're gone?" Lozano asked.

"Ed, you need to make an appearance at the precinct otherwise the hierarchy will start asking questions." Ed nodded. He knew Reece was right. "Sheriff Lozano, would you continue your research and text me anything you can find on Dracula's weaknesses. There has to be something that will put an end to him. He can't be completely invincible." His eyes moved to Todd. "Right now there isn't anything you can do here. Once we're back I'll organize training and bring you up to speed on what's out there and how we deal with them."

Todd folded his arms. "Are you sure the three of you are going to be able to handle the situation over there? I'm an expert marksman."

"So is Sarah. And Nathaniel has other useful abilities. I wouldn't go if I didn't think we could handle it. If I decide we need backup I'll call and you can follow us. That's the best I can offer right now. Our budget is limited and I can only organize flights for the three of us. Are you ok to pay for yourself, if I need you?"

"Sure. I wouldn't have it any other way. I'm not on your payroll… yet." He grinned.

"You might have to do some unpaid freelance for a while. If you're sure you want to get involved?"

"I'm sure. And I'm self-sufficient so if you need my help I'm happy to do it pro bono."

"Thanks. I appreciate it." Reece turned to look at his fiancée. "Charlotte?"

She straightened in her seat. "Yes, Reece?"

"Go see your son. Spend some time with him. Tell him I'm working away at the moment and I'll see him when I get back."

"But…"

"No buts. You've been through enough where Vlad Tepes is concerned and I don't want to put you through anything more."

Charlotte popped up off her seat. "I can take care of myself. As a member of your team I should be coming with you."

"I'm not prepared to risk your life or any of our lives. What if you're still connected to him? We have no idea what he did to you. What if he senses you're there and finds a way to use that connection again?"

"So you think I'm a risk?" She folded her arms and huffed out a sharp breath.

"To be honest, yes. Like I said, you could still be attached to him somehow and I won't risk putting us all in danger."

Charlotte's cheeks flushed with anger. Reece didn't trust her and that's the reason he was leaving her behind. There wasn't anything she could do about it, either. If she fought him on it, it would only make him dig his heels in and the distance between them even wider. "Fine. If that's what you want."

"Yeah, it is." His serious gaze met hers and lingered there. He wasn't taking unnecessary chances.

"What about bringing Andre back?" She knew how much it meant to him.

"Shit. I forgot about that." Reece paced then turned around. "I'll tell Jacques we need to postpone. I hate to say it, but this is more important right now."

"Ok. Can I at least book the flights for you? I'd like to feel as though I'm contributing in some way."

"Sure. There's a laptop over there." Reece pointed to the desk Andre used to occupy. Charlotte crossed the office and sat down. "Try to get the earliest possible flights out. We need to leave ASAP." He turned to Sarah. "Have you heard from Vincenzo?"

"I'll give him a call when I get back to St. Joseph's. Are we meeting back here and traveling to LAX together?"

"Definitely." Reece's gaze moved to his ex-boss. "Are you ok to drive us to the airport?"

"What do you think? I want to see my sweetheart off." He gave Sarah a crooked smile.

"Ok." Reece looked across the room. "How are the flight reservations coming along?"

Charlotte's eyes moved from the computer screen to him. "You're flights are all booked. You leave at 3.15 PM on Air France. I also made reservations at the Novotel Hotel at 61 Quai de Grenelle. It's not far from the Eiffel Tower." She would have loved to have seen Paris. It was somewhere she had always wanted to go. It would've been the perfect honeymoon spot for her and Reece. Tears stung the backs of her eyes at the thought and she blinked them away.

"Thanks." His gaze moved to Nathaniel and Sarah. "Be back here by twelve o'clock. We'll need to be at the airport a couple hours before our flight leaves."

Everyone headed out the door. There was much to be done. Charlotte hung back. "Reece?"

"What is it, Charlotte?" He crossed the room to her.

"Do you really not trust me?" She blinked back more tears, her emotions getting the better of her.

Reece gave a sigh. "I don't trust Dracula. We don't know if he severed all ties with you or if you're still connected to him. If you came with us and he somehow tapped into your mind who knows what could happen? We could lose him again and I can't allow that. Not this time."

"I want to help you." She stood up and came around the desk.

"Then go to your son and make sure he's ok. Keep safe. That's the best way you can help me right now." He raised his hand and was about to rub her arm but stopped himself. The gesture was too intimate for the moment. "I'll call you when we're at the hotel."

Charlotte let out a soft sigh. "Ok. I guess that's all I can ask for."

"Charlotte..."

"I know." She picked up her purse. Todd would be waiting downstairs for her. "Be safe." She moved in to kiss his cheek but he stepped back.

An uncomfortable moment.

His gaze moved to the floor in front of him then back to her. "I will. We all will."

She turned around and as she headed for the door, she glanced over her shoulder. Would Reece ever touch her again?

The PI stared at the closed door, his mind suddenly on Eva Van Helsing. Why hadn't she returned like she'd said? Where was she? He snatched his cell phone off the desk and dialed Jacques' hotel room. He knew the vampire would be pleased with the new turn of events.

CHAPTER TWENTY

Their plane landed at Vancouver International Airport to pick up passengers from a connecting flight who were also traveling to Paris. The stopover took over an hour, time they couldn't afford. How long would Dracula remain in France? Could he have left already? Where would he go next? Reece had no way of knowing until they landed and he could access his cell phone. By the time they arrived at Charles de Gaulle Airport it would be 11.05 AM, with most of the morning already gone they were on limited time.

Once the plane was in the air Reece headed to the bathroom. As he wandered along the aisle toward the back of the Boeing 777 he ran his gaze around the passengers sitting three in a row and spotted her. "What are you doing here?" His question was far more curt than he'd intended.

The author glanced up from her laptop and gasped. "What are *you* doing here?"

"I asked first." Reece folded his arms.

"Excuse me." Maggie sidled past the passenger on the aisle seat and stood in front of the PI. "I'm going to Paris to do some research for my next book. What about you?"

Reece took her by the arm and marched along the aisle to the back of the plane. His eyes roamed the other passengers and he lowered his voice. "I'm chasing Dracula. He's in Paris right now. But you should already know that." He frowned into her eyes. "Why don't you?"

"I – I don't understand what's going on. How can he be in Paris?"

The PI folded his arms. "It seems Dracula's making his own rules. This means he'll know you're on your way. He'll probably know we are too."

"How?"

"Because he has access to your book."

"What?!"

A flight attendant approached the pair. "Is everything all right? Do you need any assistance?"

"Uh, no, thanks." Reece smiled and pointed to Maggie. "I just ran into an old friend and we're catching up."

"Oh, ok, just don't take too long. We'll be serving dinner soon and you'll need to be in your seats."

"Sure, no problem. Thanks." Reece waited until the young woman moved away before turning back to the author. "If he knows you're in Paris things could get tricky. You need to keep a low profile while you're there." His frown deepened. "How long are you staying?"

"Only three days. I'm heading to Rome and Venice after that. I'm on a two week working vacation and want to get as much research as I can done while I'm in Europe. I won't get another chance for a while."

"Ok. Good. It'll be safer for you to get out of Paris as soon as you can." Reece thought for a moment. "Do you have any idea where he'd be?"

Maggie's eyes widened. "How would I know that?"

"Because you're the author."

"If he has read the book then he'll be sure not to stay where I put him in the story."

"Dammit! You're right."

"Can we talk about his later?" Maggie noticed the woman still watching them. "I think we need to go back to our seats." Her eyes moved in the direction of the flight attendant and Reece followed her gaze.

"Ok, sure. Contact me once you're at your hotel. You being here creates a whole new set of issues."

"I'm sorry about that, but I have to work. I'll call you as soon as I'm in my room."

"Good. Do that." The PI turned to walk away.

"And, Reece."

He glanced over his shoulder. "Yeah."

"Please be careful."

"That's kind of up to you, isn't it?" He gave her a thin smile and returned to Nathaniel and Sarah.

As Maggie passed the three she glanced at Sarah and Nathaniel, the priest giving her a brief smile as the author continued to her seat. What could she do to help them?

ၹ

When the plane landed, passengers jostled out of their seats into the aisle, grabbing their onboard bags in the hope of exiting the aircraft quickly. Maggie remained in her seat until the stampede was over before opening the compartment above her head and collecting her belongings. While she was in Paris she would do her best to assist Reece in locating Dracula before she continued on to Rome. It was the least she could do. With what she knew of him there had to be a way she could figure out his next move. While he was free to roam Paris they were all in danger.

The taxi ride to the Four Seasons Hotel on Avenue George V was spectacular. As she had never been to the city before everything was awe-inspiring. The sights, sounds, and atmosphere sent a shiver of joy through her which only increased when she spotted the Eiffel Tower in the distance. That was one tourist attraction she intended to visit while she was here. But the joy was overshadowed by the fact that Dracula was also in Paris. Where could he be? If he hadn't been privy to her book and this was only his way of escaping Reece and his team then they had the advantage.

As the cab pulled into the curb outside the main hotel entrance, a doorman crossed the sidewalk and opened the door for her. "Bonjour, Mademoiselle. Welcome to Paris."

Maggie stepped out of the car. "Bonjour. Merci."

The driver set her luggage down and she paid the fare, including a large tip. "Merci."

Turning around, she gazed along the beautiful, tree-lined avenue and sighed. She was finally in Paris. And although the trip was work-related, she would make sure to squeeze in some tourist spots while in the city, including the Moulin Rouge.

Once in her room, she showered, changed into some comfortable clothes and shoes, and grabbed her cell phone to call Reece. The line continued to ring until his voice mail kicked in, "You know what to do." When she heard the beep, Maggie left a brief message saying she was safely in her hotel room at the Four Seasons and would he please call her when he could.

It was just after midday and she was famished and, rather than stay and eat in the hotel, she wanted to explore the city and treat herself to some fine French cuisine at one of the quaint, alfresco bistros on the avenue nearby. She slipped on a jacket, and a pair of sunglasses, picked up her purse and headed for the door. Just as she reached it a knock echoed into the room. *Who could that be? No one knows I'm here except for Reece.* She took a step backwards and held her breath. Another knock.

She opened her mouth to ask who it was but snapped it shut again. Her gut squeezed into a tight knot and an icy shiver traveled up her spine, her body telling her something was wrong. She remained silent.

The doorknob jiggled. Whoever was in the hall was attempting to get into her room. Maggie eased herself across the luxurious carpet and as quietly as she could she set the door latch. Was it Dracula in the hallway? Did he already know she was in Paris? The knocking and jiggling stopped abruptly and the author waited, breath held, to see what would happen next, cell phone gripped in her hand. She had keyed in 112, the emergency number for Europe. Would she need to use it?

CHAPTER TWENTY ONE

Reece and the others settled into their rooms and freshened up before meeting in the lobby of the hotel. The PI was concerned about Maggie being alone in Paris. With Dracula on the loose, and no way of knowing where he was, things could get even more dangerous if the vampire knew she was here. They needed to find his location as soon as possible before the situation careened out of control. Having the author in the city created a whole new headache for him because now he had to keep track of her for her own safety and that complicated their mission of dispatching the maniacal vampire.

When he came down the escalator to the ground level of the hotel, Sarah and Nathaniel were sitting on a beige sofa in the lobby near the revolving door. They stood up as he approached.

"What are we going to do about Maggie?" Sarah asked, concern evident in her eyes. "She shouldn't be alone in a city she's never been to before while he's out there. She could be in real danger, especially if he finds out she's here."

"Yeah, I'm aware of that. But right now our number one priority is finding where he's staying. Once we know his location, and can keep an eye on him, Maggie will be safe." The PI's gaze moved to Nathaniel. "Do you have contacts here?"

"Yes. I have already spoken to someone who can assist us."

"Good." The tightness in Reece's gut dispersed. "How long before they get back to you?"

"He said as soon as he knew anything he would call." Nathaniel's eyes roamed the bright lobby. Guests were giving him curious stares. He assumed it was because of his dark clothing and sheer size. He was almost seven foot tall and broader than a Los Angeles Rams quarterback. His gaze returned to the PI.

"Ok. In the meantime, I think we should get some food to help with the jetlag and figure out our next move." Reece headed for the door. Sarah and Nathaniel right behind him.

"That's a good idea. I'm starved," Sarah said.

"Maggie left a voicemail message on my phone so after lunch I'll head over to the Four Seasons to talk to her."

The three left the hotel in pursuit of some tasty local cuisine.

℘)℃

By the time Reece reached the Four Seasons it was just after three in the afternoon. He entered the five star hotel through the elegant, black framed, glass revolving door and ran his eyes around the luxurious surroundings: gray marbled reception desks on either side of the lobby, a tiered, crystal chandelier above a beautiful, dusky pink and white floral arrangement standing center, and white marble statues adorned the foyer. He made his way through one arched doorway, walked to the lifts and pressed the button.

When he stepped out of the elevator on the seventh floor he wandered along the hallway, checking room numbers, until he came to Maggie's suite. He knocked.

The door opened and the author greeted him with a smile and a hug.

Reece eased out of her embrace and gave her a serious frown. "Why didn't you ask who it was before opening the door?"

"Because I knew it was you. Your text message said you'd be here in twenty minutes."

He stepped into the suite. "What if it hadn't been me? What if it had been whoever tried to get in here earlier?"

Maggie closed the door and followed him across the living room. "Well, then, I could only hope you'd get here in time to save me." Reece gave her a stern frown as he sat down on the cream, two seat sofa. The author eased herself into a replica Louis XV chair opposite him. The PI ran his gaze around the well-appointed room. Sophistication was a word that came to mind. The author had good taste.

"Can I get you anything?" Maggie asked. "Coffee? Brandy?"

Reece raised his hand. "No, thanks, we had lunch a short while ago so I'm good." He got straight to the point. "How soon are you leaving Paris?"

The author was taken aback by his directness, although she shouldn't have been surprised. She knew him only too well. "Uh, well, I'm flying to Rome on Wednesday morning at 6.30 AM. Why?"

He leaned forward, resting his elbows on his knees. "As I said, the sooner you leave Paris the better. For your own safety."

"I understand. I still can't believe he's here."

"Yeah, me neither. I thought he might've gone back to Romania or somewhere obscure so we wouldn't be able to find him. Maybe he already knew you were coming here." Reece glanced through the window then returned his gaze to her. "Will you be going out in the evening?"

"Yes, as a matter of fact, I made a reservation for the Moulin Rouge tonight. I've always wanted to go there and I couldn't pass up the opportunity while I'm here." A broad smile spread across her face. "Should be a lot of fun. I'm also doing a tour of the catacombs. I paid for a personal tour, just me and the guide." Her skin prickled with excitement and apprehension. "Should be fascinating… and creepy."

He raised his index finger. "Do me one favor."

"What's that?"

"Be extra careful, especially at night. Keep your wits about you and be aware of who's around you." His earnest gaze met hers. "You'd be a prize worth winning because it would give Dracula the advantage."

Maggie swallowed the tightness in her throat. "I – I promise I will."

"Good. If you run into any trouble call me. Ok?"

She nodded and her stomach did a nervous flip flop causing a wave of nausea to rise in her throat. Maybe she shouldn't go out this evening, after all.

The PI wished the author wasn't doing the catacombs tour. It was a recipe for disaster if she *was* being followed. With only a guide accompanying her, and being underground, anything could happen. Dracula seemed partial to subterranean localities when it came to orchestrating his schemes and there were areas in those tunnels that no one ventured into.

ℰℭ

As Maggie arrived at the Boulevard de Clichy her heart did a little, excited shudder in her chest. There it was, right in front of her, the *Moulin Rouge*. She snapped a couple of photos on her iPhone as she crossed the checkered roadway and stepped onto the sidewalk. She'd arrived early to wait in line so that she'd get a good seat. The queue was already quite long, but she was sure there'd be enough seating to accommodate everyone, as bookings were essential. The show started at seven and it was five now. She heard Australian accents behind her and turned around. "Hey, where are you from?" she asked the young couple.

"Sydney. Nice to meet another Aussie here," the young woman said with a smile.

"What about you? What city are you from?" her handsome partner asked.

"Brisbane. I've always wanted to come here. It's taken a while but here I am." Maggie couldn't hide her excitement.

"That's wonderful." The young woman curled her arm around her man's solid bicep. "We're on our honeymoon. Sorry. I'm Carla and this is… my husband… Jason." She glanced up at him and smiled.

"It's really nice to meet you both. And congratulations on your wedding."

"Thanks," they both said.

"How are you coping with the language?" The author was curious about people in general. Came with the territory.

"High school French, unfortunately. What about you?"

"Bonjour, merci, s'il vous plait, café au lait, and baguette are about my limit." She chuckled. "I've always wanted to learn French but never seem to have the time."

"I know what you mean." Carla pulled a small book from her coat pocket and held it up. "That's why we have this." She smiled. It was an Oxford French Dictionary.

"I wish I'd thought to bring one of those with me."

"Ask at your hotel. They may have them in the gift shop."

"Thanks. I'll do that."

ॐ

The interior of Moulin Rouge was spectacular, although rather cramped. Tables lined the floor so close together that there wasn't a lot of room between the seats. But it didn't matter to Maggie because it was a dream come true. She'd been lucky enough to get seating only one table back from the stage on the left hand side of the venue so she'd have a fantastic view of the show, and the newlyweds she'd been talking to were also on her table, so she didn't feel quite so alone. She couldn't wait for the cabaret to begin. The atmosphere was electric with anticipation.

Her excited gaze roamed the room. The venue was jam-packed. There were people everywhere already and still entering the restaurant. The lighting, bright red carpet, and red and white striped canopies overhead gave the place a carnival feel. She breathed a contented sigh and was about to turn around when she spotted someone in the crowd sitting at the end of the balcony behind her, the miniature, boudoir table lamp in the center of the small, round table accentuating the paleness of his skin. Was it Dracula? Had he followed her?

Reece recognized the number immediately and answered on the second ring. He knew the author wouldn't have called him unless something was wrong. The PI got up from the table, leaving Sarah on her own, and walked out the door of the restaurant to the street. "What's wrong?"

"I'm at the Moulin Rouge and I think Dracula is here."

The hair on the back of Reece's neck bristled. "Are you sure?"

"Well, no, because I'm not sure what he looks like now, but I had this really strange feeling when I spotted a man sitting alone in the balcony behind me."

"Did he look at you? Say something?"

"He was too far back to speak to me, but he was looking at me and turned his face away when I noticed him. I had the feeling he knew who I was. Call it intuition, if you like."

Reece paced outside the restaurant window. Sarah watched him from their table, wondering what the call was about. He looked worried. "Can you go back inside and see if he's still there. If it is Dracula he'll change location because you've seen him."

"Ok." Maggie's stomach went hollow as she headed back along the red carpet and through the matt black doors into the venue. She ran her nervous gaze around the room to where she'd seen the man. The table was empty. "He's not here."

"I'm on my way. Make sure you're around people. Don't go to the ladies room or anywhere else alone. I'll be there as soon as I can."

A shiver ran through the author and goosebumps spread up her arms. "Should I be worried?"

"If you do exactly what I've said you'll be fine."

Maggie threaded her way through the masses back to her seat and sat down, roaming her eyes around the crowded room in search of the vampire. If Reece was correct in his assumption, and she suspected he was, then Dracula was still somewhere in the building… waiting for her.

CHAPTER TWENTY TWO

Congestion on the roads slowed the cab to a crawl, and as Reece sat in the back, his gut wound as tight as a clock spring, he realized he could get out and walk faster. He shoved his hand between the front seats, dropped the Euro on the console, flew out of the taxi and continued on foot. The Boulevard de Clichy was only a couple of blocks away and if he picked up his pace he'd be there in no time. As the PI stalked along the busy sidewalk, he pulled his cell phone from the pocket of his jacket and keyed in the author's number. It rang for a long time then went to voicemail. He didn't leave a message. Perhaps the cabaret had begun and she wasn't aware of the call. He hoped that's all it was.

After cutting their dinner short, Sarah had headed back to the hotel, she and Nathaniel on standby just in case the PI needed back up. Reece raced along Rue Blanche and when he reached the multi-street intersection, the bright lights and whirling windmill of the Moulin Rouge came into view. He hurried across the road, onto the center island, then over the checkered pedestrian crossing to the venue. He entered the arcade-like entrance, stepped through one pair of double glass doors, walked down the stairs and straight over to security. After telling the guy the abbreviated version of the situation, and the author's seat being located on the theater floor plan, he was escorted inside. The show had commenced, the room resembling a dark movie theater with the lights of the cabaret giving the audience a ghostly glow.

Reece and the suit scanned the interior of the venue, not that he would recognize the author in the muted lighting, and the guy pointed to a table across the room close to the stage. "Là bas." He followed the circular, red carpet walkway past rows of packed tables, the PI close on his heel, and Reece gave a relieved sigh when he saw Maggie sitting at her table watching the show. He touched her shoulder and she jumped and spun around, but smiled when she saw him. She'd been on tenterhooks the whole time.

Reece's gaze moved back to security. "Merci. Uh, Je... uh, je dois... l – lui... parler." His high school French was extremely rusty. He needed to talk to her to find out if she'd seen the vampire again.

"À l'extérieur." The guy motioned with his head toward the entrance. "Outside," he said, his French accent thick.

The PI looked at the author with a questioning stare, eyebrows raised.

"All right." She sighed, stood up and followed the men out to the foyer. The suit left them standing by the closed doors.

"Have you seen him since you called me?" Reece folded his arms.

Maggie shook her head. "No, but I have the feeling he's still in there somewhere."

Reece let out an uneasy huff. "Then we need to get you back to your hotel. You'll be safer there because I can have Sarah stay with you."

She motioned to the doors behind her. "But the show only just..."

"I know. I'm sorry. You're not safe here and I can't be in there with you." He glanced over his shoulder at the security guy lingering nearby.

"Maybe we can buy you a ticket." The author walked over to a young woman at the counter. "Bonjour. Can I purchase a ticket for my friend?"

The woman behind the desk gave a sincere, pained expression. "I am sorry, all zee seats are taken." Maggie had suspected that would be the case as she had reserved her ticket three months before her trip.

The author's shoulders sagged. "Ok. Merci." As she turned to walk away an idea popped into her head. Her expression lightened and she turned around. "Could I buy standing room for him?" She'd waited a long time to come to Paris and the Moulin Rouge and didn't want to leave, despite the possible danger.

"We do not normally do that, but, oui... ok." The young woman nodded and smiled.

◌ଃ

Before the cabaret had begun, Vlad switched seats with a young couple who were thrilled to move to the front and cloistered himself away at the back of the balcony. When he saw the PI enter the venue with security he knew it was time to take his leave. There would be other opportunities. While the author and her bodyguard were out in the foyer debating what to do next, he crossed the room to a large, decorated column close to the exit and waited for his chance to make his escape without being seen.

When the pair returned, the author moved back to her table and the PI stood by the doors.

How could he leave now? The vampire's nocturnal vision roamed the darkened space looking for another way out. He noticed a door with Staff Only on it and cautiously made his way over to it. Perhaps it would lend him his freedom.

Reece's gaze scanned the audience. Was Dracula still in the room? If so, where? It was difficult to see people's faces in the dim light and the PI wondered if the vampire had already managed to get out.

ℂℂ

Back at Maggie's hotel suite, Reece checked the rooms, including the windows, as Dracula could use his immortal abilities to climb up or down the outside of buildings, the PI wanted to be sure the vampire didn't have easy access. He'd already phoned Sarah to ask her to come over and was awaiting her arrival. A knock on the door startled them both and the author checked through the peep hole before opening it. "Hi. Come on in."

"Thank you." Sarah stepped into the room carrying a black, leather overnight bag. "Wow!" Her eyes took in the elegant surroundings. "Very nice."

"Yes, it is. The hotel is renowned for its elegance and I've always wanted to stay here."

The PI stood with arms folded gazing out the window and turned around when the two women came in. "Sarah."

"Reece."

"Please, have a seat," Maggie said, motioning to the sofa.

The priest and the PI sat down beside each other.

"So, you saw Dracula."

"Yes, well at least I think it was him." She sat in an armchair opposite them. "He was watching me and when he saw that I noticed him he disappeared."

"It's a good thing you called Reece." Her gaze moved to him then back to Maggie. "At least it warned him off. For now."

For now. Maggie's stomach squeezed tight. She didn't like the sound of that because it meant he'd try again. "I'm not planning to stay the three days. I've changed my flight for tomorrow morning and I'm heading straight to Rome instead." She didn't feel comfortable being the target of a deranged, supernatural killer.

"I think that's a wise decision. We would hate for anything to happen to you." Sarah glanced at Reece sideways then gave Maggie a thin smile.

"Yeah, we would. And we really need to find him but if we're babysitting you we can't do our job." Reece didn't sugar coat anything.

Maggie nodded. "I understand completely. And I don't want to get in the way."

"Good. I'm glad that's settled." He leaned back and folded his arms. "I was worried when you told me you had a personal tour of the catacombs. That could've been a dangerous move."

"Once I knew Dracula might be having me followed I decided against it. As you said he's partial to underground locations and it would be the perfect place for him to abduct me without anyone knowing. At least for a while."

"Yeah." Reece turned to Sarah. "I want you to accompany Maggie to the airport and make sure she gets on that plane safely."

"Absolutely. I'm sure he'll have compatriots in Paris that work for him. If they find out Maggie's leaving someone might show up there in the morning."

"My thoughts exactly." Reece stood up. "I'd better head back to our hotel and get things in motion." His eyes moved to Sarah. "Let me know when Maggie's in the air."

"I will."

Reece rounded the coffee table and Maggie stood up and gave him a hug. "Thank you for looking out for me."

"All in a day's work." He stepped out of her embrace. "Be careful."

"You don't have to worry about that."

"Good."

She walked him to the door. "You be careful too."

"Always."

Maggie closed the door and turned to Sarah. "I'll finish packing then we can sit and have a coffee and a chat."

"Sounds like a plan. I'll just do a quick sweep of the floor. Be right back." She let herself out and headed to the other end of the hallway. Could Dracula be a guest in the hotel? Could he be lying in wait to make another move on the author? Sarah checked the whole floor and watched guests getting off the elevators, too. If the monster was anywhere in the building she *would* find him.

CHAPTER TWENTY THREE

Reece's cell phone vibrated as he reached his hotel room door and he tugged it from the pocket of his jeans. He'd taken to keeping it on silent these days. He frowned at the screen. Caller Unknown. It had to be Jacques. "What is it?"

"Have you located him yet?"

"Not yet. There have been other complications here. But we will."

"What other complications?"

"Nothing you need to worry about. He's been seen so we know he's still here. We're working on it. I'll let you know when we find him."

"I wanted to give you a heads up. Eva is missing. I assume she is on her way to Paris."

Reece paced outside his door. "How'd she find out where we were?"

"She paid me a visit and I may have inadvertently mentioned it." Jacques smirked.

"Why would you do that?" Reece could feel the flush of angry heat in his cheeks.

"Three of you are not going to be able to handle Vlad alone, you should already be aware of that from your dealings with him in Las Vegas, and she has certain *talents* that could be useful to you."

"She's a ticking time bomb, Jacques. We can't have her running about Paris picking people off, especially if she finds out who's working for him." Reece ran his hand over the stubble on his chin. The situation was out of control. "Can you find out if she is on her way?"

"I believe you may have your answer sooner than you expect." The line went dead.

Reece let out a frustrated breath and punched the keycard into the electronic lock. The door popped open.

"Hello, Reece."

Now he knew exactly where Eva Van Helsing was.

"How did you get in here?" He dropped his phone, keycard and wallet onto the credenza, crossed the room and stood with hands on hips.

"I have my *methods*." She gave him a seductive grin and eased her tightly clad, curvy frame out of the armchair she'd been occupying.

"Shouldn't you be keeping an eye on Jacques?"

"Oh, I am. I have people working for me too." She stepped up to him and curled a lock of his wavy, dark blond hair around her fingertips.

Reece took a step backwards. "Don't do that."

Her left eyebrow arched and her grin widened. "Why? Because you like it or because you have a fiancée?"

"No. Because I don't mix business with pleasure."

Eva's grin turned into a curious smirk. "That is not true otherwise you wouldn't be engaged to Charlotte, would you?"

"Let's leave Charlotte out of this."

"I am more than happy to leave her out of *this*." She stepped up to him and planted a firm kiss on his lips before he could stop her.

Reece's body reacted to the moment and he drew her closer. The heated kiss continued until the fog of passion subsided and he realized what he was doing. He pushed her away. "Don't do that again." He glowered at her.

Her glossy red lips spread into another seductive smile. "I know you liked it."

The PI couldn't argue with that. He was attracted to her but he had to keep it professional. For a lot of reasons. "We're working together. That's it." He crossed the room to the mini fridge, snatched a small bottle of whiskey from off the shelf, cracked the cap, and swallowed the amber fluid straight from the bottle, coughing as the warmth slid across the raft of tension in his gut.

"But that's not what you really want is it, Reece?"

"What I really want is to find Dracula and dispatch him before anyone else gets killed." He tossed the empty bottle into the wastepaper basket beside the credenza. "You'd do well to keep your mind on the job, if you want to remain here."

"I don't take orders from you." She stood with her hands pressed to the body-hugging fabric on her hips.

"Get used to it because you do now." Reece could feel his heart rate ticking up a notch or two. She was beautiful and he couldn't help how his body reacted to her being here. He knew it wasn't something that could mean anything, but he also knew that if he let it they could end up in bed together and he wouldn't allow that to happen. He was still engaged to Charlotte, after all, and until that was resolved he wasn't free to cheat.

A knock on the door startled him and his eyes darted toward the sound.

"It is Nathaniel." Eva sat down in the armchair again, crossed one leather clad leg over the other, and clasped her hands in her lap.

Reece walked over and opened the door. "Come in."

Nathaniel's eyes widened when he saw Eva. "When did you arrive?"

The vampire hunter gave him a sheepish glance. "Last night."

The PI swung around. "Then why are you only letting us know now? What were you doing all those hours?"

"I've been trying to track Vlad. He is not an easy vampire to find. I am of the belief he has had a cloaking spell placed on him so that no one can locate him."

"A what?" Reece stalked across the room and stood in front of her."

"It's a means of remaining undetected. A witch can perform the spell and it can become permanent, if the host so wishes," Nathaniel told him.

Reece glanced over his shoulder at the vampire. "So what you're saying is we may never find Dracula. Is that it?" He paced the length of the room with hands on hips. They had come all this way and now the monster might slip right through their fingers.

"We will find him. The vampire I have looking for him is an expert at tracking those that do not wish to be found," Nathaniel assured. At that moment, his cell phone rang. He pressed it to his ear and listened. "Thank you." He rang off.

"Vlad is staying at a boutique hotel in Saint Germain."

Reece stopped pacing. "You have the address?"

Nathaniel nodded.

"Then let's go and check the place out." The PI headed for the door.

"I'm coming with you." Eva jerked out of her chair.

Reece turned around. "I think it's best you stay here until we know the layout of the hotel. Once we have an idea of what we're dealing with we'll work on a plan."

Eva folded her arms. "I do not have to do what you tell me. But I will *for now*." She sat down. "Where is your priest friend? Maybe we can play cards while I twiddle my thumbs." She gave Reece a sarcastic grin.

"She had something else to do tonight. You'll just have to amuse yourself for a while." He gave her a serious stare. "And stay here. I mean it."

Eva pouted and huffed. "When will you be back?"

"Soon." Reece grabbed his jacket and he and Nathaniel walked out the door, leaving the vampire, vampire hunter to her own devices, which could prove to be an unwise move.

⁗⁗⁗

"Everything ok?" Maggie asked as Sarah entered the suite from the hallway. The priest was gone for some time and the author had been concerned for her safety.

"Yes. Everything's fine. I did a thorough sweep of the building starting with this level and didn't find anything suspicious on any of the floors."

Maggie's eyebrows rose. "You covered every floor of the hotel?"

"Of course I did. We can't be too careful where Dracula is concerned."

The author's stomach hollowed out and clenched into a tight ball. "Did you think he was staying here?"

Sarah nodded. "It was a possibility. But I had a call from Reece while I was checking the floors and it appears Dracula has a suite in a boutique hotel in Saint Germain, so you've got nothing to worry about."

"You know, I was so looking forward to spending a few days here but now I'm glad to be leaving tomorrow." A shiver ran through Maggie.

"Perhaps another time when things aren't so dangerous." The priest gave her a thin smile.

"Mm, hopefully."

"All packed?" Sarah crossed the room and sat down on the sofa.

"Yes. I can't wait to see Rome and Venice. It's a dream come true."

"Well, have a wonderful time. At least you won't have to look over your shoulder wondering where Dracula is lurking."

Another shiver coursed through the author. "Yes, at least there's that."

Sarah glanced at the large, flat screen television in the elegant, white wall cabinet. "Want to watch a movie or something? Relax for a while?"

Maggie glanced at Sarah and smiled. "Sure. Why not?" She picked up the remote control, turned on the TV, and pressed the movie channel.

ℰᏏ⧽Ꮯℛ

The boutique hotel in the quiet, tree-lined avenue stood seven levels high and Reece figured Vlad would be in the top floor suite. Vampires seemed to appreciate high places, perhaps because of their aerodynamic capabilities. He'd checked the internet on the way over and found that this particular hotel had an underground parking garage, appropriate for Dracula to come and go undetected, for the most part. The PI and his companion crossed the street and entered the vintage-style, elegant building. As the hotel also had a public restaurant, it gave them easy access to the inside without looking suspicious.

When the pair stepped into the sophisticated lobby a woman behind the reception desk glanced at the two men and gave them a smile. "Bonsoir, Monsieur, can I be of assistance?"

Reece walked over to her. "We'd like to have dinner. The restaurant is open to the public, isn't it?"

She nodded. "Oui." She pointed along the short hallway. "Straight ahead and first set of doors on the left. Bon appétit."

"Merci." He and Nathaniel continued along the hall to the restaurant. Once they sat for a while and ordered a drink, so as not to look conspicuous, they would leave their table and make their way discreetly to the elevator. Reece didn't have a plan. Their main purpose for visiting the hotel was to find out exactly where Vlad Tepes was so they could orchestrate some kind of surveillance and ambush the vampire away from the city.

After fifteen minutes, the pair got up and walked out into the hallway, making their way along to the caged elevator at the end. When it stopped a couple dressed for a night on the town stepped out of the lift, smiled, continued past them and headed to the front entrance.

"I cannot sense Vlad here," the black vampire said.

"Maybe he's out looking for his next meal." Reece gave his companion a sideward glance. "No offence."

"None taken."

Reece and Nathaniel entered the elevator and pressed the button for the top floor, the PI hoping the elevator door opened into the suite. It did.

"Let's do a quick sweep."

"What are we looking for?" Nathaniel's eyes roamed the shadowed living space.

"Where he's planning to go next. Maybe he has an itinerary or flight tickets. Something. Anything." Reece's voice was tight.

"All right, I will check."

"Sorry, Nathaniel." He sighed. "We just need to be one step ahead of him this time."

"I understand."

The pair searched the suite, careful not to disturb anything that would alert the vampire to their presence. There appeared to be nothing to provide any information as to where the vampire might be heading next. If they didn't make a move while he was in Paris they would lose him again and Reece couldn't let that happen.

CHAPTER TWENTY FOUR

Jacques sat in the penthouse suite of the Sunset Tower Hotel contemplating whether to go ahead with the ritual to bring his brother back while he had the chance or wait for Reece Daniels to return to Los Angeles, as had been their agreement. A smug smile slid across his handsome, pale face and he stood up, crossed the room to the door leading out onto the balcony, opened it and walked over to the balustrade. Vehicle and pedestrian traffic littered the boulevard, offering an appetizing smorgasbord for his immortal palate. He had no idea there were so many humans with A+ blood. How convenient.

He had always wanted Andre by his side and right now would be the perfect opportunity for him to fulfill that desire. He had plans for his brother. Plans that would set in motion a series of events to finish what he'd started when he was last in LA. Andre, being his identical twin, could offer certain benefits to his cause, especially if he proceeded with his scheme to raise him from the dead while Reece was in Paris. They could become reacquainted without the interference of the Private Investigator. Jacques strolled back to the end of the balcony, hands clasped behind his back, and his nocturnal vision roamed the busy street below.

Aramon, the sorcerer who would perform the awakening spell, had arrived in Los Angeles two days ago and was awaiting Jacques' order. He had all that he needed to bring his brother back from the realm of the dead so why wait any longer? It wasn't as though he owed the PI anything. In fact, it was he who had caused his death in the first place. He strutted back into the hotel suite, snatched the phone from its base and pressed the number into the keypad. "I am ready to proceed." Something stirred within him. Was it the thought of having his brother by his side or perhaps the thrill of the game he planned to initiate? Reece Daniels and his team were not equipped to dispatch the great and powerful Vlad Tepes, and Jacques knew that their being in Paris would only hasten what he had predetermined for each and every one of them. If all went according to plan, the priest would not return to the US. A smile of satisfaction spread across his face. One down and more to follow.

His brother would be raised from the dead. *Andre.*

Jacques had the sorcerer make certain adjustments to the ritual and he was keen to find out if they would work. He would see Andre soon enough and then he would know. He walked back to the balcony door and out to the balustrade. What tasty morsel could he indulge in this evening?

෫෬෬

Todd watched Charlotte from across the dining table. The sadness had consumed her and she was no longer the woman he'd known. Her life with the PI had been ripped out from under her and her spirit seemed to have been as well. He wished there was something he could do to help her find her way back. After all this time, he still had feelings for her and he would do anything to see her smile, to know, without doubt, that she was going to be all right. Charlotte seemed oblivious to his attention. She sat shifting food around her lunch plate and sighing every once in a while. His heart hurt for her. "Charlotte?"

Her disengaged gaze moved to him. "Yes?"

"What can I do to help you?" He wiped his mouth on the napkin, sat back and folded his arms.

"What do you mean?" She frowned.

"You're clearly not yourself. How can I help with that?"

Charlotte let out a heavy sigh. "There's nothing anyone can do… only Reece, and he's otherwise engaged right now."

"Do you want to go over there and talk to him?" Todd leaned forward and rested his left elbow on the table. "Because if you do I'll arrange it."

Tears stung the backs of Charlotte's eyes. He was a genuinely caring man who wanted to help her in any way he could. "I couldn't ask you to do that for me."

"You're not asking, I'm offering. If it's the only way to get you back to your old self then I'm happy to do it."

A thin smile spread across her pale, sad face and she reached across and squeezed his hand. "I appreciate that, I really do, but I just have to accept that Reece needs time to do what he has to do now then work out what to do about us next."

"What happened wasn't your fault. I don't understand why he can't see that."

"It got his best friend killed, Todd. Someone he'd had in his life for a long time." She sighed again. "So I do understand it." Her thin smile widened. "I wish I didn't but I do."

"And what about you, Charlotte? Don't you deserve a say in the matter?"

"I've tried reasoning with him... he just has to come to terms with it in his own time, I guess. There's no forcing him, and I wouldn't try anyway."

Todd stood up, walked around the table to her and held out his hand. "Come here."

A single tear slipped down Charlotte's cheek and she popped up off the chair and into Todd's arms.

"I care about you, Charlotte. I hope you know that."

She looked up at him. "Why do you think I came here?"

He smiled. "Good. If there's anything I can do you'll tell me, right?"

Charlotte nodded and nestled her face against his chest again.

Right at that moment, Todd wanted to kiss her and knew he'd have to keep his feelings in check. At least for now. Who knew what the future would hold, especially if Reece decided he didn't want to be with Charlotte anymore.

The pair stood and he stroked her silky hair while she cried. He hated how much she was hurting right now.

"Sweetheart, why don't you go spend some time with your son? Talking to him on the phone doesn't serve any purpose. He needs to see you."

"I know he does. But what am I supposed to tell him? That Reece and I broke up?"

"Well, you haven't officially broken up yet, so no. Tell him Reece is overseas doing some PI work and you're not sure when he'll be back."

"I…"

His cell vibrated on the table and his gaze moved to it. Should he answer it?

Charlotte eased her body away from his. "You'd better get that." She sniffled and sat down.

Todd picked up his phone and frowned at the screen. A number he didn't recognize. "Hello?"

"Todd, it's Enrique Lozano. Can you come over to Reece's office?"

"Sheriff Lozano. Why? Has something happened?"

"Ed's coming over and I thought it would be a good time to do a follow up."

"A follow up on what exactly?"

"Reece has been in touch. He wants to keep us in the loop in case you have to go over there."

"Does he think he'll need my help?"

"Let's discuss it when you get here. Oh, and bring Charlotte with you."

Todd's eyes moved to her as she sat watching him. "Ok. Sure. We'll see you soon."

Charlotte frowned. "What was that all about?"

"Apparently Reece has been in contact with the sheriff and he's calling a meeting."

"Oh? Ok." She stood up. "So we have to go now?"

"Yeah." Todd walked out into the entry hall. "Let me just go get my Glock."

Charlotte followed him out of the kitchen. "Why do you want to take your weapon with you?"

"I remember Reece telling me about Jacques just walking into the office without an invite. Can't be too careful."

"You do realize normal bullets won't kill him, don't you?"

"Yeah, but it'll hurt like hell for a while, won't it?" He gave her a thin smile.

"True. But it might not be a good idea to antagonize a vampire, especially not Jacques."

"Hey, now that I know about what's out there I'll do whatever it takes to keep the people I love safe." He hadn't meant to say that. At least not the word love.

Charlotte did her best not to react. She knew he still cared for her. "That's exactly how Reece felt when he found out."

Todd nodded. "Yeah, well it's a good strategy." He headed down the hallway to his room.

ℰᏒ

When Charlotte and Todd entered the Double D Investigations office Lozano was behind Reece's desk and Ed by the window. It had been two days since the PI and his team had flown to Paris, and as the sheriff said it was important that they all stay in the loop. The pair crossed the room and Charlotte sat down on one of the visitor chairs in front of the desk.

"Glad you could make it," Lozano said. "Good to see you again." His eyes moved to Charlotte and he gave her a brief smile.

Todd stood beside her with arms folded. "So what's the situation over there?"

"I'll let Reece tell you himself." The sheriff spun the laptop around and Reece appeared on the screen.

"The situation at the moment is we know where Dracula is but we have other complications happening here right now."

"What kind of complications?" Todd asked.

"Maggie's in Paris. She's leaving but Sarah is staying with her until she's on that plane and heading out."

"Who's Maggie?" Todd had no idea about the author.

"It's complicated. Let's just say the situation will be rectified this morning."

"Ok. What else?"

"Eva is here."

"What the hell!" Ed said, "I wondered where she got to."

"Yeah, well now you know. I think Jacques put her up to it to throw a spanner in the works."

"But why? Doesn't he want to get rid of Dracula?" Charlotte asked.

"I wish I knew. I'm concerned about Andre now. Jacques could have the ritual performed while we're stuck over here and who knows what the outcome will be."

"Do you think he'd do that? Didn't he agree to wait?" Charlotte leaned in to get a better look at Reece."

"He can't be trusted. Not under any circumstances."

"Good to know," Todd said. "Not that I'd trust a vampire anyway."

Nathaniel came up behind Reece on the screen.

"Sorry, Nathaniel. I'd make an exception where you're concerned."

"Thank you, Todd. Not all vampires are tarred and feathered with the same brush."

"No, I guess you're right."

"So what are you gonna do about the bloodsucking, vampire hunter?" Ed asked. "You don't want to let her run riot or Drac will know you're there."

"I think he does already, Chief. But, yeah, she's at the hotel right now under house arrest."

Ed Borenko's wrinkled brow creased even more. "And you think that's going to stop her?"

"She gave me her word she'd stay there. I'm hoping she keeps it. Sheriff?"

"Yes, Reece." Lozano came around the desk.

"Did you find out anything that could help us?"

"Not yet. But I'll keep digging."

"Thanks. We need to know Dracula's weaknesses. He has to have at least one we can use against him."

Todd stepped forward. "I'm coming over."

"It's not necessary. Just wait until I know what we're up against first."

The retired detective shook his head. "Nope. I'm booking a flight and we'll see you soon."

"We?"

"Yeah, I'm bringing Charlotte with me."

"Don't do that. Remember what I said about Dracula having a connection to her."

"I know what you said, Reece, but you need all the help you can get right now. From what I remember she's a pretty good shot." His gaze moved to her then back to the screen.

"That's not the issue. She could put us all at risk."

Charlotte huffed out a frustrated breath. "I'm right here guys, so stop talking about me like I'm not. I won't be a risk. Just give me a chance to prove it."

The PI blew out a noisy breath. What could he do? He couldn't stop Todd from bringing Charlotte with him. And he couldn't deny they needed the help. "You're right. We do need the backup."

Charlotte couldn't help but smile. She was going to see Reece again in the flesh. Her heart rate ticked up a notch.

"Ok. Then it's settled. I'll organize our flights and we'll be with you as soon as we can. Text me the hotel details so I can book rooms."

"I know where they're staying because I made the reservations," Charlotte told him.

"Nathaniel will pick you up from Charles de Gaulle Airport once we have your flight details. Thanks, Todd. I appreciate your help. And yours, too, Charlotte."

CHAPTER TWENTY FIVE

Sarah's eyes roamed the airport lounge while they waited for Maggie to board her flight to Rome. The priest wasn't taking any chances when it came to the safety of her charge. She would make sure the author was on her way before leaving the airport and heading back to the hotel. As she ran her gaze around the tube-like waiting area she spotted a suspicious looking man behind a row of potted plants watching them. Her radar was never wrong when it came to possible danger. She could feel in her gut that he wasn't there to board a flight. Was he one of Vlad's goons?

Maggie's eyes followed Sarah's gaze. "Are you concerned about him?"

"He's been there for a while now and he doesn't appear to be waiting for a flight."

"How can you tell?" She frowned.

Sarah leaned closer to the author. "Take a good look at him. You're a writer, an observer of people. What do you see?"

Maggie's eyes roamed the dark shape and his surroundings. "Well, he doesn't have anything to take onboard, not even a magazine or book, but that doesn't mean he isn't getting on a plane. Some people travel light."

"Do you know of anyone who doesn't carry something onboard?"

The author sighed. "Not really, no. In that case, I guess he does look suspicious then."

"I'd like to get closer but I don't want to leave you here by yourself, just in case he isn't alone."

A shiver traveled Maggie's spine. "I'd appreciate it if you didn't leave me."

Sarah turned to look at her. "I don't plan to. I'm here until you're on that plane and in the air."

"Thank you." The author's gaze remained inconspicuously on the dark figure lurking nearby.

"It's quarter to nine. There should be a boarding call soon."

"I hope so. I just want to get out of here now. Being the target of the most dangerous and notorious vampire that has ever existed is too much. I always thought he was only a concoction of Bram Stoker's imagination, nothing more. I mean, I wrote him as real but I never dreamed he was."

"It's astounding what's out there that people don't know about."

"Perhaps they don't want to know. It doesn't necessarily mean they don't though."

Sarah's contemplative gaze remained on the author. Could she be correct in her assumption?

CR

Once the plane took off, Sarah called Reece to let him know the author was safely in the air, and also to tell him about the man she'd seen loitering in the airport lounge. On her way to the parking garage, she noticed the dark figure was no longer standing by the potted plants. Where had he gone? Had she been wrong? Had he boarded a flight? As she walked past the row of cars, making her way to their hire vehicle, she had the feeling someone's eyes were on her. She glanced over her shoulder and ran her perceptive gaze around the large space. People were heading into and out of the airport but they were quite a distance away, and yet she was almost certain someone was in a much closer proximity to her. Could it be the man from the lounge? And, if so, what did he want?

Sarah tugged the remote key from the pocket of her pants and pressed the unlock button. Just as she opened the door a black hood was pulled over her face and she felt the sting of an injection in her upper arm before darkness enveloped her.

℘CR

When Sarah didn't arrive back at their hotel Reece tried to call her. No answer. The man she had mentioned came to mind. Why had he been at the airport? Could he be the reason she hadn't returned yet? He kept trying her cell every five minutes without a response. "Nathaniel, I'm worried about Sarah. I can't get her on her phone and she told me a man was hanging around the lounge while they were waiting for Maggie to board her flight."

"Perhaps we should go out there and take a look around."

Reece's eyes met his. "We need to organize another car." He picked up the hotel phone.

A car was out front when the pair came downstairs and the PI took the passenger seat. "You can drive."

Nathaniel wasn't fond of driving in traffic chaos because his vampire instinct was to run over everything in his path, but he climbed in beside Reece anyway and started the engine. Once at the airport, he pulled into a parking space on the level where Sarah would have parked and he and Reece got out of the car. The vampire stood, eyes closed for a moment, then said, "This way." He'd picked up Sarah's vibration. "She was anxious. Someone was watching her." He pointed ahead of them. "The car is still here."

When they reached the rental they found the driver's door open and no sign of Sarah.

Reece's eyes roamed the parking garage. "The guy she saw had to have had others with him because there's no way they would've taken her without a fight."

"Unless they drugged her."

The PI frowned at him. "It had to be Dracula's men."

"Without doubt."

Reece waited a moment, the nerves in his gut twisting into an anxious tangle. "Do you think he'll kill her?"

"He may want to bargain for her life."

"They have a long history. She's been looking for him for years, has interfered in his plans, and has made attempts on his life on many occasions. Maybe he just wants her out of the picture."

"He is a shrewd manipulator, do not forget that, and he will stop at nothing to get what he wants. And what he wants right now is to live. So I believe he will contact you to organize a meeting."

Reece swallowed hard. "A face to face with Dracula."

"Yes."

"Not something I'm looking forward to."

℞

Sarah woke up in the boot of a fast moving sedan. How long had she been unconscious? And where were they taking her? Her racing heartbeat boomed against her ribs. It had to be Dracula's orchestration, who else could it be? She swallowed dry saliva, her mouth gagged. Her cramped shoulders ached from her hands being secured firmly behind her back. They knew her abilities and had compensated for them. Would the monster kill her? Icy beads of perspiration dotted her brow and the feeling of dread washed over her. She had been on his trail for over a century and now it would end with him laughing in her face in triumph.

She knew Reece would be worried about her by now and she hoped Nathaniel could pick up her vibration and follow it, the way Arianne had done in Las Vegas when Reece was taken. Without her special weapons she was at the mercy of her soon-to-be host. A sudden thought crossed her anxious mind. *Maybe he'll use me to get to Reece. Maybe he wants to make a deal.* She prayed that was the reason for her abduction… and not her death.

℞

Reece wondered if Nathaniel could pick up Sarah's energy so they could follow it. They had nothing to go on. *Nothing.* And Sarah's life hung in the balance. If Dracula hadn't taken her to make some kind of deal she was as good as dead. "Nathaniel, do you think you can follow Sarah's trail? Can you still feel her vibration?"

"I have tried to pick up any residual energy but there does not appear to be any."

"Nothing at all?"

The vampire shook his head. "I am sorry."

"It's ok. You can't do what you can't do. We'll head over to Dracula's hotel and remain there until we get some kind of movement."

"Todd and Charlotte are arriving today, are they not?"

"Dammit, you're right. Their flight takes about ten and half hours so they won't get here until later this evening but I said you'd pick them up." The pair stopped at the hire car the priest and the author had traveled in to the airport. Reece squatted and peered beneath the four wheel drive. "You take our car back to the hotel and I'll follow you." He reached under the side of the wagon and dragged out the remote key. He remembered his phone had slipped underneath the car when he'd been abducted in Vegas.

As he was about to climb into wagon car his cell phone vibrated. He had a text message: *Hi Reece, Maggie here. Arrived safe and sound. Thanks for your help. Good luck with everything.* At least that was one less complication he had to worry about. He glanced at Nathaniel. "Maggie's safe in Rome."

"That is good news."

"Yeah. Let's get going we have work to do."

CHAPTER TWENTY SIX

Charlotte gazed out of the oval plane window at the passing clouds. She had only been on two other flights in her life, one when she and Dan got married and holidayed in Hawaii for their honeymoon and the other when she was kidnapped and drugged at LAX. At least she assumed she had been taken to Las Vegas by plane. Her eyes moved from the passing fluffy white clouds to Todd sitting beside her and she wondered, for the briefest moment, what it would have been like if she'd taken him up on his proposal all those years ago. What would her life be like now? She shook the thought from her mind – she was engaged to Reece, if he still wanted her, and she couldn't let her heart stray to places it didn't belong. Although quite a few years older than her, Todd was still an attractive man who kept himself in good shape. She felt safe in his arms for some reason, probably because his life, up until now, had been normal. Why did he want to get involved in all of this? Once you knew the truth it was a never ending nightmare.

His eyes were fixed on a movie on his tablet, something not long out of the box office, and hadn't noticed Charlotte watching him. They still had five hours in the air before landing in Paris. *Paris.* Charlotte had always hoped to visit the city of light one day under far different circumstances to these. She'd hoped to go there with Reece on a romantic escape at some point. She sighed and turned her welling gaze back to the window, blinking away the tears before they could spill down her face. Would things work out between them?

When Todd touched her arm she jumped and shifted in her seat. "Yes?"

He pointed to the flight attendant and cart. "Want a drink?"

"Yes, thanks. Coffee's fine."

After setting the drinks down on their trays, Todd frowned at Charlotte. He could tell something was on her mind. "Are you all right?"

"I'm not sure. I'm worried about the kind of reception I'll receive from Reece when we arrive. He said we should take it one day at a time and see where it leads but…"

"You think he said that to appease your feelings?"

"Possibly, yes." She picked up her coffee and took a cautious sip. "He doesn't look at me the same way anymore. I see it in his eyes whenever we're together."

"He just needs time to work it out, Charlotte, that's all. I'm sure he'll make the right decision."

Charlotte's frowning gaze met his. "But for whom?"

Todd squeezed her hand. "For the both of you."

"I wish I could believe that. He's pretty adamant when it comes to his values and beliefs. He believes I got Andre killed and I don't think he'll change his mind about that. And, inadvertently, I did."

"Don't do that. It wasn't your fault. He's a logical man, he'll figure it out. Have a little faith in him."

"I do… it's just… I know him. And because I know him so well I think he'll break off our engagement when all of this is over."

"Don't put it out there, Charlotte. Hold onto the hope that you'll be the choice he makes. He still loves you and he just needs to remember that."

Charlotte needed a change of topic. "What are you watching?" She pointed to the tablet sitting next to Todd's coffee cup on the tray.

His eyes moved to the screen. "Oh? Uh, the latest Tomb Raider."

"Any good?"

"It's not quite the same as the others, but, yeah, it's entertaining."

"Then I'll let you get back to it."

Charlotte went to turn away but Todd gently grabbed her arm and stopped her. "Things will work out, Charlotte. Just keep believing that."

"I'll do my best." She gave him a thin smile.

Todd sat and watched her for a while before returning to the movie. Her coming back into his life stirred up feelings inside he still had for her, although he would never tell her. All he could do was be her shoulder to cry on while he could. Reece would be a fool if he let her walk out of his life, but if he did Todd would be there to pick up the pieces.

⁅⁏⁆

Reece sipped the lukewarm coffee he'd picked up on the way to Dracula's hotel, screwed up his nose and sat the cardboard cup back in the console. He and Nathaniel had been sitting around for hours, and nothing. No sign of the vampire. No black limousines had entered or left the premises in the time they had been outside and he wondered if Vlad was at another location. If they didn't find Sarah soon there was no doubt in his mind she'd be dead and he didn't want to be the one to have to tell Ed.

He glanced at the dashboard digital clock. 11.00 PM. Todd and Charlotte would be at the hotel by now. Just as the thought entered his mind his cell rang. "Reece Daniels speaking."

"Hey, it's me," Todd said. "We're almost at the hotel. Where are you?"

"We're doing surveillance on Dracula's hotel. There have been some new developments."

Todd frowned and his gaze moved to Charlotte. "What kind of developments?"

"Sarah was taken from the airport after seeing Maggie off."

"What?"

"That's why we're staking out his hotel. We think he orchestrated the abduction. It's too much to go into right now but Sarah and he have a history. He's either going to use her as a bargaining tool or kill her. Either way we need to get a location as quickly as possible. You and I both know the first forty eight hours are crucial and it's already been over twelve."

"Yeah, it is. Do you have anywhere in mind?"

"No. I know very little about the city except for what it offers in the tourist brochures, which means they could be anywhere. I have to do something about the safety of my team. This is becoming commonplace and I don't want to lose anyone else."

"I had a thought about that."

Reece frowned. "What was it?"

"Maybe you and your team can have microchips implanted with a tracking device so that if anyone does go missing they'll be easy to find."

123

The PI couldn't believe he hadn't thought of it himself. "Sounds like a solid idea. Once we get this situation under control I'll look into it."

"Glad I could offer something. So what can we do to help?"

"Eva is in my room. And before you get any ideas it's not what you think. She showed up out of the blue and I'm pretty sure Jacques encouraged her. I told her she was under house arrest for now. That's if she listened to me and is still there. She's been chasing Dracula for years. Maybe you could talk to her and see if she has any ideas about where he could be. Give me a call if you find out anything in the next twenty minutes, otherwise I'm calling it quits and heading back to the hotel."

"Ok, will do." He waited a beat then said, "Do you want to talk to Charlotte?"

"Not right now. Just see if you can get anything out of Eva. We need to find Sarah before something happens to her, if it hasn't already."

"We'll see you when you get back then."

"Yeah, you will." Reece rang off and turned to Nathaniel. "Do you think Eva might know where Vlad is?"

"It is possible. She has been documenting his movements for years and would have a vast knowledge base of how he operates."

"That's what I thought. Maybe we should head back now. She'll play with Todd and won't tell him anything."

Nathaniel's left eyebrow arched. "She plays with you too. What makes you think she will tell you what you want to know?"

"I don't but someone has to lean on her for information."

Reece's cell phone went off again. "Reece..."

"It's me," Todd said, "Eva's not here."

"Dammit! We're on our way back." He rang off and frowned at Nathaniel.

"She has gone?"

"Yeah. Let's get going."

$$\mathcal{SOCR}$$

Todd and Charlotte met Reece in the hallway outside the PI's room. "Have you checked the hotel to see if she's in the building?"

"Yes, she doesn't seem to be," Todd told him.

"I knew I couldn't trust her. I should've tied her up or something."

"She is an immortal," Nathaniel offered, "She would have found a means of escape no matter what you did."

Reece gave a heavy sigh. "Now we have two deranged vampires on the loose in Paris and we don't know where either of them is."

"Vlad is deranged but Eva is cunning."

Reece realized he had her number in his phone. He tugged it from the pocket of his jeans and found it in the address book. No answer. Of course not. He ended the call and shoved the phone back into his pocket. "Well she isn't answering her phone."

"We could get the police to track her GPS," Todd said.

The PI turned around. "Yeah, maybe, unless she's found a way to have the signal blocked." He hadn't bothered to let the Paris police commissioner know he was in his city. Perhaps it was a bad call now that they needed official help.

"Why don't you let me give them a call?" Todd offered. "Just give me the cell number and I'll see what I can do."

"What are you going to tell them?"

Todd's right eyebrow arched. "That she's a fugitive from the US who has entered Paris illegally and I'm trying to locate her to extradite her back to home soil. Looks bad for them so they'll be only too eager to help."

Reece and Todd gave each other a thin smile. It could work. "What if they want to know more?" the PI asked.

"They won't. Trust me."

Reece pulled up the number and Todd keyed it into his phone. "Thanks. Won't be long." The retired detective headed to his room.

Charlotte, Reece and Nathaniel stood in uncomfortable silence. "I will be in my room if you require any further assistance." The vampire turned and strutted down the hallway.

"How was the flight?" Reece asked, feeling awkward, his gut churning.

"Good." She gave him a brief smile. "Long."

He nodded. "Yeah."

"I know it's late but I'm starved. Want to grab a bite to eat?" Charlotte hoped he'd say yes.

"I should wait in case we get a location on Eva." His gaze moved along the hallway in the direction Todd had taken.

"Oh, yes, you're right. Do you think Sarah's still alive?"

"I'm hoping so. I think Vlad will want to make a deal and that's why he took her."

"What kind of deal?"

"His life for hers."

"Oh? I hope you're right. Sarah's a valuable member of our team." She gave him another self-conscious smile. It felt clunky and strange talking to him. Nothing was the same between them anymore.

"Yes she is and we can't lose anyone else."

Charlotte frowned into his eyes. "I'm truly sorry, Reece. I am. If I could change what happened I would. I've already told you that."

Reece reached out and gripped her arm gently. "I understand that, but…"

"You still don't trust me? You think I'm in league with him?"

"No. But, as I said, you could still be connected to him. That's not your fault, but your being here could jeopardize everything and everyone."

"Do you really believe that? Do you hate me that much?" A single tear slipped down her right cheek and she swiped it away.

"I don't hate you, Charlotte, I…" He stopped himself before he said something he couldn't take back. He knew he was still in love with her but it didn't change anything.

CHAPTER TWENTY SEVEN

The black limousine traveled the debris covered road up to the abandoned LA Zoo and stopped at the dilapidated, graffitied entrance. The sun had almost vanished behind the distant horizon, and as the last of its yellow rays slipped into the hazy, maroon aura, Jacques stepped out of the prestige sedan, tugged the brown leather satchel off the back seat, and gazed around the expansive treed remains of the once popular venue. It was the perfect location to perform the ritual for his brother's return from the realm of the dead. The zoo appeared deserted at this time of night, but maybe not for long. It seemed to be an intriguing attraction for urban explorers who investigated deserted properties in the hope they were haunted and he couldn't allow anyone to find them here. If someone happened to stumble upon them it would be the last thing they'd see.

Jacques waved off the driver – he would call him when he was required – and wandered into the deserted grounds following the path Aramon had instructed him to take. Andre would no longer be able to venture out into the daylight. His brother would be a creature of the night... just as he was. A smug smile spread across his pale, handsome face. Andre would be imprisoned in darkness, too. Not that Jacques minded, he preferred the shadow of night. It afforded him a certain ambiguity from the mortals of the world who professed to be human. He huffed out a disenchanted guffaw. Some were more monster than he was.

His cell vibrated in his jacket's inner pocket. He snatched it out and frowned at the screen. "Yes, I am almost there. Is everything ready? Good.

I will see you soon." He dropped the phone back into his pocket and strode along the path and around the corner to an unfenced set of enclosures near the picnic grounds.

Aramon stepped out of the shadows to greet him. "It is good to see you again, Jacques. How long has it been? Were we not in the land of the Pharaohs when we last met?"

Jacques pursed his lips as the question circled his mind in search of an answer. "Possibly a hundred years, give or take, 1917 perhaps. Yes, I believe it was. Fuad the first had just become Sultan."

"Yes, you are right. I remember now. He succeeded his brother, Sultan Hussein Kamel, after his death. Come. Everything is in readiness." The sorcerer turned on his heel and headed back through the rocky outcrop into a graffitied space behind the wall.

Jacques followed.

An altar dressed in black surrounded by six, burning black candles stood in the center. Upon it sat three glass vials – one containing Andre's ashes, the second containing his blood, and the third containing Jacques' blood, an assurance that his brother would belong to him and would do whatever he desired.

Aramon shrugged into his colorful, ancient robes, placed the gold and emerald headdress on his head, walked around the altar and stood behind it. He opened the first vial and spread the ash in a straight line along the cloth then opened the second and third vials and poured the blood into the ash. Jacques remained in the shadows, his curious gaze fixed on the ash and blood. The sorcerer closed his eyes, raised up his chin and thrust his hands into the air. "I call upon the gatekeeper of the realm of the dead. Hear my plea. With ash and blood I beseech thee to release the vampire, Andre Delacroix, back into the living realm. Hear me oh great one. I call on thee to quicken him by joined blood and set him free from the bonds of death."

The blood-soaked ash began to bubble and white smoke rose from the amalgam, spiraling upward.

Aramon repeated the incantation twice more. A complex spell of this nature always worked better when recited three times.

The ash and blood spread across the altar. The flattened outline of a male figure formed, expanding into a three dimensional silhouette.

Jacques darted out of the shadows toward the altar, his eyes wide. *So this is how I returned.*

Aramon thrust out his hand. "Remain where you are."

Squelching and cracking sounds echoed around the rocky walls as the embryonic shape became whole.

"Aaahhh!" Andre screamed as searing pain enveloped him. Bloodless skin wrapped itself around muscle and bone as ribs formed and limbs extended. Another horrific scream of pain escaped his lips.

Jacques cringed at the sound. He hadn't remembered his reawakening. Would his brother, once it was complete?

As the tissue and skin solidified, Andre lay naked on the altar, his eyes closed.

"Is he all right?" Jacques asked, a frown of familial concern crossing his handsome face.

"I believe so." Aramon placed both the palms of his hands on Andre's chest. "Rise up, Andre, you are whole."

Andre opened his eyes and sat up. When he saw his brother he frowned. "What happened? Where am I? How are you here?" He turned his head toward the sorcerer. "Who is he?"

"That is something we can discuss later, little brother." He tossed the satchel at him. "Get dressed." Andre was only minutes younger than Jacques but he liked to remind him of that fact whenever he could.

Andre's eyes widened. "I died." He pressed his hand to his chest where the wound had been. "Dracula... Dracula killed me."

"Yes, he did. And he will pay for that mistake." Jacques walked over to the altar. "I am glad you have returned. There is much to talk about."

Andre's eyes roamed the gloom. "Where's Reece? Does he know about this?"

"As a matter of fact he does. He is in Paris at the moment hunting Dracula."

A bloody tear slid from Andre's left eye. "Arianne."

"Yes, an unfortunate circumstance. Who would have thought Vlad would murder his own blood."

"Can this sorcerer bring her back?" His eyes moved to the robed man standing beside him.

"I am afraid not."

"How is this possible? How are you here?" Andre opened the satchel and tugged out the clothing inside.

"The same way you are, dear brother. I still have loyal adherents who were waiting for the opportune time to bring me back. I've been alive for over a year now."

"And you didn't bother to let me know?" He gave Jacques a resentful glare. "Why did you do this? You must want something."

"Why does everyone keep saying that?"

Andre gave his brother a skeptical frown. "Because it's the truth."

"I made an arrangement with your friend. He would dispatch Vlad and I would return you to the human world."

"And he's killed Dracula?"

"Not yet, no. But I have the utmost confidence that he will."

"We couldn't before. What makes you think we can now?"

"Eva Van Helsing."

"Abraham Van Helsing's great granddaughter?"

"Great, great, great, great granddaughter. Yes. She has certain abilities that will be useful in orchestrating the demise of Dracula."

"What kind of abilities?"

"She's a vampire for one thing. But beside that, she knows as much about him as he does himself. She can track him."

Andre pulled the black T-shirt over his head then jumped down off the altar and slipped on the pants and loafers. "Where's Sarah, Nathaniel and Ed?

"The priest and Nathaniel are also in Paris. The lieutenant is still in Los Angeles, along with Charlotte and a new team member, Todd Lassiter... oh, yes, and sheriff Lozano."

"The sheriff's here?"

"Yes. Now hurry along we have to go." He turned his gaze to Aramon. "Thank you."

"It was my pleasure, Jacques."

"We will see each other again."

"Just don't make it another hundred years." He gave the vampire a thin smile.

"Of course." Jacques turned on his heel and headed outside.

Andre followed his brother out of the enclosure remembering his encounter with the werewolves all those years ago and having to wipe

Reece's and his partner, Dave Colson's memory because of it. His eyes roamed the dark, treed picnic grounds.

"Come with me." Jacques pulled his cell phone from the pocket of his jacket and keyed in the number for his driver then strutted along the path heading for the main entrance, his brother in tow. "We are ready to be picked up."

Andre caught up to him and the identical twins walked side by side out to the meeting point. His friend would be glad to see him… and he him.

CHAPTER TWENTY EIGHT

Eva Van Helsing strolled the sidewalk on Avenue du Colonel Henri Rol-Tanguy, heading to the official entrance for the Paris catacombs. She knew Vlad's habits all too well, after centuries of pursuing him, and had a sense that he might have a location deep within the tunnels of which no one was aware. The depth of the underground tomb of more than six million souls equated to a five story building and traveled over 186 miles below the city, which meant he could be anywhere inside the maze of bones. There were gated, locked sections that no one could enter, restricted areas that contained loose bones and skulls piled to the ceiling and others with no bones at all where limestone rock was once excavated.

Reece had been trying to reach her. Should she call him with her suspicions? No. She needed to be sure before she allowed the PI and his team access to the underworld city of the dead and the danger that lurked within it. They had already lost loved ones, despite them being vampires, and she wasn't about to let more innocents die at the hands of a ruthless, bloodthirsty fanatic. Eva stopped opposite the dark green metal façade on the tree lined corner that lead into the safer sections of the caves and ran her discerning gaze over it. She would dress as a regular Parisian tourist, purchase a ticket online, return in the twilight hours of the evening, as the last admission was at 7.30 PM, and once inside, would find a place to wait out the flow of curious humans before making her way to the inaccessible areas of the catacombs and to where she believed Vlad held the priest captive. She had placed a listening device into the PI's phone while he had been sleeping so she would know what they knew.

Her cell vibrated against her hip and she tugged it from her body-hugging leather pants to check the caller ID. Reece. Again. She hesitated before pressing the button. "Hello."

"Why haven't you been answering my calls? And why didn't you wait at the hotel as we agreed?" The angry tension in his voice did not go unnoticed.

"You mean as you ordered. I am following a hunch. If it plays out the way I hope it will I will call you with directions."

"You know where he is?"

"I am not sure yet. When I am I will contact you." Eva ended the call before the PI could protest and sighed as she pushed her cell back into the pocket of her pants. She resented being told what to do. She had been on her own for a long time and could take care of herself, without the interference of others.

The ghoulish queue of patrons extended far beyond her gaze and would be waiting in line for at least two hours before gaining access to the subterranean exhibit. She, on the other hand, would walk right up to the barrier and have immediate admission. Eva turned on her heal and strutted back along the sidewalk, heading to the hotel. She had a room on the floor above Reece and the others, although he was unaware of it, so she could hear what was going on below her. Sounds, like heat, traveled upward. It wouldn't be difficult for her to climb out of her window and descend the wall to the PI's room beneath hers if she heard any kind of trouble, which is how she had gained access to his phone.

ℰℭ

Reece folded his arms and gave a heavy sigh. "Why can't that woman just do what she's asked?"

Nathaniel eyed him sideways. "Because she is an old vampire who has lived a solitary life for hundreds of years in pursuit of Dracula and others of his kind and she listens to no one."

The PI's disgruntled gaze moved to his companion. "Thanks for the reminder. I know all that, but it still doesn't give her the right to jeopardize our mission."

"Maybe she will locate Vlad. Perhaps you should give her the benefit of the doubt this time."

Reece huffed out a frustrated breath, his eyes still on Nathaniel. "You really believe that?"

"I would trust that is the situation."

The pair was in their rental car outside the boutique hotel waiting for Dracula's return. If he returned.

Reece's focus moved back to the hotel. *What are we doing here?* Vlad had no intention of returning when he had a prisoner to torture. *Where is he?* "Let's head back to the hotel. It's pointless sitting around here doing nothing."

"You are sure?" Nathaniel turned his curious gaze to Reece.

"Yeah. We can make better use of our time working on a plan of our own."

"Very well." Nathaniel started the engine and pulled away from the curb.

"I think Todd's idea of microchipping ourselves is a sensible one. Don't know why I didn't think of it myself."

"It would be of great benefit in keeping track of everyone during dangerous situations."

"Yes, it would."

"I believe having Todd Lassiter on our team will be an advantage."

"Me too."

"He has knowledge and resources that will assist us."

Reece nodded. "Yeah, he does. And he's trustworthy."

Nathaniel waited a beat, then said, "Have you given any further consideration to what you are going to do about Charlotte?"

Reece sighed. "Not really. We've had a lot to deal with since we got here and there hasn't been any time to think about anything else."

"Now you have seen her again how do you feel about that?"

The PI turned his head and gave Nathaniel and steely stare. "What are you... my shrink?"

"I am only concerned for the both of you."

"Well I appreciate that but my love life is no one's concern."

"I am sorry. It was not my intention to cross any boundaries."

"I know. It's fine. To be honest, I wish things were the way they were before everything fell apart."

"So you still love her?"

"Love isn't something you can turn on and off. Of course I do but…"

"You cannot forgive her for Andre's death?"

"It's not that. Well, yes, it is that." He gave another heavy sigh and shook his head. "I can't trust her anymore."

"But why? You know what happened was not her fault. She was under Dracula's influence. He had control of her mind and she was unaware of what she was doing."

"I know, but it doesn't change the fact." He shrugged. "I don't understand why I feel this way, but I do."

"Perhaps you need to let your heart rule your head for once." Nathaniel gave him a sideward glance then returned his eyes to the road.

Reece didn't have an answer for that. He had always been a man of logic. Was Nathaniel right? Could he allow his heart to make the right decision?

CR

The hotel elevator doors slid open and Reece and Nathaniel were met by Todd and Charlotte stepping into the hallway. "Hey, Reece, no luck with you know who?" Todd asked cryptically as other hotel patrons exited the elevator around them.

Reece's eyes moved from the ex-detective to his fiancée then back. "No, he didn't show."

Charlotte stepped up to him. "Todd and I were heading out for some dinner. Want to join us?"

"Uh, no, but thanks for the offer. I need to take a shower and change and get on the net for a while."

"Oh, ok. Are you sure? We were told there's a great little bistro down the street." Charlotte wanted to spend some time with him, even if they weren't alone.

"You enjoy your dinner. I have to work." He gave her a thin smile and stepped into the elevator. Nathaniel followed.

Reece and Charlotte's eyes met between the gap as the doors moved together.

"May I ask a question?" the black vampire queried.

"What is it?" Reece felt the tension increase in his shoulders as he pushed the call button for their floor, knowing Nathaniel was about to make a logical assessment.

"Why do you allow your fiancée to have dinner with a man she had a previous relationship with?"

There it was.

"Charlotte can do whatever she wants. I'm not her keeper. And they're friends, Nathaniel, just friends." Reece folded his arms.

"Are they?" His left eyebrow arched. "Humans are confusing."

Reece turned to look at him. "How so?"

"You are still in love with Charlotte and yet you are pushing her into the arms of a man who cares for her. It does not make sense." He frowned.

Reece didn't like hearing the truth. It was a bitter pill to swallow. "Like I said in the car… my love life is no one's concern." Nathaniel was right, though. He was pushing her away and if he continued to do so Todd would be there to catch her when she fell.

"As you wish." Nathaniel hoped the seed of doubt he had planted would take root and Reece would make the right decision about his and Charlotte's relationship.

CHAPTER TWENTY NINE

Andre stood on the balcony of his brother's penthouse suite gazing down at the busy boulevard below. Being dead had been only a blink of an eye for him and now he was back in the land of the living and his best friend didn't even know he was alive. His eyes roamed the street. Humans were oblivious to the things that lurked in the shadows... waiting. So many people disappeared each year and not all by human means. And now he was one of those creatures of the night. He swung around at a sound behind him. Jacques was there.

"You were thinking about your friend?" he said, moving alongside his brother.

"Yes. I should let him know I'm back."

"It would be better not to distract him for the time being. He and his team are hunting Dracula and they need to keep focused. There will be ample time for a reunion later."

Andre frowned at Jacques. "Why did you bring me back? As I said at the zoo, there has to be a reason."

Jacques' left eyebrow arched. "Why can't you believe I did it for you?"

His brother folded his arms and leaned against the balustrade. "Because you *never* do anything for anyone but yourself."

A slight smirk tugged at his lips. "All in good time, brother, all in good time." He turned to walk away.

Andre grabbed his arm and swung him around. "No. I want to know now. What are you planning? If it has anything to do with Reece and the others you can forget it. I'd rather be dead."

The smug smirk widened. "It may not be that simple."

Andre's eyes widened. "What have you done?"

"I did what was necessary."

Andre frowned. "Which means what exactly?"

"As I said, all in good time." Jacques turned on his heel and strutted back into his suite.

Andre's suspicious gaze remained on the open doorway. "What had his brother done?" Turning around, his gaze moved back to the pedestrians below. A primal urge surged through him as he listened to all the beating hearts pumping blood around those bodies. His bloodlust had reared its ugly head once again and he had to fight to control it. Without his serum he would revert back to a blood drinker... a dangerous one. The feeling intensified.

"Here." Jacques tossed a blood bag across the balcony to him. "This should keep your craving in check. For a while, at least."

Andre ripped the blue plug from the clear, plastic tube and threw it across the balcony, then stuck the tube in his mouth and sucked the bag dry in seconds. He tossed it aside, stalked toward his brother and grabbed him by the throat. "What have you done to me?"

Jacques' dark eyes met Andre's. "Take your hands off me."

Andre tightened his grip. *"Tell me."*

"I did what I had to." He shoved his brother away from him and took a step backwards.

Andre rushed at him.

Jacques propelled himself into the air. "Let us not do this now, brother. It will serve no purpose"

"I want to know what you've done to me. I don't feel like myself anymore." Andre hurtled his body into the air.

"I saved your life. You should be grateful." Both brothers hovered in the dark sky.

"Grateful? You brought me back for your own purpose not because you missed me. Why should I be grateful?" Andre wanted to attack Jacques, the desire overwhelming, and he knew something was wrong. The need to kill had never been this strong before, but right now he wanted to end his brother and was having a difficult time controlling the rage rising inside him.

Jacques could sense the hostility in his brother and felt a sense of satisfaction. His plan had worked. Andre was now his to control. "Little brother…"

Andre's eyes glowed red, not their usual pale blue. "*Don't* call me that."

"Very well. Andre, I brought you back because you are my brother and because I need you with me, but, yes, I do have other reasons… and I will explain them to you. But for now, you must trust me."

A deep scowl formed on Andre's handsome face. "Trust you? You tried to kill us all the last time you were here. Remember? How can you expect me to trust you?"

Jacques snapped his fingers and both vampires descended to the balcony floor. "You will. In time."

Andre stood before his brother in a trancelike state, eyes glazed.

Jacques turned to walk back into his suite but stopped and turned around. "Come." He glanced up at the dark sky. "It looks like rain."

Andre followed Jacques into the hotel as though he were being led by an invisible leash.

❧⁂☙

Eva remained behind the line trudging the narrow, damp, well-lit passage into the underground tomb of bones. Her vampire nature struggled to contain the bloodlust around so many beating hearts pumping the sanguine fluid through their veins, the scent so potent it wafted into her nostrils causing a wash of saliva across her tongue. She was hungry. The tour guide continued his spiel as he led the group deeper into the catacombs telling the enthralled tourists about the Cataphiles – groups of thrill seekers who entered the restricted areas of the subterranean city illegally through old manholes or trapdoors of unused train stations, and, if they were caught, how they were fined a hundred Euro by police patrolling the tunnels at night. Once Eva found a means in which to detach herself from the humans she would do so. If she remained around the scent for much longer there would be a massacre because she wouldn't be able to contain her bloodlust. She always maintained a tight leash on her thirst and never ventured into the nefarious terrain of drinking directly from mortals. Not unless there was no other option.

The guide led them further into the macabre depths below the city imparting historical facts to the camera flashing group about the reason the bones were placed in the catacombs – cemeteries had been overflowing and created a health risk to the citizens of 18th century Paris. Eva held back, allowing some distance between her and the entourage. Once they were out of hearing range, she would break the lock on the gate beside her with her bare hands and disappear into the unlit, off limits sections of the tunnels.

Inside the dank, black passage her nocturnal vision widened, allowing her to see through the gloom. Eva knew she had a lot of ground to cover so she whipped through the darkness, making her way deeper underground, the time taking half as long as it would if she were human. When she came to another gated section she stopped and used her immortal hearing to listen for the echo of a heartbeat. Sarah had to be somewhere within the vast expanse of tunnels. This was the perfect place to hide her where no one would hear her if she screamed.

Eva came upon an engraved street sign in the rock wall face: Rue De La Voie-Verte D 1874-1875. From what she had researched online, there should be chambers that no one had entered in this section of restricted tunnels. She continued along the passageway, her nocturnal gaze widening even more, the graffiti on the walls impressive. *What a shame the people who venture down here to deface the city of the dead didn't put their talents to better use.* After moving through the passageway for some time, she heard voices echoing out of the dark somewhere ahead. She stopped and used her super-sensitive hearing to determine where they were coming from.

Was it Vlad's voice she could hear?

She whipped along the tunnel to a crossroad and stopped again, taking in the sound of the voice traveling toward her. To the left. As she moved closer she pressed her back against the wall and waited to see if she could hear others in the chamber. Perhaps it was a group of Cataphiles hanging out down here smoking pot and drinking beer. If her heart actually beat, it would be racing right now. Eva sidled along the rocky wall, palms against the rough surface and stepped closer to the echoing voice.

"You have been a thorn in my side for far too long, *Priest*. But I will use it to my advantage."

"Why don't you just kill me and get it over with?" Sarah's voice was weak, shaky.

"Because I have plans for your meddling private eye and the others who follow him."

Eva hovered above the debris strew floor so as not to make any noise and eased herself forward so she could peer around the column. Sarah was tied to a chair in the middle of the chamber, her face swollen and bleeding, one eye black, blood trickling from the right corner of her mouth. She had taken a beating from one of Dracula's henchmen who stood behind her. Whatever the father of all vampires had wanted from her she had not given up. That was commendable. True loyalty.

"You think he'll walk into your trap?" Sarah chuckled and coughed out more blood.

"He will… for you. He is loyal to his own detriment." Vlad smirked.

"I'm not that important to him. We've never really seen eye to eye. I think you're mistaken about where his affections lie."

Vlad's left eyebrow arched. "And I believe you are lying."

"Why would I? I have nothing to gain."

"I think he is planning an all-out assault and, once he has this location, will be here with his small army to fight for your life."

Eva knew Reece would come for Sarah. But what Vlad didn't know was that she had contacts in Paris as well and would call on them for assistance to destroy him once and for all. The vampire hunter headed back in the direction she had come from. It was time to let the PI know where their nemesis was hiding and to orchestrate her plan of attack. Dracula would not escape this time.

CHAPTER THIRTY

Reece stood in front of his team and was about to speak when his cell vibrated in his jeans pocket. He pulled the phone free and answered it. "Reece…"

"It is me," Eva said. "I know where Dracula is."

"Where?"

"I am on my way back to the hotel. You are there, are you not?"

"Yeah, we're in my room. We were about to put some strategies in motion."

"Don't do anything until I get there." She rang off.

The PI sighed and shoved the phone back into his pocket.

"What was that all about?" Charlotte asked.

"Eva. She says she knows where Dracula is. She's on her way back and asked me not to do anything until she gets here."

"And you believe her?" Charlotte folded her arms. She knew there was something going on between her fiancé and the vampire hunter … or the leather-clad vixen, and she didn't like it.

"Why wouldn't I? She has nothing to prove by lying to me."

"How do we know she isn't in league with him? How do we know he didn't turn her?"

Nathaniel stood up. "He did not. And I think we should hear what she has to say."

Todd turned from the window. "Are you sure about that?" He wanted to defend Charlotte's insinuation.

"Yes. The vampire who sired her is of the French aristocratic bloodline de Tourville."

Charlotte gave him a sheepish glance. She wanted Reece to doubt the woman… vampire. Whatever she was. She was too beautiful to be anywhere near him. "Oh."

Reece gave her a severe frown and Charlotte diverted her gaze to her lap. It was obvious she had annoyed him with her questions about the vampire hunter. It seemed being in the same space did that these days. Would she ever see the love he once had for her in his eyes again or would he always look at her the way he was right now?

Nathaniel noticed the exchange between them. "Your question was a valid one, Charlotte. You had no idea about her immortal lineage. And we cannot be too careful when it comes to trusting someone we do not know well." The serious look on Reece's face softened and Nathaniel was pleased he could diffuse the tension between them.

The door opened and Eva sauntered into the room.

Reece's gaze moved to her. "So where is he?"

"First of all, Sarah is alive. I have seen her. She is a little worse for wear but she is all right." Relief showed on everyone's faces.

Reece folded his arms. "That's good news… where is he?"

"I have made contact with other immortals I know who live in Paris. We will have the assistance we need to defeat him."

"Who are they?"

"Does it matter? The bigger our number the more likely we are to succeed."

"Yeah, it matters. I want to know we can trust them."

"You have my word." Eva crossed the room and stopped in front of Reece.

"Like I had your word you'd stay here?"

"That is different. I am trying to help you."

Reece gave a heavy sigh. "If we don't work together things can go wrong. People can die." He stared into her pale eyes. "Now where is he?"

"In a restricted section of the Paris catacombs."

"You mean the underground city of bones?" Todd asked, his voice apprehensive.

Eva nodded. "Yes."

"There's over 180 miles of tunnels under the city how do you know you'll be able to find your way back to his location?" Todd had seen a documentary on the catacombs. Their length was enormous.

"I'm a vampire with certain senses which allow me to do that." Her right eyebrow arched. "Are you claustrophobic, Mr. Lassiter?" Her glossy red lips spread into a shrewd smirk.

"I'm fine."

Reece frowned at him. "Are you claustrophobic?"

"To some degree, yeah. But as I said, I'll be fine."

The PI gave him a concerned stare, hoping it wouldn't become a problem, then turned to look at Eva. "You're sure you can get us in?"

"Of course." She unrolled the map of the catacombs she had downloaded off the internet and printed. "He is here." Eva pointed to the place she had circled in red lipstick. "And I have discovered a way in other than the tour, but it is a bit… tricky. Not for the faint of heart."

"What does that mean?" Reece's eyes remained on her.

"You will need certain items of clothing. And headlamps. Some areas are a tight squeeze." Her gaze moved to Todd. "Still up for it, Mr. Lassiter?"

"Absolutely." Although underneath his façade he wasn't so sure. What did she mean by 'a tight squeeze'?

"I'm coming too," Charlotte said.

Reece crossed the room to her. "I'd prefer it if you didn't. It's dangerous and, as I've said more than once, Dracula could still be connected to you, which would give him the advantage and time to plan some kind of escape … or retaliation."

Charlotte felt tears sting the backs of her eyes but she wouldn't allow herself to show emotion. Not now. She had to prove herself. "I want to help you."

"I know you do. And you can by doing what I ask."

She let out a frustrated huff. "But…"

"Please, Charlotte, just do as I ask. It'll be safer for everyone, including you."

"So when do you want to go?" Todd asked.

"The sooner the better," Reece told him. He turned to Eva. "When can you get your people there?"

"I call, they come." She shrugged.

"Ok. Tomorrow night. We'll need to gear up first. Get the clothing and headlamps. What time does the last tour go in?"

"Seven thirty and it lasts for forty five minutes."

"So, after nine?" Reece's gaze ran around the others in the room and then moved to Charlotte. He knew she wanted to redeem herself, but now wasn't the time. She could be the one component that could get them all killed and he wasn't about to take the risk.

CR

The circular white glow of the headlamps only stretched so far in the pitch black, claustrophobic tunnel. As they trudged the damp, muddy floor a squirming feeling of apprehension curled through Reece's gut, the walls pressing in on him and the others as they continued to move deeper underground highlighted the feeling of foreboding. The vampires Eva had asked to help were already in place. It was just a matter of them getting to the location, without Dracula realizing something was amiss, and finishing him before he could kill Sarah and vanish for good.

Once they were close, they turned off their headlamps and followed Eva blindly through the gloom, careful not to make any sounds that would echo along the narrow passageway.

A shrill scream shattered the dense silence, traveling along the walls like an evacuation siren warning them to get out. Everyone stopped. "What was that?" Todd whispered.

"I hope it wasn't Sarah," Reece said.

"Take each other's hand," Eva told them. "Reece, you take mine and no one let go." She whipped through the tunnel to Dracula's hiding place. Where was her team? She peered around the corner of the column into the dark cavern, her eyes widening. "Oh, no!"

The PI flicked on his headlamp and stepped around her, his shocked gaze meeting the horror within. Sarah's body sat slouched to the side, her head lying on the floor beside her chair. The five vampires Eva had asked to assist them were piles of smoldering ash, and Charlotte... what was she doing here? Charlotte stood in the middle of the floor with a wooden stake in her hand smiling. Had she killed Sarah too?

Reece gasped, his heart racing, his breathing ragged as he sprang up in bed. What the hell had he just dreamed? Did it mean he was right about Vlad's connection to Charlotte?

CHAPTER THIRTY ONE

A knock on the door of his room startled Reece. He frowned at the emergency evacuation poster on the back before walking over to open it. He hoped it wasn't Charlotte. He didn't want to get into a heated discussion about his reasons for not wanting her to come along on their mission to kill Dracula. How many times could he explain it to her before she understood? He swung the door back. "What are you doing here? I told you I'd let you know when there were any new developments." He turned and crossed the room to finish dressing, leaving the door open. The sun hadn't come up yet, but after the dream he'd had he couldn't get back to sleep.

"Reece, it's me."

The PI swung around, his heart hammering in his chest. Was it him? "Andre?"

An uncertain smile crossed his friend's handsome face. "Yes."

Something warned Reece to be careful. Jacques had masqueraded as Andre before. "How do I know it's really you?"

"Jacques had the ritual performed to bring me back."

"That doesn't answer the question, does it?" He wanted to believe it was his friend but he wasn't sure he could trust his own gut. "Tell me something your brother couldn't know. Something you told me that no one else knows about."

"When Jacques killed our family I had to go to the crypt and decapitate my parents and little sister. I was sick at the time. The change was beginning, but I had no choice. My brother couldn't know that, but I told you about it at Adrian's when you first discovered what I am."

Reece ran his questioning gaze over the vampire at the door then rushed over and wrapped his arms around him. "It's good to have you back, buddy. I missed you... so much."

Andre eased out of his friend's embrace. "You may not think so after I tell you what he's done."

„ₒₓ

Lozano sat on the sofa of Andre and Reece's apartment feeling useless. He'd come to Los Angeles to help the PI out and now he was twiddling his thumbs waiting for any news on the Dracula situation overseas. He wanted to do something constructive for their cause. But what? His cell phone vibrated on the coffee table in front of him and he snatched it up, not recognizing the number on the screen. "Hello?"

"Hey, it's me," Ed Borenko said. "Wanna get some dinner? I'm feeling itchy. I feel like I should be doin' something."

"Yeah, me too. Sure. Where do you want to meet?" The sheriff breathed a relieved sigh. At least it would kill some time and he'd be with someone else who knew what was going on so they could talk about it.

"Why don't I swing by and pick you up? Then we can decide."

"Sounds good."

"Ok. I'll see you in about twenty minutes." Ed rang off.

While he waited, Lozano thought he'd give Reece a call. It had been a while since they'd heard anything on this side of the world and he was worried. The phone went to voicemail. He hung up. *What's going on over there?* The sheriff wandered down the hallway to the back bedroom to change before going down to the sidewalk to wait for the Lieutenant.

ₓ

When Ed pulled his sedan into the curb Lozano climbed in. "How's it going?"

"Yeah, can't complain. What about you?"

"I'm like you, itchy. I came here to help and I'm sitting around waiting for news."

Ed sighed. "I know what you mean. I wish I could've gone with them, too. But duty calls." He gave the sheriff a crooked grin.

"I've been trying Reece's cell but there's no answer. I hope they're all ok. Even if they're not there's nothing we can do about it from here."

"Are you thinking about going over?"

Lozano let out a long sigh. "I wish I could but I can't take any extra leave."

"So, then, we wait until he calls. Nothin' else we can do."

"But it sucks, doesn't it?" Lozano clipped in his seat belt.

"Sure does." Ed pulled out into the traffic and headed for a café he knew served a mean steak with all the trimmings – mashed potato, fries and vegetables. A hearty meal.

As they traveled along Sunset Boulevard, Lozano's phone buzzed. He tugged it from the pocket of his jacket. "Reece," he told Ed, pressing his cell to his ear. "Hey, how's it going over there?"

"Yeah. Good. We've got a lead on Dracula's whereabouts and we're organizing an assault. Sorry I haven't got back to you. It's been crazy here."

"Understandable. How is everyone?"

Reece didn't want to tell him about Sarah's abduction. He didn't want Lozano to mention it to Ed and have him worry. He also didn't want them to know about Andre's arrival until he could figure out what he was going to do with the information his friend had imparted on him. "All good. What about there?"

"Ed and I are just on our way to get some dinner. Is Sarah around? Maybe she could say hi."

"Uh, not at the moment, no. Everyone's still asleep. It's only 4 AM here."

"Oh, ok. So when are you planning to attack Dracula?"

"Tonight. He's laying low in the Paris catacombs. Not the most ideal place for an assault but nothing we can do about it."

"That's underground, right?"

"Yes, it is."

"Be careful down there. Is there anyone you can let know where you're going? In case you need help."

"No. Where we're going is illegal. It's in the restricted areas beneath the city."

"Just be safe."

"We'll do our best. Eva's organized some vampire backup so at least we won't be outnumbered."

"You trust her?"

"I wish I could say yes but I can't. I'm keeping my eye on her."

"Then be extra careful."

"Definitely. Have you found anything that could be useful in defeating Dracula?"

"Not yet, but I'll keep looking."

"Thanks. There has to be something that will kill him. Hey, I've got to go."

"Keep us up-to-date, ok? Even if it's only a quick text."

"Will do." He rang off.

Lozano's gaze moved to Ed. "Something's not right over there. I could hear it in what Reece wasn't telling me."

Ed frowned into the sheriff's eyes. "Like what?"

He shrugged. "I don't know. But there was something in his voice."

"So what's happening over there?"

"Oh, yeah. Dracula's hiding in the catacombs and their planning an assault tonight their time, which is tomorrow here, I guess."

"Sounds dangerous, especially being underground with that monster."

"Yeah, it does."

Ed pulled the sedan into a side street off Sunset Boulevard and parked. He and Lozano sat for a moment before getting out of the car and wandering back to the main road. The Saddle Ranch Chop House was a great place to grab a meal and Ed was hungry. He and the sheriff headed along the sidewalk and entered the barn-like building, the inside resembling an old time saloon. It even had a bucking bull ride in a round wooden pen just inside the door. The pair found a table by a multi-paned window looking out onto the strip and sat down to peruse the menu.

"What do ya feel like?" Ed asked, raising his eyes from the appetizing list in front of him.

"It all sounds so good. I don't know what to try. What do you suggest?"

"The prime rib. It'll hit the spot."

"Ok. Will do." Lozano gazed around the restaurant. It had a certain seedy western feel to it but he liked it. Reminded him of places back in Vegas.

Over dinner, Ed and Lozano discussed their concerns about what was going on in Europe. The two men felt as though they weren't contributing to the mission and it didn't sit well with either of them.

Ed took a swig of beer. "You know, I've been thinking about quitting the force and working with Reece full time. The trouble is he can't afford to pay me. I'd do pro bono but I need to eat, too, ya know?"

"How long before you retire?" Lozano licked the BBQ sauce from his fingers before wiping them on a napkin.

"Couple of years. Why?"

"Couldn't you apply for early retirement? Seeing as it's a short amount of time?"

"What are you sayin'?" Ed frowned at him.

"Well, you'd get a pension out of it. So you'd have money to eat." He chuckled. "Maybe you could look into it."

"Yeah, maybe I will."

"After everything I've learned, I've been thinking about quitting too."

"Yeah?"

Lozano nodded. "I can understand why Reece did it. Once you know what's out there how can you continue to do a job that restricts you from getting rid of the creatures lurking in the shadows picking us off one at a time? You can't, and I don't want to."

"Can you afford it?" Ed plucked a fry off his plate and bit it in half.

"Yeah, I think I can. I've squirreling away as much as I can for years so I'd be ok."

"So you'd want to come here and work with us?"

"Maybe. Or I could start my own PI business in Vegas."

"Sounds like you've been giving it a lot of thought."

"I have. I can't sit back and do nothing now that I know." His gaze met Ed's. "Can you?"

"You're damn right. I'm going to talk to my superior first thing tomorrow and see what I can find out."

"When I get back home that's exactly what I'm doing."

"What do we do in the meantime?"

"I need to find some way to eliminate Dracula. I've gone over what we have but nothing stands out so far."

"He's been around a long time. Maybe there isn't a way."

"He has to be vulnerable to something. We just need to find out what that is."

※

"There's something else you should know." Andre crossed the room and pulled the curtains closed.

"What is it?" Reece gave him a curious frown.

"I'm no longer a daywalker."

"What about your serum?"

"I don't have it."

"I do, but it's back in LA." Reece gave a heavy sigh. "Ok. Well it's lucky that we're going in at night then, isn't it?"

Andre's eyes widened. "You're trusting me to help you after what I told you Jacques did to me?"

"Yeah, I am."

"What if I turn into just as bigger monster as Dracula while we're down there? What if this is my brother's way of getting rid of you?"

"Like I said, I know you, Andre, and I know you wouldn't do anything to hurt me."

"You can't be sure of that anymore."

"I am sure of it." He hoped his loyalty to his best friend wasn't misguided. He also hoped that what Jacques had done was reversible.

Andre shook his head. Reece was acting like a fool. If he didn't trust himself why should his friend?

A knock echoed into the room and Reece walked over to open it.

Todd Lassiter stood in the doorway. "What's he doing here?" He pointed at Andre believing he was Jacques.

"Come in." Reece closed the door and moved back to his friend. "This is Andre, Todd. Jacques had the ritual performed while we've been gone, another breach of trust." He eyed Andre sideways.

"Wow! So he was telling the truth." Todd crossed the room and ran his gaze over the vampire standing in front of him.

"Yeah, he was." Reece sat on the end of the bed and pulled on his boots. "We need to have breakfast and then go and buy the gear we need for tonight." His eyes rested on his friend again. "Andre can't come with us."

"Why not?" Todd frowned into Andre's eyes. There was something about him that seemed off to him. Was he a liability to their mission?

"Andre used to take a serum so he could appear... human... be in the daylight. Unfortunately, he doesn't have it right now so..."

"Well I guess it's lucky we're going into the tunnels at night then, huh?"

Andre wondered if all cops thought alike. He could tell Todd was or had been in law enforcement. It wasn't difficult. They all had similar mannerisms.

"Sorry. I should've introduced you. Todd Lassiter, ex LA detective." He motioned to his friend. "Andre Delacroix, my best friend... and vampire."

"You weren't kidding when you said they were identical twins."

"I never kid about anything."

"Guess not. I'll go wake up Charlotte." Todd turned and headed for the door.

"We'll meet in the restaurant downstairs in, say, twenty minutes?"

"Sure. See you there." When he opened the door Nathaniel was outside in the hallway. "See you downstairs for breakfast." He stepped around the huge vampire.

"I do not eat breakfast."

Todd continued down the hall.

Nathaniel turned his gaze to Andre. "I thought I sensed your presence."

"Hello, Nathaniel."

The vampire stepped inside and closed the door. "I also sense Jacques. You have his corrupted blood running through your veins."

"Unfortunately, yes, but there's nothing I can do about that." Andre folded his arms and stretched his spine against the scrutinizing stare.

"Let us hope it does not create problems."

"What do you mean?" Reece stepped up to him, hands on hips.

"Andre does not trust himself. He is concerned that he may jeopardize the people he cares about."

Reece glanced over his shoulder at his friend. "Is that true?"

"I already told you that you can't trust me. Why won't you believe that?"

"Because I've known you for a long time and I know the kind of person you are on the inside. You'll do everything you can to resist whatever it is Jacques has done to you."

"It may not be enough." Having been with Jacques for hundreds of years, Nathaniel knew what his ex-master was capable of and wondered what he had planned for them all.

CHAPTER THIRTY TWO

Eva had managed to get her hands on a tool to open the manhole they were about to descend into the bowels of Paris through. They had to be quick as the illegal entry was situated on the corner of the busy intersection and they were in plain sight. Reece and Todd stood in front of the opening to block the view of drivers passing in their cars and were the last to drop into the pitch black circle. The small metal rungs of the extensive ladder that disappeared into the deep, dark hole were precarious at best and Reece slipped a couple of times, almost falling on top of Todd and Andre as they made their way down the cylindrical, Alice in Wonderland rabbit hole.

After trudging the damp, eerie depths, they came to a metal staved gate standing open to welcome intruders into the off limits sections of the underworld city of the dead. The PI surveyed their immediate surroundings – the medieval, numerical carvings on the wall left by limestone miners hundreds of years ago and the graffiti tags by cataphyles more recently were ominous and Reece felt his gut twist into a tight tangle of nerves. *What if it all goes horribly wrong down here?* Despite his belief that Andre would stand with them against Dracula, he still couldn't get it out of his head that Jacques' blood ran through his friend's veins, which could potentially put them all in danger.

Eva led the group further into the tunnels, traveling quickly along the narrow, sandy passage that looked like it could lead into an ancient Egyptian burial tomb, the tension in the dense atmosphere around them palpable. Everyone was anxious, including Nathaniel. What would be waiting for them when they reached the chamber Dracula had Sarah hidden away in? The group continued onward through the gloom, some tunnels were marked with street signs such as Rue Nationale, indicating the roads above, but for the most part it was a dark, never-ending maze that anyone could get lost in and never be seen again.

They came upon a passageway piled with skulls and bones that almost reached the ceiling, whatever lay beyond was unknown to anyone. Eva stopped short and Andre came to an abrupt halt behind her, Nathaniel, Todd and Reece pulling up sharp so as not to run into him. "What's wrong?" Reece asked.

This is as far as Nathaniel can go I am afraid. She shone her flashlight at the narrow square window no bigger than a pet door cut into the limestone. "I think we'll all have some difficulty getting through there, don't you?"

Reece squeezed past the others. "Then why did you bring us this way?"

Eva's narrowed dark stare met his. "I was unaware of this. It did not show up on the map."

"Let me take a look." Nathaniel pressed his back against the jagged stone wall and eased his bulky frame past Todd and Andre in the claustrophobic space. His eyes roamed the sandy yellow wall from floor to ceiling then he thrust out his large fist and punched a bigger hole in the limestone. "Now I will be able to get through."

"Let's keep moving," Reece said, slithering through the gap on his belly. Once on the other side, his nightmare the previous evening tore through his brain like a speeding locomotive and his body gave an involuntary shudder. He glanced around himself in the dark. Was his dream some kind of premonition? His heart rate ticked up a couple of notches at the thought.

When everyone was through, Eva roamed the flashlight around their faces. "You need to be as quiet as you can from now on. Sounds echo down here and we want to take Dracula by surprise, not have him waiting for us." The four men nodded. "Good. Let us press on."

೮ာၥ

Charlotte paced her hotel room, her breathing shallow, her heart racing. She wanted to be there with Reece in those tunnels, wanted to stand by his side and offer her support but he had denied her that. A tear slipped down her right cheek and she swiped it away, frustration mounting inside her. A knock on the door startled her and she swung around, her eyes moving to the safety lock. It was in place. She let out a relieved sigh, crossed the room to check the peep hole, and frowned when no one was standing on the other side. Something slithered in her solar plexus and she stepped away from the door. "Who is it?"

No answer.

Charlotte eased herself across the room to her purse sitting on the dresser and squeezed her pistol out of it, checking the clip and aiming. "I said who is it?"

"Hotel management, Miss Delaney, I need to speak with you," the male voice replied.

"What about?" She moved silently back to the door and peered through the tiny circle of glass. "Stand in front of the door so I can see you."

"Very well."

Before she could react, the door burst open knocking Charlotte to the floor and the gun from her hand which skittered across the carpet out of her reach. Two men dressed in black combat gear, their faces hidden behind ski masks, charged into the room.

She opened her mouth to scream but was silenced by a large, gloved hand pressing against her lips.

ಸಂ

A faint yellow glow danced across the yellow limestone wall opposite the opening to the chamber and as the group reached it, Eva motioned for everyone to stop. Something was wrong. She couldn't sense Dracula's presence nor could she sense anyone else. She turned to look at Reece. "He's not here."

Reece's severe stare met hers. "What?!"

"It appears no one is."

The vampires Eva had asked to help emerged from the shadows, their leader stepping up to her. "When we arrived he was already gone."

Reece let out a frustrated huff, pushed past Eva, and stalked into the cavernous space. Sarah was hunched over tied to the chair, her face swollen and bloody. He rushed over, knelt in front of her and felt her throat for a pulse. "No. No, no, no! This can't be happening." His strained voice echoed around the chamber.

The others stood just inside the graffitied opening.

"So the monster got away. Again." Todd's disbelieving eyes roamed the shadows. "What do we do now?"

Reece stood up and turned his frowning gaze on him. "Right now I've got other things to worry about. Sarah's dead. How do I explain that to Ed?"

"You won't have to."

The PI swung around. "But…"

Sarah's face was already healing and her swollen left eye receding back into its socket. "Remember what happened at the night club and what I told you?"

Reece flipped through the archives in his head. The attack by MacKinnon. Sarah had died at the hands of a hybrid vampire but came back to life hours later and frightened the hell out of everyone. He nodded.

Nathaniel crossed the rubbish strewn, sandy floor, ripped the ropes from around Sarah's body, and helped her to her feet.

"Thank you, Nathaniel," she said, giving him a brief smile.

"I am glad you are all right." He went back to stand with Andre, Todd, and Eva.

"Ok, would someone like to fill me in on how this is possible?" Todd asked.

"It's a long story. One we don't have time for right now," Reece told him. "The short version is Sarah has vampire blood running through her veins and it keeps her alive even if she dies."

"I knew about the blood but how can it bring her back from death?"

"I don't have the answer." Sarah crossed the cavern to him. "But I'm grateful it has. I've been chasing Dracula for most of my life and now he's slipped through my fingers once again."

"I don't understand." Todd frowned into her eyes.

"As Reece said, it's too long a story to tell right now."

"So what now?" Andre asked.

"He's heading back to Romania. He has a fortress there and he thinks he'll be safe." Sarah stepped up beside Reece.

"How do you know that?" He gave her a curious stare.

"Because he thought I was dead." She smiled.

CHAPTER THIRTY THREE

"Have you seen Charlotte?" Todd asked as he rushed into Reece's hotel room, leaving the door open. "She's not in her room and she isn't downstairs either."

"No, I haven't." Reece frowned at Todd and stood with hands on hips. "Have you tried her cell?"

"What do you think? Of course I have and it's ringing inside her room. Do you know anyone who leaves their phone behind when they go out?"

Something unsettling slithered in the pit of Reece's gut. "Did anything look out of place to you?"

"Not that I noticed. Why, what are you thinking?" His heart rate ticked up a notch.

"I'm not sure. Let's go take a look."

The pair hurried down the hallway to Charlotte's room.

"Here. Look at this." Reece pointed to the rift in the wooden doorjamb and turned to look at Todd. "The lock has been forced. If you weren't looking for it you wouldn't be aware of it."

"You're right, I didn't see that." He sighed. "As a cop I should have."

"You didn't see it because you weren't expecting her not to be here."

A worried expression crossed the ex-detective's face. "Do you think Dracula…?"

"Yeah, I do. And that means he's taken her with him."

"Hell, Reece, what are we going to do?"

Andre came along the hallway. "What's going on?"

Reece's concerned frown met his friend's inquisitive stare. "It looks like Dracula's taken Charlotte *again*."

"What?!" Andre pushed open the unlocked door and the three rushed inside.

Reece crossed the room and picked up Charlotte's pistol off the floor. "She must have tried to defend herself." He checked the clip. "But she didn't get a shot off." He set the weapon on the dresser beside her purse and picked up her phone. "She didn't get a call, either."

"We're going after them, right?" Todd crossed the room and gazed out of the window, praying she was all right. The inky night seemed ominous now that Charlotte was missing.

"If I had the resources I would fly out tonight, but I don't," Reece told him.

Todd spun around. "We have to do something. He'll kill her if we don't. Or worse, turn her into a... a bloodsucking monster." His eyes moved to Andre. "Sorry."

"It's ok. I wouldn't wish immortality on anyone." He walked over to his friend. "I'll talk to Jacques."

"No!" Reece was adamant.

"Yes." Todd crossed the room to the pair. "We have to go after him, rescue Charlotte, and finish what we came here to do."

Reece let out a heavy sigh. "I'm already indebted to Jacques..."

"I don't care." Todd's face flushed with anguish and anger. "We're obligated to help her. She's a part of this team."

"There's no question about that but there has to be another way. I don't want to owe anything more to Jacques."

"What other way?" Todd folded his arms. "You said yourself you don't have the resources so how are we going to get there?"

Reece ran the idea around his brain. He didn't like it but Todd was right. His gaze moved from the ex-detective to his friend. "Ok. Ask him." He knew he had no other option, but at what cost?

࿇

Bucharest was one hour ahead of Paris. It was already 10.30 AM and it would take over two hours to get there by plane. The airport was chaotic as travelers hurried through the massive structure making their way to board their flights. Eva had given Andre a Lapis Lazuli ring like the one she had given Nathaniel so he was able to go with them to Romania to battle Dracula, and save Charlotte before something happened to her that couldn't be undone. Eva had said she would meet them at the Europa Royale Bucharest Hotel once they arrived. Reece had no idea how she was making her way there, but seeing as she was a vampire, after all, she would probably fly, literally. He chuckled inwardly at the thought. Why did she feel it necessary to go ahead of them? What devious plan had she set in motion that he didn't know about? And would it put their lives in jeopardy? He had learned not to trust anyone... except for the people closest to him.

The boarding call echoed through the passenger lounge, and Reece and the others made their way over to join the queue. He'd thought about asking Sarah to stay behind after the ordeal she had been through, but knew it was out of the question as it was her fight more than theirs because the monster had killed her family all those years ago. He knew Sarah was a tough cookie, but what would it take for her to break?

Charlotte prodded the back of his mind and he hoped she was all right. Her abduction had brought his feelings for her flooding back and he knew they had to repair the estrangement between them and move forward with their life together. If anything happened to her he would never be able to forgive himself for not doing it sooner. He *was* still in love with her, and her being taken again forced him to admit it to himself. Something he hadn't wanted to do for many reasons, the most important – keeping his head in this dangerous game.

$$\mathcal{SOCR}$$

The prestige limousine drove up the steep drive to the elaborate, peaked castle entrance and stopped at the stone steps. One arched wooden door swung back and a manservant, dressed in a dark blue suit, descended the stairs with an open, oversized black umbrella and waited for the front passenger door to open. Vlad was covered from head to foot, including leather gloves, but a bright shaft of sunlight still managed to make contact with the diaphanous skin on his wrist and singe the flesh as he stepped under the canopy of dark material, the smell like that of seared steak. He tugged at the sleeve cuff of his long jacket to cover the burn. "Bring her inside and lock her in one of the bedrooms on the mezzanine floor," he ordered, his eyes moving to the back passenger door. "And make sure there is no way for her to escape."

His manservant bowed his head and said, "As you wish, Master." Handing the umbrella to Vlad, he stepped from under its shade and proceeded to open the left hand rear door of the vehicle.

Charlotte squinted as the glare poured into the heavily tinted limousine. She was bound and gagged. How could she be in this position again? She wished she'd taken Reece's advice and gone to see Tommy instead of traveling to Paris. She knew Reece would come for her. Her heart crashed against her ribs as an arm stretched across the backseat and gripped her with forceful fingers. "Get out of the car, madam." The Romanian accent of the manservant was thick and reminded her of Bela Lugosi's portrayal of Dracula.

Once inside, the man led her up to a room close to the main staircase. "I am sure you will be comfortable in here." He tugged the tape from across her mouth, the sting of adhesive biting her skin and ripping out fine hairs, then cut the thick, white plastic tie binding her arms behind her back with a sharp, red-handled pocket knife. "Do not try anything," he warned as he turned on his heel and stepped into the shadowed hallway.

Charlotte heard the lock snap into place and knew she was trapped.

CHAPTER THIRTY FOUR

The group checked into the Europa Royale Bucharest Hotel and Reece asked at the reception desk which room Eva Van Helsing was staying in. To his surprise, she wasn't registered at the hotel. Where was she? Reece didn't like having her running around the countryside without knowing what she had planned. To his mind, she was an obstruction rather than an advantage because he had no idea what she was up to and he didn't like it.

Everyone's rooms were on the same floor so they picked up their bags and headed to the elevator. "Let's freshen up and meet in the café for some coffee and a brief on what to do next," Reece said as he stepped into the lift and pressed the button.

Half an hour later, the group was at a table sipping coffee and discussing their plans. Without Eva they were flying blind because she was the only one with the information they needed to locate Dracula's hiding place. Tourists were under the impression that Bran Castle was the home of the monster they had come to free the world from, but that was a misrepresentation. The castle of Vlad Tepes, known as Poenari Citadel, was a crumbling ruin set high on a hill in Arefu, Argeş County, but was not the place he would be right now. It was a popular tourist attraction boasting a climb of 1,480 concrete stairs to get to what remained.

"So, here you are," a female voice echoed along the quiet restaurant. Eva sauntered up to their table, pulled out a chair and perched her leather-clad frame on the seat.

"Where have you been? And where are you staying?" Reece's severe stare met hers.

"I have friends here so I am visiting them."

"Do you know where," Reece lowered his voice, "Dracula is?" His eyes roamed the other handful of patrons scattered around the café.

"Yes, as a matter of fact, I do."

Reece's right eyebrow arched. "Well?"

"I will impart that information when we are ready to leave."

Reece slid back his chair, stood up, and pressed his hands to his hips. He was angry. "Why don't you stop playing these ridiculous games and help us?"

Eva's red glossed lips spread into a smirk. "Because I enjoy my diversions." She stood up so that she was on the same level as the PI. "Besides, what other fun am I having?"

"This is not a game," Sarah told her. "We need to find where Dracula has taken Charlotte and finish him once and for all."

Eva frowned at the priest. "And we will."

"*Where* is he?" Reece's voice was tight. He was tired of her manipulation and wanted answers.

"The journey will take about two hours. He resides in an old monastery in the mountains. It is a fortress and we will need a specific plan of attack if we intend to get in and out alive. He is not alone there."

Reece's gaze moved around the faces at the tables then back to Eva. "Then sit down and tell us everything you know."

"I have to be somewhere but we will discuss it later when I return." Eva turned to walk away but Reece grabbed her arm. She gave him a death stare.

"Where are you going now?"

"There are people who can assist us. I need to talk to them."

"What people?"

"You mean other vampires?" Todd asked.

Eva's severe gaze moved to him. "They are the only kind who can offer what we need. Do you think there is anyone here who will assist us?"

A squirming feeling in the pit of Todd's gut made him feel nauseous. Was she setting them up? He didn't trust her and knew Reece shouldn't either. "You're keeping your cards close to your chest, Miss Van Helsing, and I, for one, don't feel comfortable with it."

"I am here offering my help and this is what you think?" She tugged out of Reece's grasp, giving him a disgruntled stare, and marched out of the restaurant.

Reece looked at Todd. "That went well."

"I'm sorry, but I don't trust her."

The PI frowned. "And you think I do?" He folded his arms. "We need her skills and knowledge to get the job done. That's the *only* reason I'm keeping her around. Remember that saying: keep your enemies closer?"

"She has not given you cause to doubt her." Nathaniel spoke up. "She does not have to be here."

"There's something she's not telling us. I feel it in my gut, Nathaniel. She's definitely up to something."

"What makes you think she would sabotage our mission?"

Reece let out a sigh. "I don't know. Something doesn't feel right about her. I think she's hiding the real reason she's here."

"Van Helsing blood runs through her veins, she is a hunter of vampires. That is what she does. I do not sense anything dishonest about her intentions."

"Let's hope you're right about that." Reece took his seat. "I guess we wait until she returns." He picked up the cup in front of him and sipped his coffee.

"So what do we do in the meantime?" Andre asked, leaning against the back of his chair and folding his arms.

Reece's eyes moved to his friend. "We wait. What else can we do? We don't know where Dracula is, nor the layout of his castle, so there isn't much point in trying to work on a plan of attack without that information, is there?"

"I beg to differ," Sarah said, "I think we should be working on some way of finding out where he is. If we wait for Eva we may never know."

Reece's right eyebrow arched. "And who do you think we should ask? The locals?"

She shrugged. "Why not? There are a lot of superstitious older folk still living here with knowledge about Vlad. I know because I've spoken to some of them before and I think they might be able to help us. If we sit here we're wasting valuable time we don't have."

The PI let out a heavy sigh and kept his serious gaze on her, wondering if she was right. "Ok. Where do you think we should start?"

"The older parts of Bucharest first then out into the country." Sarah stood up. "Coming?" She glanced at the others around the table with a questioning stare.

Todd stood up. "I'm in. I don't think we should wait around for Eva Van Helsing to show up. We need to find Charlotte before something happens to her."

Reece looked at his friend. "Andre?"

"If we wait it could be too late." He stood up.

"Nathaniel?"

"If that is what you wish to do I will accompany you." He had reservations about rejecting Eva's offer to help because he knew what she could do when she felt betrayed. She was not one to be crossed.

Ⅎ)Ⅎ

Vlad pushed the large, rusted key into the lock, turned it and swung the door open, his eyes roaming the high ceilinged, spacious bedroom and spotting the woman standing by the window. He stepped into the room and with a wave of his hand the door banged closed behind him, startling Charlotte. Her thoughts somewhere else, she gasped and spun around, pressing her small frame against the cold brick wall beside the window.

"Why have you brought me here?" Her words were breathy, shallow, nervous. She took another tentative step backwards, the heavy maroon drapes brushing against the side of her trembling body.

The vampire moved to the foot of the four post bed and stopped. "You belong to me, Charlotte. You have my blood running through your veins. You are mine to do with as I please."

"No! I am not yours." She felt a rush of adrenalin surge through her even though she was afraid of him. "I would rather die than belong to you."

A smile of satisfaction spread across his ruggedly handsome face. "Ah, but that is where you are wrong, my dear. I could turn you at any moment by snapping your neck and then what would your boyfriend do? And what about your son?"

Tears welled in Charlotte's eyes and one slipped down her right cheek. "Why are you doing this?"

His left eyebrow arched. "Why?" He took another step toward her. "Because I have intentions for you all. None of you will pursue me once I have implemented my plan."

"What plan?" Charlotte continued to edge away from the monster and was pressed into the corner now.

"You will find out soon enough." Vlad turned on his heel and crossed the room. "They have come for you just as I suspected they would." The door opened with a motion of his hand and he was gone, the snap of the lock echoing around the room.

Charlotte remained where she stood, her heart beating way too fast. She inhaled a deep breath through her nostrils, filling her lungs to capacity, and blew it out in a long, slow whoosh. Her body trembled so hard her teeth chattered. She wrapped her arms around herself and tears slipped down her cheeks. Reece was in Romania looking for her. But they were all in grave danger.

CHAPTER THIRTY FIVE

Sheriff Lozano leaned back in Reece's office chair, his phone pressed to his ear, as he listened to what the PI had to say. The group had traveled to Romania on the hunt for Dracula and Charlotte's whereabouts. They were in dangerous territory. Lozano was worried. Reece asked if he'd discovered anything new that they could use to eliminate the vampire of all vampires.

"So far I've found nothing," Lozano replied, "except that from what I've read it seems he had some kind of enchantment placed on him that prevents him from dying. That's how he's managed to escape death for so long. But I do have a suggestion of my own."

"What's that?" Reece asked, leaning against the side of their rental car waiting for Sarah to get back from speaking to some of the locals. She knew the language. He was impressed but not surprised. She had, after all, traveled around Europe in search of Dracula for quite some time.

Although Nathaniel, Andre and Todd were meant to accompany them, Reece had decided they should prepare for the road trip to wherever it was they would be traveling. It was easier for Sarah to communicate with the people who had the information they needed and he was sure they would recognize Nathaniel for what he was and not want to talk.

"Why not just cut off his head and burn the remains? I'm sure he's not going to come back from that." Lozano offered.

"You think it's that simple?"

"It could be. I mean, let's face it, he was human once and if you cut off our heads we die."

"I'll keep that in mind when I'm face to face with him. Burning his body may not give us the permanent outcome we expect. Remember both Jacques and Andre have risen from the ashes just like the mythological Phoenix."

"Hey, it was just a thought." Lozano could hear the skepticism in Reece's voice.

"I appreciate what you're doing, Sheriff. Keep up the good work. I'm sure you'll come across something."

It was obvious to Lozano that his suggestion wouldn't be a consideration. "Thanks. Yeah, I will. If I find anything more useful I'll text you."

"Great." Reece's gaze moved to the street. Sarah was on her way back. "I've got to go. Talk later."

"Reece."

"Yeah?"

"Be careful."

"Always." He rang off and pushed his cell phone into the back pocket of his jeans. As Sarah got closer he said, "Get any answers?"

"Yes, as a matter of fact. There's a monastery about fifty miles out of town. It's not a tourist attraction and some of the locals believe it's where Vlad hides out when he's in Romania. It's built like a fortress with watchtowers set in strategic places around the twenty foot, fortified wall so it's not going to be easy to get into."

"Why would a monastery need that kind of protection?" Reece frowned and folded his arms.

"I don't know. Perhaps it was a place of refuge back in the day. It's believed to be a few hundred years old."

"We'll round up the others and head out there." He moved away from the car.

Sarah grabbed his arm. "Reece."

"What?" His question was tighter than he'd intended. "Sorry. What is it?"

"The small village that sits in the valley below the monastery is believed to be under Vlad's influence. Which means…"

"We have to find a way in without being spotted." Reece opened the car door for her.

Sarah gave him a curious frown and climbed into the passenger seat. He never opened doors for her before. "That's going to be difficult considering we have no idea what the layout of the land is like."

"Yeah, I know." He moved around the hood of the car and climbed in beside her. "We need to do some research, find a map online and study the area before we even consider making any kind of attempt to enter the monastery." He wasn't about to lose anyone else that he cared about. That was a given. He started the engine and pulled away from the curb.

ℰᴑᏫ

Back at the hotel, Reece called everyone into his room to discuss their next move. They would need abseiling equipment for the monastery wall. The clothing they wore in the catacombs was perfect for climbing into the grounds and would offer obscurity in the dark as the sleeved tops, canvas cargo pants, and beanies were charcoal gray. Todd had suggested night vision goggles. They'd be shadows in the night and hopefully fly under Dracula's radar until they located Charlotte and instigated their attack.

"Before we get started, has anyone seen Eva?"

A unanimous 'no' drifted around the room.

Reece stood with hands on hips and gave a heavy sigh. He wondered what she was up to. "Ok." Why was he so concerned about what she might be doing? Because he had everyone's lives in his hands and he couldn't afford to make any more mistakes.

"While you were gone I found a map of the monastery and the land surrounding it at the local library," Todd said, unrolling the paper in his hand across the round table that had been placed in the center of the room. "It's rough terrain but there is a narrow road leading up to it. The only problem is it runs through the village."

Everyone moved to the table to study the landscape.

"That means we're going to have to hide our car off road and do the climb on foot," Reece told them.

"Not necessarily," Nathaniel said. "I can fly each of you one at a time up to the plateau. We will be less obvious that way."

"I don't know about that." The color in Todd's face drained slightly.

"Afraid of heights, Mr. Lassiter?" Nathaniel gave the man a curious, arched eyebrow stare.

"Not heights, no, but what if you dropped one of us?"

"I can assure you that will not happen."

"I think I'd prefer to take my chances doing the climb."

"We don't have the time, Todd." Reece came around the table to him. "The quicker we can get up there the better our chances of getting into the compound undetected. If we're seen by anyone Dracula will know before we make it up the wall."

"I could run him up the hill," Andre offered. His immortal speed was faster than a car.

"What? You mean piggy back me?" Todd shook his head. "No way."

"Then what do you suggest?" Reece was annoyed at the ex-detective's negative attitude to their situation.

Todd shrugged. "Like I said, I can do the climb."

"We'd be in and out before you reached the plateau. That's not going to work."

Todd's eyes roamed the faces in the room and he raised defensive hands and sighed. "Ok. I'll go with Nathaniel."

"Thank you." Reece returned to his position on the other side of the table. "Can we get on with this now?"

"Sure." Todd folded his arms and gave the PI a sour stare.

"Ok. Andre, did you find out how many live in the village?"

"Yes. There's a hundred or so people."

"Good. At least we know how many we're dealing with, just in case."

"They will not see us if we ascend from the other side of the hill," Nathaniel offered.

"Agreed. The only thing we're unsure of at this point is how many guards he has up there. He wouldn't leave himself unprotected."

At that moment, the door burst open and Eva strutted into the room. "Of course he has guards with powerful weapons. What would you expect?"

Reece swung around. "Where have you been?"

"I've been arranging some help."

The PI's gaze moved to the open doorway. "Where are they?"

"They are on standby awaiting my call."

"How many?"

"Six. And they can fly so it will be easy for us to get to the monastery from the air. When are you planning to go?"

"Once we have a solid plan we'll head out." Reece still wasn't sure he could trust her but right now they needed all the help they could get.

"Very well. Text me when you require my assistance and we will meet you on the far side of the hill." Eva turned around and strutted toward the door, Reece's eyes following her red, leather-clad ass as she disappeared down the hallway.

"Man, she's a piece of work, isn't she?" Todd assessed.

Reece's gaze returned to the group. "Yeah, she sure is." He couldn't allow his attraction for her cloud his judgement.

"Do you really think she'll help us?" Todd's eyes remained on the open doorway and he crossed the room and closed the door.

"Good question. I have a feeling we're just pawns in her game."

"That's what bothers me," Sarah said. "She's a loose cannon and could end up getting us all killed, including herself. I've seen what Vlad can do to humans and vampires alike."

"Not if we can formulate a backup plan." Reece pulled up a chair and sat down at the table. "Let's get to work."

CHAPTER THIRTY SIX

The woman in Jacques' embrace was oblivious to what was about to happen. His dark vampire eyes had drawn her in and she felt warm and safe in his arms. Even when his canines locked into place, the young woman didn't flinch and when he pierced her flesh she gave a pleasurable, satisfied, aroused sigh. The feeding process could be incredibly sensual, if a vampire so desired. Something stirred inside him as he swallowed the life-giving elixir and a vision appeared in his mind. One he had no inclination to remember. Patricia.

She had been brought to his bed chamber by his then loyal assistant, Nathaniel, for his pleasure but there had been something about her... something that made him want to keep her with him and not kill her, but she had declined his offer of immortality. She had fought for her life, something none of the others had done. They had begged for him not to kill them. A sharp pain gripped his gut, the feeling like someone had twisted a knife into the revitalized tissue and muscle and he shoved the woman away from him. She fell into a disheveled heap on the floor, blood trickling from the small, circular wounds on her throat, and lay there in a euphoric daze.

Why had the woman he'd unwillingly killed so long ago return to his thoughts now? Whatever the reason, it had promptly quelled his thirst.

As Jacques' mesmerism faded, the young woman sprang to her feet, her eyes wide with horror, and dashed out the door barefoot, her hand pressed to her throat. He didn't attempt to follow her. Who would believe her anyhow? By the time she reached the lobby the bite marks would be gone and her black dress would conceal any evidence of blood. He stepped out onto the wrap around balcony of his suite into the night, wandered over to the balustrade, and gazed down at the traffic below, both vehicle and pedestrian. It had been a long time since he'd had an immortal mate. Cassandra had been the closest to it but she had been killed during the ritual to turn his brother into a dark immortal. Perhaps it was time to find someone willing to abandon their humanity for an eternity with him. Was there such a mortal?

Eva Van Helsing's face appeared like an effigy before him and he wondered why she had spared his life. She could have killed him that night in the street when he'd followed the young woman to drink from her. Why hadn't she? He glanced over his shoulder at the windows of his hotel suite and a smug smirk spread across his handsome pale face. He was in possession of something she wanted even though she wasn't certain he had it. And while he did have it, it assured his immortal longevity. It was something he could use to protect himself when the inevitable confrontation arrived, which it would eventually. Even though Eva had sworn never to negotiate with blood drinkers but he was sure she would for this.

He turned around, wandered back to the doorway and stepped inside. Crossing the living room, he stopped at the credenza, pressed the front right hand side of it and a panel popped open. He keyed in the security number for the safe into the luminous, green keypad, opened the door and took out the tattered, black leather volume. Abraham Van Helsing's journal contained information about how Vlad Tepes became the creature he is and the means by which to end his life, among other treasure troves of knowledge regarding the immortal world. Jacques understood its value and planned to use it to his advantage before returning it to its rightful owner. Why hadn't he imparted such valuable information on to the PI? Because he wanted Reece and his team out of his way. And Dracula would deliver what he desired. He had his own plans for the father of vampires.

CHAPTER THIRTY SEVEN

Evening had set in by the time Reece and his team arrived at the base of the wooded hill, out of sight of the village residents on the other side, the monastery looming like a dark monolith high above them. The moon, hidden behind ominous, charcoal gray clouds drifting across the inky sky gave off no light and they were at the mercy of the muted night as they made their ascent to the plateau a hundred feet below the towering, white-washed fortress. Eva's crew was in place awaiting Reece's order to move in but the vampire hunter was nowhere to be seen.

The PI approached an immortal that appeared to be in charge. "Where's Eva?" he asked, his anxious voice tight.

Dumitru glanced over his shoulder, his pale eyes examining the PI from head to foot before turning around completely to address him face on. "She has other business to take care of and will not be joining us tonight."

Reece folded his arms and frowned. "She was meant to be here to help us with our mission."

"That is our responsibility. We have been fully briefed."

"About what exactly?" Something in Reece's gut slithered. He should have known better than to trust her. Somewhere in the back of his mind he knew he shouldn't have but did anyway.

"We are to transport you and your team up to the plateau and then convey you individually over the wall to a safe location within the compound before moving inside."

"That wasn't the plan."

The vampire's left eyebrow arched. "That is the only plan we have. Once inside, we are to locate your team member, expedite you all to safety, and make every effort to capture Vlad."

"Capture?" Reece's frown deepened into a scowl. "No. The plan was to kill him."

"Ms. Van Helsing gave strict instructions that he was not to be harmed. We are to apprehend him and transport him to a secure location."

"What location?" The slithering feeling in Reece's gut tightened into a knot of twitching nerves. Eva had betrayed him and had set other plans in motion for the monster. Why? What possible reason could she have to want him alive?

Dumitru gave no reply to the PI's question.

Reece waited a moment, expecting an answer, then turned around and stalked back to the others. "Eva's not here. She's given instructions to the vampires that are meant to be helping us not kill Dracula."

"What?!" Everyone said together.

"I hate to say it, but I knew you should never have trusted her. I had a feeling she wasn't playing for our side," Todd said.

Reece gave him a severe stare. "Saying *I told you so* doesn't help right now, does it?"

Todd returned a sheepish glance but didn't reply.

"Do you know what her plans are for him?" Nathaniel asked, feeling also betrayed because he had vouched for her believing she would assist them.

Reece's eyes moved to the vampire he'd been speaking to then back to Nathaniel. "No. If they know anything they're not telling."

Sarah let out a frustrated huff. "Then what do we do now? Trust them to get us in and out unharmed or…"

"I don't know, to be honest. I don't trust them and that makes this situation all the more dangerous." Reece ran his hand around the back of his neck and gave a heavy sigh. His main priority was extracting Charlotte without getting anyone killed. This new turn of events placed all their lives in jeopardy. What else had Eva planned that he wasn't aware of?

He had spoken to her on the phone the day before and she had given no indication that she wouldn't be with them when they implemented their mission to take out Dracula. Her knowledge of the vampire was the reason they'd planned this assault in the first place. She knew more about him than Sarah did and that was the only reason Reece had trusted her. Without Eva being present the situation could go horribly wrong.

Andre spoke up. "We should follow through, Reece. We need to get this done. If we don't do what we came here for Dracula will continue to pursue us until he has finished us all. His abducting Charlotte again should prove that. He's not about to walk away without some kind of fight, no matter how long it takes."

"Andre's right," Sarah said. "He will be relentless."

Reece ran his gaze around his team. "Nathaniel?"

"I have to agree. We came here to dispatch the villain. And both Sarah and Andre are correct in their thinking. Vlad will continue to pursue us until he had ended us."

The PI gave another heavy sigh. "Then we need to watch each other's backs up there. I don't trust Eva's guys to do that. We have no idea what she's put in place. Maybe she wants us out of the picture so she can take down Dracula herself and gain the notoriety for ridding the world of the most notorious vampire to ever exist." He huffed out a humorless laugh. "Would look good on her vampire hunter resume, don't you think?"

The vampire he'd been speaking to came over to the group. "Are we ready to proceed?"

Reece's eyes moved to him. "Yeah. Just give us a minute."

"Of course." Dumitru tilted his head, ran his gaze around the faces standing with the PI, then turned on his heel and stalked back to his team secluded among the trees.

Everyone pushed their wireless coms into their ears and did a check to be sure they could hear each other.

"Ok, we have communication. At least if we get split up for any reason we can stay in contact." Reece studied the group of immortals standing in the shadows. What had Eva told them to do... and where was she? "Let's go."

ℰᏯᏩ

Jacques stood at the ceiling to floor draped window at the edge of the sun's bright reflection across the carpet and gazed out at the blue sky. He knew now, by his brother's resurrection, that he was unable to walk in the daylight. He preferred the night so it was of no consequence. Better not to ponder over things that were unattainable to one's reach. He had lived in the shadows for hundreds of years and felt comfortable in their anonymity so why change his habits now?

He turned his head and glanced over his shoulder at the knock on the door, then crossed the elegant, bygone era style suite and reached for the handle only to stop before his long, slim fingers could connect with the metal. A lengthy silence ensued before the female voice echoed into the room from the other side.

"I know you are in there, Jacques. Where else would you be during daylight hours? Open the door."

"What do you want?" He knew her visit would be of no benefit, for many reasons.

"I want to offer you a deal for something I need from you. Now, are you going to invite me in?"

Jacques allowed her words to circle his devious mind for a moment, pondering what it was she could possibly have to offer that would persuade him to open the door, allow her access into his sanctuary, and place his immortal life in danger? "I do not believe there is anything you could offer that would be of any value to me."

"Not even the lives of your nemesis and his team? Would that not be enough for you to hear what I have to say?"

⃸⃺

Reece's cell vibrated against his hip. He snatched it from the pocket of his charcoal gray cargo pants, his frowning gaze on the screen. Lozano. The PI's eyes roamed the group around him, immortal and human alike. "I need to take this." He stalked away from the two teams and wandered further into the trees before answering. "What have you got?"

"Abraham Van Helsing wrote a journal that contains the only way to kill Dracula. He figured it out all those years ago but his writings disappeared. Do you know if Eva is in possession of it?"

"No, I don't. I think she would've told me if she had it." Reece wondered if that were true and what other secrets she had kept from him. Why wouldn't she tell him if she knew how to kill the monster?

"You would think so, wouldn't you?" Lozano gazed out of Double D Investigations' office window. The blue sky was dotted with white clouds and the sun was high in the sky. All in all it was a pleasant day in LA. "Can you ask her?"

"No, I can't ask her. She's…" He wasn't sure he should say anything about her not being with them. He knew the sheriff and Ed would worry. "She's already up top."

"Oh. Ok. Well, when you see her, ask her. If she has it you'll be able to get rid of Dracula once and for all." A thought crossed his mind. "Wait. Didn't Eva say Jacques had something that belonged to her and she wanted it back?"

Reece frowned, trying to recall if he remembered her saying that. Come to think of it, he did. "Yeah, you're right. Maybe Jacques is double crossing us all."

"From what you've told me about him and from what I've seen myself I wouldn't put anything past him."

"Thanks for the info, Sheriff. I appreciate it. I'll keep in mind what you've told me. If Jacques has the Van Helsing journal we could all be in serious trouble."

"Do you want me and Ed to go over there and find out?" Lozano suddenly felt the need to be more useful than he was right now, his bravado getting the better of him.

"No. *Do not* go over there. If he does have the journal let him think he has the upper hand, for now."

"Ok, if you're sure."

"I am sure. I don't want either of you putting your lives in danger while I'm not there."

"All right. Be careful, Reece. We're thinking of you and hoping this is all over soon."

"Thanks. We will. Tell Ed Sarah says hello."

"Will do." He rang off.

Reece pushed his phone back into his hip pocket and joined the others.

"Everything ok?" Sarah asked, eyeing him with a concerned frown.

"Yeah. All good. Just Lozano telling us to be careful. I told him to tell Ed you said hello."

"Thanks." She gave him a brief smile, her nerves on edge. This was the battle she'd been waiting for most of her life and now she was here.

Once safe on the plateau, the vampires transported Reece and his team up over the wall and into the stables at the back of the compound. They would take out the guards one at a time around the perimeter, so as not to draw attention to themselves, then take the lead entering the monastery. The PI and his team would follow close behind.

The interior was cloaked in darkness with no servants or other attendants anywhere in the main building. Not unusual for a vampire to live in shadow. Nonetheless, Reece couldn't shake the feeling they were walking into a trap. He and his team flipped down their night vision goggles, everything around them glowing bright green through the lenses, and followed the vampires further into the ancient edifice, his gut squeezing the air from his lungs. This was Dracula's domain and they were out of their depth, even though they had Eva's team, Nathaniel and Andre, Reece couldn't be sure about the six immortals the vampire hunter had employed... nor could he be one hundred percent certain about Andre either. Jacques' blood coursed through his friend's veins and the PI had no idea what that would do to him.

⁊ʘ

Eva stood outside Jacques hotel suite facing the elegant, paneled door, then shrugged her shoulders and turned to leave. "Very well, if you do not wish to rid yourself of the private investigator so be it." She strutted over to the elevator and poked the down button with her index finger several times.

The lock snapped back and Jacques appeared in the doorway. "Tell me how you plan to execute such a scheme."

A satisfied, red gloss smirk spread across Eva's lips before she turned around. She knew he couldn't resist her offer. "Would you prefer we discuss it here in the lobby where we may be overheard or are you going to invite me inside?"

⁊ʘ

The place appeared deserted. The two teams continued to the main staircase and stopped at the foot of the steps. Dumitru turned around. "We will go ahead and survey the upper levels of the building before your group comes up."

Reece shook his head. "Not going to happen. We go together." His gut told him not to trust them and he *never* ignored his instincts.

179

The vampire's left eyebrow arched. "Very well, but do not say I did not warn you."

"I won't." He waved his team on.

The six vampires took the stairs first, followed by the PI, Andre, Nathaniel, Todd and Sarah. All was deathly quiet and still above. Where was the monster? Where was Charlotte? What if they'd been led on a wild goose chase? What if Dracula never came here? What if this was Eva's plan all along?

Reece pushed through the center of the vampire team members to their leader. "There's no one here."

"It would appear that way but looks can be deceiving."

"What do you mean?" The PI frowned.

Dumitru tilted his head to the side. "There is a human heartbeat."

Reece's eyebrows rose. "Where?"

The vampire pointed upward to the next level.

"Then let's go." He wanted to get to Charlotte.

Dumitru gripped Reece's arm. "Wait."

"For what?" The PI tugged out of the vampire's firm grasp.

"Vlad will be here... somewhere. We must take precautions." His vampire eyes roamed the hallway and the left corner of his mouth hitched into a crooked smile. "I have an idea."

Reece stood with hands on hips. "Tell me."

∽◯

Charlotte's heart thundered in her chest as she sat on the side of the huge, four post bed, hands tied behind her back, her mouth covered with a strip of duct tape. Dracula was immersed in the shadows across the room along with several immortal members of his legion. Reece and the others were about to be ambushed and there was nothing she could do to stop it.

Her tear-filled eyes roamed the gloom in the room and her thoughts turned to her son. After tonight she would never see him again. What would he do without her? She closed her eyes and his sweet face appeared in her mind. *Tommy*. A single tear slipped down her right cheek before a surge of adrenalin kicked in. She couldn't give up now. She had to help fight for their lives. She leapt from the bed into the shadows.

CHAPTER THIRTY EIGHT

Jacques gave Eva's question some thought. He wasn't one to put his immortal life in danger, not for any reason. He searched her attractive face and met her questioning gaze. He knew he couldn't trust her. Perhaps her offer was just a ploy to enter his suite and finish him off permanently. His suspicious eyes remained on her. "If I were to invite you in I would require reassurance that you would not make an attempt on my life. Are you prepared to agree to those terms?"

The thought of ending Jacques was tempting but she had other plans for ridding the world of him. Her glossy smile widened. "I suppose I can make an exception… on this occasion." She sauntered across the small lobby and stood at the threshold of his room. "But I also need something from you."

"Yes, I am aware." He made a sweeping motion with his left hand and hesitated for the briefest moment before saying, "Won't you come in?"

Eva's eyes studied the luxurious, bygone era suite with its ceiling to floor heavy drapes, expensive furnishings, and private outdoor balcony. She was surprised to see one pair of drapes open, but then, the room was mostly cast in shadow so there wasn't much chance that Jacques would be sizzled by the sun. The idea caused her to smile but as the door closed behind her a feeling of unease washed over her cold skin. Her host was a vampire of little morals and would do anything to protect himself. She turned around. "So, are you ready to hear my proposal and return to me what is rightfully mine?"

He gave a nod and motioned for her to take a seat.

The vampire hunter crossed the room and sat down in one of the armchairs opposite the coffee table and sofa.

"Would you like some refreshments?" Jacques walked over to the bar and poured himself a very old, very expensive, double shot of whiskey.

"No, thank you. It is a little too early in the day for me." She crossed one, long leather-clad leg over the other and placed her hands in her lap. The one thing she was sure of was that she should never accept a drink from Jacques Delacroix. Because it could be her last.

Jacques moved to the other armchair and sat down, placing his glass on the table between them. "Now, what is this deal you have to offer? I am curious to learn how you plan to eliminate Reece Daniels and his team."

"First things first." She held out her hand. "My journal."

"Ah, yes, the journal." He raised the etched, crystal glass to his lips and swallowed a large mouthful of amber fluid. "I came into possession of it by shear good fortune as it happened and I have pondered it many times. Enlightening reading material."

"Why did you not use it to get rid of Vlad when you had the opportunity?"

"We were allies for a time… comrades in arms, so there was no need."

Eva's left, sculpted eyebrow arched. "And now?"

"Now?" A capricious smile crossed his handsome face. "He has what I desire. To be king of all vampires. It's that simple."

Eva knew his inflated ego would be his undoing. She was counting on it. "How did you get journal?" She was sure that how ever the book had come into Jacques possession it was not by good fortune. Someone would have died for it.

"Your four times great grandfather was robbed while traveling across the Carpathian Mountains and the journal was one of the items among the possessions taken." He paused to remember the night he had acquired it, his eyes focusing on the luxurious carpet beneath his feet. "I was in a tavern in Michalovce observing the patrons, in search of my next meal, when a rugged-looking man stumbled through the door with a large sack over his shoulder. He attempted to sell his wares to the customers but, alas, had no takers. His asking price for the items he offered was a bit *steep*. My curiosity piqued as I watched him roam the tables, people shaking their heads, and when he was about to leave I called him over to my table."

"So you paid him for the journal?" She doubted it.

"Not exactly, no." A smirk stretched across his pale face as he recalled their interaction in the unlit alley beside the tavern on that snowy night. "The peddler would not have lived long, anyhow. His blood had been tainted by disease."

"So you stole it from him... and drank him dry?"

"Is that what you think of me?"

"I believe I know you well enough to realize the scenario would have played out almost exactly as I imagine." She didn't say yes, although the thought crossed her mind.

His left eyebrow arched and he stared into her eyes. She did know him all too well, it seemed. "Then I will not try to dissuade you."

She raised her hand again, palm upward. "I would very much like to see it."

"In due course." He rested his elbows on the arms of the chair and clasped his fingers in front of him. "Tell me about your plan."

ℰℭ

Once Charlotte's location was discovered, the vampires entered the adjoining two rooms. The strategy was for them to access the chamber from the outside while Reece and his team came in through the only entrance. Dumitru could sense Dracula and several immortals within, so they would take them from both sides in a preemptive strike. Both teams could communicate through their earpieces and when Dumitru gave the order his team would crash through the windows and Reece's team would storm in, guns blazing with silver cartridges. They knew it wouldn't take out the monster, but it would eliminate his combatants, and wound Dracula enough to capture him.

As the windows burst inwards, spraying shards of glass across the room, and Reece's team stormed through the door, everyone stopped mid-motion.

Dracula emerged from the shadows holding an ancient, jeweled dagger to Charlotte's throat, his men assembled behind him, weapons raised. "I would advise you not to take another step, otherwise I will slit her throat and you wouldn't want me to do that because she has my blood coursing through her veins." A crooked, satisfied smirk crossed his lips.

Reece stood his ground for a brief moment before lowering his automatic and motioning for Sarah and Todd to do the same. Nathaniel and Andre didn't need weapons to fight. "Don't do anything stupid, Vlad. If you kill Charlotte your life is over."

The vampire's smirk widened. "Foolish human, I am unstoppable. Have you not learned that by now?"

"I don't believe that."

"You should." He pressed the point of the dagger into the soft flesh of Charlotte's throat and a single trickle of blood slid down her skin and soaked into the white fabric collar of her shirt.

The PI's intense gaze remained on the monster. "You won't get away with this."

"Oh?" His right eyebrow arched. "But I have already. Now step aside or I will make her one of us."

Reece's gut tightened with furious frustration. He wanted to lunge across the room, rip the vampire's head off his shoulders and end him for good, but he couldn't. Charlotte would be dead before he made it half way and would turn into a creature like Dracula, and he couldn't let that happen, for her son's sake.

They had lost the battle again. At least for now.

Vlad made his way across to the open doorway using Charlotte as his shield, the dagger remaining at her throat. Before stepping into the hallway, he turned around. "Do not try to follow me. Her humanity is in your hands, Reece Daniels." With that said, he and Charlotte were gone.

Reece rushed out into the corridor but the pair had vanished.

Dracula's men threw down their weapons and raised their hands in defeat. Dumitru's men charged across the room and dragged them away in shackles. At the doorway, Dumitru stopped. "We will find where Vlad is and rescue your fiancée. You have my word."

The PI frowned into the vampire's eyes. "He won't be as easy to find. And who knows what he'll do to Charlotte in the meantime?" Reece headed out the door, Sarah, Todd, Andre and Nathaniel behind him. How could he have been so stupid as to think killing Dracula would be a simple process? It hadn't been in Las Vegas, what made here any different?

CHAPTER THIRTY NINE

On the flight back to Bucharest, Eva studied her grandfather's journal. She hadn't expected Jacques to hand it over so easily, but he believed what she had told him about her plan and she was thankful. As she perused the worn pages, she realized Abraham had been Dracula's adversary for a long time and had learned all he could about the vampire's weaknesses and strengths. Vlad Tepes was a true monster. He had literally killed thousands during the time he was human, and also over his immortal lifetime. If Jacques took control of the immortal realm he would do exactly the same and Eva was not about to let that happen. Vlad, too, had been raised from the dead, which was the reason why he was invincible. She was grateful that Jacques had no idea of his true power.

An announcement over the PA requested all passengers store their belongings and fasten their seatbelts for the landing. Eva slid the tattered journal into her flight bag and stuffed it back into the overhead compartment. She now had the weapon she needed to rid the world of Vlad Tepes and Jacques Delacroix. A smile spread across her face at the thought. She would finally be free to pursue other degenerate vampires roaming the earth and get back to what she did best. Both her nemeses would be gone... for good.

ଓ

Eva strutted along the hotel hallway and stopped at Reece's room. She stood outside and hesitated before knocking. She had been informed that their plan to rescue Charlotte and capture Dracula had failed. Not the outcome she had been expecting. The PI would be pissed at her for leaving them to tackle the monster alone – well, not totally alone – but without her knowledge and presence. She knew he didn't trust her, although he had no reason not to. Well, perhaps now he did. Eva raised her hand to knock but the door opened before her knuckles connected with the wood.

Reece's severe frown told her everything she had been thinking. "So you decided to show up after the fact. Thanks for that." He pushed past her and closed the door behind him.

"I had important business elsewhere."

"Yeah, so we were told." He headed along the hall.

Eva followed. "If you would let me explain."

Reece swung around. "Explain that you left us for dead? Explain that Dracula has transfused his blood into Charlotte and if she dies she comes back a monster? Explain that he seemed to know what we were doing and was well prepared for us when we arrived? Go ahead. Explain all that." He pushed his hands onto his hips and waited for her reply, eyeing her with derision.

"I flew back to Los Angeles. I went to see Jacques. He gave me the journal." She tugged the book from her flight bag and pushed it toward him. "We needed this."

Reece's eyes moved to the leather-bound volume and he snatched it from her hand. "How'd you get this? Jacques wouldn't just hand it over. He'd want something in return." The PI flipped through the yellowed pages perusing the old-fashioned handwriting and crude sketches.

"I made him an offer he couldn't refuse." Her glossy red lips spread into a knowing smirk.

Reece's gaze darted from the book to her. "What kind of offer?"

"*That* I cannot tell you right now. But trust me when I say that we can rid the world of both monsters for good with this." She tapped her index finger on the page of the journal he had turned to.

The PI's eyes narrowed. "What have you done?"

"You should have a little faith. You will find out soon enough." She eased the journal out of his hands and dropped it back into her bag. "We need to get everyone together so we can devise a strategy that will actually work the next time we face Vlad Tepes."

"And how do you propose we do that when we have no idea where he is?"

"Do not concern yourself. I have ways of finding out." She turned around and strutted back to the elevator.

Reece stood and watched her. What was she up to? And why was his gut telling him not to trust her?

�☜☞

Andre sprang from his pillow with a sharp gasp, his anxious, vampire eyes roaming the deep shadows of his hotel room, his body glistening with sweat. If he had a heartbeat it would be thundering in his chest right now. What had he dreamed? While Jacques was dead Andre hadn't dreamed, something vampires were not meant to do anyhow, but now that his brother was back, now that he was back, the dreams had started again. Jacques blood coursing through his veins had to be the reason for the horrific nightmares of blood and death.

He swung his legs over the side of the bed, stood up, and walked over to the window. The Bucharest full moon shone like a beacon in the inky sky, its iridescent, milky aura a halo around it. What was happening to him? He could feel his self-control losing its battle against whatever it was playing with his mind and he wasn't sure he could continue to sustain who he once was. It was becoming more and more difficult to keep a hold of himself. A sound in the silence startled him and he swung around. "Adrian?!"

His mentor's hazy form emerged from the shadows. "You must fight what's happening to you, Andre. You cannot allow your brother to manipulate you and pull you into the darkness of his world."

"Don't you think I know that? But the sorcerer's magic is far too strong."

"*You* are strong. You always have been. You can fight it. You *have to* fight it."

Andre waved the comment off and turned back to the window. "You're not real. You're dead."

"That may be, but I will always be with you. You just need to remember who you are, Andre. I know you'll do whatever it takes to do the right thing, to keep the ones you love safe."

"But what if I can't?" Andre turned around to find the room empty.

Tears stung the backs of his eyes and he whispered his fear again. "What if I can't?"

၆၁

The middle of the night was the perfect time for Eva to implement her plan. Her team of vampires was waiting for the go ahead and, once she gave it, the scheme she had devised would be the beginning of the end for all concerned. She gave the order and the immortal group surged through the hotel like unseen phantoms to the PI's and his teams' rooms, entered without a sound, and injected each of them with a drug that would keep them asleep until after they were transported to the secret location she had prepared for them. Although Nathaniel and Andre were vampires, their bodies were still organically human so the double dose they had be given, just to be sure, would take effect and keep them unconscious as well.

Once they were out of the city, she would contact Jacques and, as agreed, he would fly to Bucharest to witness the proof of her promise. It couldn't be more perfect. She would have both monsters in the same place at the same time. One would destroy the other. How poetic. Then she would deal with whoever remained.

The underground, fortified defense bunker was the ideal place to take the unconscious group. It was not too far from Bucharest, just far enough to be anonymous to the populace of the city. She felt a pang of remorse for what she was about to do to Reece and his friends but she had no choice. There would always be casualties of war. Especially in a supernatural battle.

Eva's team transported one person at a time, wrapped in a sheet inside a laundry trolley, along the hallway to the service elevator, traveled down to the basement, and out to a truck parked in front of the metal roll up door leading to the alley behind the hotel. When everyone was secured inside, Eva and her team climbed on board and the truck made its way out of town. They needed to get to the bunker before sunrise as the vampires she had hired were nightwalkers.

After traveling for thirty minutes, the truck turned onto an unlit, narrow road, its headlights forging a dull, yellow trail ahead of it on the unpaved surface. Charcoal clouds drifted across the face of the full moon causing a sudden shift into darkness. As the laundry truck came up over the rise, a black sedan with headlights glaring stationed in the center of the road blocked its path. The truck rolled to a halt. Eva stood up and leaned between the front seats. "Why did you stop?"

Dumitru pointed in the direction of the vehicle standing twenty feet away.

Eva's gaze moved through the windshield and a feeling of dread washed over her. "Back up now!" she ordered, her voice anxious, fear pouring over her.

A van appeared behind them. They were trapped.

CHAPTER FORTY

Sheriff Lozano frowned at the screen on his phone. Why wasn't Reece answering his cell? His eyes moved from the digital display to the opening door. Ed Borenko stepped into the office carrying a tray of coffee and scones. When he noticed the concerned expression on the sheriff's face, he strutted over, dropped the cardboard tray onto the desk and stared into Lozano's worried eyes. "What's wrong?"

"I've been trying to get onto Reece and he's not answering." He leaned across the desk, snatched a coffee container from the tray and took a cautious sip.

Ed shrugged. "Maybe they have no cell service where they are."

"Maybe, but it's been a couple of days since we heard anything from him. I hope he's ok."

"Hey, Daniels can take care of himself. He's learned a lot over the years. He'll be fine."

"I hope you're right." Lozano sighed. "I wish we could go over there to help out. Like I said before, I feel useless sitting around here waiting for news. It annoys the hell outta me."

Ed plonked himself into one of the chairs in front of Reece's desk. "Yeah, me too. I hate twiddling my thumbs."

"Did you look into early retirement like we discussed?"

"Oh, yeah, I did. I'm going to fill out the paperwork next week." He picked up his coffee. "I'm looking forward to working here full time. The city needs all the help it can get."

"You know, I've been seriously thinking about moving here so I can help too."

"Ed's right eyebrow rose. "You have? I thought you wanted to start somethin' in Vegas."

"Yeah, well, I did, but I think I could be of more use here in LA. Besides, I could use a change of scene."

"Well I'm sure Daniels would be happy to have you on board."

The sheriff's face lit up. "You think?"

"Sure. The more the merrier, I say. We need a solid team."

"I've been worried about Andre being over there with Reece. You know, with him having Jacques' blood running through his veins and all. Why do you think Jacques did that?"

Ed shrugged again. "Who knows what runs through the mind of a sociopath? Maybe he thinks he can manipulate him into doing what he wants. Maybe he can, I don't know."

"Then Reece and the others could be in real danger with him around." He reached across and tugged a scone from the paper bag.

"Not much we can do about it." Ed plucked the other scone out of the bag and took a bite.

Lozano was silent for a moment.

Ed could almost see the cogs turning in the sheriff's mind. "What are you thinkin'?" he asked.

"I have some savings tucked away. We could be packed in no time and on the next flight out. I still have a couple of weeks' vacation time up my sleeve and if all else fails I'll try to work something else out. What do you think?"

The chief leaned forward. "You're serious? You want to buy me a plane ticket and head over to Bucharest?"

Lozano shrugged. "Sure, why not? It's better than sitting here doing nothing."

Ed swallowed the last of his coffee, allowing what the sheriff had just said to circle the processing center of his brain. "I'd pay you back, you know."

The sheriff waved it off. "You don't have to. At least if we go there we won't be sitting here worrying about them. What do you say?"

Ed tugged his oversized body out of the chair. "I say to hell with this, let's go."

"What about the precinct and not having any leave left?"

"You let me worry about that." Ed dropped the last of his scone onto the paper bag and brushed the crumbs from his hands. "I'm going in to speak to my supervisor. See you back here in an hour."

"I'll go pack up my stuff and come right back."

"Ok. See you soon." Ed marched across the office, pulled open the door and disappeared down the stairs. He was a man on a mission. A mission to help the people he cared about.

Lozano stood up and walked over to the window. Ed had just climbed into his sedan and was pulling away from the curb. The sheriff felt good about the decision he'd made. He and Ed needed to be useful and they couldn't do that in LA.

℘

Ed threw open the office door, jostled a bulging, gray suitcase through the doorway and dropped it on the floor, puffing and panting. "Geez, that was hard work." He pulled a handkerchief from the pocket of his dark blue pants and mopped his sweaty brow. "When we get back I'm signing up to a gym. I need to get fit."

Lozano eyed him without comment. He knew if he agreed Ed would be annoyed so he kept his mouth shut. "I've booked our flight and hotel so we're all set. The cab should be on its way."

"Great. It'll be good to feel like we're doing something, huh?"

"Yeah, it will." He was curious. "How'd it go with your superior? Did you have any trouble getting the time off?"

"I filled out the early retirement paperwork. Told him I had family commitments that wouldn't wait for a couple of months and if I couldn't file now I'd quit."

"And he agreed?"

"Yeah." Ed shrugged. "Well what else could he do? I've been on the force a lot a years, they owe me. I already got the fake gold watch a few years ago so a pension will be nice. What time do we leave?"

"Three fifteen. The flight will get us to Bucharest close on midday tomorrow."

"Ok." Ed ran his eyes around the office, hoping he'd see it again. Trailing Dracula was a dangerous exercise and who knew if any of them would make it out alive. At least he'd be with Sarah and that was a plus. He'd been missing her. His gaze moved to the sheriff. "Ready to go?"

Lozano nodded. "Yep." He grabbed the handle of his suitcase and wheeled it over next to Ed's.

The chief studied the solid, black plastic case on wheels. "I gotta get me one of those. Lugging this around is a killer."

The pair headed out the door, Ed glancing over his shoulder at the muted glass panel with Double D Investigations inscribed across it and prayed they would all make it home safe and sound. No loss of life this time. They'd already lost good people and it still hurt like hell.

Lozano made a mental note to give Reece's cell another try before they boarded their flight. He was still concerned about why the PI wasn't picking up and hoped all was well over there, as well as could be expected, under the circumstances. *We'll find out soon enough, I guess.*

CHAPTER FORTY ONE

A dark shape stepped from the idling, black sedan and stood behind the open passenger door. Dressed in similar, charcoal colored attire to Eva's team, he blended into the shadows of the night; obvious to her he was also an immortal. She could sense the menacing vibrations around them and knew they were in serious trouble. If the order was given they would all die. The male figure moved around the car and stood between the bright auras of the headlights. "You will follow us," he shouted at the windscreen of the truck. "If you do not do as I say you will die here."

Dumitru's severe, frowning gaze met Eva's. "What do you want us to do? Attack?"

The vampire hunter didn't answer right away, her mind ticking over the worst case scenarios and possible outcomes if they attempted to fight back. How many occupants sat inside the car and the van? More than she and her team, she assumed. And what would happen to the unconscious PI and his friends if she and her team were massacred out here? She shook her head. "We surrender."

Dumitru swiveled in the driver's seat. "But…"

Eva raised a silencing hand. "We cannot afford to have anyone killed. We will go with them and find out what they want."

"We are setting ourselves up for a dangerous fall, Ms. Van Helsing. Once we are at the second location we are more likely to die."

"That may be but we have no choice at this point. We are surrounded and possibly outnumbered. Do you really want your immortality to end here tonight?"

Dumitru didn't answer. Instead, he turned his intense stare back to the figure ahead of them. To his mind they should stand their ground and fight.

"Good. I will step out and give him my decision." Eva opened the side door of the truck and climbed down onto the dirt road. She pushed her hands deep into the pockets of her leather jacket and walked to the front of the vehicle. "Are you working for Vlad?" She already knew the answer.

The masked combatant spoke with an even tone, not revealing anything in his voice. "You do not need to know that. Are you conceding?"

"I am not conceding anything. We will follow you as requested." How civil the conversation was, considering their lives hung in the balance.

"A sensible choice. I will have two of my men ride with you."

Eva moved closer to the masked, male figure, her dark gaze meeting his immortal eyes and she frowned into them. "That won't be necessary."

"On the contrary, it will ensure your safe arrival at the destination point." He turned on his heel, strutted back to the open door of the sedan and climbed in.

Eva let out an exasperated huff, hoisted herself up into the front passenger seat beside Dumitru and banged the door shut. "Two of his team will be riding with us."

"What…?"

At that moment, the rear door of the laundry truck rolled up with a clatter and the armed pair climbed into the back.

The vampire hunter had hoped to devise some kind of defense plan while traveling to their undisclosed destination, but now that would be impossible. They were at the mercy of their host and she believed it was Dracula who had orchestrated the abduction.

✺

Jacques listened to the continuous ring on the other end of the line and gave a frustrated huff. Why was Eva Van Helsing not answering her phone? He pulled his cell from his ear and frowned at the screen. Where was she and why hadn't she called him back to report that the PI and his team had been dealt with? Excluding his brother, of course.

He tossed his phone onto the coffee table and paced the length of his hotel suite. Had he been deceived? There was only one way to find out. Jacques snatched up the receiver to the phone on the credenza and dialed reception. "Yes, hello, would you organize a first class flight for me to Bucharest for this evening? I do not mind what time. Good." He hung up. The only way he would get an answer to his question, it seemed, was to go there himself.

ℰↃ⊂ℛ

Ed Borenko gazed out of the airplane window, watching the soft white clouds drift by like frothy ocean waves on a blue sea. He sighed and turned to glance over at his new found friend, Enrique Lozano. It seemed fate had brought them together, and from what he'd learned about the sheriff, it also seemed they were destined to work together to fight the supernatural fight. Lozano was an intuitive and could do a lot for their team. He hoped Reece, Sarah, and the others were all ok and that it was a false alarm that had led to him and Lozano flying to Europe. Somewhere beneath the slithering feeling in his gut, caused by a fear of flying, he knew otherwise. He could sense something was wrong. And he believed it had something to do with the vampire, vampire hunter, Eva Van Helsing. He'd felt right from the start that she couldn't be trusted.

Lozano noticed Ed watching him. "Everything ok?"

The chief's face flushed slightly. "Yeah, sure. Just hoping all's well over there and that we're flying to Europe for no other reason than to offer our help."

The sheriff nodded and a pained expression crossed his face. "Yeah, me too." It wasn't like Reece not to call or answer his cell phone and Lozano was pretty certain something was amiss.

A flight attendant stopped the beverage cart beside their seats, offering a pleasant smile. "Would you gentleman like coffee, tea or juice?"

Ed's eyes moved from Lozano to her. "Got anything stronger?"

ℰↃ⊂ℛ

The tall wire gate rolled open, allowing access to the compound, and the black sedan drove through followed by the laundry truck and the van. Once inside, the gate squealed shut behind them and Eva knew there was no way

196

out. Not yet, anyhow. The combatant who had spoken to her got out of the car and walked up to the passenger door, circling with his index finger for her to wind down the window.

"Get out."

"What are we doing here?" Eva tried to stall the inevitable for as long as she could. Once they were taken inside she knew they would be caged like animals.

"You will find out soon enough. Now, all of you get out of the truck."

Eva's gaze moved to Dumitru. "You heard him."

He gave her a disapproving stare. They should have fought when they had the chance.

As she was about to climb down out of the truck, the back door rolled up and the two armed soldiers motioned with their weapons for the others of Dumitru's team to climb out.

"We have come here peacefully," Eva said, "I hope we can come to some arrangement."

The vampire didn't answer. "Take them inside."

Eva counted the vampires on his team. They would have been well outnumbered and killed if they had attempted to defend themselves. "What about the others?"

"Do not concern yourself with them. They will be taken care of."

"What does that mean?"

"As I said, you will find out soon enough."

At that moment, a soldier came up beside Eva, gripped her arm, and tugged her toward the two story concrete building nestled into the rock face beneath the mountain.

When the compound was empty, Andre and Nathaniel jumped out of the truck to survey their surroundings.

"This has to be Dracula's doing," Nathaniel told him.

"Yes, it is. Charlotte's here."

"We need to find a place to hide until we can come up with a way to get inside without being captured."

A quiet voice behind the pair caused them both to swing around.

"Reece." Andre was surprised his friend was already awake. The drug they'd been given was strong and had made Andre feel sluggish, even though it hadn't completely knocked him and Nathaniel out. They had feigned unconsciousness. He knew who had loaded them into the laundry truck. Eva Van Helsing. But he wouldn't tell Reece that because they needed her teams' help to get out of this situation alive.

"What happened?" he asked, rubbing his fingers across his forehead to massage the fog from his medicated brain.

"We don't know. But this is the work of Dracula. I can sense Charlotte."

"Yeah, I figured." He stepped backwards and peered into the truck. "Sarah and Todd are still unconscious." His eyes returned to his friends. "We need to find a way out of here."

"The fence is electrified and the gate opens by remote, which the leader of the team that brought us here has." Andre's eyes roamed the area beyond the fence line. "There isn't much out there. And by my estimation we'd have to be miles away from the city."

"We're better off out there than in here," Reece told him.

"What about Eva and her team?"

"Not much we can do about that right now. If we don't get out of here we're dead."

"What about Charlotte?"

"We'll come back for her."

A noise behind the trio startled them.

"Hey, it's only me," Todd said, jumping down out of the truck. "What happened? How did we get here?"

"None of us know. But Dracula's behind it."

"Figures. Who else would it be?" He rounded the truck and stood with hands on hips. "So what do we do now?"

"I think we should find a way out of here until we can come back prepared to fight," Reece said.

Todd's eyes moved to the gray concrete building. "Is Charlotte inside?"

"Andre thinks she is."

"I don't think it, Reece. She is inside."

"Ok." He looked at Todd. "Yeah."

"Aren't we going in to get her out before we leave?"

Andre's gaze moved to the ex-detective. "There are too many of them. We'd be captured or killed before we could make it into the main atrium of the building."

Todd frowned at him for a moment, the cogs in his head ticking over, then turned to Reece. "What if we eliminate some of Dracula's men and change into their uniforms? Our faces would be hidden behind masks so no one would realize it was us... not right away, anyhow."

The PI shook his head. "I don't know. It sounds too dangerous. We'd be setting ourselves up to be captured."

"Look, once we're disguised, we can get inside, locate Eva's team and set them free so they can help us. We'd have a certain advantage for a short period of time because no one would be expecting it. It's worth a try."

"It could work," Nathaniel said. "As long as we follow certain protocols and are careful."

Reece let out a heavy sigh. "All right. But we need to watch our backs in there. One false move and we're dead."

Todd frowned at the building and ran his gaze around the compound. "Why aren't there any guards at the entrance?"

The others turned around to look at the gray structure. "He's right. Dracula wouldn't leave the outside of this place unprotected. It's got to be a trap." Reece ran his eyes over the outside of the building. "Why would they just leave us out here by ourselves?"

"Because he wants us to get inside," Sarah climbed down out of the truck. "He's reeling us in like a fish on a hook."

"Then we have to outsmart him." Reece paced behind the truck. "We have to do the unexpected."

CHAPTER FORTY TWO

When Ed and sheriff Lozano arrived at the hotel they made a beeline for the reception desk, not only to check in but to also find out if anyone had seen Reece and the others in the past couple of days. The male reception attendant told them that Mr. Daniels and his friends had left the hotel and had not yet returned. He assumed they had taken a scenic tour of some kind and would be back when it ended. The pair thanked him for the information, took their electronic door keys, and crossed the lobby to the elevators.

"I knew something wasn't right," Lozano told Ed. "Reece always calls to let us know what's going on. It wasn't like him not to."

"Yeah, you're right. I had a nagging feeling in my gut too."

Once upstairs, they made their way to Reece's room. Lozano told Ed that if they found a staff member on the floor he would ask them to open the door. If necessary, he'd use official police business to get inside.

Following the hallway along to the PI's room, they stopped outside. Everyone on the team was staying on this floor. Ed pointed along the hall to a cleaning cart and Lozano wandered down to it. The door to one of the rooms was open so he knocked. A maid came out of the bathroom with a wet cleaning cloth in rubber-gloved hands. "Yes? Can I help you?"

"I hope so. I'd like to get into my room. I seem to have misplaced my key."

"Oh? Which room?"

Lozano motioned for her to follow him out into the hallway.

"See where my friend is standing? That one."

She glanced along the hall then returned her gaze to the sheriff. "It's your room?"

"Yes," he lied.

"Ok." She walked along the hallway and stopped at the door, gazing at both men before she opened it. "You're sure this is your room?" She had the feeling the man was lying to her.

"I'm Sheriff Enrique Lozano, Las Vegas PD." He flashed his badge. "And this is Lieutenant Ed Borenko, Los Angeles PD. We're here on official police business and we need to get into this room. It could be a matter of life or death."

The woman's eyes widened. "Oh!" She pushed the electronic key into the lock and the door popped open. "I hope everything is all right."

"So do we. Thanks." Lozano smiled.

The woman walked back along the hallway, but before stepping into the room she'd been cleaning, glanced back at the pair hoping she had done the right thing by letting them into another guest's room.

Once inside, with the door closed, Ed and Lozano began searching for any clues as to where Reece and the others had gone. The pair spotted the map on the table at the same time and rushed over to it. Running their gazes over the markings on the topography, they assumed the team had headed back to Dracula's hiding place.

"So, do we follow them out there?" Ed asked, turning to look at Lozano.

The sheriff shrugged. "I don't know. I thought Dracula escaped from there and took Charlotte with him."

"Well, yeah, but maybe they thought he'd go back."

Lozano gave the chief a skeptical frown. "You really think so? From what we know of Dracula's habits, he would find another location no one knew about."

Ed huffed out a frustrated breath. "Geez, then I don't know. We're flying blind here."

"Yeah." Lozano thought for a moment. "We need to work forward following what they've already done and see what we can come up with. They could be in danger."

"Ok, ok. So where do you wanna start?"

"Let's keep searching and see if we can find anything else."

The pair rummaged through drawers, closet, credenza and all of the paperwork on the table – nothing that would indicate where the PI and his team had gone presented itself.

"What do we do now?" Ed asked. "We've hit a brick wall."

"Yeah, I know." The sheriff shook his head. "At this point, I'm not sure." His forehead rose as an idea jumped into his head. "Maybe we should check everyone else's rooms, too, just to be sure."

"Ed frowned. "Daniels' room seems to be the hub of activity. Do you think it'd be worth the time?"

"Probably not. Then we need to follow their footsteps. Go to the monastery and take a look around."

"And what do you think we'll find there?"

"Your guess is as good as mine. All I know is we can't just sit here and do nothing."

Ed agreed with that. They hadn't traveled all this way to another country to wait around until someone died. "Precisely. But before we do can we get somethin' to eat? I'm starved."

A thin smile crossed the sheriff's face. "Sure. Yeah. I forgot about food."

As they were about to leave, a noise behind them startled the pair. They both swung around.

"That's Reece's cell," Ed told Lozano.

"We didn't see it anywhere. So where's the sound coming from?"

Both men crossed the room to the bed and wandered around it. "Here," Lozano said, lowering himself onto his knees, lifting the valance, and reaching under the side of the bed.

"So now we know for sure something's happened to them. Reece never goes anywhere without his phone." Ed's solemn gaze met the sheriff's.

₭)ӕ

Jacques sat in first class, his vampire gaze roaming the other passengers seated around him. Oddly enough, there were only three and he thought that if he had the opportunity, he would take a small amount of blood from the only A Positive female sitting to his right when he had the chance. He decided it would be advantageous to initiate a brief conversation with her once the others were asleep, and drink from her while the flight attendant was busy elsewhere. No one would be any the wiser, as his bite healed itself within seconds of him retracting his fangs from the donor's flesh. Usually, it didn't matter to him whether or not he left behind any evidence of his incursion because he would drain his victim to the last drop, but he knew it was out of the question while on board the aircraft. He couldn't bring attention to himself, otherwise he would have to mesmerize everyone on the plane... or kill them. A smirk crossed his handsome face at the thought. He would definitely have his fill, if that were the case, and wouldn't need to feed for quite some time. And what would the news reports say? His devious mile widened.

Bored, he tugged his cell phone from the inner pocket of his jacket and scrolled through the onboard movie selections for something to do. Sensing he was being watched, he averted his gaze from the screen and noticed the attractive A Positive looking at him. She gave a coy smile when their eyes met. Jacques returned the smile, pocketed his phone, got up from his seat and crossed the aisle. "May I?" he asked, gesturing to the empty seat beside her.

She gave a single nod and he sat down next to her.

"Hello, I'm Jacques." He didn't offer his hand as he knew the reaction he would get from his chill touch. Better not to tempt fate.

"Hi, I – I'm Amanda." Another coy smile.

"Nice to meet you, Amanda. So, you're traveling to Bucharest? For business or pleasure?"

She nodded. "Pleasure. I have family there. Well, my father. He's a research assistant at the University of Bucharest."

"How interesting. And what about you? What do you do?"

"I'm a fourth grade teacher on vacation. I haven't seen my dad in a year so I thought I'd travel to visit with him and to see the beautiful city he lives in now."

"Sounds wonderful."

"What about you? What do you do?" She couldn't believe how handsome the man sitting beside her was. He could be on the cover of a fashion magazine. Her heart gave a little thump.

"I'm CEO of a personnel company." It wasn't a lie. Once Dracula was out of the picture he would be the master of their immortal realm.

"Really? I wouldn't have picked you for that line of work."

"Oh?" His left eyebrow arched. "What line of work would you have picked me for?" He was fascinated by her idea of him. Humans were so fanciful at times.

"Perhaps an actor... or... a musician. You certainly have the look for both." A slight flush of pink spread across her cheeks.

"I appreciate your appraisal." Jacques gave her a seductive smile. His eyes roamed the cabin. The other two passengers were asleep. He knew the attendant would return at any moment so he seized the opportunity. Staring into Amanda's eyes he drew her in, wrapping his arms around her and pulling her closer as his canines extended. He pushed the sharp points into the soft flesh of her throat and gave a pleasurable sigh as the warm, life-giving fluid slid down his throat. Her blood was exquisite and he found it difficult to stop himself.

His immortal hearing alerted him to the sound of approaching footsteps. He eased the woman out of his embrace and whipped across the aisle to his seat, wiping any evidence of their tryst from the corners of his mouth as the attendant pushed back the curtain and stepped through the doorway.

She glanced around the cabin and wandered over to him as he seemed to be the only passenger still awake. "Is there anything I can get for you, Mr. Delacroix? Coffee? A snack perhaps?"

"Thank you, but I've already had a snack." He smiled up at her.

∞)(∞

The next afternoon, after being up most of the night going over everything on the table in Reece's room and coming up empty-handed, Ed and Lozano headed down to the lobby. They'd get some breakfast, well, lunch at this point, and hire a car. Once they organized that, they'd take the map and head out to the monastery to see if they could pick up any clues. They had until 7.30 PM, when the sun set, and it would take about an hour to get there. Was it a waste of time? Maybe. But Lozano didn't know what else to try. The only thing they could do right now was follow the teams' trail to see where it led.

As the pair were about to walk out the door, Jacques entered the lobby. All eyes met and everyone stopped in their tracks.

"How are you here?" Ed asked, stunned to see the vampire out in the daytime. It was just after midday.

Jacques raised his left hand to reveal a white gold, Lapis Lazuli signet ring.

How did he get his hands on one of those? Ed didn't like the fact that Jacques could now walk around during the day. That could prove to be a danger to them all.

"Where'd you get that?" Ed knew the vampire wouldn't tell him but it was worth a shot.

"I have my sources." He gave the lieutenant a shrewd smirk. It had been a bargaining tool he'd used during his negotiations with Eva regarding Van Helsing's journal.

"What are you doing here?" Ed asked in a gruff unwelcoming tone. He hated Andre's brother for what he'd done the previous time they'd faced him.

"I came to see my brother. I am sure I don't need your approval. Is he here?" Jacques wasn't about to tell the lieutenant that he'd arrived in Bucharest to see Eva Van Helsing and that she was the one who had given him the ring. "And I might ask the same question. I thought you two were in LA."

"Yeah? Well we're not, as you can see." Ed didn't believe a word he'd said. Jacques' presence in Bucharest was for some other reason and none of it good. "What are you doing at *this* hotel? There're dozens in the city."

"I came here, as I've already explained, to see my brother. He'd mentioned you were staying here so I thought I would too. To be close by." He'd learned their location from the vampire hunter, but he didn't feel the need to share that piece of information with them either.

"Really?" Ed folded his arms over his podgy belly and gave him a skeptical sneer. "Why don't I believe you?"

Jacques' head tilted to the left and his intense gaze remained on the lieutenant. "I have no idea. Now, if you'll excuse me I would like to check in." He side-stepped the pair and headed to the reception desk.

Ed glanced over his shoulder, eyeing Andre's brother with contempt then turned his gaze back to Lozano. "Him being here can't be a coincidence. I'll bet the vampire hunter has something to do with it. Maybe she was the one who gave him that damned ring."

"I was just thinking the same thing because it looks the same as the one Nathaniel's wearing. I knew there was something about her that didn't sit right. Reece should never have trusted her."

The pair stepped out onto the street and headed along the sidewalk to a local café.

"You know, I don't believe what he said. Andre would never tell him anything about our mission."

Lozano frowned at him. "Don't forget he has his brother's blood running through his veins now, so who knows what he's capable of."

Ed considered what the sheriff had just said. "You're right. Besides that, he has come back from the dead. That's gotta do somethin' to you, don't ya think?"

"Yeah, for sure. Don't get me wrong, Reece is a great guy but far too trusting. Andre has changed but he doesn't want to see that. Unfortunately, his loyalty will get him killed one day, if he's not careful."

Ed couldn't argue with that. He'd been in dangerous situations with the PI for that very reason. "What about this place?" He pointed to the al fresco shop front with hanging, potted red Geraniums and tables and chairs scattered along the street.

"Looks ok."

The pair sat down at a small, round, white metal table on the sidewalk.

"Jacques being in the city could jeopardize what we came here for," Ed said as he perused the menu. Nothing looked familiar.

"Or... maybe he can help us. Andre's missing too, don't forget."

"Ed's right eyebrow rose. "Want to explain?"

"He's a..." Lozano lowered his voice and leaned in, "vampire with certain abilities that we don't have. He could be useful to us, especially now he can walk around during the day."

"Oh? Now I get where you're goin'."

"You see what I'm saying?"

"Yeah, yeah. He could work to our advantage for once."

Lozano poked the air with his index finger. "Exactly."

A satisfied smirk crossed the chief's stubbled, rugged face. It was about time they turned the tables on that monster. "I like the way you think, Lozano. Good call."

CHAPTER FORTY THREE

The pair approached the vampire's room and Ed knocked on the door. Jacques didn't answer. Ed knocked again and they waited a couple more minutes. He turned to Lozano and frowned. "Looks like he's not here."

"I wonder where he went." The sheriff glanced along the hallway in both directions.

Ed shrugged. "Beats me. He'd know the city better than we do."

"Yeah, you're right. He's been here before."

They headed back to the elevator and Lozano pressed the call button.

"Him being out during the day is a dangerous thing. Gives him the opportunity to kill whenever he wants." Ed was having difficulty getting his mind around that. He remembered the teens Jacques had drained when they'd first encountered him in LA all those years ago. It was a time when the vampire could only venture out at night and he'd still managed to murder too many. He was a killing machine and now he could do it at will.

The elevator door slid open and Jacques stepped out. "Well, fancy meeting you on my floor. To what do I owe the intrusion?"

"We were lookin' for you," Ed told him.

Jacques' left eyebrow arched. "Oh? Why?"

"We need to talk to you about something," Lozano said.

Jacques' gaze moved from the lieutenant to him. "Really? And what would that be?"

A couple came out of their room and headed down the hallway towards them.

"Not here. Can we talk in your room?"

Jacques' dark stare moved from the sheriff back to Ed Borenko.

"It's important." Ed swallowed hard. He hated having to say the words that were stuck in his throat. "We... we need your help."

Jacques gave the lieutenant a smug smirk and held the elevator door for the couple. When it closed he said, "Well, then, you'd better follow me."

Inside his room, Jacques dropped the keycard onto the credenza and turned to look at the pair standing by the closed door. "Do come in. I won't bite."

Ed and Lozano crossed the room.

"Don't bother to sit. I'm sure this will not take long." Jacques also remained on his feet. "So, what can be of such dire circumstance that you've come to ask for my help?"

Ed cleared his throat. "We..." he glanced sideways at his companion. "...we believe Reece and his team, including Andre, have been taken from the hotel to a secret location and..."

Jacques raised his hand, motioning for Ed to stop talking. "What do you mean they've been taken?"

"Just like I said. We think Eva is behind the abduction."

Andre wasn't meant to be included in our plan. What had the Van Helsing woman been thinking?

"Jacques?" Ed frowned at him, his gut telling him Jacques may have been involved. "Do you know anything about what happened here?"

The vampire folded his arms and walked over to the window. It felt good to have the sun on his face for the first time in hundreds of years. He closed his eyes for a moment and relished the warmth penetrating his cold skin, then turned around and walked back to where he had been standing. "You won't like what I tell you, so let us not get into that right now. What kind of help do you want from me?" He had no option but to help them in order to get his brother back. Eva had betrayed him, as he'd suspected, and now he was obliged to assist the lieutenant and the sheriff in their quest to locate their missing friends. He had hoped by now the PI and his team would have been eliminated.

"Can you pick up Reece's or Andre's vibration? Arianne had that ability. So does Nathaniel."

"Yes, I am aware Nathaniel has that ability but, alas, I do not."

"Then we're screwed," Ed said, letting out a huge huff.

"Perhaps not all is lost." Jacques moved closer to the pair. "I have read Van Helsing's journal." A conceited smirk crossed his handsome face.

"And that helps us how?" Ed gave him a skeptical frown.

"Because it mentions several of Vlad's secret locations. Van Helsing traipsed around Europe seeking out his hiding places and managed to find at least five of them. Two here in Bucharest."

"Yeah, we already know about the monastery. Where's the other one?"

"The Carpathian mountains, of course."

ℰᏅᏣᏧ

Reece and his team had made their way safely to the mountain rock face not far from the building. All was quiet so they knew it was a setup. As they inched their way closer, the PI stopped at a craggy outcrop, his gut twisting into a tight knot of tingling nerves. "Nathaniel, what do you think Dracula will assume we would do?" Reece asked. They had to find a way to outsmart the monster and the only way they could do that was to devise a plan he wouldn't anticipate.

"I believe he would expect us to climb onto the rooftop and make our way inside inconspicuously, possibly through the ventilation system or a trap door, if there is one."

"Ok. So you think Todd's idea of overpowering some of his men and changing into their camouflage gear will work?"

"If we have the opportunity to subdue members of his militia, I believe it will give us the advantage. For a limited time, at least."

"That's all we need. Then we have to find a way inside." Reece peered around the rocks and surveyed the front entry point. Why were no guards present? He turned around. "I'm still concerned that there's no one guarding the perimeter. It's not like Dracula to leave himself defenseless. This feels like the monastery. It was too easy then and it's too easy now."

"I have a suggestion," Sarah said.

"Ok, I'm listening."

"We need a decoy."

Reece frowned. He had a feeling he knew where her theory was going. "Go on."

"What if I surrender myself and while they're dealing with me you slip inside and find a place to hide until you can execute our plan?"

The PI shook his head. "*Not* an option. We stay together."

"Can you think of a better way to get into the building?"

"No, I can't. But you're not sacrificing yourself for the greater good. He'll kill you. He already thought he did and now he'll realize you're not entirely human and find another way to finish you. Think about Ed."

"He knows. How else could I pursue him for all this time? If we don't stop him…"

"I know all that, but there has to be another way."

Todd stepped up beside Sarah. "If there is then let's hear it because we're running out of options here."

Reece gave the ex-detective a severe stare. He didn't want to admit that both Todd and Sarah were right. Their choses were limited. He reached out and gripped her shoulders. "I can't lose anyone else, Sarah. And I can't let Ed down. He loves you, and I know you love him. You going out there alone isn't a viable solution. We'll bide our time until the right opportunity presents itself."

Todd frowned at Reece. "That's it? That's your plan? We don't have that kind of time. What about Charlotte… and Eva and her team? Do you think he's going to keep them alive indefinitely? We have to do something now."

At that moment, three of Dracula's men came out of the building, weapons in hand, and stood at the entrance.

"Look," Todd said, pointing in their direction.

"It looks like an opportunity has presented itself." Reece motioned for Andre and Nathaniel to follow him, using baseball-like hand signals. The trio moved around the rock face, keeping to the shadows at the base of the mountain. Once they were close enough, they each dashed across the ten foot gap one at a time to the side wall of the building and waited.

One of the guards turned his head and peered over his shoulder in their direction. Had his vampire hearing picked up Reece's pounding heartbeat? After a brief moment, he turned back to talk to the other two standing with him.

Reece kept his eyes on the three. "Ok. We need to make this quick."

"We are ready," Nathaniel said.

The guard who had looked their way turned around again. He had picked up their voices. He motioned with his head for the other two to follow him, weapons raised.

"You know what to do." Reece's gaze moved from Andre to Nathaniel and they both nodded.

ℰᗩᏟᎡ

Ed's face creased into a skeptical frown. "Yeah? But where? Doesn't the mountain range cover eleven hundred miles?" He folded his arms over his protruding belly.

"That is true, but Van Helsing's journal mentions certain geographical landmarks which will make it easier for us to locate Vlad's hiding place." Jacques raised a hand to his goateed chin. "When can you be ready to leave?"

"We hired a car so we can leave anytime," Lozano told him.

"Good. I'll meet you in the lobby in twenty minutes. Wear something… inconspicuous."

"What does that mean?" Ed asked.

"Something that will blend into the night."

"Right." He and Lozano headed out the door and down the hallway to the elevator. "I don't trust him."

"Me neither, but right now we need his vampire senses to help find Reece and the others." Lozano poked the down button, his eyes moving to the numbers above the door.

"We need to watch our backs with him around. My gut's telling me he had something to do with all of this."

The pair stepped into the elevator.

"Don't worry. We'll have protection." The sheriff pushed back the left-hand front of his jacket to reveal a Glock pistol tucked into its holster. "Silver."

"Now you're talkin'." Ed gave him a crooked smile.

CHAPTER FORTY FOUR

Eva sat alone in her cell. Where had they taken her team? Had they been executed? For the first time in centuries she felt vulnerable, defenseless and afraid. Was it Vlad's intension to attempt to unnerve her? To get her to choose sides? She jumped to her feet. *That will never happen.* Her thoughts turned to the PI and his crew. *What has happened to them?* Eva had had no plans to kill them. She was there to help. To rid their world and humanity's of such monsters as Vlad Tepes and Jacques Delacroix. She'd needed a ploy to get Jacques to travel to Bucharest. Her notion had been to move Reece and his team out of harm's way and now they were in the thick of it. Had Jacques arrived in Romania as planned? And if so, would he realize they were in trouble and devise a way to rescue them?

The padlock outside clanged against the metal door. Someone was about to enter her cell. Eva pressed her back to the concrete wall for protection. The door swung open on squealing hinges, the sound echoing around the box-like room.

"You will come with me." It was the vampire that had ordered them out of the truck on the road.

"Where are you taking me?" Eva stepped away from the wall. Could she subdue this immortal and secure her escape? It was worth a try. Without hesitation, her right leg swung out and connected with the side of his left knee. It buckled, bringing him crashing to the floor, but before she could race out the door he grabbed her booted ankle and tugged her to her knees. She flipped over, baring her fangs, her fist connecting with the middle of his face causing blood to trickle from both nostrils. He ran his hand under his nose, frowned at the dark smear across his knuckles and was on his feet in an instant. So was she. They stared into each other's pale immortal eyes, circling the small space. Fangs bared. She needed to anticipate his next move otherwise she would be trapped once again.

The soldier lunged and she darted out of the way, shoving her foot into the center of his back, knocking him to the floor. Before he could spring to his feet, she rammed the sole of her boot into the nape of his neck. "If you move I will crush your spine."

He raised a defensive hand. "What do you want?"

"Where are my men and the others?"

"I cannot tell you."

Eva pressed her foot down harder. "Do you really want to die for nothing?"

"If I tell you I am dead anyway."

"So be it." A sharp snap resonated around the concrete walls. The broken neck wouldn't kill him but it would render him useless for a short period of time. She would leave him to his fate. Eva dashed out the door, padlocking it before heading along the dimly lit corridor. She had to find Dumitru and the others.

℘ℭ

Reece waved Sarah and Todd over. They had to be quick. "Todd, you change into his gear. Andre, you change into his. He pointed at the dead immortals lying on the ground. "And grab their coms and radios. We need communication in there." He passed a device to Nathaniel. "Once we're inside and have eliminated more of Dracula's soldiers I'll let you know." He needed all of his team together.

"Very well. We will remain here." Nathaniel pressed the small communication capsule into his ear and ran his gaze around the compound. He had a bad feeling.

"What about me?" Sarah asked.

"You can disguise yourself in one of the uniforms, too. Just wait here with Nathaniel until we secure ground level." Reece changed into the camouflage gear, pulled the mask up to his eyes, picked up the automatic M16A4 rifle, gave Andre and Todd an intense stare and said, "Ok. Let's go." His gut churned as he eased his body around the corner of the building followed by Todd and Andre. Would they finally defeat Dracula and rid the world of a monster? Charlotte jumped into his head. Where was she? Was she still herself? He prayed for Tommy's sake she was. All he could do right now was hope. That's all they had.

₧)₨₧

Eva used her vampire senses to locate Dumitru and his team. When she reached the cell, she forced the lock and threw open the door. "Let's get out of here. We have to find Reece and the others."

Dumitru stood. "And how do you expect us to do that?"

She shrugged. "How else? We search and take down anyone who gets in our way."

"We are unarmed. And what about Vlad?"

"We do not need weapons, we are immortals. We will deal with Vlad when the time comes."

The other members of the team climbed up off the floor.

"Let's go." Eva peered around the door into the dim corridor. "Now."

₧)₨₧

Nathaniel and Sarah had joined Reece, Andre, and Todd and were making their way to the elevators across the deserted lobby. They had managed to take out five of Dracula's men but had no idea how many more were in the building. When they reached the double oversized lifts, the PI was surprised to see that the two story building was only a façade. There were at least fifteen levels below ground. "There has to be a floor for holding prisoners. It's most likely in the lower basement, so we'll head down there first and see if we can find Eva and her team."

Todd and Nathaniel stood facing the main entrance, weapons in hand, scanning the foyer. No time for surprises. The first elevator jerked to a stop, the large, metal door sliding open to reveal no one inside. Reece and his team filed inside. Traveling into the bowels of Vlad's enterprise would put them in a life-threatening situation and they needed to keep their wits about them. No one knew where Dracula or his men were. The elevator descended into darkness and came to an abrupt stop on the LB level. The door slid open and Nathaniel turned to the others. "Ready?"

Reece peered around the opening. The dim corridor extended in both directions.

Todd walked over and gazed along the darkened passage. "Maybe we should split up."

The PI swung around. "No. We stay together. I'm not risking anyone's life here."

"We can cover more ground if…"

"I said no."

"Ok. So what do we do? We're wasting time."

"We'll go left first and see what's down there then we'll take the right."

Sarah stepped up to the pair. "Todd's right. We can cover more ground if we split up. We have communication so whoever finds Eva and her team first can let the rest of us know. We have weapons, we're not defenseless."

Reece gave a heavy sigh. He wanted to keep everyone safe but knew they were right. "All right. Let's make it fast. We'll meet back here in ten minutes."

Everyone agreed. Todd, Sarah, and Nathaniel took the left and Reece and Andre took the right. Peering over his shoulder, the PI couldn't see the others heading in the opposite direction. His stomach squeezed into a tight knot of nerves. They were setting themselves up to be ambushed and he didn't like it.

"Where do you think Charlotte is being held?" he asked Andre.

"I can't say for sure, but she is here."

The PI eyed his friend sideways. "How're you feeling?"

Andre turned his head and stared into Reece's questioning eyes. "I'm fine. Don't worry, I'm not about to do anything to get us killed, if that's what you're concerned about."

"That's not what I meant. I'm concerned about you. You're my friend."

Andre gave him a thin smile. "Sorry. I guess I'm projecting what's bothering me onto you."

Reece's right eyebrow arched. "So you're worried about yourself?"

"I do have my brother's blood running through my veins. Of course I am."

As Reece came to an intersecting passage he heard a noise echo toward him. He and Andre raised their weapons and stood their ground waiting for whoever was approaching them.

The vampire hunter stepped into the dim light.

"Eva!"

"Reece! How did you get down here?"

"We took out some of Dracula's men and used their camouflage gear to disguise ourselves. It's gotten us this far."

"Where are the others?" Eva gazed into the gloom behind the pair.

"They went the other way." He turned to Andre. "Let them know we've found Eva and her team."

Andre activated his com and told Sarah, Todd, and Nathaniel to head back to the elevator. They'd meet there.

"Have you seen Vlad?"

Eva shook her head. "No."

"He has to be here somewhere. Charlotte's here."

"Yes. I can sense her."

"Is she... is she ok?" Reece frowned into Eva's eyes. He could've asked Andre but the thought only just crossed his mind.

"Her heart beats. She is still human, if that is what you mean."

The PI gave a relieved sigh. "Good to know." He waited a beat. "How did we get here?"

"That is a long story. One we do not have time for right now." Eva gave him a sheepish glance.

"It's a simple question. We were in the back of a laundry truck. Who put us there?"

The vampire hunter raised her chin, her eyes remaining on him. "I did."

"What?!" He ran a hand across the stubble on his chin. "You're working with Jacques, aren't you? That's why you went to LA, isn't it?"

"It is not what you think. I needed a way to get Jacques here, so I told him I would help him get rid of you and your friends."

"And that's why he gave you the journal?"

"Yes. We needed its knowledge."

"I can't believe you'd do something like that without telling me. How can I trust you?"

"Because you have no other choice, Reece Daniels. Between us both we must rid the world of Dracula and Jacques Delacroix for all time. There is no room for them here."

She was right. They did need to work together if they were going to complete their mission and get out of this alive. Even so, he knew he'd have to watch his and his friends' backs because he couldn't trust her anymore.

"There are many levels to this underground complex. We need to find Charlotte and deal with Vlad. How do you want to proceed?"

CHAPTER FORTY FIVE

Lozano was behind the wheel with Ed in the passenger seat beside him. Jacques sat in back watching the pair as they traveled the road to Dracula's secret compound at the base of the Carpathian Mountains. Ed kept checking the rear view mirror, even though he couldn't see Jacques' reflection in it, and that unnerved him. Being in such close proximity to Andre's brother made his over-sized belly quiver. His gaze moved from the mirror to Lozano and the sheriff gave him a sideward glance.

"How long till we get there?" Ed asked Jacques, turning and gazing between the front seats over his shoulder.

"It is another couple of hours." He could sense the unease in both men and he relished the sensation. "Don't worry, I'm not hungry. I had a snack on the plane that will keep me satisfied for a while longer." He smirked to himself.

"Thanks for sharing." Ed swallowed hard. They were sitting ducks.

"As I already told you, I am here to help get your friends back. You are safe with me." *For now, anyhow.* He needed to get to his brother.

Ed swiveled in his seat and faced Jacques front on. "Why'd you do it?"

Jacques' left eyebrow arched. "Do what, exactly?"

"Give Andre your blood? It wasn't part of the resurrection ritual, was it?"

"I wanted him by my side again as my brother. My twin. Is that so hard to believe?"

Ed shook his head. "Sorry, but I don't buy it. You've got something else up your sleeve."

The lieutenant was more astute than Jacques had given him credit for. "I can assure you I do not."

Ed's face wrinkled into a skeptical frown. "Yeah? Don't think so."

"Well, you will have to wait and see, won't you?" Jacques folded his arms and gazed out of the window at the swiftly passing forest of trees. At his command, Andre would do whatever he wanted and that would be Reece Daniels' downfall. A satisfied smirk spread across his pale, handsome face. He would finally be rid of the meddling PI and his friends, and his brother would once again belong to him.

℠℣

Charlotte woke up inside an open coffin lined with red velvet, a white satin pillow beneath her head. A scream threatened to escape her lips but she held it in and sprang up, her anxious eyes darting around the dim space that contained no windows, a tall, brass candelabra with three, burning white candles standing on the floor behind her head. Where was she? How did she get here? She pulled herself up and climbed out of the casket, giving a shiver as she gazed over her shoulder at the deep mahogany chamber. A terrifying thought crossed her mind. Had Vlad turned her? Is that why she had been lying in a coffin? A cold sweat poured over her and a tear slipped down her right cheek. She swiped it away. What would happen to Tommy if she was a… a vampire?

She crossed the room to the gray metal door and tugged on the handle. Of course it was locked.

A sudden thought shot adrenalin through her body and she pressed two fingers to her wrist. She had a pulse. She laughed as relief washed over her. She wasn't a monster she was still human. Thank God! But then the realization of being Dracula's prisoner pulled her out of her reverie. How could she get out of here and get back to her son? Where were Reece and the others? Were they looking for her? She had to believe they were. They had to be, unless something had happened to them. Charlotte pounded on the door. "Can anyone hear me? Let me out of here." She had to figure out a way to save herself.

CR

Reece stopped in his tracks and swung around. "Did you hear that?"

Everyone behind him pulled up short.

"Yes. It sounded like it came from down there." Sarah pointed along the shadowed corridor.

"It was Charlotte's voice." Todd stepped up to him. "I'm sure of it."

"Andre? Nathaniel?"

"It did sound like Charlotte," Andre said.

"Let's go." Reece stalked along the passage. "Charlotte? Charlotte where are you?"

Charlotte's ears pricked up. Was that Reece? Her heart beat ticked up several notches. "Reece, I'm here. I'm here," she called frantically through the door. He had come to rescue her.

"Down here!" Reece broke into a run.

The group followed him.

"Charlotte?"

"In here. I'm here. Please get me out." She pressed her cheek and her palms to the cold metal as tears of joy slid down her face. "I'm here," she called out again.

Reece stopped outside a locked door and leaned in to hear. "Charlotte, are you in there?"

"Yes."

"Step back."

"All right." She moved aside.

The PI aimed his rifle at the lock.

"Wait!" Eva gripped his arm. "If you fire that you'll be letting Vlad's men know where we are."

"They already know. We've been using their transmission devices, so where are they?"

Eva's eyes widened. "That was a stupid move. Do you want to get us all killed?"

"Let's face it. Dracula wants us here. That's why he hasn't sent anyone to capture us. Now let me get Charlotte out of there."

Eva stepped aside. There was no way Vlad would allow them to leave this underground prison. She knew they were trapped.

ℰℐℂℛ

The sheriff pulled the rental into a dirt clearing among the tall European Beech trees and turned off the engine. The gated compound stood fifty feet along the single lane road. He glanced over at Ed, his stomach doing a nervous flip flop, then turned in his seat and looked at Jacques. "So what do we do now we're here?"

The vampire's gaze moved from him to Ed then back again. "We wait."

Ed swiveled in his seat and frowned at Jacques between the front seats. "For what?"

"I have help coming. What do you think the three of us could do alone?"

"Why didn't you say somethin' then?" Ed's gut shrank beneath his belt.

"Would you have come with me if you'd known?" Jacques' left eyebrow arched.

"Ok. I get that. But you said we were working together so don't keep things from us. How do you expect us to trust you when you do this kind of stuff?"

"Fair comment." Not that he cared what the lieutenant thought.

"So how many are coming?" Lozano asked.

"Ten."

Ed's brow wrinkled even further. "You know ten vamps living in Romania?"

"I have forged *many* alliances over my immortal lifetime, but, unfortunately, it was all I could organize on such short notice."

"Do you think they'll be enough?"

"They will have to do. We are out of time."

A knock on the back passenger window startled Ed and Lozano and their eyes moved to the sound. The sheriff pressed the button on his armrest and the pane of glass glided into the door.

"We are here. What is the situation?"

"We do not know. Vlad has captured several humans and a team of vampires led by Eva Van Helsing."

"The vampire hunter?"

"Yes. Is there a problem?"

The vampire leaning into the window shook his head. "No. We are here to assist you in any way we can."

"Thank you."

"What is your strategy?"

"To get inside, of course."

At that moment, two of the vampire's men appeared beside him and he pushed himself out of the window to speak with them. After a couple of minutes he leaned in again. "The fence is not electrified. We should be able to get over it at a point where we will not be seen."

"Good." Jacques flung the back passenger door open and stepped out of the car, his eyes moving to the two law enforcement officers in the front seats. "Are you coming?"

Ed and Lozano glanced at each other then stepped out of the rental. "How are we getting over the wall? It looks high." Ed knew he couldn't climb it.

"You'll be carried across." Jacques turned on his heel and followed the vampire into the woods to his team.

The sheriff frowned at Ed. "What does that mean?"

"Some vamps can fly."

"You mean…"

"Yep."

Lozano's gaze moved to the metal fence ahead of them and he swallowed hard. He wasn't good with heights. He turned to look at Ed. "And you're ok with that?"

Ed shrugged. "Sure. If it's the only way we can get inside."

The sheriff let out a nervous huff. "Ok."

❧

Charlotte threw herself into Reece's arms and sobbed. "I never thought I'd ever get out of here. I never thought I'd see you or Tommy again. When I woke up in that coffin I thought… Thank you for coming for me." Her tear-filled eyes looked up at him.

Reece held her tight. It felt good to have her in his arms again. He'd missed her body close to his. "I made you a promise, Charlotte. I'll always come for you, no matter what?"

Eva stepped up to the pair. "There is no time for happy reunions. We need to keep moving."

"Is there another way out of here?" Reece's eyes moved to the vampire hunter and he eased Charlotte out of his embrace.

"I do not know. There has not been enough time to investigate, but from what I have seen so far it appears there are only the lifts. These corridors go around in a square back to the elevator banks."

"All right. Let's get back there and see if we can get upstairs."

Eva had misgivings. She knew Vlad only too well and assumed that by now the elevators would be inoperable. "What if the power has been cut to them?"

"Then we prize open one of the doors, lift the hatch in the ceiling and climb up." Reece was determined to get to Dracula one way or the other.

"Very well. But I doubt we will make it. It is a long way back to ground level."

"We don't have a choice, Eva. We need to end this today.

☙

Once over the wall, the vampire squad, Jacques, Ed and Lozano circled the compound around the rock wall and entered the building. Where were Vlad's men? The building appeared deserted. Perhaps that's what Vlad wanted them to believe. Perhaps his men were waiting to ambush them when there was no way to escape. The ground level was indeed empty and Jacques had a bad feeling about the entire situation. His intense, immortal gaze roamed the lobby and fell upon the elevator bank to his left. Wandering over to one lift, he glanced at the numbers on the panel. So, the building extended underground. He turned to the others. "We need to get below."

"The elevators do not appear to be working," the lead vampire offered. "I have someone who can check the electrical circuits." He waved one of his team over. "This is Vasile. He is an expert with electrical devices."

"Good. See if you can get the elevators working." Jacques watched Vasile open a panel in the wall with the tip of his combat knife. Inside looked like a larger version of a computer's motherboard. "Can you fix it?"

"I will not know until I check all the circuits."

"How long will that take?"

"It depends on if anything needs to be repaired."

"Then get on with it. We need to get below." Jacques strutted away from the pair. All he wanted was to get to his brother, nothing more. The others could deal with Vlad on their own.

Twenty minutes ticked by and Jacques was frustrated. He marched over to Vasile.

"How much longer? We are running out of time."

The vampire glanced over his shoulder. "I am about to test it now."

"Good. Hurry up."

Vasile flipped a switch and the numbers on the elevator panel lit up.

"Let's get inside. We will go down to the lower level and start there." Jacques stepped into the first lift, Ed and Lozano behind him.

The other vampire and his men stepped into the second lift.

℘

Reece, Eva and their teams made their way back to the elevators. "They're moving," Reece said.

"It must be Vlad and his men." Eva took a step backwards.

"Then we'll confront them head on." Reece raised his automatic rifle. "Wait until the doors open then fire."

Todd, Sarah and Andre raised their weapons.

Eva's team stepped into position beside them, their retrieved weapons raised ready to fire.

The tension in the air was palpable as the numbers on the elevator panel descended.

Reece's heartrate ticked up several notches and his breath caught in his throat. This was it. Their moment of truth.

CHAPTER FORTY SIX

Only three more floors to go and the elevator doors would open. The final battle was about to begin. Reece's gut tightened and he swallowed hard. "Are we ready?" Everyone gave a resounding 'yes.' "Ok, let's do this. On my count. One, two..."

"Wait," Andre shouted. "It's not Dracula."

Reece swung around and frowned at him. "How can you be so sure?"

The doors slid open and the PI turned to see who was inside. "What are you doing here?"

Jacques stepped out. "Well that's a nice thank you for coming to the rescue."

Ed and Lozano appeared behind him. "Reece." Ed rushed up to him and pulled him into a tight man hug. "I'm so glad you're all ok. We, Lozano and I, decided to fly over here to help you and when we found you were missing we had no choice but to set out on a rescue mission. Jacques arrived to see Andre so we thought we could use his skills and contacts to get the job done."

The second elevator door opened and the vampire team stepped out.

"Who are they?" Reece's severe stare met Jacques'.

"They're the cavalry."

"Have you seen any sign of Vlad or his men?"

"The ground floor level is completely deserted. But that doesn't mean they are not here." Jacques gave Eva a dark stare before returning his gaze to the PI. "We need to get back upstairs before anything else happens to prevent us from leaving."

Reece had to agree. "Ok. Let's get out of here."

Everyone piled into both lifts. Reece and his team with Jacques, Ed and Lozano.

"Why are you here, Jacques?"

"As the lieutenant already told you, I came to offer my assistance."

"But why?" Reece's stern gaze met the vampire's.

"I was concerned for the safety of my brother." He glanced at Andre over his shoulder.

Reece gave him a skeptical frown. "You don't care about anyone but yourself. There has to be another reason."

He returned his gaze to the PI. "As I told the lieutenant, there is not. Why so suspicious?"

"Because I know you."

"You mean you think you do."

"If what you say is true then... thanks." The expression of gratitude stuck in his throat because he didn't believe a word of it. He knew there had to be another reason for Jacques being in Romania.

"You are welcome."

The lift jolted and came to a complete stop.

"What just happened?" Charlotte asked, her breath short and sharp, her eyes darting around the claustrophobic space.

"I don't know." Reece looked at Jacques.

"Don't look at me. I had nothing to do with it."

"Can you get in touch with your guys?"

"No. Can you contact Eva?"

"They took our phones, so no." Reece huffed out a frustrated breath.

Several sets of footsteps dropped onto the outer ceiling.

"Reece raised his automatic rifle and fired in a zig zag pattern above them. Everyone dropped to the floor, debris raining down on them as the lights went out.

"What are you doin', Daniels?" Ed asked, his voice gruff. "Do ya wanna kill us all with ricocheting bullets?"

"That wasn't the plan, no. I was trying to prevent us from being killed by Dracula's men." He lowered his weapon.

"I doubt you had any effect on them," Jacques told him. "Unless there is silver in that rifle."

Reece turned his intense gaze to the Swiss cheese ceiling, trying to ascertain if the militia was still up there. "I don't hear anything, do you?"

"They will be waiting for our next move."

At that moment, the lift started its ascent again.

"Yeah, at ground level it seems." Reece checked his ammunition and roamed the pallid faces of his friends. "We have weapons. So let's use them. The moment that door opens we fire. No second thoughts. Got it?"

Everyone nodded.

"You will not have enough ammunition to defeat them all," Jacques said.

"Do you think the others are on their way up?"

"What do you think? Vlad is not about to offer a level playing field." Jacques' left eyebrow arched. "Is he?"

"So we get off before we reach the top." Reece pushed buttons on the elevator's console but it wouldn't stop.

"Any other ideas?" Todd asked.

Only seven more floors before they reached ground level.

The PI whipped a combat knife out of a pocket of his pants and began undoing the control panel screws. "Maybe I can smash some circuits and stop the elevator."

"It's worth a try," Ed said, moving over and taking Reece's rifle from his hand.

With the console cover removed, Reece studied the circuits and wiring. He cut a red wire then a blue one. The lift kept moving. He turned his knife around and rammed the handle into the circuitry. The elevator ground to a halt. "Ok, let's climb up and see if we can open one of the doors."

The metal exterior of the lift's ceiling was riddled with bullet holes but managed to support their combined weight, nonetheless. Reece gazed up at the next level door. "If we climb up there we should be able to get that open and get out of this lift well."

At that moment, a loud crash was heard from within the cubicle below their feet. Reece peered inside. Jacques and Andre were gone.

"What the hell?!"

Todd leaned closer to the trap door. "Where'd they go?"

The PI shook his head. "Your guess is as good as mine. I knew Jacques was up to something."

CR

"Where are we going?" Andre asked as Jacques held him tight against his side and flew down to the floor they had just traveled up from. "We're meant to be fighting alongside Reece and his team. They won't stand a chance without us."

"And we will. But for now I have to release the other vampires from the stalled elevator."

"So we're going back to help Reece?" Andre wasn't sure he could trust his brother.

"Of course." Jacques hoped that by the time they reached ground level the battle would be over and the PI and his *friends* would be dead. He needed to delay his vampire team from reaching them in time.

"Why don't I believe you?" Andre could sense something was wrong.

"I don't know. I am here, am I not?" He lowered his brother onto the lift well floor and peeled back the metal door as though it were the skin of an orange. "After you."

Andre stepped out through the misshapen hole into the elevator lobby, Jacques close behind him. "Now what?"

"Now we release my team along with that meddling vampire hunter and hers. If we plan to vanquish Vlad then we will need everyone's assistance." Jacques walked across to the elevator and ripped the door from its track. The vampires and Eva and her team were gone. Jacques' dark gaze roamed the cubicle. The ceiling trap door was open. "It appears they've escaped." His long, slim index finger shot up and Andre leaned in to look at where he was pointing.

"They'll be able to help Reece and the others."

"Yes, won't they?" Jacques was not happy about this new twist in his plan. "Well, then, we had better join them." He gripped his brother's arm and lifted them both through the opening in the ceiling.

The second level elevator door had been forced open. Jacques dropped himself and Andre just inside. "There must be a set of stairs around here somewhere."

"Then let's find them and get up there." Andre rushed forward into the gloom.

"Wait." Jacques followed him.

"For what? We need to go now."

Jacques grabbed his brother's arm to stop him and stared deep into his eyes. "You will not attempt to help Reece if it appears he will be killed. Understood?"

Andre nodded blankly at his brother.

"Good. Carry on."

"What just happened?" Andre asked.

"What do mean. We're on our way to help your friends."

Andre frowned into Jacques' eyes. "Yes, I know, but something happened."

"I do not understand, brother. As far as I am aware nothing happened."

Andre shook the foggy sensation from his brain and continued forward. He seemed to have blacked out for a moment. What had his brother done to him?

By the time Andre and Jacques made it up to the lobby the fight was over. Reece, Charlotte, Sarah, Nathaniel, Todd, Ed and Lozano stood in the center of the circle of bodies covered in blood, some of it their own. They had fought to the death and had successfully defeated Dracula's army. Eva and her team stood near the glassed entrance, and the vampires Jacques had enlisted were in front of the closed elevator doors. Jacques' eyes roamed the mound of bodies looking for his nemesis.

"Where is Vlad?" he asked Reece.

The PI ran his hand over his sweaty, blood-streaked face. "He isn't here."

"But that cannot be. This is his lair, his hideaway. He has to be here somewhere."

"As you can see he's not." Reece huffed out a frustrated breath and pulled Charlotte into his arms. "You ok?"

She looked up at him and nodded. "Yes, I'm fine."

Eva strutted over to Reece. "It is a good thing he was not here. If you kill him Charlotte and anyone else who has his blood running through their veins will die."

Reece swung around and glared at the vampire hunter. "So why didn't you tell me that before? What if he had been here?"

"I only discovered it when I overheard some of his men in conversation." She folded her arms and raised her chin. It was a lie, of course. She had read it in her grandfather's journal.

"And you forgot to share that important piece of information with me before we came up here? You could've told me at any time while we were searching for Charlotte."

"Well now you know." She strutted back to her team.

"How are we going to stop him if we can't kill him?" Charlotte's wide eyes met Reece's and a single tear slid down her cheek.

"We'll figure out a way. There has to be something we can do." His stern gaze met Jacques'. "Did you know about this?"

"I may have heard something in my travels, but you cannot believe everything you hear. I assumed it was a ploy to keep Vlad from being killed."

Reece gave a heavy sigh. "Or you wanted Charlotte to die, just like you want the rest of us to."

"I came here to help you. Don't forget that." Jacques stalked over to the PI.

"Yeah? How strange, then, that you weren't here when we needed you."

"I took Andre with me so we could release the others and make it a fair fight."

"Keep telling yourself that, Jacques. We both know that's not the real reason you're here."

"I think we should get back to Bucharest and decide what to do next," Eva suggested. "Vlad will not return here. He will be on his way to another of his safe locations."

Reece turned around. "And where would that be, exactly?"

Eva shrugged. "I do not know."

"So we've lost him? Is that what you're saying?" He folded his arms and glowered at her.

"All is not lost… yet." She smirked.

CHAPTER FORTY SEVEN

The lone traveler sat at the rear of the elegant, Gulfstream G650 private jet in one of the comfortable, large, cream leather passenger seats and gazed out at the night sky. He would fly back to Los Angeles and orchestrate his next plan of attack. The PI and his team would learn of his departure soon enough and would be on their way back to the United States in search of him, and when that eventuated he would be ready for them. It was time to end this charade.

A pretty, brunette flight attendant came toward him with a tray. Sitting in the center was a tall glass of what looked like red wine, but it was not. He had mesmerized the crew when he had first stepped on board, so there would be no discrepancies in each of their recollections should they be queried by authorities about the nature of the flight and its passenger. He was merely a business man on route to a meeting.

Vlad smiled up at the attractive, young woman and as she leaned in to set his drink down on the small table between the seats he pulled her to him and sank his fangs into the soft, warm flesh of her throat, drinking deeply. He hated cold blood and much preferred consuming the life-giving elixir form its source. She would not remember what had occurred.

He eased her petite frame out of his embrace; his tongue slipping from the corner of his mouth to erase any trace of her blood from his chin, then smiled up at her, thanked her for the drink, and allowed her to return to the small kitchen at the back of the plane. She was a tasty morsel and he would imbibe once more before landing in the City of Angels. After all, he needed to increase his strength for what lay ahead.

ഇൗരു

Intel relayed by one of Eva's contacts in Bucharest told them Dracula had left the city by private jet and was on his way back to Los Angeles. Reece's gut tightened into a tangle of tingling nerves when he heard the news. Why hadn't the monster ran? What was he planning?

There wasn't anyone else in the city that the vampire could use to manipulate them. So why go there. A thought dashed across his mind. Tommy, Charlotte's son was there and the PI knew that Dracula would use any means necessary to get what he wanted. The look on his face frightened Charlotte.

She crossed the room to him. "What is it?" She reached out and touched his arm. He let her.

"Nothing." He couldn't bring himself to tell her his suspicions.

"I know you too well to believe that, Reece. What's wrong?" Her eyes met his and she frowned into them.

"Honestly, it's nothing." He pulled her to him and held her. Something he hadn't done in a while. It felt comforting.

Charlotte wasn't accepting his word. She tugged herself out of his arms and stared into his eyes. "I need you to be honest with me. You realized something… what is it?"

The others in the room turned to look at the pair.

"Everything ok, Daniels?" Ed asked.

"Yeah, everything's fine."

"No it's not," Charlotte said. "I can tell there's something on your mind so share it with us. We need to know."

Reece gave a heavy sigh and folded his arms. What could he do? Charlotte wasn't letting this go. "Ok. We've learned Dracula is on his way back to LA, right?" Everyone nodded. "At first I wondered why because there isn't anyone there he could use to manipulate us into submission, but…"

Charlotte gasped and raised her hand to her mouth. "Oh, my God! You think he's gone back there for Tommy, don't you?"

Reece's eyes roamed the faces in the room before returning to Charlotte. "Yes, I do."

Todd sprang from the foot of the bed. "Then we need to get back there ASAP!"

"And we will. We have our return flights; we just need to organize a time."

"Then what are we waitin' for, Daniels? Let's get goin'." Ed was on his feet and marching across the room to the door. Sarah behind him.

"All right. I'll give the airline a call and try to get the next available flight out. If not, we'll stay at the airport on standby in case something opens up. Let's meet in the Lobby in fifteen."

"Make it ten," Todd said as he dashed across the room and out the door.

Reece's gaze returned to Charlotte. "I didn't want to upset you. I hope you understand."

She nodded. "I do. But when it comes to my son, our son, you need to be honest with me. I can handle it."

"I don't doubt that." His heart ached for her right now and he hoped they could intercept Dracula's plan before Tommy's life was placed in more jeopardy. "Go get packed. I'll see you downstairs."

Once everyone cleared the room, Reece called departures to arrange their flight. As luck would have it, they could be on the next flight out at 6:00 AM. He glanced at the luminous red numerals on the bedside clock radio. 4:27 AM. They would need to hurry because Dracula already had a head start.

The next port of call was to phone Mrs. Jenkins. He calculated the time difference. It would be around 6:30 PM yesterday in LA right now. Tommy should be home. "Hi, Mrs. J, it's me. Where's Tommy?"

Mrs. Jenkins could feel something was wrong right away by the sound of Reece's voice. "He's at an after school event working on a Science project for the upcoming carnival. I was just on my way to pick him up. Why?"

"I need you to get to the school ASAP and take Tommy somewhere none of us know about. Do you have a place you can go?"

"Yes, I know a place. What's going on, Reece?"

"Dracula's on his way back to LA. I believe he's coming for Tommy." Mrs. Jenkins had been very receptive when he and Charlotte had sat her down to discuss what they did and to warn her about the things that were in their world. She'd told them she had always believed in such things. Humanity couldn't be that arrogant as to believe we were alone in the universe.

The old woman gasped. "Oh no!"

"Yeah. I need you to go *now*."

"I'm leaving right away."

"Thank you. Keep your cell phone handy. I'll call you once we're back on home soil."

"Please be careful. Tommy needs you."

"We will. Just keep out of sight and don't tell anyone where you're going."

"Don't worry. I won't." Mrs. Jenkins ended the call, dropped her cell into her purse, shrugged into her coat and headed out the door. She was determined to keep Tommy safe.

ℰ◯ℭ

The Gulfstream G650 taxied along the runway and stopped beneath the shadow of the hangar at the private airstrip. A sleek, black sedan with fully tinted windows idled nearby, the driver waiting beside the open back door for his passenger to depart the plane. After over fifteen hours in the air, Vlad wanted to head to his secret location in Mission Beach to prepare for the final confrontation with the PI and his team. In hindsight, he wished he had eliminated Eva Van Helsing from the equation when he had her prisoner because she was relentless in her pursuit of him and would not stop.

He had also been made privy to the fact that the priest had contacted someone at the Vatican to obtain information that could potentially end his immortal life. Thankfully, that information never reached her and the person involved had been, shall we say, excommunicated. A satisfied smirk crossed Vlad's ruggedly handsome face but disappeared in an instant when he recalled that the vampire hunter had her grandfather's journal. He would need to make certain adjustments to protect himself.

The jet's circular door hissed open and he descended the nine steps onto the tarmac, crossed the asphalt to the waiting limousine, and stepped inside. His plan to abduct Charlotte Delaney's son and hold him to ransom, so to speak, would prevent them from initiating an all-out attack on him. The boy would be his insurance policy – at least for the now.

Inside the sleek, black sedan, Vlad used the car phone to make contact with associates that could offer their assistance. Once everything was in place, he would contact the PI and arrange a tradeoff. The vampire's life for the boy's. He poured himself a glass of blended, Cabernet Franc and enjoyed the mouth-watering, peppery flavor. It wasn't blood but it would suffice.

He thought it best to choose a rental property with an unassuming demeanor, nothing over-the-top this time. Nothing to draw attention to himself until he was prepared. The driver pulled into the driveway, climbed out and opened the back right-hand door for his passenger. Vlad stepped out of the limousine and handed him a hundred dollar bill. "Thank you."

"You're most welcome, sir," the driver said, tipping his hat.

"I will require your services tomorrow evening. Can that be arranged?"

"Of course. What time would you like me here?"

"Nine PM. I have a late business meeting."

"Very well. I'll be here." He climbed into the limousine and drove away.

Vlad's eyes roamed the three story, gray and white wood-clad house. It would do. He walked over to the mailbox, opened it and retrieved the keys, then climbed the front steps, pushed the key into the lock and swung the glass paneled door back. Simple but elegant. Polished wood floors gave the home a warm feeling and the furnishings reminded him of a bygone era, which he much preferred. He stepped into the entry hall and pushed the door closed behind him. It would be his home for only a few days.

The boy would be taken from the school and brought to this location. Vlad would then make the call to Reece Daniels clarifying his demands. It was not a negotiation. If they did not withdraw the boy would be his. A fate worse than death the PI believed. The vampire knew that a ten year old was too young to be a blood drinker, but if need be he would follow through with his threat.

CHAPTER FORTY EIGHT

Reece, his team, Eva and Jacques arrived at LAX just after 10:00 AM, picked up their van from the long term parking garage, and made their way over to Double D investigations. They had no time to lose in finding Dracula and a way to contain him until they could figure out how to end him without the people he had infected falling prey to his demise. The PI knew the vampire hadn't returned to Los Angeles on a regular airline and wondered where the plane had landed. There were a number of private airstrips in the state and Dracula could have set down at any one of them.

He opened the glass paneled door to his office, swung it back, and motioned for everyone to step inside. He'd be right back; he had a call to make. Descending the stairs, he stepped out onto the sidewalk and keyed in the number. "Mrs. J, everything all right? You're at the safe location?"

"Yes, we are." She sounded flustered. "Tommy's been asking all sorts of questions and I don't know what to tell him."

Reece sighed into the phone. "Put him on. I'll talk to him." How was he going to explain it to a ten year old? The question circled his brain for a moment. Be honest with him, at least as much as he could be.

"Hey, Reece, how's it going? Is mom with you?"

"Uh, no, she's upstairs. I just stepped out to get some fresh air and thought I'd give you a call."

"Can I... ask you something?" Tommy's voice sounded tentative and Reece knew what was coming.

"Sure, buddy, anything. You know I'd never lie to you, right?"

"Yeah, I know."

"So what's the question?"

"Well, Mrs. J says we have to stay here for a while and that I can't go to school. What's going on?"

"While your mom and I were in Vegas, we encountered a bad man. One who tried to hurt us…"

"But you're both ok, right?"

The urgency in Tommy's voice caused Reece's heart to clench.

"Yeah, buddy, we're fine."

Tommy gave a relieved sigh. "That's good."

"He threatened us and said he'd hurt the people we love so…"

"So you want to keep me safe so he can't fine me?"

"Yeah, we do. What I want you to do for me is not to worry. Ok? We're on his trail right now and we'll capture him soon then everything will go back to normal." He knew nothing would ever be normal, so, technically, that was a lie. Hopefully it would be considered a small white one by the man upstairs.

"Ok, Reece, I'll do my best."

"That's all we can ask for. Oh, and one more thing. Please listen to Mrs. J. She loves you, too, and wants to keep you safe."

Tommy nodded, even though Reece couldn't see it. "I will. I promise."

"Thank you. Look, I have to go. But I'll ask your mom to give you a call. Ok?"

"Ok. Tell her I miss her."

"I will. She misses you too, so do I. See ya, buddy. Can you put Mrs. J back on?"

"Yep, sure. See ya."

"What did you tell him," the old woman asked.

"I told him a partial truth. That a bad man had threatened to hurt the people we love and that you brought him to the place he's at now to protect him."

Mrs. J breathed a relieved sigh. "Thank you, Reece. I'm glad he knows something, at least."

"He's a good kid. He'll do what's right. I don't expect you'll have any problems with him while you're there."

"I know he's a good boy and I'm sure he'll listen to me. He always has."

"Ok. I've got to go. I'll be in touch again in the next couple days. If you have any issues you know I'm only a phone call away."

"I know. Thank you."

"Be safe."

"You too."

When Reece turned around Charlotte was standing on the steps behind him. "How much of that did you hear?"

"A little." She stepped down onto the sidewalk. "How is he?"

"Worried. But he's doing his best to be brave. I told him you'll call him soon."

Charlotte nodded. "I will. It's just…"

"Yeah, I know." His eyes met hers. "Look, I'm sorry for the way things have been between us. I've been a bit of an ass." He gave her a thin smile. "When this is all over I'd like us to try again. See what happens."

"So you're not breaking off the engagement?" She stepped closer to him.

"No. I don't think I ever intended to. I think deep down I knew the truth but with everything that had happened…"

"You needed someone to blame."

He gave her a sheepish glance and sighed. "Yeah, I guess so."

She stepped closer still. "So what does this mean for us?"

Reece pulled her into his arms. "I still love you, Charlotte. I don't think I ever really stopped. I was hurting and irrational and I'm sorry for everything I put you through."

Charlotte eased herself out of his embrace, tears welling in her eyes. "I'm still in love with you too, Reece. I never stopped, either." A fragile smile spread across her face.

Seeing the tears in her eyes caused a pang of guilt inside Reece. He leaned in and pressed his mouth to hers in a gentle kiss.

A soft moan escaped Charlotte's lips and she wrapped her arms around his neck, pulling him closer.

From the window above, Ed and Lozano smiled at each other. The lieutenant knew Reece would come to his senses sooner or later and he was happy for them both.

Sarah came up beside him. "What are you two smiling about?"

Ed pointed through the pane of glass and Sarah's gaze moved in that direction.

A smile spread across her face. "I'm so glad they've worked things out. I was worried that they wouldn't."

"Nah, I always knew Reece would make the right decision... in the end."

Sarah's eyes moved to Ed. "Oh, you did, did you?"

"Yep." He nodded.

"Well, you're a wise man, Ed Borenko. And that's why I love you." She leaned in and kissed his stubbled, chubby cheek then walked back over to the others.

Ed's face flushed a slight pink color.

"Aw, are you blushing?" Lozano teased.

"Who me? Not on your life." Ed cleared his throat. "Hey, they're on their way back upstairs."

The pair darted away from the window and joined the group.

Reece opened the door for Charlotte and followed her inside, his eyes roaming the other faces in the room as he closed the door behind him. "What's going on in here?"

"Nothin', Daniels, we've been waiting for you." Ed folded his arms across his podgy belly.

"Why do you look like the cat that just swallowed the canary?" A frown furrowed the PI's brow.

"I don't know what you're talkin' about." The chief's face wrinkled into a curious frown.

"Fine, then. But I don't believe you." Reece crossed the room and sat down at his desk.

"All good. You don't have to." Ed walked over and stood beside Sarah.

"Ok. We need to gather intel on where Dracula's plane set down. What I'd like you all to do is call the private airstrips and enquire when the last plane landed on their runway. They might tell you or they might not. It's our only option at this point. Wherever he landed will be his location. He won't risk coming back to LA, but will want to be close."

Jacques folded his arms. "I don't have time for this." He headed to the door.

"Wait. Where are you going?" Reece jerked out of his chair and stood up.

"I will let you know what I find out." Jacques opened the door.

"You can't just walk out in the middle of a crisis." Reece came around the desk and strutted up to the vampire.

"Of course I can. I am not one of your," his eyes roamed the room, "lackeys. And I don't take orders from you." He stepped out into the hallway.

"Jacques."

"I will be in touch." With that said, he disappeared down the stairs and out the door to a waiting limousine he'd called while Reece was otherwise engaged.

The PI sighed. Having two monsters on the loose could prove extremely dangerous.

CHAPTER FORTY NINE

Reece stood with arms folded frowning at his friend. He couldn't understand why Andre would ask him to do such a thing. What was he thinking? "You can't ask me to do that."

Andre gave him a severe stare. "There's no other way. You have to do it."

The PI shook his head. "I can't."

"Can't or won't?"

"Both. You're by best friend, Andre. When Dracula killed you that night at the observatory I thought I'd die too. You were gone and I had no idea what to do. How can you ask me to do something like this now?"

"Because if you don't who knows what I'm capable of? I have Jacques' blood running through my veins and I can't risk your lives. I'm a sleeper cell, Reece, just waiting for the trigger. You and I both know that."

"What I know is you wouldn't do anything to jeopardize the lives of the people you love."

Andre stalked over to him and grabbed his arm. "You don't know that anymore. I'm a ticking time bomb waiting to explode... what happens when I go off?"

"We'll deal with it *if* and *when* it occurs." Reece eased his arm out of his friend's tight grasp.

Andre frowned into his eyes. "You're prepared to accept that kind of responsibility? Risk the lives of the people we both care about just to keep me alive?"

"Damn right I am. I love you, Andre. You're the brother I never had and I won't lose you again."

The echoing voice inside Andre's head grew louder. "Kill him. Kill HIM. KILL HIM!"

Without a moment of hesitation, Andre lunged at Reece, knocking him to floor. He sank his fangs into the PI's carotid artery, drinking deeply, his eyes closed, savoring every mouthful of the warm, life-giving, sanguine fluid.

Reece's eyes rolled back into his head as his life force slipped away with every swallow. "Andre... please... don't." The words were a weak, jagged whisper.

Andre's eyes snapped open and he sprang up in bed. If he had a heart beat it would be thundering in his chest right now. Was he the monster he believed himself to be? Would he turn on the people he loved because his brother's blood coursed through his veins? What else had Jacques implemented during the resurrection ritual? He threw back the covers, climbed out of bed and walked over to the window. How could he stop himself from doing something that could never be undone?

Adrian's voice startled him and he swung around.

"I have total faith in your ability to control the beast inside you, Andre. Your brother cannot influence your conscience, only you can do that."

"You're not real. Why are you haunting me? Why do you have the faith in me that I don't have in myself?" He missed his mentor and friend and could only assume that was the reason for these impromptu ghostly visits. Adrian had always been his voice of reason.

"Because I know the man you've always been and always will be."

"Yeah? Well I wish I knew who that was right now. I'm missing time and I can only assume it's because of Jacques. What if I kill someone close to me during those misplaced hours?"

"You won't, Andre. You're stronger than your brother, even if you don't believe it."

His eyes moved to the floor as he contemplated Adrian's words. "I wish I could be that confident." When he looked into the shadows his mentor was gone.

Andre gave a heavy sigh and returned his gaze to the dark night beyond the window pane. What if Adrian was wrong?

ᏕᎧᏟᎡ

The next evening, just on sundown, Reece called a meeting in the living room of their apartment. While they waited for Eva to arrive, he paced the length of the room as he spoke, his eyes roaming the faces of his friends. "We have to find Dracula ASAP. Who knows what he has planned. We've hindered his scheme to abduct Tommy so he'll be pissed and looking for other ways to get at each of us. To divide us... and we can't let that happen. He's a manipulator and he'll do whatever it takes to win this battle."

"Eva would be the only one who would have an idea of where he might be," Ed said. "We need to interrogate her." The ex-lieutenant still didn't trust the vampire hunter despite her assistance so far. There was something about her he didn't like. And his gut was never wrong.

"I don't think interrogation will help our cause, Chief. Whatever Eva knows she isn't sharing." Reece was now certain she had her own agenda. But what?

Lozano got up off the sofa. "From what I can see she's the only one who can offer the best advice on how to proceed. She has her grandfather's journal. That should have something in it to help us take down Dracula."

A knock on the door startled Reece and everyone else in the room. The PI turned around, stalked over to it and peered through the peephole before opening it. "Why are you here?"

Jacques motioned to the living room beyond the threshold. "Aren't you going to invite me in?"

"You took off yesterday and left us to it. Give me one good reason why I should?" Reece folded his arms and glared at the vampire.

"Perhaps because I have these." He held up a bound wad of A4 sized sheets of paper.

"And what are those?" Reece motioned with his head toward the pages in Jacques' hand.

"A copy of Van Helsing's journal, well most of it, I didn't have time to finish photocopying all the entries." Jacques gave him a smug smile and his left eyebrow arched. "Now are you going to invite me in?"

Reece sighed and stepped aside. "Come on in." He wasn't comfortable allowing Andre's brother into the only safe house they had left, but he had no choice. In order to contain Vlad Tepes they needed everyone on board, including Jacques. Knowing they couldn't kill the monster, they had to come up with a different plan of attack and the professor's journal could hold the answer to their prayers.

"How'd you get those?" Ed asked, eyeing the vampire with contempt. He was definitely one they couldn't trust.

"Before I agreed to hand over the journal to Eva I thought it best to have a backup plan, just in case she didn't want to share. It's a pity I couldn't get them all." He crossed the room and stood in front of the others.

Reece followed him over and held out his hand. "Give them to me."

Jacques' left eyebrow arched. "Why would I do that?"

"Didn't you come here to help get rid of Dracula?"

"Of course I did. But that doesn't mean handing over the only bargaining tool I have. I will share the information with you, but I will hold onto these, if you don't mind."

"And what if I do mind?" Reece folded his arms.

"Then I can leave and you can continue whatever it was you were doing before I arrived. It is up to you, Detective." His eyes remained locked onto the PI's.

What other option did they have? They were at the mercy of Andre's brother's ego once again. Reece knew he couldn't be trusted but, unfortunately, they were running out of time. "Ok. You win."

Sarah stood up and came over to the pair. "Jacques, if you expect us to instill trust in you, you need to offer your assistance without conditions. Remember we're helping you achieve your goal, too."

Jacques' intense gaze moved to the priest. He hated being reminded of that. He gave her a thin smile. "Very well. Here." He shoved the pages at her, turned and marched over to the closed door. "Do not say I don't do anything to help."

Reece turned around, placing his hands on his hips. "And where are you going now?"

"That, Detective, is none of your concern."

"Don't you want to help take down Dracula? Don't you want us to trust you?"

Jacques gave the PI a dark stare then said, "I will return in due course." He opened the door and disappeared down the hallway.

Reece stepped out into the hall. Jacques was gone.

Moments later, Andre told Reece he had to leave for a while.

"Where are you going?" The PI wanted to know.

"I have a theory I want to follow up. I won't be long. I promise."

"Maybe I can come with?"

"As I've already said I won't be long. Don't you trust me?"

"That's kind of a loaded question, given the circumstances, don't you think?"

Andre gave him a sullen stare then turned and headed for the door. "I'll be back as soon as I can."

"Ok." Reece wanted to tell his friend he couldn't go, but he had no right to stop him. Was it Jacques' pull on Andre causing him to want to leave? Was he lying about what he planned to do?

CHAPTER FIFTY

The back passenger door of the idling, black limousine swung open and Jacques peered out, waving Andre inside. "Get in." He had something for his brother to do, something that would assist him in getting rid of Vlad and the PI's team once and for all. He knew if the vampire was dispatched everyone he had ever sired or those who had been given his blood would be also. A satisfied smirk crossed his pale, handsome face. Reece Daniels would be lost without his precious Charlotte, and once weakened by grief the whole team would fall apart and become easy targets.

Andre sat beside his brother as though in a daze, staring ahead of him, Jacques' blood causing him to sink into his shadowy subconscious far removed from reality. Jacques gave him a sideward glance, wondering what was actually going on inside his brother's head during these moments. Was he in a dreamlike state, hovering somewhere between this world and the next, or was he transported into a dark void, his mind still and unthinking? Jacques' belief was his brother was in some kind of suspended animation, or a form of hypnosis while in this state, unable to think or feel. At least that's what he hoped.

He felt the need to test his theory so he removed a lapel pin from his jacket and jabbed the sharp point into the skin of Andre's forearm. Nothing. *Interesting.* He returned the pin, clasped his hands in his lap, and gazed out of the window at the passing restaurants and stores on the boulevard. They were almost there.

As the limousine pulled into the Sunset Towers' drive, Jacques snapped his fingers. Andre blinked, frowned, and gazed around the interior before turning his perturbed gaze to his brother. "What happened? How did I get here?"

"I picked you up. Do you not remember?" He gave Andre a faux curious frown.

"No, I don't remember. Where?"

Jacques changed the subject. "You said you needed to get the Van Helsing journal from Eva."

"I did?"

"Yes. You said the pages that I gave you didn't offer anything useful that would vanquish Vlad."

Andre's questioning gaze remained on his brother. "I said that?"

"You did." The back passenger door opened and Jacques stepped out under the terracotta colored marquis then peered into the car. "Coming?"

"Where?" Andre slid across the back leather seat and climbed out.

Jacques motioned to the hotel. "Up to my penthouse so we can devise a plan to get that journal back, of course." He had planted the seed, now he had to see it through to fruition.

℘

After unlocking the door and swinging it back, Jacques motioned for his brother to step into his suite ahead of him and followed him in. "Have a seat. I will only be a moment." He crossed the room, and disappeared into his bedroom.

Andre wandered over to the sofa and sat down on the end cushion and ran his gaze around the penthouse. It had been a while since he'd been here and he didn't much care for the unsettling feeling it provoked. He got up and walked to one of the floor to ceiling doors, opened it, and stepped out onto the wrap around balcony. Sunset Boulevard was glistening with neon signs and moving headlights. He swung around when he heard Jacques come up behind him. "Eva won't hand over the journal willingly," he said.

"No, I suspect she will not." His brother folded his arms. "But, perhaps, you can persuade her."

Andre frowned at him. "How do expect me to do that?"

Jacques stared deep into his eyes, gripping his brother's shoulder and pinning him to the spot. "When you get to Eva Van Helsing's you will break into her apartment and steal the journal… and before you leave you will kill her." He stepped back and removed his hand.

Andre blinked several times. "What just happened?"

"What do you mean?"

"Something happened." His gaze snapped to Jacques. "What did you do?"

"Why must I have done something?"

"Because I know you."

Jacques handed his brother a piece of paper. "Here is Eva's address. I know she hasn't told anyone where she is staying."

"How did you get this?" Andre raised the note paper in his hand.

"I had her followed, of course." Jacques gave his brother a smug smile. "Do I need to tell you to be careful?"

"Why would you even be concerned for my safety?"

"I didn't bring you back from the dead just for Reece Daniels' benefit."

"No, I'm sure you didn't." Andre strutted across the balcony and disappeared through the door he had stepped out of.

Jacques stood and watched him leave, smiling to himself.

℘)(℞

As Andre stepped into the taxi and it pulled away from the curb the headlights of a nearby car flashed on and it merged into the traffic a couple of cars back. It followed at a safe distance, so as not to be spotted, and continued its pursuit of the yellow Prius. Where was he heading?

The cab turned a corner to the left, drove along the tree-lined street to an apartment block, and stopped out front. The vehicle behind it pulled into the curb about five cars along and the driver turned off the headlights and the engine.

Andre got out of the taxi, closed the passenger door and gazed up at the five story, cream colored building. It was late and most of the residences windows were in darkness. Was Eva there? He climbed the front steps and walked along the path to the glass paneled door leading into the entry hall. It was locked. He stepped out of the alcove and perused the exterior. He could fly up to the roof to see if there was a way in from there.

He ascended into the air and landed on a sun roof. The green wood door to the stairwell was closed. Andre made his way over to it, reached for the handle and turned it. It opened. Checking for any sounds, he stepped into the semi-lit space, closed the door behind him and descended the concrete stairs. Eva lived on the top floor.

Her door was at the end of the corridor, so Andre whipped along the hallway and stopped outside, pressing his ear against the Christmas red wood door to see if there was any movement inside. Nothing. He turned his head and ran his gaze along the hall before slipping the lock picking tools from his pocket. Within seconds the lock snapped back and he opened the door and stepped into the apartment.

The shadowed figure on the floor below waited for Andre to enter and close the door before climbing the staircase onto the landing above.

The apartment was in darkness, as would be expected. A vampire didn't require any light to see by. As he moved through the living room, checking drawers and bookshelves and any other place he could think of a voice broke the silence. "What are you doing here?" It was Eva.

"I came for the journal. We need to find a way to bind Vlad as we can't kill him." Andre put down the book he'd picked up off the desk and turned around slowly.

"I cannot give it to you." Eva crossed the room to him. "You must know that."

"We have to find a way of stopping him. There has to be something in that journal that will offer a solution."

"Did Jacques send you?" Her nocturnal eyes glowed in the dark.

"No. It was my idea to come here." His gaze met hers.

"You are sure about that?" She took a step backwards.

Andre lunged at her, grabbing her by the throat and knocking them both to the floor. A table nearby skidded sideways and a lamp crashed onto the polished wood.

At that moment, the front door burst open and Reece raced into the room, pulling Andre off Eva. He had planted a tracking device in his friend's phone and had felt guilty for doing it. Now he was glad he did. "What are you doing?"

Andre turned and sprang at Reece, his fist connecting with the PI's left cheek, air and blood whooshing from his lips.

Eva darted across the room, grabbed Andre by the back of his shirt and flung him away from Reece. He hit the sofa and fell to the floor.

Reece rushed over to him. "Andre, are you all right?"

His friend looked up at him in a daze. "What happened? What did I do?"

The PI extended his hand and helped his friend to his feet. "You tried to kill Eva."

"What?!"

"It is true," Eva said, folding her arms. "If your friend hadn't stopped you I might have killed you instead."

Reece's severe stare met hers. "You'd would've done that?"

She raised her defiant chin. "If I had to protect myself, yes."

Now he knew she couldn't be trusted. He turned to his friend. "Andre, why'd you come here tonight?"

"I'm not sure. To get the journal, I think."

"Did Jacques send you?"

"I didn't think so at first, I thought the idea was mine, but now I'm not so sure."

"You were with him before you came here?"

Andre nodded. "Yes, he said he was going to help me with a plan to get the journal."

"Then that explains everything." Reece folded his arms. "He sent you here to get rid of Eva."

"I knew something wasn't right about all of this. I had another one of those blank moments while I was at his penthouse. He must've put the suggestion in my mind while I was out of it."

"Obviously. He wants to kill Dracula to obtain his position in the immortal world and he knows that if he does others will die, including Charlotte."

Andre gave his friend a sheepish glance. "I'm sorry, Reece."

"Should you not be apologizing to me?" Eva stepped up to him.

"I'm sorry. Truly."

"Very well, then. Let us go and copy some of the pages so you have something to return to your brother with."

"You're going to give him what he wants?" Andre's eyes widened. Eva had no idea Jacques had already copied some of the pages.

"Of course not. But I will let him believe I am." She gave him a glossy red smirk.

ᛞ

When the pair reached Reece's 1966, Midnight blue Mustang convertible, the PI stopped and turned around. "What were you thinking, Andre? You know Eva's been around longer than you. She has abilities and powers we know nothing about. She could've killed you tonight."

Andre's gaze moved to the sidewalk. "I get that. And to be honest I wasn't thinking. Whatever Jacques did to me... as soon as I walked into that apartment I had no conscious notion of what I was doing. I'd been programmed."

"You need to stay away from your brother. He's planning to kill anyone who gets in his way, including me and our friends. You have to know that."

"I know. But when he calls I go. His blood coursing through my veins makes me submissive to him and I can't stop myself. Adrian told me I'm stronger than him but I don't know if I am."

"Adrian?" Reece folded his arms.

Andre raised his hand. "It's a long story."

"I'm listening." The PI frowned into his friend's eyes.

"I've been seeing him."

"What do you mean you've been seeing him?"

"Lately, he's been my reason. He appears when I'm feeling out of my depth and offers advice. He told me I'm stronger than Jacques. I know he's not really there but..."

Reece shook his head. "Hey, if he can talk some sense into you I'm all for it. You *are* stronger than your brother. You just have to believe it."

"That's what Adrian said and I'm trying to. But Jacques has total control over me right now and I don't know how to stop him."

"We'll find a way, Andre. I promise you that." The pair climbed into the car and headed to their apartment.

CHAPTER FIFTY ONE

The floor to ceiling door blew outward, a gust of wind causing the heavy drapes to dance across the opening. Jacques spun around, his eyes wide for a moment. The scenario reminded him of a scene from a cheesy, old-time horror movie. All it needed now was a thick, cloud of mist to drift through the doorway to make it perfect... perfectly ridiculous. "What is it you want, Vlad?" He knew the father of all vampires couldn't enter until he invited him in, which he wouldn't. While he inhabited the hotel suite it was his home and there were certain protocols within the supernatural realm that had to be obeyed, no matter who you were.

"I want to discuss a negotiation with you. Will you not invite me in to talk... for old time's sake?" He lingered at the threshold to the living room, unable to step across the invisible boundary.

"You can speak from where you are." Jacques would not risk his own immortality by placing himself in a dangerously compromising position with a new adversary.

"Very well, if that is what you wish."

"It is. What do you want to discuss?" Jacques remained in the center of the room, far enough away so as not to be drawn in by his old comrade, now his nemesis.

"Your quest to end my life. And how we can come to a mutually beneficial arrangement."

"It is time for new blood, so to speak." A smirk crossed Jacques' pale, handsome face. "Pardon the pun. You have held the reins for too long,

Vlad. The world has evolved but you have remained indifferent to those changes. Our brethren are eager for an innovative leader."

"Consistency is the key to maintaining order within our world, Jacques. You should have learned that by now. I will not be that easy to usurp. But, by all means, try." He made a sweeping flourish and gave a devious chuckle.

At that moment, a knock echoed into the penthouse. Jacques' head whipped around and he glanced over his shoulder at the door. *Who would be coming here at this time of night?* His disturbed gaze moved to the clock on the bureau. It was after midnight.

"Are you not going to answer that?" Vlad asked, his right eyebrow arching.

"No, I don't think I will." All of a sudden he had a sense of foreboding.

"Come now, Jacques, what are you afraid of?"

His gaze moved back to Vlad. "Nothing. You and I are in the middle of a discussion. Whatever it is, it can wait."

ℜℚ

The next morning, Reece drove Andre to the Sunset Tower so he could deliver the pages to Jacques that Eva had copied for him. Reece parked his Mustang in the side street on the opposite side of the boulevard and the pair crossed the road and entered the hotel lobby. While they waited for the elevator to arrive, Andre turned to look at his friend. "Do you think he'll buy it?"

"Your guess is as good as mine. He's your brother. What do you think?"

"I'm not sure. It might give us some time. Maybe long enough to find Vlad before Jacques does."

"Let's hope so."

The elevator door glided open and the pair stepped inside.

"Jacques is determined to rid the world of Dracula so he can rule the immortal realm. He's a control freak. Just look at what he's doing to me... his own brother."

The button lit up for the penthouse floor and the door opened. Both men stood agape. The door to Jacques' suite had been ripped clean off its hinges and was lying in the open doorway.

Andre rushed forward. "Jacques? Jacques, are you in here?"

Reece pulled his Glock from the back of his belt and motioned for his friend to step out of the way. "Jacques?" he called into the suite. No answer.

The PIs stepped into the living room and were startled by a woman dressed in a dark gray skirt suit standing in the middle of the room. "Who are you?" she asked, her voice tight. "Did you do this?" She motioned around the suite at the decimation.

"I'm Reece Daniels." He turned to look at Andre. "And this is my partner, Andre Delacroix. We're private investigators." He flashed her his PI license.

"I'm Julia Crosby, hotel manager." She gave Andre a curious frown. "Delacroix? Are you related to Jacques?"

"Uh, yes, he's my brother."

She shook her head as if to rattle logic into it. "Of course you are. You look exactly like him. Silly me."

"Do you have any idea what happened here?" Reece asked.

"No, I don't. I got a call from the client in the next suite. We have two penthouse suites, you see. They found the door like that," she said, pointing to the fallen, paneled wood door, "when they were heading downstairs this morning for breakfast."

"Did they tell you if they heard anything?"

"No, they didn't. I did ask that very question and they told me they took sleeping meds, so they were sound asleep all night. Jet lag."

Reece ran his detective's gaze over the upturned space. "Mind if we take a look around?"

Julia raised her hand. "Be my guest. The police will be here soon so don't take too long."

"We won't. Thanks."

The pair waited for the manager to leave the suite and step into the elevator before turning to each other. "This has to be Dracula's handiwork," Reece said.

"Agreed. Where would he take Jacques, I wonder."

"Good question. We need to look around and see if we can find anything then head over to Eva's. We're going to need her help."

The penthouse yielded nothing that could offer any assistance as to the whereabouts of Andre's brother. Their next stop, Eva Van Helsing's.

ℰᏗᏟᎡ

Eva opened the door and eyed Andre sourly as the pair entered her apartment. Lucky for him Reece had arrived when he did or Delacroix might have died... again. She closed the door and followed them across to the sofa. "So, to what do I owe this unexpected visit?"

"Dracula has taken Jacques," the PI told her.

She shrugged. "So? If he kills him it would be one less monster to deal with."

"As much as I'd like to agree with you, we need all the immortal help we can get to detain Dracula. You know certain things about him, so does Jacques. Things that could assist us in our quest to rid the world of the one true monster, once and for all."

"Ah, but you cannot kill him. That is your Achilles heel. What is to say he does not get free at some point? Then what do you plan to do. Eventually someone *will* kill him." Eva folded her arms across her ample, red leather clad bosom.

"Maybe by then we'll find a solution to the problem of freeing those he's initiated. And those who have his blood running through their veins... like Charlotte."

"What is your plan?"

"To put him on ice. Literally."

Eva's eyes widened. "You mean freeze him?"

"Yeah. We place him in a coffin, chain it, put a large cross on the top and store it in a meat freezer." He wasn't about to tell her about the compound.

The vampire hunter's left eyebrow arched. "That could work."

"We thought so." Reece folded his arms. "Do you have any idea where he might be?"

CHAPTER FIFTY TWO

Just on sunset, the van pulled into the curb outside the tattoo parlor and Eva slid the side door open and climbed out, the guy she had a meeting with was already standing on the sidewalk, hands in pockets, his arms sleeved with a variety of black ink and colored tatts. He stepped up to her. "What have you got for me?" he asked, holding out his hand and wriggling his multi-ringed fingers.

The vampire hunter slid a business-sized, yellow envelope from the pocket of her jacket and whacked it into his palm. "What do you have for *me?*" Her sculpted right eyebrow arched.

"The guy you're lookin' for is stayin' here." He handed her a grimy piece of food wrapper with an address scrawled onto it. "But he's not alone."

She plucked it from his hand and perused the writing. "Do you know how many are with him?"

"Two. Three, maybe." He shrugged.

"I did not pay you to give me estimates. I need answers."

The guy raised his hand, his index finger extended. "Give me a minute." He turned around and walked back into the shop.

Eva's suspicious gaze remained on him through the store window. Would he try to skip out on her without providing the information she had paid him for?

Reece clicked the passenger door open but didn't step out of the van. He wound down the window. "What's going on?"

"I'll be right back." Eva whipped along the sidewalk and disappeared down a side street.

The guy was looking over his shoulder as he threw open the screen door and high-tailed it out of the tattoo parlor. When he turned his head, his eyes grew wide.

Eva grabbed him, raised him off the ground, and slammed him up against the brick wall. "Now that was not very nice, was it? I paid you for information that you didn't provide. And you thought you could get away with not fulfilling your end of the deal." She clicked her tongue, her eyes changing color, and bared her fangs.

The acrid smell of urine mixed with fear wafted into her nostrils and her gaze moved to his crotch. A dark wet patch had spread across the blue fabric of his dirty jeans. "I – I…"

"You what?" She lowered him onto his feet but kept a firm hold.

"I'll find out. I promise I will."

"You had better." She snatched the envelope from his hand. "And when you do you will get this back."

The guy nodded, his eyes still wide. Eva released him and he fell into a heap on the rubbish-strewn ground, his heart pounding like a drum beneath his sweaty singlet.

"Now get out of here. And don't call me until you have the answers I seek."

The guy scurried to his feet, losing traction on some old newspapers, then took off down the alley.

Reece came around the corner. "What was that all about?"

"He only delivered half the information." She held up the greasy piece of paper. "We have an address though." Her lips spread into a glossy black grin.

დʘ

The van pulled up across the street. The unassuming, two-story house was not at all what Reece expected as Vlad had leased a mansion the last time he was in LA. Eva leaned between the front seats and ran her gaze over the nondescript building. Nathaniel turned to look at the PI. "It appears he is keeping it low-key."

"Yeah, if this is the right address." Reece's eyes met Eva's in the rear view mirror. "Do you think that guy was on the level?"

She shrugged. "Who knows? I did my best. All we can do is take a look around and see if he is here."

"Kinda risky, don't ya think?" Ed said, peering through the side window. "Especially if he has bodyguards."

A shiver ran through Sarah. "This seems out of character for Dracula," she offered. "It's not like him to leave himself vulnerable."

"I know, but, like Nathaniel said, he could be playing it low-key." Reece's gaze moved back to the unlit house across the street. "He obviously never expected us to find him, at least not so soon."

"So, are we getting out of the car or are we just going to sit here and admire the view?" Eva asked.

Reece glared over his shoulder at her. "We need to be sure everyone's going to be safe before we do anything."

"Very well, allow me to suss out the property for you." She slid back the side door and stepped out of the van. "I won't be long." She disappeared in a blur.

"I wonder if he brought Jacques here," Andre said.

"Good question. It doesn't look like a place you could hide a prisoner."

"Yes, so where's my brother?"

"Your guess is as good as mind at this point." He leaned around the seat. "We'll find him, Andre. Don't worry."

Reece's gaze moved back to the house on the opposite side of the street as he watched for Eva to return. He was concerned about why it was taking so long. Even though he loved Charlotte there was still that attraction he couldn't shake, no matter how hard he tried. He'd sent his fiancée to stay with her son while he and his team came over here. She had been resistant at first, but after he'd explained that it could be a potential threat to her, and Tommy needed her, she'd agreed. He wanted to keep her as far away from the monster as he could until they could find a way to release her from his supernatural hold. And he didn't want to know where Mrs. Jenkins had taken the boy in case he was captured and tortured for information, that way he couldn't say anything because he didn't know their whereabouts.

Something moved across the hood of the van and Eva appeared at the passenger window. "He's not here, but this is the right place."

"How can you be so sure?" Reece frowned.

"I got inside and had a look around." She gave him a smug smile.

The PI sighed. "Ok, we'll come back when it's daylight."

Eva climbed into the back and the van drove away.

"We need to know how many he has with him." Reece leaned between the seats to look at Eva. She was beautiful… but he knew he couldn't trust her, not totally.

"I can go back to that tattoo place and see if he has anything else for me."

"Isn't he meant to be calling you?"

She folded her arms. "Yes, but I think I scared the crap out of him by turning in front of him."

"You did?" Reece's eyes widened. "Why would you reveal yourself like that?"

"It was the only way to intimidate him into doing what I want. He knows better than to mess with me now."

"Ok. So when do you want to go?"

Eva glanced at the dashboard clock. 10:42 PM. "Why not now? The place is twenty four hour."

Reece's gaze moved to Nathaniel. "Ok, let's go."

℘ↄ℞

He knew better than to run this time. His eyes widened as he watched the beautiful… *vampire* walk into the tattoo parlor and step up to the counter. "Hi, can I have a private word outside?" she said.

His head bobbed like one of those stupid dogs some people have on their car dash and he came around the counter, eyeing the customers and tattooists as he followed her out to the street. "I didn't expect you to be back so soon." His words came out in one long rush. "I thought you wanted me to call you."

"We need the information ASAP."

His body gave a nervous twitch. "Oh, ok. I was going to catch the dude in the morning, but let me see what I can do." He turned to walk back into the shop then turned around. "Don't worry. I'll be right back."

She gave him a knowing smile and a single, curt nod.

Within minutes, he was back. "The dude said if you can wait till tomorrow he'll get what you need."

"All right. Tomorrow. What time?"

"I'll call you as soon as he contacts me."

Eva gave him a dubious frown.

"Hey, I want my money so I'll call."

"Then I will wait to hear from you. But do not keep me waiting too long."

He nodded and swallowed hard. "I won't." He knew what would happen if he didn't follow through. He'd be dead.

Eva strutted across the sidewalk and climbed into the van.

The guy let out the breath he'd been holding and watched the taillights disappear into the traffic before returning to his stool behind the front counter.

CHAPTER FIFTY THREE

Lozano and Todd got up off the sofa and studied the serious expressions on everyone's faces as the group entered the apartment. What had happened? "How'd it go? Is he there?" the Sheriff asked.

"Looks like it," Reece told him. "But he wasn't there tonight."

"Did you get a chance to check the place out?" Todd wanted to know.

"Eva found a way inside and had a look around."

"So what are you going to do now?" The ex-detective was keen to contain Dracula somewhere where he couldn't hurt anyone ever again. Especially Charlotte.

"Don't know about you but I plan to get some shuteye, I'm beat," Ed said, glancing at Sarah who looked equally tired and withdrawn.

"I'm referring to Dracula." Todd stood with hands on hips.

"Eva has a contact who's going to get intel on how many he has with him. Once we know that we'll work on our next strategy."

"What about Jacques?" Lozano crossed the room to join them.

"As far as we could tell he wasn't there. Not the kind of place you can take someone without it being noticed."

"We need to get Dracula on ice as soon as we can... for Charlotte's sake." Todd was concerned something could happen to the vampire in the meantime, and that would mean his ex-partner's death and he would do everything he could to prevent it. "If someone gets to him before we do, and I'm sure there are other hunters out there, Charlotte will die."

"I know that, but we can't go bursting in there and not expect collateral damage. I'm not prepared to risk any of your lives." Reece crossed the room to the hallway. "Get some sleep. We'll talk about it in the morning."

☙❧

Jacques woke up locked inside a cage in a pitch black basement. He ran his nocturnal gaze around the underground space. Where was he? What had happened? It took a few seconds for his mind to connect the dots. Vlad! He'd sent his henchmen to abduct him. That maneuver had been something Jacques had not anticipated. Now he was at the mercy of a deranged psychopathic vampire. One who was aware of his plan to have him dispatched so he could control the immortal world in his place. Would he be left here to perish in an agonizing death of starvation? A tremor ran the length of his tall, lithe frame, the thought terrifying. The memory of him holding Tobias captive without blood in the underground chambers of St. Gabriel's church came to mind, Karma certainly was a bitch. For the first time in his immortal life he was afraid. His eyes darted around his underground tomb. No windows. How could he get free?

The door opened, light from the corridor spilling into the dark interior, and a figure appeared in the doorway. "Vlad told me to deliver this to you." He tossed something across the room that landed with a liquid plop at the vampire's feet. The door banged shut. Jacques snatched the blood bag off the floor, twisted the blue cap, and stuck the tube into his mouth, sucking vigorously. The chill, metallic taste was not at all satisfying or comforting but it would have to suffice if he was to keep up his strength. Why would Vlad feed him? What was his plan?

☙❧

Pounding on the front door brought Reece racing down the hallway into the living room in his boxer shorts, Glock in hand. Everyone else in the apartment came out of their rooms at the same time. Ed and Lozano, who were still sharing the fold out sofa bed, sprang from sleep. "What's goin' on?" Ed asked, a groggy urgency to his voice.

"I don't know." The PI crossed the living room and leaned in to peer through the peephole, breathing a relieved sigh when he saw it was the vampire hunter. "It's Eva." He snapped back several locks and swung the door open. "Why are you here so early? What's up?"

Eva strutted into the room. "We need to get over to Vlad's while it is daylight. He has five protectors with him. If we can eliminate them we can contain him while he sleeps and transport him to a confined location."

Todd rubbed sleep from his eyes. "Well, hell, we can deal with five. There are more of us than them."

Eva's left eyebrow arched and her gaze fell on the ex-detective. "Not if they are immortal, which I suspect they are."

"I have weapons to help with that," Sarah said, stepping into the living room fully dressed.

"That is good, but we do not know what kind of immortals they might be. Vlad is known to create hybrids from time to time and the five he has with him could be difficult to defeat."

"What kind of hybrids?" Reece was concerned for the safety of his team as well as himself. They had dealt with hybrids before – MacKinnon's vampires – and they had not been so easy to kill.

"They would most likely be vampire, but who knows." Eva shrugged. "Vlad has a way of turning the tables. They could have abilities far beyond what we know or they may be daywalkers, which would mean they would be awake now."

"The weapons I have were designed to take out any kind of supernatural creature." Sarah was adamant. "We used them in the church when Dracula set his vampires on us and we defeated them. We should be able to take out five, regardless of what they might be."

Eva gave the priest a sour, sideward glance. "Let us hope so." She stepped up to Reece. "Nice boxers by the way." A seductive smile spread across her pretty face as she ran her index finger down the center of his six-pack to the elastic waistband. He was in great shape for a human of his years.

Reece frowned into her eyes for a moment, glanced down at himself, removed her hand from his body, then turned on his heel and headed to his room. "I'll be right back."

Sarah walked over to the vampire hunter. "Leave Reece alone, he's engaged to be married."

"Engaged does not mean he is taken." Eva raised her defiant chin.

"True, but you need to have some kind of moral code where he's concerned. He's off limits, especially if you want us, his team, to watch your back."

"Is that a threat?" Eva glowered at the priest.

"No, not a threat, but advice you need to consider. We protect our own, first and foremost." Sarah walked over to Ed. She had no time for Eva Van Helsing. The huntress was a schemer and, to her mind, a liability.

Several minutes later, Reece returned to living room, showered, dressed, and ready to go. "Let's hurry up with breakfast and get over there. We'll discuss a plan of attack while we eat."

As everyone was about to step into the kitchen, Sarah's cell rang. She snatched it from the pocket of her jacket and frowned at the screen. She didn't recognize the number. "Hello?"

"Deacon Johnson?" the Italian voice queried.

Her frown deepened. "Yes. Who is this?"

"Scusi, my name is Pietro. I work at the Vatican."

Sarah's heart lurched in her chest. "Is this about Vincenzo?"

"Si, it is. I am sorry to have to give you bad news over the telephone but Vincenzo was found deceased in the archives a few days ago."

Tears stung the backs of Sarah's eyes and she blinked them away. "Can you tell me what happened?"

"We do not know."

"You must have some idea." She sniffed back the urge to sob. "Was he shot, stabbed, strangled?"

"No, none of those things."

Sarah's eyes widened. "Was he bitten?"

Silence.

"Pietro? Pietro, are you still there?"

"Si, I am here."

"Was he? You know what I'm talking about, don't you?"

Silence again.

"Pietro? Answer me."

"I – I must go now. I am very sorry." The line went dead.

Ed's frowning gaze rested on her. "What was that all about?"

A single tear slipped down Sarah's right cheek. "Vincenzo's dead."

The lieutenant walked over to her and pulled her into a tight embrace. "I'm so sorry, sweet lady. I know you cared about him."

"I heard you trying to get information out of the caller. Did they answer your question?" Reece folded his arms.

Sarah was now sobbing quietly against Ed's chest.

"You think he was bitten?" The PI was disturbed by these new turn of events. If someone at the Vatican can be killed by immortals what does that say?

The priest pulled her tear-streaked face away from the man she loved and stared into Reece's eyes. "Yes, I do. And I believe they... or some of them are in league with Dracula."

ಬಿ೦ಜ

Jacques finished the remainder of the blood and tossed the empty, plastic pouch aside. As he sat on the floor with his back pressed against the metal staves, he gazed around the gloom. Something seemed familiar about the place. What was it? It was just a basement, after all. He searched his mind for the answer but it eluded him. How long had he been down here? Would his brother know he was missing? Would he even care? His brow rose as a thought jumped into his head. Andre was attached to him, in more ways than one, he could summon him. Why hadn't he thought of that before now?

He sprang to his feet. His brother would be *his* savior this time. A smile spread across his face. He would soon be free to implement his plan.

ಬಿ೦ಜ

In the faint early morning haze, the street seemed ominous. No movement anywhere, which to Reece's mind seemed a little out of character for the area. Shouldn't someone be walking a dog or taking a morning jog or putting out the trash? Maybe he didn't know LA as well as he thought he did. He shrugged off the uneasy feeling and peered around the front seat. "Ok. We'll move in quietly from both sides and head round back. Keep your eyes and ears open, we can't afford any casualties right now."

"I could go in first and do a quick sweep of the premises. They would not even know I was there," Eva offered, her gaze darting to the priest then back to the PI.

Reece wondered why she was being so helpful all of a sudden. And what that look was between her and Sarah, which hadn't gone unnoticed. "Yeah, that's a good idea. It'll give us some kind of indication of where everyone is."

"Vlad will be upstairs. The master suite is fitted with block out drapes."

"Good. Don't be long."

Eva was back within a couple of minutes. "I saw one in the entry hall, one out by the pool. I think they may be human. There has to be more inside the house. Vlad would not leave himself open like this. He'd have several bodyguards."

"Ok." Reece ran his gaze around the group's anxious faces. "Everyone know what you have to do?"

They nodded.

"Watch each other's backs out there."

Andre and Eva left the van first. It was best that they go in gradually so as not to draw attention to themselves. After a few seconds, Sarah and Ed crossed the street and disappeared into the manicured front yard. Reece watched Lozano and Todd make their way over then he and Nathaniel climbed out of the van and followed them in. Each had ear coms so they could communicate with each other. "Can everyone hear me?" Reece asked, his voice low. A 'copy that' came back from all. "Ok, move in slowly."

CHAPTER FIFTY FOUR

Jacques stood up and walked across the cage, curling his fingers around the iron bars that held him captive, and staring into the darkness before him. The surrounding walls looked as though a tidal wave had surged through the basement at some point. Why did that set off alarm bells? His nocturnal vision roamed the pitch black space and something nudged the back of his brain. Decadent Desire? He was in his old night club. The one Dracula had tried to destroy by fire.

Now he had a destination he could telepathically relay to his brother. Andre and his friends would come and save him from a vampire gone mad. Jacques thought about that for a moment. Vlad Tepes had always been a little mad, even before he turned. Sticking bodies on spikes and sitting down to eat a meal in front of a sea of rotting corpses? Vampires could be ruthless, cold, calculating, but they always ended their victims relatively quickly, not allowing them to die an agonizing death that lasted for days. Most of the time, anyhow.

Why would Vlad bring him here? What was the purpose of it?

Jacques moved back across the cage and lowered himself onto the floor, crossing his legs and resting his hands in his lap. He closed his eyes and allowed himself to slip into an immortal meditative state. He needed to remain aloof to the situation at hand, otherwise he would deplete his energy and who knew if he would be given anything more to sustain himself. The guy that had thrown the blood bag at him earlier had been human, so if all else failed, perhaps he could concoct a way to lure him over and take a bite. The thought brought a smile to his face. He did love drinking directly from the source.

He assumed Reece Daniels and the others would be on the hunt for Vlad. Did they know he was here or were they on a wild goose chase around Los Angeles trying to find his location? Jacques berated himself inwardly… how could he have so blind to Vlad's tricks? Why hadn't he picked up on the fact that the vampire had come to his suite? He should have realized he wouldn't come alone. And what if Andre decided not to help him? He was resistant to his hold on him, in certain respects, questioning him about those blank moments in time. His brother was strong-willed, whether he knew it or not, and if more determined he could break their blood bond. But for now, Jacques would use it to free himself, while he still had the option.

ℰↄ☏

Eva came around the building and up behind Reece, tapping him on the shoulder, startling him. The PI swung around. "What are you doing here? You're meant to be with Andre."

The vampire hunter stepped closer. "Let me go out there. I could use a little fun before all hell breaks loose."

"What are you talking about?" Reece frowned into her pale eyes.

"I'll distract him and finish him so we can enter through the back." Before Reece had a chance to object, Eva brushed past him and headed around to the patio and pool area.

"Eva, no," Reece said into his com. Of course she paid no attention.

"Hi." She said in a seductive voice as she sauntered up to the heavy standing at the sliding glass door.

His gaze moved to her. "Who are you and how'd you get in here?"

"I'm an old friend of Vlad's." She glanced behind herself. "There is no fence on the side of the property so I thought I would just come around." She stepped closer. "Is he here?"

The suit pressed the com in his ear. "Hey, I've got an intruder. Want to come out here?"

"But I am not an intruder. He knows me." She gave him a sexy smile. "Surely you believe me."

Another suit came through the doorway. "What are you doing here?"

"As I told your friend, here, I came to see Vlad. I'm an old friend."

"He didn't mention you to us."

"I do not know why. He knew I was coming to see him. We arranged it weeks ago." Her fangs snapped discretely into place. She motioned to the door with her head. "Maybe you could check with him."

"He's…" The guy stopped himself. If he gave her any information he'd be a dead man.

Eva's left eyebrow arched. "He's what?" She stared deep into his eyes.

A dazed demeanor crossed the guy's rugged features. "He's sleeping."

The first suit swung around. "Hey, don't tell her that!"

"Too late." She sprang at him and sank her fangs into his thick neck, draining him in seconds before jumping the second bodyguard and doing the same. She stood up with a satisfied gasp and wiped a small drop of blood from the corner of her voluptuous, glossy red mouth. "You can come out now," she called to the others. "I've eliminated the threat."

Reece stormed up to her. "That was risky, Eva. Next time do what I ask."

"It served its purpose, did it not? Now we can get inside."

"She's right." Ed hated to admit it but it was true.

The PI gave his ex-boss a sour glare over his shoulder.

Ed shrugged. "Just sayin'."

"Let's move in. And be on alert. There's bound to be more inside." Reece stepped through the opening, remembering Eva had said there were five here. The others followed.

They entered the kitchen/living area, Reece moving ahead of his team, Glock raised. Whether the other three hiding here somewhere were vampire or human the silver bullets in his weapon would take them out either way. He pressed on, glancing over his shoulder at the group behind him, and motioned with his head for the other four to go through the galley into the formal living room from the second doorway. Ed, Sarah, Todd and Lozano nodded and made their way over to the closed door.

Reece stomach was as tight as a drum, his gut telling him something was definitely wrong. The place was too quiet. Where were the other three? Upstairs? He reached the bottom of the staircase, stopped, turned around and whispered, "We need to get up there fast and take out the last three." He stepped onto the first carpeted tread. Todd turned around, raised his pistol, which had a silencer attached, and stood at the base of the staircase while the others climbed up ahead of him.

As the seven reached the first landing, the low pop, pop, pop of Todd's gun caused everyone to swing around. A hulk sprang from an open doorway and hurled himself at the ex-detective, knocking him to the ground, his gun sliding across the white tiled floor.

Reece jumped the banister and landed just behind Todd, firing off his Glock while his team member scurried to his feet. The hulk kept coming. Nathaniel flew down the stairs and grabbed the guy by his collar, tossing him backwards into the front door, glass raining down on him. He was back on his feet in seconds and stalking towards them.

Another hulk appeared out of nowhere, grabbed Reece and tossed him across the entry hall like a ragdoll. Andre thrust himself up over the railing and onto the back of the huge vampire. Eva had been correct about Vlad creating hybrids.

She climbed the stairs while the fray continued. She had to get to Vlad and end him before anyone could stop her. Charlotte be damned, she had a mission to complete and there were always going to be casualties of war. Sarah reached out and grabbed the vampire hunter by the booted ankle and she fell to her knees. Turning, she kicked out at the priest and scrambled to her feet. Sarah raised her weapon and yelled. "Stop! Or I will shoot you."

The vampire hunter stopped in her tracks and raised her hands. "It won't do you any good. There will always be more who come after Vlad."

"Not where we're taking him." She kept her sights on the woman.

A hulk flew over the railing and landed with a thud in front of Sarah stealing her attention away from Eva for the briefest moment. Nathaniel slammed past her, grabbed the vampire and hurled him back down the stairs. When Sarah looked up Eva was gone. She climbed the stairs two at a time, Ed behind her, Lozano following him. They couldn't let Eva kill Dracula.

The trio reached the open doorway.

Eva was in the center of the room with hands on hips. She turned when she heard them behind her. "He's not here."

"That doesn't change the fact that you were going to kill him," Sarah said, her weapon aimed at the vampire hunter's unbeating heart.

"Oh, please, if it were not for Charlotte you would do the same. Do not be a hypocrite. Have you not been trying to dispatch the father of all vampires for many, many years now?"

"This is what I meant by we look after our own, Eva, but you wouldn't understand that concept."

Todd pushed past the group and raced into the room, panting. "Where's Dracula?" He peered over his shoulder at the trio standing in the open doorway. "Did she…?"

Sarah shook her head. "He wasn't here."

"So, wherever the third bodyguard is that is where Vlad will be." Eva strutted past them and down the stairs.

"She's some piece of work, isn't she?" Lozano said.

"Yeah, and dangerous too," Ed agreed.

Reece came up behind them. "Let's get out of here. I don't think Dracula will be coming back. He's got to be wherever he has Jacques."

Andre was at the bottom of the staircase. "We can't trust Eva. We need to do something about her."

The PI gave his friend a serious stare. "Yeah, we should, but what? She does whatever she likes and gets away with it. How do we stop her, apart from locking her up somewhere?"

"That's not such a bad idea," Ed told him. "She's a liability we can't afford to have around. She's going to get one or more of us killed."

"He's right, Reece," Sarah agreed. "She's a loose cannon."

"I get that. But she's a vampire, too, don't forget. She could take us all out if she wanted to."

Todd stood with hands on hips. "So we're just going to let her run amok?"

Reece let out a heavy sigh. "Let me talk to her. See if I can get her to agree to not killing Dracula, at least. She might listen to me."

"You really think she'll go along with that?" Todd was skeptical. "And why would she listen to you, Reece, she wants Charlotte out of the way so she can get her hooks into you."

"Hey, that's not true." The PI strutted over to him.

"Uh, yeah, it is."

"It's not."

Sarah stepped between the pair. "Yes… it is, Reece. I've already had to warn her off and she told me you weren't married so you were fair game. Todd's right. If she could, she'd kill Charlotte herself."

Reece gazed around the faces standing in the entry hall, turned around without another word and climbed through the shattered front door. There were times when he hated hearing the truth. This was one of them.

"Well, that went well," Ed said, an element of sarcasm to his gruff voice.

"We have to do something about Eva ourselves," Andre told them. "She won't listen to Reece. She'll kill Dracula at the first opportunity and Charlotte will really be dead." He remembered having to ID the body they thought was her in Vegas.

"What do you suggest?" Sarah wanted to get the vampire hunter out of the picture so she was no longer a threat to their plan of containing the monster.

CHAPTER FIFTY FIVE

The door swung open and a dark shadow stretched across the floor, haloed in the bright rectangle of light. Vlad. Jacques was his feet in an instant and stood his ground. Never show fear to a predator. He should know, he'd seen it too many times when taking the life of a victim. Would the vampire offer some answers? He could only ask. "Why have you brought me here?"

Vlad stepped into the gloomy space and stopped just far enough from the perimeter of the cage. "Have you not considered the answer to your question?"

"I don't know what you mean."

"Perhaps you need more time to reflect." He turned on his heel and walked back to the open doorway.

"Wait. Will you not tell me?" He despised being played games with. Another tactic he also often used. Karma popped into his head again.

"Oh, very well. If I must." He turned around and walked back to the cage. "This is where I tried to end Reece Daniels and his team, and this time I will not fail. This time I will dispatch you all. And once I have accomplished that task I will create an army of immortals that will suck this city dry and then move to another and another..." He cackled a demented chuckle as he crossed the cellar and closed the door, leaving his captive alone in the dark once more.

Jacques knew it was time to summon his brother. Not only did they have to rescue him, they had to stop Vlad from creating an epidemic.

Something he had wanted to do himself, but in a controlled fashion. Vampires would always need humans as a food source.

He sat down in the same position he had been in earlier when he retreated into an immortal meditation. Once he was on that transcendental plain he would step into his brother's psyche and provide him with his location. Not aware of what time it was, he hoped his brother was in immortal repose so he would have the chance of connecting with him in the realm between consciousness and death, as was the case for vampires when they *slept*.

"Andre? Andre can you hear me?" he asked with his mind.

Nothing.

"Andre? Wake up! Listen to my voice. I need you to find me."

"I hear you." His brother stepped out of the haze.

"Vlad has me prisoner at Decadent Desire."

In his mind, Jacques moved closer to Andre. "You have to come and set me free otherwise he *will* kill me."

Andre nodded. "We will."

He reached out and rested his hand on his brother's arm. "Be careful, little brother, Vlad is a maniac."

"Is there something else?" Andre asked, sensing a feeling of foreboding in Jacques that was unusual for him.

"Vlad is planning to create an epidemic of vampires."

"What?! How?"

"I do not know. He may have already set his scheme in motion."

"We have to stop him!"

"Yes, you do."

"We're coming for you, Jacques. Hold on."

"Thank you, little brother." He knew he did not deserve Andre's help but was grateful for it. An emotion he rarely, if ever, felt.

෫෨෬

Charlotte couldn't sleep. She had tossed and turned for hours unable to find the right spot to drift into oblivion for a while. She was worried about Reece and the others and what might happen to them when they confronted Dracula. Tommy was still asleep, softly snoring as he always did... a sound she loved so much. They were sharing a room in the place Mrs.

Jenkins had hidden them. She threw back the covers and swung her legs over the side of the bed wishing she was with Reece right now. He'd called her earlier to let her know their progress and she was concerned for their safety. Dracula was a monster and would do whatever it took to be rid of them all.

She slid her feet into her slippers, shrugged into her robe and crossed the room to the door, gazing back at her sleeping son with a smile before opening it and stepping into the hallway. He was her world and she would do anything it took to protect him from the nightmare existence they were now a part of. The thought crossed her mind of how Tommy would undergo a dramatic change when he turned sixteen. How could she prepare him for that? She walked out through the kitchen to the back door, opened it and stepped out onto the porch. The night was dark, thick, charcoal gray clouds covering the quarter moon. Her body gave an involuntary shiver. A sudden sound behind her made her swing around.

"Mom? What are you doing out here?" Tommy stood in the open doorway rubbing his sleepy eyes.

"I couldn't sleep. Go back to bed, honey."

"Can I stay here with you for a while?" He stepped outside and closed the door with a soft click.

"Sure. If you're not sleepy."

"I'm ok." He moved up beside her. "It's dark out here."

Charlotte wrapped her arm around her son's shoulders. "Yes, I was just thinking the same thing." Another shiver. Her gaze wandered the shadows of the yard. She couldn't see anything out of the ordinary. *Don't create dramas that aren't there,* she told herself.

A twig snapped somewhere close by.

Charlotte's anxious eyes roamed the yard once more. Nothing. She turned to Tommy. "Let's head back into the house."

"What was that noise?" Her son's wide eyes studied the yard.

"Probably a neighbor's cat." She was about to reach for the door handle when something from behind whipped her off the porch.

"Mom!" Tommy screamed.

$$\mathcal{SO\,CR}$$

275

Andre burst into Reece's room. "Wake up. I know where Jacques is."

The PI rolled onto his back, giving a sleepy gasp, and sat up. "Jesus, Andre, give a guy a heart starter why don't you."

"Sorry, but we need to go. *Now.*" He marched out of the room and down the hallway leaving the bedroom door wide open.

Reece flicked on the lamp, it was still dark outside, dragged the sheet around himself as he stood up, walked over and pushed the door closed. Jacques had used their blood connection to summon Andre. As the PI recalled, he always had that ability because he'd turned his brother. What was the difference now? Double strength blood? Or something the Sorcerer had performed during the ritual? He threw the sheet onto the bed and pulled on his boxers. No time for a shower. They needed to get to where Jacques was and get him out of there before Dracula made his absence permanent.

He stopped dressing for a moment and wondered why it was so imperative to save him. After everything he'd done to them the PI knew he couldn't be trusted. A heavy feeling of self-reproach fell over him. He did understand why... because Andre was Jacques' brother and, right now, his friend wanted to save the only relative he had left in the world. It wouldn't be fair for Jacques to die twice. He sighed and continued dressing. They only had a few hours to rescue Jacques before the sun came up. When he reached the living room, everyone was ready to leave. "So where's your brother?"

"I'll show you." Andre crossed the living room and opened the door.

Nathaniel was parked at the curb when the group got to the street. "Good morning, let us go."

Everyone climbed into the van, Reece in the front passenger seat. "Where to, Andre?"

"The night club."

Reece swiveled around and peered through the seats. "Decadent Desire?"

"Yes."

"But the building's a burnt out shell."

"And the perfect place to hide Jacques," Sarah said. "The cellar was unaffected by the fire."

Reece's gut was a tangle of twitching nerves. His gaze moved to his friend. "Vlad could've forced Jacques to send for you? He could be there waiting for us?"

"It's a risk we'll have to take if we want to get Jacques out of there."

The PI nodded, even though, in the back of his mind, he still wondered why they had to be concerned about Jacques' welfare. The vampire was more than capable of looking out for himself. He clipped in his seatbelt and gazed out of the windshield. But, then again, one rescue did deserve another. "Yeah, ok. Let's go.

ဆာလ

The alley was pitch black, the streetlight standing outside the building had been disconnected since the fire. This was the perfect place to be ambushed. Reece ran his scrutinizing gaze along the alleyway through the windshield. Nothing he could detect. He turned to look at Nathaniel. The black vampire shook his head after scanning the area with his nocturnal vision. The PI nodded and the group filed out of the vehicle one at a time and stood off to the side. All eyes were on the charred, brick skeleton of the once popular venue.

As Reece climbed out of the van his cell phone vibrated in his back pocket. He ignored it. No time for calls right now.

A set of stark headlights rounded the corner at the far end of the alley and headed toward the van full-throttle. Everyone darted backwards expecting it to impact their vehicle, but the car stopped within inches of the grille. Eva flung the driver's door open and stepped out of the black sedan, other vampires followed. "You did not think you were going in there after Dracula without me, did you?"

Reece gave Nathaniel a severe stare. He had to be the one to have contacted her.

"It was necessary. We needed backup," Nathaniel told him.

Reece walked over to the vampire hunter and stood with hands on hips. "We're not even sure he's here."

Eva raised her chin. She knew Vlad's scheming, maniacal mind and habits better than anyone. "Of course he is here. This is a set up. Can you not feel it in the vibrations around you?"

The PI frowned. "You mean Jacques is working with him?"

"I do not believe so. But the father of all vampires knew he would summon his brother. He counted on it."

Reece folded his arms. "And how do you know all of this?"

She smiled, even though it was too dark for him to see her face. "Because I have someone on the inside."

He was stunned and impressed at the same time. The woman was resourceful; he had to give her that.

"Where do you think Jacques would be?" Eva's eyes moved around the group.

Sarah stepped up to the pair. "The only place he could be... the cellar."

"Vlad is bound to be waiting for us inside. We need to go in strategically." Eva waved her team over. There were four. "You, you and you," she said pointing at each of them, "head around to the front of the building. "You, come with me."

"Where are you going?" Reece wanted to know where everyone was at all times. The situation depended on it.

"There is another exit on the opposite side of the building is there not?"

"Yeah."

"That is where we will enter."

"Are you wearing your com?"

"Of course. My guys are on the same frequency so they will hear you." She strutted away, the last member of her team behind her.

Reece spun on his heel, his cell phone vibrating in his jeans pocket. Once again he ignored it. They had a dangerous job to do. "Ok, listen up. I think Todd and Sarah should join Eva."

The pair nodded and moved off.

"Andre, Ed, you come with me." He looked at Nathaniel. "You take Lozano and follow the three in that Eva sent out front."

"Very well." Nathaniel marched toward the street, Lozano close at his heels.

"This could be a case of do or die, Andre. Let's hope your brother's all right and we can get him out before all hell breaks loose."

The three headed over to the alley doorway that led into what remained of the building. Reece stopped and turned to his friend. "Are you ok?"

Andre frowned. "What do you mean?"

Ed frowned too. "Yeah, Daniels, what do ya mean?"

Reece's gaze moved from his ex-boss back to his friend. "You're not going to turn rogue on us in there are you? Jacques hasn't programmed you to help Dracula get rid of us, has he?"

"First of all, I don't know what my brother has done to me. What I do know is I'm here to help you, my best friend and brother, and the other people I care about get the job done. We need to capture Dracula and lock him away where he can't hurt anyone ever again."

"That's all I needed to hear. Come on."

CHAPTER FIFTY SIX

"Can everyone hear me?" Reece flicked the com in his ear as he strutted along the passage heading into the night club. He got a 'copy that' from the rest of his team and Eva. "Good. Wait until I give the ok before going in. We need to do this in sync so we enter at the same time. Copy?" Eva didn't respond. "Eva?" No answer. "Shit!" He stopped at the blackened metal door and glanced over his shoulder at Andre and Ed. "Ready to do this?"

Andre and the chief gave a single, sharp nod.

The PI gave the order. "Everyone, move in. And watch your backs."

Each group moved into the hollow space, weapons raised. No sign of Dracula, his bodyguard or anyone else.

Reece did a 360 degree turn in the center of what was once the dance floor. His mind wondered back to the first night he'd done surveillance on the place and had met Cassandra. Little had he known then she was a vampire. They'd come that close to making love, except she'd slipped him a mickey and he woke up in his Mustang outside his apartment building. The work of Jacques. And now they were here attempting to rescue him.

The teams met in the middle of the large, burnt out space.

"We'll head down to the cellar and get Jacques. You wait here... and be ready for anything." Reece, Andre and Nathaniel made their way across the obstacle course of charred debris, furniture and other items strewn across their path.

The door stood ajar. Reece frowned at the refraction of light shining through the small, broken window in the top of the metal panel. When he pulled the door back, he could see the source. Two battery operated work lights stood either side of the cellar door. Vampires didn't need any illumination to see by so who else was here? The bodyguard?

"Stay close." Reece eased himself down the steps, Glock in hand ready to shoot anything that appeared in his path, Andre and Nathaniel right behind him.

The trio continued to move forward with caution. Who knew where Dracula or anyone else could be hiding?

When they reached the door, Andre called to his brother. "Jacques, are you in there?" An ominous sensation wandered the length of his body.

No answer.

He gave Reece a suspicious frown. "I don't think Jacques is here."

The PI raised his gun, shot the padlock off the hasp, and kicked the door open.

"So good of you to come." A voice echoed out at them.

Reece pulled his cell phone from the pocket of his jeans, shone it into the dark space and gasped.

Vlad stood in the center of the cellar holding Charlotte in front of him.

This maneuver was something they hadn't seen coming. How had he found where she and Tommy were?

"Let her go," Reece said. "Haven't you done enough to her?"

"But I am only getting started. Make your way back upstairs, if you please."

Reece's gaze moved to Andre then to Nathaniel. The monster was once again one step ahead of them. The three turned on their heels and climbed the stairs.

"Did you find…?" Sarah stopped mid-sentence when she spotted Vlad and Charlotte.

Andre swung around. "Where's my brother?"

"He is *alive*… for the moment. His life rests in your hands and what eventuates here."

"What does that mean?"

"You will find out soon enough."

A swarm of vampires appeared from every entry point and stood to the right of Dracula.

"As you can see I came prepared."

"What do you want?" Reece yelled, frustration getting the better of him.

"Why, Detective Daniels, I want you all dead. Is it not obvious?"

Eva kept her cautious gaze on the monster and his vampires as she eased herself around behind the other members of their group. Vlad would not escape her this time. He had run amok for far too long. She felt a pang of remorse for what she was about to do, but drastic times called for the only thing that would save humanity from the clutches of a deranged, supernatural serial killer... her ending his undead life once and for all and sending him to hell where he belonged.

She whipped Sarah's crossbow from her hand and fired off two shots at Dracula.

"No!" Sarah shrieked as she watched the special arrows rocket toward Charlotte and the monster.

Things seemed to move in slow motion.

Reece threw himself at Charlotte to knock her out of the way and only just made it as the arrows slammed into Dracula's chest one at a time with a fleshy thud, black blood spraying into the air around him.

Charlotte fell to the debris-ridden floor as the PI let her go and attempted to pull the arrows out of the monster's chest. He had to save the woman he loved... for Tommy's sake.

As the arrows were tugged free, black ooze spewed from the gaping holes and within seconds Dracula ignited and disintegrated into a pile of ash.

All hell broke loose as his vampires leaped across the room fangs bared.

There was no time to think. Reece threw himself into the fray defending the people he loved.

Charlotte jumped to her feet and hurled herself at a vampire that was about to stick a dagger into Reece's back, knocking him to ground.

Nathaniel whipped across the room and tore the head off the vampire underneath Charlotte then helped her to her feet. More vampires kept coming.

Sarah tossed an orb into the air and screamed out for Andre and Nathaniel to take cover. Just as the pair disappeared into the passage the sphere opened and ultraviolet shafts of light radiated from the metal ball. Shrill shrieks of agony echoed around the night club as flesh and muscle peeled from the skeletons of the vampires and their bloody remains burst into flames.

Charlotte screamed and sank to the floor, Reece hurtling himself across the room to where she lay.

"Charlotte, no." Tears spilled down his face.

"Take care of Tommy for me. And tell him how much I love him." Her voice was a whisper. "He loves you."

"I – I will. I love you, Charlotte. I always have. I promise you I'll do everything I can to look after Tommy." He pulled her close and kissed her forehead.

She smiled up at him. "Thank you. I love you, t…" Giving one last gasp she closed her eyes and died in his arms.

The Gypsy in Vegas had warned him someone he loved would die and he'd thought it had been Andre. Now he knew who she'd meant. His tear-filled gaze fell on Eva. "You did this," he roared, racing across the room and grabbing the vampire hunter by the throat. Why hadn't she died when the orb went off? A thought crossed his mind… the daywalker ring she wore. So Nathaniel and Andre were immune to the weapons, too.

"I did what I had to do," she said, her voice raspy because of his hold on her.

"I should kill you for what you've done." He glowered at her.

"Dracula had to die and you were not going to end him for the sake of *one* human."

"One human? That woman was my fiancée and the mother of a boy who's never going to see her again." His grip tightened. He wanted to rip her head off.

Nathaniel stepped up to him. "Reece."

The PI turned his head and spat the word, "What?"

"Andre has a plan for her."

"What kind of a plan?"

CHAPTER FIFTY SEVEN

Vincenzo had managed to email Sarah with the incantation to close the rift between hell and earth, and for that she was grateful. She had texted him to ask for it when she realized he couldn't get the pages she needed. He must have tried, though, and in the end it had cost him his life. A single tear slipped down her cheek as his smiling, handsome face popped into her head. She would miss him. She swiped the tear away and sniffed back the urge to cry. She had never been one to give in to her emotions but these days she couldn't help herself.

Andre had come up with a plan to send Eva Van Helsing to hell before the fissure was sealed. Right now, she was in the middle of the Sahara Desert, where they had intended to send the succubus, awaiting the moment when she would be transported to Hades. He wondered what would happen when she met Dracula there. It didn't matter; they would both get what they deserved.

They hadn't found Jacques at Decadent Desire and because Eva had dispatched the only one who knew his whereabouts it would remain a mystery until Jacques summoned Andre. If that ever happened. The vampire hunter's quest for Dracula's demise nullified any human element of emotion she may have carried and had caused her to instigate the most despicable act of betrayal. They had suspected it, but no one believed she would actually go through with it. When the opportunity presented itself they had hoped she would do the right thing. She didn't.

If they'd been able to get Vlad on ice, locked away where no one could have found him, Charlotte would still be here to be with her son and finally marry the man she loved. There was no time to grieve. There was still work to be done.

"Eva deserved what she got," Ed said with conviction as he set the mug of coffee down in front of Sarah who was on her laptop organizing what she needed to deliver the incantation. It would be a two-fold process transporting Eva to hell and closing the rift before any other creatures could escape.

"I always felt we couldn't trust her." She picked up the mug and took a cautious sip of the hot coffee.

"Yeah, me too, but Reece..."

The PI stepped into his office and closed the door. "But Reece what?"

"Nothin' just talkin'," Ed told him, sitting down on the chair next to Sarah. "How'd it go with Tommy?" Tears stung the backs of his eyes and he blinked them away. *Poor kid.*

Reece let out a heavy sigh. "Not good."

Sarah looked up from the computer screen. "Is there anything we can do?"

"Not really. He just lost his mom and that'll take time to adjust to." Reece crossed the office and sat down behind his desk.

"Why didn't you stay with him?" Sarah's gaze followed the PI across the room.

"Because we have work to do. I want to make this city safe for Tommy for as long as I can." He squeezed his thumb and index finger into his tired eyes. "Charlotte would've wanted that." She was really gone this time. How could he get his mind around that? A sob stuck in his throat and he coughed to stop the sound from escaping. "Where's Andre?" His bloodshot gaze roamed the office. He'd been crying in the car on the way over.

"He went to St. Joseph's to pick up some stuff for Sarah," Ed told him. "For the incantation."

"Oh, ok." The PI slid his laptop across the desk toward him and lifted the lid. When the screensaver of him with Charlotte and Tommy popped up he burst into tears.

Sarah rushed over and wrapped her arms around his shoulders. "I'm so sorry, Reece. Something like this should never have happened. If only Nathaniel hadn't told her we'd be at the night club."

"Hey, he was only tryin' to help." Ed crossed the room and stood beside her. "Why don't you let us handle things her, Daniels, and you go back and spend some time with Tommy?"

Reece sniffed back the urge to sob again and lifted his head out of his hands. "I don't know what to say to the kid to make him feel better. My heart's aching just as much as his is and I feel like I'm making things worse."

"You're the closest thing he has to a dad, Reece, he needs you," Sarah offered a voice of reason. "And anything you do is going to seem worse right now because it is."

The PI nodded. "Yeah, it is."

"Go talk to him, be with him, let him know you're there for him. We got this," Ed told him. "We're not about to let the Van Helsing bitch get free. So don't worry about her. She's where she belongs."

"We need to close the rift before the end of the week." Reece leaned back in his office chair and ran his hand over his moist face. His heart hurt like hell.

"The funeral?" Sarah would be officiating.

He nodded. "I want everyone there, for Tommy's sake. He needs to see how much Charlotte was loved."

"And we'll be there." Ed was emphatic about that. He'd called the precinct to round up as many people who knew Charlotte as he could. She'd get the sendoff she deserved.

"Good." Reece stood up. "Ok, I'll head back. Call me if you need me for anything."

"We will," Ed lied. They'd take care of what needed to be done so Reece could be with Charlotte's son for as long as he needed to be.

ᏕᎧᏝᎧᏠ

Reece pulled up outside Mrs. Jenkins' house, turned off the engine and stared at the front door. What could he say to the boy to help ease his pain? What could he do to ease his own? He let out a heavy sigh, pulled the keys from the ignition and climbed out of his Mustang. A heavy cloak of dread washed over him. Charlotte was gone. She was never coming back. Tears slipped down his cheeks and he swiped them away. He had to be strong for Tommy. As he reached the porch steps, the light overhead flashed on, the door opened, and Tommy raced up to him, wrapping his arms around his waist.

Reece pulled him into a tight hug and the pair stood in silence for a long time, Mrs. Jenkins watching from the door, wiping her puffy red eyes with a floral handkerchief.

"Hey, buddy, how're you doing?" The PI said, finally.

Tommy's tear-streaked face gazed up at him. "I miss my mom."

"Yeah, me too." He eased Tommy out of his embrace and lowered himself to the boy's level. "I know it's hard right now, but she's always going to be with us… in here." He rested his palm over Tommy's heart. "We'll never forget her. Ever."

Tommy's lip quivered and he threw his arms around Reece's neck, pressed his face into his shoulder and sobbed.

Tears rolled down the PI's face, his heart aching for the boy and for Charlotte.

Mrs. Jenkins came out onto the porch. "Why don't you come inside? I'll make us some hot chocolate." She didn't know what else to say.

Reece picked the boy up and carried him into the house.

CHAPTER FIFTY EIGHT

Jacque's dark gaze rested on his brother... his twin... his doppelganger. "I release you."

Andre frowned into his brother's eyes and folded his arms. "You release me? You've always had the ability to do that?"

A smirk tugged at the left corner of Jacques' mouth but he stopped himself. This was not the time. For once in his long, immortal life he was attempting to do the right thing where his brother was concerned. "Yes, I have." The look of disgust on Andre's face did not sit well with him.

"You know, all I ever wanted was for us to regain what we once had. To be brothers. But you wouldn't allow that to happen."

Jacques' left eyebrow arched. "That's all I ever wanted, too, Andre. That is the reason why I came to Los Angeles in the first place."

"Do you remember how we used to be?"

"Yes, I remember. But it was a long time ago. We were human then. We are two different immortals now."

"I loved you."

"And I you, little brother. I still do in my own... demented way." The smirk he'd prevented moments ago slid across his handsome, pale face. It was not one of derision but one of sincerity. Something new for him. "That is why I'm letting you go. And why I'm leaving."

Something inside Andre ached for the brother he once loved. The brother he wished he could have back. "You're leaving?"

"I am. You need to get on with your life without interference from me."

"What if I asked you to stay?" Andre wasn't sure how he felt about his brother leaving for good. He had lost Jacques once when he'd burned in the sun and, at the time, had hidden his grief from his friends. He realized that old saying: Blood is thicker than water was true.

"You know I can't even if I wanted to, which I do not. It is time for me to take my leave. I have plans to implement."

"Will I see you again?"

"It is better that you don't. We are nothing alike, you and I, you are good, kind, caring, and I am the exact opposite. You will be better off without me."

Andre stepped closer to his brother, his emotions conflicted. He wanted to embrace him but knew it was only because of the feeling of impending loss. He was taken aback when Jacques pulled him into his arms and held him tight.

"Be safe, little brother. Take care of yourself and the people who love you."

Tears stung the backs of Andre's eyes and a single, bloody trail slid down his right cheek.

"Goodbye, Andre." Jacques released him, turned on his heel and stalked away. Before climbing into the black, elegant sedan, he turned and took one last look at his brother, then stepped into the car and it drove away.

Andre turned and headed along the sidewalk to the van, Reece standing beside the passenger door, arms folded. "What did he want?"

"To say goodbye."

"He's leaving?"

Andre nodded, the painful lump in his throat preventing him from answering.

"Are you ok?"

His friend took a moment to compose himself before replying. "I don't know."

Reece could see the pain on Andre's face and in his eyes. "Did you ask him to stay?"

"He said he couldn't...

Andre sprang up in bed, his eyes roaming the shadows in the room. "Jacques?" He frowned, threw back the covers and climbed out of bed. "Are you here?"

No answer.

Had Vlad lied about Jacques being alive? Was he dead? Had he come to him in a dream to say his final goodbye? The answer to that question would remain unanswered.

$$\mathcal{SO}\mathcal{CR}$$

"Mom… mom… mom!" Tommy jolted up off the sofa, tears spilling down his face.

Reece rushed over to him and scooped him into his arms. "It's ok, buddy, it was just a dream." He stroked the boy's hair, feeling his body tremble.

Tommy eased himself out of the PI's embrace. "I had a dream about mom," he said, swiping at the tears slipping down his cheeks.

"Want to talk about it?" Reece sat back.

The boy nodded. "We were in this beautiful garden and she walked up to me. She was dressed all in white. She looked beautiful." He wiped at his nose. "She said she was at peace and not to worry about her. She told me to take care of you."

Reece's eyes widened. "She did?"

"Yeah. She said you needed someone to take care of you."

"She said that?"

"Yep."

"You know what I think?"

"What?" Tommy swiped at another tear sliding down his face.

"I think we should take care of each other. How does that sound?"

Tommy nodded again. "Good. I'd like that." He thought for a moment, then said, "Are you going to be my new dad?"

Reece didn't know how to answer that question. He had no idea what Charlotte had arranged. He would only know that when her will was read. "I don't know yet, buddy. We'll see what happens. But I hope so."

"Me too." He wrapped his arm around Reece's abdomen and snuggled into his side.

Charlotte had come to say goodbye to her son in his dream. It was believed people and pets did that after they passed away. Would she come to him once he could close his eyes and sleep? He hoped he'd see her one last time.

CHAPTER FIFTY NINE

Nathaniel pulled the van up at the perimeter of the clearing, turned off the engine and looked across at Sarah sitting in the passenger seat. "We are here."

"Yes, I can see that." Her eyes roamed the circular patch of grass amid the trees, her insecurities getting the better of her. Could she close the rift? She had the incantation, she had all the supplies needed... she had to, she had no choice.

Ed's head appeared between the seats. "Are we doin' this or what?"

Sarah glanced over her shoulder at him. "Of course we are. I just need a minute." She had gone through the cleansing process – even as a priest, a woman of the cloth, she was only human, well, mostly human, and had committed sin. It was essential that she be in a purified state to perform this particular incantation or she could be dragged into hell herself.

Todd slid the side door back and stepped out, followed by Ed who passed the box to the ex-detective and fumbled his way out of the van.

Sarah opened the passenger door and climbed out.

Nathaniel would remain in the vehicle. He couldn't be present because he was a supernatural creature not bound to the earth.

The three walked into the center of the circle of trees. The spot was perfect for the ritual. Sarah asked Todd to set down the box and she removed a large, white folded sheet from on top. "Would you help me lay this out, please?"

Both Ed and Todd followed her over and as she opened it they each took a corner and spread the sheet across the grass. In the center, Sarah had painted a black pentacle with ancient symbols surrounding it. Symbols that would trap the creatures, transport them back to hell, and seal the doorway. For how long? She didn't know.

"What's that gonna do?" Ed asked, frowning at the image in the center of the sheet.

"That is going to send all of the creatures inhabiting the earth back to hell and the incantation will close the rift." She pulled her robes out of the box and shrugged into the alb and the chasuble, then kissed the stole before placing it around her neck. She was ready to begin. Her stomach flipped over and wave of nausea rose in her throat. "Ok. Let's do this."

Giving instructions, Sarah told the pair where to place the items they had transported out to the woods. Candles at the four corners (earth, air, fire, water), brass bowl and dagger in the center of the pentacle, and the special blend of herbs sprinkled around the outside. And just to be sure, a circle of salt outside the sheet so Todd and Ed would be safe during the ceremony.

Sarah stepped up to the bowl, picked up the ancient dagger and sliced down the palm of her left hand, allowing the blood to drip into the circular, brass receptacle. "O God who hast given unto me the gift of discernment to understand good and evil; through thy Holy name grant that this incantation to rid the Earth of evil may become true and veritable in my cleansed hands through thy Holy Seal. O Lord, be thou unto me a tower of refuge, and grant me strength to fulfil my duty as your servant."

A light breeze whipped the leaves around her and both Todd and Ed's eyes widened.

Sarah raised her hands into the air. "Hear me O creatures from Hell, Behold the Symbols and Names of the Creator, which give unto ye Terror and Fear forever. Obey, by the virtue of these Holy names and return to whence you came."

The ground shook beneath their feet and a bolt of lightning prodded the earth not far from where they stood. Ed lost his balance and grabbed Todd's arm so he wouldn't fall.

"The door to Hell is sealed by the servant of He who created all things. We praise his Holy name. Amen."

The rumble of thunder could be heard in the distance and heavy, gray clouds drifted over the clearing.

"Is that it?" Ed's rugged race screwed up into an incredulous frown.

Sarah nodded. "It should be."

"What's happening with the weather?" Todd asked.

"There'll be a storm tonight to cleanse the city."

"I was expecting something bigger," Ed told her.

Sarah gave him a thin, amused smile. "Well, God doesn't always do things in a BIG way."

Ed shrugged. "Fair enough, I guess." He frowned. "So Eva was sent to hell too?"

"She was."

"How do you know for sure?"

"Because I sent her there before we got out here."

"One less bloodsucker to deal with. Good riddance, I say. The only helpful thing she did was give Andre and Nathaniel day rings."

Todd and Ed picked up the items and sheet and returned them to the box while Sarah removed her clerical garments, folded them and sat them on top. The pair walked back to van.

Sarah stood for a moment in the center of the clearing hoping the incantation had worked. By the signs that had appeared it seemed to have and she had to believe that God heard her. Her eyes roamed the tree-lined space. Did the atmosphere around her feel cleansed? She couldn't be sure. Faith and hope was all she had.

"You coming?" Ed called out.

"Yes, I'm coming." Sarah crossed the clearing to the van, gazing back before climbing in.

"It went as you expected?" Nathaniel asked.

"I think so." She clipped in her seatbelt.

"But you are unsure?" The black vampire gave her a curious frown.

"You felt the tremor, saw the lightening, didn't you?"

"Yes."

"Then all I can tell you is I think it worked."

"Very well. If not, I imagine we will find out soon enough." He turned on the engine, did a U-turn through the trees and headed back to LA.

Sarah thought about that.

CHAPTER SIXTY

Reece squeezed two fingers into the collar of his white business shirt and pulled the fabric away from his skin. It felt like it was strangling him. He much preferred T-shirts and jeans and was uncomfortable in a suit and tie, but as he was attending the reading of Charlotte's Will he wanted to honor her by arriving well-dressed, clean-shaven, and ready to be the dad Tommy needed. The boy was beside him and pushed his hand into Reece's when the office door opened. "Mr. Daniels, I presume?" the lawyer said, offering the PI his hand.

"Yes." He turned to look at the boy gripping his hand so tight. "And this is Charlotte's son, Tommy."

"I'm Phillip Pembroke. I've known Charlotte and her family since she was a little girl. I'm so sorry for your loss." He motioned to the open doorway. "Won't you come in?"

Reece stepped into the well-appointed office with a view of the city, Tommy in tow. The lawyer closed the door and walked around his desk but didn't sit down. "Can I get either of you anything? Coffee, water ..." he said, glancing at Tommy, "a soda perhaps?"

"Uh, thanks, but we're fine." Reece glanced at the boy sitting beside him also dressed in a suit and tie – the same suit and tie he'd worn to his mother's funeral only a few days before.

"Very well. Let's get on with it, shall we?" Phillip took his seat and pushed a pair of expensive-looking, gold framed spectacles onto his nose.

Charlotte had no siblings and her parents had passed away years ago, long before Reece and she had met. He and Tommy were it.

Phillip Pembroke opened a manila folder on his desk. "Charlotte has made certain provisions for Tommy. There is a college trust fund that cannot be accessed until his eighteenth birthday. She has also left a small sum for his care in the vicinity of a $100,000 that will be transferred over to you Mr. Daniels."

"Please, call me Reece." Being here, wearing a suit, having Tommy hearing all of this, made Reece feel even more uncomfortable. Charlotte should still be here raising her son herself.

"Thank you, Reece." Phillip's gaze returned to the Will. "She has also made you Tommy's legal guardian."

Reece smiled for the first time in days. "I'm more than happy to become his guardian." He ruffled Tommy's hair and the boy smiled at him. It was a sad smile tinged with a hint of happiness. At least they could be together... grieve together.

"She knew you would." He closed the folder. "That's it. I have some documents for you to sign and then it's all done."

Walking along the corridor to the exit, Tommy stopped and tugged Reece's hand.

Reece turned around. "What is it, buddy?"

"When you and mom were in Las Vegas I asked her a question."

"What kind of question?" Reece lowered himself to the boy's level, unbuttoning his jacket as he did.

"I asked her if you'd mind me calling you... dad. She said you'd love it if I did. Would you?"

Tears stung the backs of Reece's eyes and he blinked them away. "Of course I would. I love you and I'll always be here for you. As far as I'm concerned you are my son."

Tommy threw himself at Reece, hugging him tight. "Thank you... dad."

A thin smile crossed the PI's rugged features. Whatever the future held they would deal with it together. Dan being a wolf popped into Reece's head and he dislodged the thought. That was a few years away yet.

When they reached the sidewalk, Sarah threw open the van's passenger door. "How'd it go?"

"I'm Tommy's legal guardian."

Ed's face appeared over Sarah's shoulder. "That's good to hear. Let's go celebrate."

Andre slid the side door open. "Congratulations!"

Reece's eyes widened. "I thought you were on a case."

"Do you think I'd miss this special day? Nathaniel's on it. Now, what Ed said, let's go celebrate."

"I'm not in the mood to celebrate, guys, but thanks."

Tommy glanced up at Reece. "Can we do it in honor of mom?"

Reece gave a soft sigh. "Of course we can, buddy. If that's what you want."

"Yep, I do."

"Ok." He took off his jacket and climbed into the van behind his son, his and Charlotte's son.

෨)෬

Reece lay on his back in bed staring up at the ceiling, unable to sleep, grief preventing him from closing his eyes. A single tear slipped from the corner of his right eye and he brushed it away. His heart ached for Charlotte but he had a responsibility to their son now and there was no time for him to grieve. He had to be the father Tommy deserved.

He gave a heavy sigh and turned over. Charlotte was beside him.

"Hey, you," she whispered, giving him a loving smile.

The PI's eyes widened. "How…?"

"I couldn't leave without saying goodbye to the man I love, could I? I've been waiting to talk to you."

Reece reached out and pulled her into his arms. "I'm glad you did. I hoped you would."

"I want you to know how proud I am of you for all that you've done to keep our city safe. You're a man of honor and that's the reason I fell in love with you." She touched his cheek.

"I miss you, Charlotte. I wish you'd never been involved in any of this. I wish I could've protected you and Tommy from all of it."

"I know. And I love you for that. None of what happened was your fault. You have to go easy on yourself."

He sighed. "I wish I knew how. I feel responsible."

"You're not. You never were."

"How am I going to live without you?"

"You have our son to raise. Make him your focus and you'll be fine. I love you, Reece Daniels. I always will." She smiled and pressed her lips to his in a gentle, loving kiss.

Reece jerked awake and sprang up off the pillow, his eyes roaming the shadowed room. "Charlotte?"

It had been a dream. She had come to say goodbye to him. He pressed his face into his hands and sobbed. Even though his heart ached, he felt elated that he had gotten to see her one last time. He knew he would always love her and he would do everything he could to be the kind of father she hoped he would be.

For now, life would return to some kind of normal. As normal as it could be until the creatures of hell found another means of escape into their world. He knew the future held its own difficulties, things Charlotte feared for her boy, but he and Tommy would face them together head-on as a team – father and son.

AUTHOR'S NOTE

This is the final book in the Dark Legacy series *for now*. I'll be working on the third instalment in the Moon Grove Paranormal Romance Thriller series and a standalone vampire novel that has been sitting on the back burner for a while over the next twelve months or so. It doesn't mean there won't be more to this series some time down the track as I've already had ideas for future storylines. I hope you've enjoyed reading this series and I also hope you'll check out the other books written under my pen name Maggie Anderson. Oh, and by the way, if you enjoyed this conclusion to Soul Chaser please leave a review wherever you purchased you copy. Thank you.

Happy Reading!

www.ingramcontent.com/pod-product-compliance
Lightning Source LLC
Chambersburg PA
CBHW031253170626
46807CB00001B/119